BELLA OSBORNE

I've been jotting down my stories as far back as I can remember. Somehow life took over, I got a sensible job in project management and the writing has remained a passion. Writing your own story really is the best fun ever! But it's a close run thing along with talking, eating chocolate, drinking fizz and planning holidays!

I live in The Midlands with my lovely husband and our wonderful daughter, who thankfully, both accept me as I am (with my mad morning hair and a penchant for skipping).

www.bellaosborne.com
@osborne_bella

It Started at Sunset Cottage

BELLA OSBORNE

AVON

A division of HarperCollins*Publishers*
HarperCollins*Publishers*
1 London Bridge Street,
London SE1 9GF

www.harpercollins.co.uk

A Paperback Original 2015

First published in Great Britain by
HarperCollins*Publishers* 2015

Copyright © Bella Osborne 2015

Bella Osborne asserts the moral right to
be identified as the author of this work

A catalogue record for this book is
available from the British Library

ISBN-9780008158637

Set in Minion by Born Group using Atomik ePublisher from Easypress

Printed and bound in Great Britain

MIX
Paper from
responsible sources
FSC
www.fsc.org   FSC® C007454

For all those that said I could do it, this is your one and only opportunity to say 'I told you so' so please feel free to take it! This book is dedicated to all of you which is my way of saying a big ginormous thank you!

Chapter 1

The small group watched as Sebastian entered his final resting place and all those gathered bowed their heads respectfully; it was a truly great send-off.

"We have entrusted our brother, Sebastian, to God's mercy," Andy's voice intoned, "and we now commit his body to the ground; earth to earth, ashes to ashes, dust to dust. In sure and certain hope of the resurrection to eternal life, through our Lord Jesus Christ, who died, was buried and rose again for us".

"Amen," came the chorus.

A cool breeze caressed the bushes and its whispers politely interrupted the silence. Clouds drifted by, scattering shadows on the ground and letting light through from the spaces between to dance on the grass. Five-year-old Amy stood on the edge of the grave, her curly brown hair, under control for once, fastened in a neat ponytail. Her usually beaming smile was missing from her solemn little face. She wiped away a tear with the sleeve of her best dress and turned to the three adults.

"We will now sing 'Morning Has Broken'," she announced with supreme composure, took a deep breath, filled her lungs and...

"Sweetie, we've sung it once already for Sebastian." Amy fixed her mother with a hard stare. Unperturbed, Sarah continued, "I think Sebastian has had a pretty good send-off for a hamster, don't you?"

Amy thought for a moment then nodded her agreement.

"We've been out here for 20 minutes and he's all buried now. Time to go back inside." Sarah took out a clean tissue from her jeans pocket and wiped the tears from Amy's face. She handed her the tissue and instructed her to blow. "How about we celebrate Sebastian's life and toast him with some milk and custard creams?" she suggested, willing her daughter to oblige.

Amy's face screwed up in horror. "Toast him!"

Sarah stifled the impulse to laugh. "Toast also means having a drink in his honour."

Amy's face cleared as the understanding of the other meaning of the word "toast" and the words "custard cream" hit home. "Okay, Mummy. Can I show Kate my new hamster?" she asked.

Kate had been Sarah's best friend since Brownies and was also Amy's godmother, so had been summoned to Sebastian's funeral when he'd been found dead that morning. Her face was pale and looked more so against the dark colour of her winter coat. Her still- beautiful, pale blue-grey eyes had lost a little of their old sparkle. Her light-brown hair fell around her shoulders and strands blew across her face in the breeze. A cursory sweep of lipstick showed she'd attempted to make an effort before leaving her house. She stood, shivering slightly, staring at the tiny grave, her hands thrust deep into her coat pockets as though reaching for warmth.

Amy tugged one of Kate's hands free. "Don't look sad. Mummy bought me a new hamster. Come and see."

The little girl marched towards the house, giving her godmother no opportunity to protest. Kate, thankful for the intrusion, forced a smile onto her face and allowed herself to be towed up the thin garden. The remaining two adults exchanged smiles.

"Great job as vicar, Andy, nice sermon," said Sarah, wrapping her fleece tighter around her tiny frame, as a cloud moved overhead and left a chilly shadow across them both.

"My pleasure. I've been to too many funerals, but this is one of the nicer ones." Andy gestured at the small back garden. A strip of grass took up most of it, with a border on one side filled with plants and flowers and an old fence that looked as if it was only being held up by the wayward clematis and honeysuckle sprawling over its rickety surface.

"Shall I do the final honours?"

When Sarah nodded, he picked up the spade and nudged the earth into the tiny grave. He managed not to disturb too much of the flower bed as he tamped soil over the Jaffa Cake box that had taken on the role of hamster coffin so well. A strand of wayward hair fell over his eyes and he pushed it off his face. Andy was what his mother called a strapping young fellow. He was six foot four, lean and muscular, his tousled, unstyled light-brown hair had fair streaks running through it.

"Kate looks pale," Andy said, patting the soil into place. "It's James's birthday tomorrow…would have been," He concentrated on the patting. Sarah bit her lip; she was rubbish with dates.

"Maybe she was just cold – it'd freeze the arse off a polar bear out here."

Without looking up, Andy said, "Cold weather apart, how do you think Kate really is?"

"Oh, I don't know." Sarah shrugged. "I know how much I miss James and it's been, what, 18 months since the accident? And I know it's a million times worse for Kate… and for you."

Sarah could have kicked herself; Andy's pain at losing his brother had to be as deep as Kate's at losing her partner. She reached out to touch Andy's arm. "Sorry."

"It's okay." He gave a half-smile, gestured for her to continue, then carried on levelling off the earth.

"Sometimes I think she's amazing and really getting on with her life and then other days I can see that lost look in her eyes and I don't like to leave her alone."

Andy stopped patting the earth down on Sebastian's grave.

"You don't honestly think she'd…" he didn't finish the sentence; he just looked at Sarah and frowned as he tilted his head.

"No! Sorry, don't think that. She's not *that* bad. Well, it is bad, because she's lost her partner. I mean. Bad, but not top-yourself bad. Oh bugger! I'm so crap at this," said Sarah as she started marching on the spot, for no apparent reason other than to mask her embarrassment. Andy laughed at her.

"Go on, carry on," he said,

"No, she wouldn't do anything stupid. Deep down I know she still loves life. She spends time making everyone else's life better. In fact, she probably spends too much time caring for others. Look at that voluntary-helper job she does at the convalescent home," Sarah found it hard sometimes to understand how Kate could work just for the fun of it, when she herself was trying, not very successfully, to hold down two jobs and was barely making ends meet. "She spends hours there talking to people, making tea and tidying up. Funny really, because she doesn't even tidy up at home, she has help from that Concetta woman.

"Maybe Concetta is company for her" said Andy.

"Have you ever met the woman?"

"Only a couple of times, but I know James thought a lot of her,"

"She is the Devil in an apron," said Sarah emphatically, pushing her two index fingers up through her short, dyed-blonde hair to indicate horns.

"She can't be that bad,"

"I'm serious, Andy. I never really understood what the word 'glower' meant until I met Concetta. One look from her and you could be lying on a slab with a tag on your toe!" Sarah scrunched up her shoulders as if physically hit by the horror of her faux pas "Sorry! Again."

"Sarah, it is okay. Don't feel you have to apologise every time you say something about death. Trust me, it's okay. Honest." His smile was sincere. This wasn't the first time Andy had tried to put Sarah at ease over her slight lack of tact and, given Sarah's ability to put her feet in it at any, and every, given opportunity, it most likely wouldn't be the last. "Anyway, you were saying about Concetta?" Andy prompted.

Sarah relaxed her shoulders and retraced her thoughts "Yes, Concetta just mumbles at you in Spanish, and I bet it's not nice things she's mumbling."

"But she is Spanish, Sarah, so it's not that much of a surprise," chuckled Andy. "James seemed to like her. He said they often talked about her life in Spain."

"That's because James spoke fluent Spanish, he employed her and he talked to her. Now that he's gone, Kate and Concetta just nod and point at things and that's about it. So, to answer your question of about an hour ago, no I doubt when she's there that she's company for Kate. Personally, I'd rather share a cell with Hannibal Lecter."

"I'm glad she didn't give up the convalescence home tea round, I think she gets a lot out of helping others. She's also probably trying to keep herself occupied, give her a purpose aside from the writing." Andy said leaning on the spade.

"Slave labour, if you ask me, making cups of tea for old, sick people. Most of them are asleep, so I don't think she is exactly getting scintillating conversation out of them, either." pondered Sarah.

"There you go, one finished grave," said Andy admiring his handiwork. "Do you have a cross or something?"

"No, it's okay. I'll remember where Sebastian is. Come on, let's get a coffee and warm up, I'm colder than a..."

"Polar bear's arse?"

"Exactly!"

Sarah opened the door to the small kitchen and was welcomed by the waft of warm air. She flicked the switch on the kettle and took three random mugs from the mug tree. Andy took off his muddied boots and went to the sink to wash his hands. Kate was sitting rigid at the kitchen table with a very anxious Amy hovering over her.

"What's going on here, then?" asked Sarah as she gently pulled her daughter's ponytail.

"Kate is holding my new hamster, but I don't think he's very happy."

The small honey-coloured creature was sitting stock-still, its pretty, unblinking eyes looked as though they had been swept round with a dark kohl pencil. Not a muscle was moving.

Sarah intervened and picked the hamster out of Kate's sweaty palm.

"Let's rescue the poor terrified creature and put the hamster back in his cage, too," said Sarah, as what little colour Kate had started to come back to her face. "Better?" Sarah added.

"Thanks, I'm not good with animals. Actually, I am good with animals, I guess I'm just not good with rodents," said Kate, joining Andy at the sink to wash her hands free of the sensation of miniature clawed feet.

"Don't take it personally, Curry hasn't had much handling so he's not too good with humans yet," Sarah said, setting him down on the floor of his sawdust-lined cage and carefully shutting the door. Curry scampered off into his plastic house to recover from his ordeal.

"Curry?" questioned Kate.

"Ask my genius of a daughter." Amy grinned from ear to ear.

"So why have you called him Curry?"

Amy looked a little disappointed. "You need to say his name and then say what he is. Like Amy, the little girl," she explained.

"So that would be Curry, the hamster," Kate dutifully replied. At this Amy collapsed into fits of uncontrollable giggles. Sarah brought the mugs to the table and Kate followed her as her hands now felt cleansed of eau de hamster.

"I know she's going to do that every time someone new meets him. She thinks it's hysterical. Go on, strange child, go and hang your coat up, wash your hands and then come and choose a biscuit." Amy skipped off, still chuckling to herself.

"You know, that's really quite clever," said Andy, joining them at the table.

"I agree. It's inspired. I'm just glad she didn't call him Roger!" said Sarah.

They all laughed, but the laughter dwindled quickly. In the pause that followed, they all took a swig of their drinks in a synchronised motion. The hamster funeral had left the three of them feeling a little odd. Their normal, easy air and chatter was lost today, replaced by unwanted silences. Sarah was the first to crack and break the peace.

"Amy's a smart cookie, she's running rings around her father already; outgrew him academically about a year ago."

"How is Shaun?" asked Kate out of habit, rather than out of any genuine interest.

"Still an arsehole." said Sarah, taking a swig of coffee. Kate nodded her understanding.

Andy leapt to defend his friend, "He's not so bad really. You can't deny that he loves Amy and he's a good plumber." Okay, the last point was not a terribly imaginative one, but he liked Shaun and he had seemed really cut up when he and Sarah had separated. He knew that Shaun was lacking in sensitivity and was sometimes a bit of a borderline bully, but only because he took things too far. Andy had welcomed his support since James had died, but had felt it would betray his friendship with Sarah if he admitted that they were still regular drinking buddies, so this he kept to himself.

"Andy, I know you're trying to be nice, but Shaun is a bastard. He lets Amy down on a regular basis, he's behind with the mainte-nance again and he's a low-life," Sarah resolved to end her diatribe.

"Couldn't be lower if he was limbo-ing under a slug," said Kate and I loathe him, she thought.

"Let's change the subject. Any news?" Sarah said, turning the attention to Kate. Kate stopped sipping her tea, put her mug down and waved her hands in a bit of a jazz-hands way, which grabbed their attention. This was just the opportunity Kate had been waiting for now that she was with her two closest friends.

"Yes, I have news," Kate said, her face changing as her smile spread.

"Ooh, exciting. Let's guess," said Sarah.

"Okay, but only two guesses each, otherwise we'll be here till Christmas," said Kate. "Andy, go on, you guess first."

"Err, well, err…"

"I'll have to hurry you, time is running out," said Kate.

"Okay, okay, you're going away on holiday?"

"Uh, er, wrong answer. Sarah, your chance to steal the lead."

"You've finished book number five?"

"Uh, er, wrong answer. I really do need to get a wiggle on with that, my editor's patience is wearing thin. Back to you, Andy," Kate had produced a wonderful plan for book five; it was colour-coded with arrows linking key characters and important events. She was very proud of her plan; she just needed to muster the same enthusiasm for writing the story.

"You've met someone else?" said Andy cautiously.

Kate was a little surprised by this one, "Er, no, wrong answer," she said, trying not to react, although she wasn't sure if she was meant to give a long speech about James. Kate was never sure how people expected her to respond to things like that, so she just ignored it. "Sarah, last guess,"

"Oh, God, you're not buggering off to live in Australia with your parents are you?" her face looking dismayed at the thought.

"No, don't be daft. You're both rubbish at this game. So I win," she said, helping herself to a custard cream and slowly eating it as the other two stared at her. She loved keeping them in suspense; this was fun.

"Kate, out with it! I'm worrying here," said Sarah.

"Don't be silly, nothing to worry about, it's good news. You remember my second novel?"

"*Love.com*!" shouted Sarah.

"Yes, ten points and straight to the top of the leader board you go,"

"There's talk of making it into a film."

"Wow!" mouthed Sarah. "You could have famous actors and actresses playing your characters. How about George Clooney and Gwyneth Paltrow?"

"Beautiful, but too old for my characters. They've only just sealed the deal, so it's a bit early for choosing the leads," but Sarah was already lost in a mini-fantasy.

"I know! What about Timothy Calder and Emma Watson!"

"Nice combination, but let's not get carried away just yet."

Sarah stared into space and Kate clicked her fingers in front of her nose. "Hey! I was just picturing Timothy Calder..." said Sarah before drifting off again.

"He's naked isn't he?" said Kate.

"Well, obviously. My fantasy. My rules. Don't pretend you don't lust after him, either, Miss Marshall, you're not immune. I've seen that Agent X DVD in your bedroom."

"That's research," said Kate as a grin spread across her face and Andy tried to take a drink from his empty mug.

"Okay, tell us everything," said Sarah, shuffling forwards in her seat with curiosity.

"Marcus Leonard, he's another author with the same agent as me," said Kate. "You've met him, Sarah."

"Um, grey hair, wears tank tops and bow ties. A bit of a lovey and obviously gay," précised Sarah.

"Good description but definitely not gay. Very married, to a very lovely American woman."

"Really?" said Sarah looking genuinely surprised. "My gaydar is rarely faulty; he must be borderline."

"Anyway, he was the screenwriter for the Agent X films and other stuff. He's kept things moving on the *Love.com* film front, when I didn't really have the interest in it at all, to be honest." Her friends sat silently, willing her to hurry up the story. Recognising their impatience, Kate continued. "Marcus and my agent have been speaking to people in the film industry. A couple of companies have been in talks over the last couple of months. Anyway, we've agreed a deal with one of them and they're going to make the film. Sometimes they just buy the rights but the film never gets off the ground. I'm just waiting to hear what happens next." There was stunned silence, broken only by a little girl chanting, "Ibble, obble, bibbly, bobble" over two biscuits. Andy was the first to speak.

"Kate, that's wonderful news, I'm really pleased for you." Kate shrugged, trying and failing to be nonchalant. Sarah jumped up and hugged her friend tightly as she tried not to cry. It seemed silly to cry over happy things, when Kate was constantly being so brave.

"I'm so proud of you," said Sarah, briskly wiping away a stray tear with her sleeve.

"Well done," said Andy, as he leaned across the table and lightly kissed Kate's cheek. "He would have been made up. You know that, don't you?"

"I know," said Kate. She knew exactly how James would have reacted. He would have been overexcited and keen to tell everyone. Kate had always loved to write but did it as a hobby and never felt her work was good enough to be published. That wasn't why she did it, but James had read one of her novels and loved it. He'd packaged it up and sent it off to a series of agents and one of them had taken Kate on and persevered to get her first book published. After that she was able to leave her office job and really give the writing a chance.

Kate wrote to escape into another world. Not that she needed to escape. Her own world had been pretty near to perfect. She and James had met at a party, but had both realised within hours that they had something special. Kate had been a calming influence on the manic James and he, in turn, had inspired a confidence in Kate that had previously been lacking. They had got engaged within a year and set the wedding date for the following summer. This had all been shattered when James had died in a motorcycle accident nine weeks before their wedding. Her newfound confidence appeared to have died along with James.

For the second time that day, it was Amy who broke Kate's train of thought and brought a smile back to her face. Amy was standing in front of her holding something large and yellow about an inch from Kate's nose.

"What's this?" enquired Kate, trying to move back slightly so that she could focus on the yellow mass, but Amy brought it closer still, both her hands clenched tightly around it.

"You hold it, Kate, it's very heavy," she said, as she let go. Kate reacted quickly and caught the lump in mid free-fall. It was heavy, Amy was right, and it was made of pottery. Its surface was scored and blobbed with yellow glaze and a single spike protruded from what Kate supposed was the top. As if reading Kate's mind, Amy announced, "It's a pineapple! I made it," to which both Kate and Andy feigned mock awe.

"Of all the fruits to pick, she picks a sodding pineapple," said Sarah, "not a pair of cherries like her friend Freya, or a strawberry like Lauren. No, Amy wants to make a pineapple."

"I like it," said Kate, feeling a little defensive towards Amy, who had got bored again and had left the kitchen, taking her heavy pineapple back to its place on the hall table.

"They charge the parents by weight," explained Sarah.

"Oh," said Andy and Kate in unison.

"Exactly. Six pounds, forty-two pence I paid for that sodding pineapple."

"That's more expensive than Waitrose," said Kate.

"It'll last longer, though," said Andy helpfully. "I thought it was a hand grenade!"

The adults sniggered and passed around the biscuits for a second time.

"Mummy, what flower do you think Sebastian will be?" said Amy, plonking herself and her collapsing custard cream on her mother's lap.

11

"Mmm", thought Sarah, "probably a winter pansy."

"What's that like?" said Amy reaching for her third custard cream.

"They are very pretty little flowers that bloom during the winter and they come in all colours, but often purples, blues and yellows."

"That sounds nice. I think Sebastian will like being a pansy," and with that she jumped off Sarah's lap and went off to play. Kate and Andy looked perplexed by the conversation, so Sarah began to explain.

"When Goldie the Goldfish died, when Amy was about two and a half, we buried him in the garden and I went with the conventional line of 'Goldie has gone to heaven.'"

"Makes sense," agreed Kate. Andy nodded.

"But a few days later Amy walked into the kitchen in tears. She was covered in mud and held in her hands a slightly decomposing Goldie the Goldfish. She had dug him up to check that he had actually *gone* to heaven."

"Ah, I can see where there's a flaw in the plan," pointed out Andy.

"Exactly. So now, when one of the family dies, our spirit goes to heaven and we become a flower. Which also avoids us being dug up quite as easily," said Sarah, looking over her shoulder to check that Amy was still out of earshot.

"Nice touch," agreed Andy.

"That's really quite a lovely thing to do," smiled Kate, thinking how nice it must be to be Amy and have all your concerns explained away by someone who loved you enough to protect you from life's unknowns. Sarah scooped up the empty mugs, pushed back her chair and gestured to the window. Kate and Andy followed Sarah to the kitchen window, where she pointed out Goldie, who was now just a stalk but last summer had been a dwarf sunflower and Gerry the Gerbil, who was a primrose.

"It depends what time of year they die as to what type of flower they become." All the adults nodded and were a little shaken by the voice that suddenly came with such gusto from behind them.

"Kate, what kind of flower is James?"

Chapter 2

Kate peered out onto the typical October day and was grateful she didn't need to be anywhere that morning. The sky was dark with rain clouds that seemed intent on depositing most of their cargo in the few square yards of Kate's front garden. She needed to get some chapters of her current book written and that would keep her busy until the tea round tonight. As she watched the swirl of raindrops, her scene was interrupted by a large, bright-yellow umbrella that turned into the drive and approached the house at speed, a pair of sensible black lace-up shoes on a mission to convey their owner into the dry as quickly as possible. Kate leapt into action, ran to open the front door and beamed her usual greeting at the yellow umbrella. The umbrella swung around and was vigorously shaken for just a fraction longer than was needed to remove all the water droplets. Despite the exceptionally large umbrella, its owner's coat was wet beneath it where the driving rain, helped by the fierce wind, had sought out opportunities to dive underneath and hit their intended target.

"Hace mucho frio," said the small Spanish woman, giving the umbrella another violent shake.

"Yes, it is cold," said Kate taking the umbrella out of harm's way and guiding Concetta into the hall. Concetta said this most mornings and, because of this, it was the one Spanish sentence that Kate understood.

Concetta was in her late fifties, Kate guessed, but it was difficult to date her exactly as her skin was what you would describe as well weathered and had the colour and texture of a walnut. The walnut fixed Kate with a stare "Té?"

"The kettle is on," said Kate still smiling and she pointed into the kitchen and Concetta followed her directions, muttering something inaudible under her breath.

The women drank their tea in silence and desperately tried to avoid eye contact. They both found it difficult to think of things to talk about, given the limited vocabulary between them – Concetta spoke no English and Kate no Spanish. Today Concetta was wearing one of her vast collection of loud dresses. If there were such a thing, thought Kate, this one would be a Hawaiian dress. It was emblazoned with oranges, lemons and the odd palm frond. It was a fruit salad of orange, yellow and green, in stark contrast to the day outside. Kate would have loved to have seen inside Concetta's wardrobe as she never failed to surprise Kate with her amazing array of brightly patterned dresses. It must be like a drag queen's ball in there, she thought. Kate wished she had learnt a little Spanish from James; just enough to exchange pleasantries with the poor woman; maybe offer her a choice of biscuit without having to wave the wrappers under her nose. Kate pointed above her head, "Changing the bed covers today, I guess" she said slowly as if addressing a child.

"Si," came the reply, as Concetta gave an awkward smile, took a last swig from her mug and disappeared upstairs, hurriedly putting on her apron as she went. Kate relaxed, her shoulders dropping to their normal position instead of the "to attention" pose they had automatically assumed as Concetta had entered the house. She tucked a loose tendril of hair behind her ear and took the mugs to the sink.

Kate was interrupted by the front-door bell. A very wet Sarah stood on the doorstep, her ancient blue Beetle coughing and

15

spluttering on the drive behind her. Her usually spiky blonde hair had been quickly reduced to limp tufts by the rain and her denim jacket was a very much darker blue than usual. She held out a soggy brown-paper bag to Kate.

"Can't stop, late for school. I mean work. Late for everything today, really," she said. "These are for you. I have too many. You need to put them in very soon. Like today." Before Kate could ask Sarah what was in the bag she was already back in her car, shaking her head like a Labrador. With a scurry of flying gravel, a small bang from the exhaust and a large cloud of bluey-black smoke, Sarah was gone.

Kate returned to the kitchen with the mystery soggy parcel, opened it slowly and peered inside. Kate wasn't too sure, at first, what it was full of. It was either shallots or bulbs of some description. Kate was no gardener, but she was a good cook and on closer inspection they were definitely not shallots. She studied the dozens of bulbs in the bag and then turned to the window to watch the stair rods of rain still thundering down outside and hoped she could remember where her wellies were.

A couple of hours later, Concetta's departure was announced, as usual, by the slamming of the front door and Concetta's feet pacing across the gravel.

"Bye," shouted Kate belatedly, as she always did, wondering if Concetta ever heard her. Kate had played Angry Birds on the iPad and done some celebrity-stalking on Twitter, which had occupied a few hours, and she was rather pleased with her new profile on Linked In until she realised that she'd lost three hours and was still no closer to writing the three chapters she had promised to email to her editor by the end of the day.

Now the coast was clear, she decided to venture downstairs and get herself some lunch. As soon as she opened the fridge door she was joined in the kitchen by Marmalade, a large female ginger cat that James had brought home from a rescue centre. Marmalade had two main functions: sleeping and eating, both of which she performed to Olympic standard. The fridge opening had triggered her unique food radar-detection system and she had appeared in an instant. Opening any tin elicited the same response. Marmalade was not a fan of Concetta's and always spent those mornings sleeping under a spare bed in an attempt to avoid being shooed. Marmalade rubbed around Kate's legs on tiptoes, purring as she did so. Kate fixed herself a sandwich and stared back at Marmalade as she eyed Kate's lunch with interest. She decided that her procrastination in the book department was not going to improve, so she might as well brave the weather and plant the bulbs.

Despite the quagmire that she had managed to create, and the rain that had trickled down her neck, she discovered that she had enjoyed planting the bulbs. She had tried very hard to plant them randomly and not in neat rows, but it went against all her carefully honed neuroses. However planting the bulbs had felt as if she was making a nod to the future. That she would actually be looking forward to seeing them grow and bloom in the spring. Well done me, thought Kate to herself, as she headed off out for the tea round. St Gaudentia House, the convalescence home, was fairly close to Kate's village, just a ten-minute drive and practically the halfway point en route to Sarah's house. It was a Victorian hospital that had been renovated and was now a convalescent home whose main occupants were elderly people. Kate had been a helper for over three years, ever since she went to do some research for a book idea that had eventually turned into book number three. She had continued to visit and had enrolled as a volunteer because she enjoyed talking to the patients and felt that it gave her a purpose in life apart from work. Since she had left her office job to take up writing full time, she had had little interaction with people, which James had felt wasn't healthy. The tea round was something Kate could do on her own and it gave her the added bonus of feeling she was doing something useful.

Some patients rarely had visitors and to have someone who visited them regularly made a big difference to their day, giving them a short respite from their problems. The irony of this was not lost on Kate, who on some days over the last few months had looked more wretched than the patients had. She found that on the tea round she could become someone else. For just an hour she could switch on a happier version of Kate. In the early months after James's death it was an effort to haul herself over to St Gaudentia's, but she always felt better for it, and each week it became less of a struggle to switch on the smile and make the tea. Kate enjoyed the routine and simplicity of the night-time tea round and chatting to the patients, but most of all she liked to see the patients improve. Most made a recovery, even if sometimes it was an excruciatingly slow one.

Kate filled up the urn from the water boiler and loaded up her trolley with supplies. She always started at the far end of the ward in the rooms, which were usually reserved either for those who had just come in to the home or for those less fortunate who were soon due to leave, and not in a taxi. Kate tapped the first door and, receiving no answer, went in anyway. The whiteboard nameplate above the bed read "Deirdre Harris" in pink marker pen, and a lady who Kate hadn't seen before seemed to be sleeping. Kate checked her records in case she couldn't have any fluids and then gently said, "Deirdre, would you like a cup of tea?" The lady didn't open her eyes, but as Kate turned to leave she replied.

"No, but I could murder a G & T," she opened one eye and smiled at Kate.

"Sorry, I'm all out of the good stuff. It's tea, coffee, hot chocolate or some malty drink that smells like boiled sawdust," said Kate, returning the smile.

"Black coffee, no sugar then, please," came the reply as Kate moved back to the trolley to make the drink.

"Only school teachers and doctors call me Deidre, everyone else calls me Didi."

"There you go then, Didi," said Kate, handing her a plain white cup and saucer. "I'm Kate."

18

Andy had woken up earlier than he planned to, due to the rain lashing against flimsy, rotting windows but, since he was awake, he thought he might as well make an early start. He had purchased the house at auction two months ago and despite hours of hard work it didn't really look greatly changed from the day he moved in. "Moved in" probably wasn't the right phrase as it had only been him, a bin bag of essentials, his armchair and a bed.

The intention was to move from floor to floor and room to room, until the whole house was completed and this had been a good idea, but the amount of time it was taking to make even the shell of the house stable was beyond Andy's worst nightmares. He had seen it from the outside before the auction and had fallen in love with the location and the fields that lay beyond the weed jungle that would one day be a garden. It looked as though the outside needed a lick of paint and there were a couple of tiles missing from the roof but, with some time and care, it would look beautiful. I would probably want to paint the rooms inside a different colour anyway, thought Andy, so that wasn't really additional work.

Little did he know, when the auctioneer dropped the gavel, that he had just bought something that, were it human, would be on the critical list, with someone hovering mighty close with a pair of heart-zapping defibrillation paddles.

After two months he was over the initial shock and was now firmly in denial. He had felt it necessary to trivialise the issues his visitors had highlighted with dramatic gasps at the crumbling plaster, horror at the lack of ceilings and occasional screams at the array of dead rats and birds who had met their maker there. Probably driven to suicide by the depressing air of the house, Andy had later thought. He was fed up saying, "Don't worry, I have a friend in the business who can put that right" or "That's easily fixed, I can do that myself". At least now the house was watertight, as Andy had replaced the entire roof – trusses, joists and tiles – which, in one fell swoop, had cost him a huge chunk of the renovation budget, as well as his left thumbnail.

Andy was a carpenter by trade, having faced the early disappointment at the age of ten that there wasn't much call for bouncy-castle testers. Work was sporadic as a carpenter and he liked that lack of schedule to his life. He had drifted for a time after James's death and had taken a few extended holidays on his own, to try to get his thoughts together. James was both his elder brother and his best friend, and his death had torn something out of him that he now searched to regain. Andy quickly discovered that having time away to think meant that you did exactly that, nothing but think, and soon realised that actually the last thing he needed was time to think. Thinking only turned to sadness, maudlin thoughts and, eventually, a state of abject depression. This conclusion had led to his hasty decision to buy the house in order to give him something to occupy his mind and hands for a few months or, as it was starting to appear, the foreseeable future.

Andy had decided that, with the roof now finished, this week he was going to tackle the cellar. That way, when finished, he had one large area he could easily shut off from the rest of the house and have a small sanctuary to return to. He nudged the old cellar door just a fraction too hard and watched it leave its hinges behind as it fell away from its frame and slid down the staircase. Not the start to the day he was hoping for, he thought, as he trudged down the stone steps after it.

The door had been the least of his worries, Andy realised, as he splashed into the water at the bottom of the cellar. Funny, he thought, that wasn't there the last time I came down here. He pulled a torch from his jeans back pocket and pointed it into the gloom as the water efficiently found its way into his boots. He stood there for a moment, taking in the unhappy scene – the whole cellar area was flooded. Andy was puzzled; it had rained before, perhaps not quite as violently as today, but there had been rain and his previous inspection of the cellar had revealed only traces of damp, not signs of total flooding. He suddenly realised where the water might be coming from and said aloud, "Bloody Shaun!"

Shaun had, after weeks of polite reminders, finally turned up at Andy's to sort out the plumbing to the kitchen and the outside tap so that, very soon, Andy could start mixing concrete in the garden. He should have known there was something wrong when Shaun had nipped off to get a washer two days ago and not returned. Andy, being a trusting soul, had believed that Shaun had been held up with something more important and that clearly the washer wasn't an immediate need. Now he knew that clearly it had been.

Over the last few days, the smiles and pleasantries between Kate and Didi had turned into full-blown chats. Didi was 70 years old and had undergone a complicated heart-bypass operation, with reconstruction and replacement valves. She had a history of lung problems and lived alone, so she needed some support over the coming months while she regained her full strength. Kate was surprised at how much she was looking forward to seeing Didi and decided that, to give them more time for a natter, tonight she was going to do the tea round from the other end of the ward. She hoped the shock of the change of routine would not upset too many patients. They weren't terribly receptive to change – when the paper towels in the toilets had been changed from white to green it had been the talk of the home for days.

There had been a few changes over the weekend, Kate noted, as she served everyone on the main ward. Margaret had gone home, as planned, now that she could manage her walking frame on her own. Betty, too, had gone, but unfortunately, not home. Kate swung her trolley out of the last bay and rattled off the private rooms in quick succession before tapping on the glass of Didi's door.

"Come," came the deep reply.

Kate shot a startled head around the door to see Didi's beaming smile.

"Good Lord. I thought you had a man in here."

"Chance would be a fine thing" Didi said, wriggling to try to sit herself up on her pillows. Didi had a kind face and thick, grey hair that was speckled with white and cut short, but arranged in big waves, giving her the air of a retired film actress. She was now managing to put on a little make-up, which always made you feel a whole lot better. She had told Kate that she never felt properly dressed without her face on. Over her nightdress she had a pashmina neatly draped across her shoulders. Very Hollywood, thought Kate.

"Pass me that paper, would you?" Didi indicated the local evening newspaper that was on her table. "Have a look at the lonely hearts' section. I've circled a couple of maybes."

"Didi, that's very kind of you, but I'm not looking for anyone right now."

"Not for you, you silly thing. For me!" declared Didi with a mischievous grin.

"Fair enough," said Kate handing a black coffee to, along with the evening newspaper.

"I can see that you're taken, my dear. I bet your fella's lovely, like you, isn't he?" said Didi, patting Kate's left hand with its engagement ring, as Kate clasped her chipped tea cup.

"Yes. Er, he, he...," stumbled Kate, with difficulty.

"Oh my!" exclaimed Didi covering her mouth with her hand in mock horror, "Did I just put my size nines in it? He left you this morning, didn't he? Ran off with the au pair?" she laughed, and Kate couldn't help laughing too at the sheer mischief of Didi and wondered how she would feel if that had been true. Then she thought of Concetta and James running away together and it made her laugh all the more.

The pub was warm and welcoming despite the stale-beer smell that radiated from the ancient carpet. The Blacksmith's Arms was a "locals" pub: lots of wood, low ceilings and a horseshoe bar that served both public and lounge bars. The real fire crackled a convivial greeting – the only such one Sarah was likely to receive. Melanie scurried out of the way as Sarah lifted the hatch and went behind the bar.

"Hi, Mel," she said brightly to the back of Melanie's head as she disappeared out the back.

"What time do you call this?" said Phil. Sarah winced and held up her hands in surrender. Phil had been the landlord at the Blacksmith's Arms for 16 years. He was a large, round Yorkshire man and most of the time he was a jolly soul. Unfortunately, it appeared that today was not one of those times.

"I'm really sorry, Phil. It was Shaun – he was late collecting Amy."

"I thought you had a child-minder?" interrupted Phil, puzzled.

Melanie reappeared with a tray of clean glasses and started to replace them noisily on the racks above the bar.

"I did. But they let me down because of a hospital appointment, so I called Shaun first thing and he said he could have her, but then he was late picking her up."

Melanie tutted behind Phil and he raised a hand to signal her to stop.

"Look, Sarah. I know it's not easy with the little 'un, but I have a business to run and I can't show favouritism either."

"I know. I'll work twice as hard. I am sorry,"

"I know you are, lovey. I'll dock your wages. Can you take the food orders out?" He said, patting her arm with his chubby hand. Melanie looked over at Sarah with a look that could curdle milk and Sarah opened her mouth to repeat her explanation, but Melanie turned away. Melanie finished replacing the glasses and followed after Phil.

"Phil, have you got a minute?"

"Not if you're gonna bitch about Sarah. I've said my piece to her, so that's the end of it."

"It's just that that's exactly what he said would happen," gabbled Melanie, in her excitement to share her knowledge.

"Who said what would happen?"

"Shaun. He was in here earlier and he said that Sarah was having one of her episodes and wouldn't let him see Amy. He'd offered to have Amy, but she'd refused," Melanie's eyes gleamed with anticipation, searching Phil's face for a reaction.

"Righty-oh, then. Best you get back to it. There's people waiting to be served."

"Is that it, then? You know she was lying about it being Shaun's fault, but you're not going to sack her?"

"No. She's a good barmaid." And with that, Phil started whistling as he headed down to the cellar.

Sarah was tired but happy as she left the pub at the end of her shift. Melanie had been a bit strange with her, but that really wasn't anything new and other than the work had been steady. It was good to go to work and have a steady shift, one that was busy enough that you didn't watch the clock, but not so busy that you felt like a single worker bee looking after the hive on your own.

It was just after ten past seven when Sarah shut the front door behind her and she decided that there was time to have a look in the loft and see what she had up there for Christmas. She knew she had been on a spending spree in the January sales, but now she couldn't for the life of her remember exactly what she had bought. She did have a vague memory of lots of cheap, pink tinsel and she hoped she hadn't bought too much of it. Sarah had lost the step-ladder when Shaun moved out, as he had taken everything that belonged to him with him, anything of theirs and anything of use or value. This had left her with little more than some worn-out furniture, some stacking Tupperware and her compilation CDs.

She hauled one of the old wooden kitchen chairs up to the top of the stairs and plonked it under the loft hatch. Sarah wasn't short, at five foot six inches, but she needed to be a little higher to help drag herself up into the loft. She searched the bedrooms for something suitable and returned with a collection of the biggest books she and Amy owned. She piled them up, with *British Hit Singles* and the *Concise Oxford Dictionary* giving good foundations at the bottom and Amy's illustrated atlas on the top.

Sarah climbed onto the chair, steadied herself, then reached up and pushed the hatch to one side. She carefully put one foot, then the other, onto the books and, when she felt stable, pushed herself up. She found herself suspended by her forearms, with her legs dangling. To quickly get herself out of her predicament she felt for the back of the chair with her right toe and gave herself the final bit of height and thrust that she needed to propel herself up into the loft space. Unfortunately the force of this thrust was also enough to send the chair toppling over and bouncing down the stairs, taking the books with it. Sarah heard the commotion, but was unable to watch as she grappled to get herself into a safer position. She eventually peered down through the loft hatch to survey the disaster.

"Buggeroo," she sighed as she checked her watch. Shaun and Amy will be back in ten minutes, she thought, so I may as well make myself useful till then. She stood up as far as she could, which was about three-quarters of her height, making her feel like a hunched-up old lady and carefully moved from joist to joist in search of anything Christmassy.

The first half hour went quite quickly as Sarah discovered four boxes of Christmas cards with scary cartoon Christmas trees depicted in various poses, five cards that said from "all of us" and an assortment of January bargains. On reflection, twenty-four lengths of magenta tinsel, six bunches of plastic mistletoe and a parachuting Santa Claus didn't seem such first-class acquisitions as they had at the time.

As the time ticked away, Sarah found herself sorting through the many dusty boxes piled up precariously across the joists. She opened a battered case that had been on one cheap flight too many to find some of her old clothes, including some maternity clothes she had worn when she was carrying Amy. Great, she thought, as the chilly loft air swamped her, there must be something warm to wear in here. She pulled out a bright-green sweatshirt with Kermit the Frog's face covering the front. Sarah smiled as she remembered wearing the sweatshirt non-stop after she'd found it in a charity shop. As she pulled it on, over her thin jumper, she surveyed the upside-down Kermit and remembered how Shaun had mocked her for being so childish.

She opened the top of a large box to find a collection of Amy's first scribbles and pictures. Shuffling over to a small piece of chipboard that was balanced where the joists met, she sat down, dipped into the large box and pulled out picture after picture. Some were random scribbles with crayons and pencils, but there were some original pieces – one with lentils and pasta shapes stuck on it, lashings of orange paint and a fish shape covered in pieces of kitchen foil and a large letter A for Amy scrawled on the back. Sarah held the lentil-and- pasta picture and felt the tears come. Her baby was growing up so fast, it seemed like yesterday they were making the picture and giggling when Amy splashed the paint across the kitchen table. She remembered how Amy had been so proud and had wanted to show Shaun but, when he eventually came home, he was drunk and could barely focus on her work of art.

Sarah sifted through Amy's first attempts at writing her name, her first self-portraits and one drawing of all three of them with stick legs, large heads and even bigger smiles. She felt the silent tears drip down her face. "Where did it all go wrong?" she asked herself. She dried her face on her Kermit sweatshirt and set about repacking the box.

She went through boxes of long-lost stuff and started to make a box for the charity shop and one for the rubbish bin. Sarah found random wedding presents that had been consigned straight to the loft: an insulated gravy boat and an ornament of two gold jumping dolphins who looked as though they were smiling – really creepy. Other classics included a tea-towel holder in the shape of a cat's bottom and a pair of pink champagne glasses engraved with their initials. Unfortunately, being Shaun and Sarah, each glass had SS on it, making them resemble bizarre gay Nazi memorabilia. These were all that remained of the wedding presents from Shaun's family, as most of the others comprised cheap fizz that had long since been poured down the sink or Shaun's neck.

Sarah found an abundance of photos that had never quite made it into an album. Some made her laugh out loud and others triggered the odd stray tear. The memories came flooding back like a raging tsunami and brought with them a myriad emotions. So many happy memories, but so many of them counterbalanced by an unpleasant one, thanks to Shaun. Was that yin and yang, the universal balance, or karma, she wondered? Or perhaps just her being "bastard blind" and now she could see.

She found herself in the deepest, darkest corner of the loft as she crouched down to feel a box tucked into the edge of the eaves. Still balancing on the joist like an amateur gymnast she lifted up the surprisingly heavy box and looked inside. The surprise that met her almost made her drop the box through the ceiling, with her following close behind. Sarah steadied herself and then warily peered inside again. She wasn't exactly sure what she was looking at, but it was definitely furry and very dead, whatever it was.

Sarah shuffled back to the precarious safety of the chipboard and the saucer of light from the tiny bare light bulb to have a closer look, whilst still being careful not to touch the offending item. She could now see that it was a stuffed otter. It was the fiercest-looking otter she'd ever seen and certainly no cuddly Tarka. With its teeth bared and eyes wide it had the look she'd seen on many a sales shopper in early January. It must have been stuffed a very long time ago, as its fur was bald in places and there was a lot of white dust all over the wooden plinth it was mounted on, suggesting that the stuffing inside was escaping.

Sarah decided that it must have been left by the previous owners and no wonder it had been; it really was the stuff of nightmares. She wobbled as she swung the heavy box over to the rubbish pile and then had a pang of guilt. The poor thing did give up its life to be immortalised on a lump of mahogany, so she put it with the charity items.

Sarah sat on the edge of the hatch with her feet dangling into space and listened to the phone ring out for the second time. It was now nine o'clock and she was seriously pissed off. There had been no sign of Shaun, who had clearly had no intention of getting Amy back for seven-thirty, as she had requested. She had now passed the adventurous stage, when at about a quarter-past eight she had thought she would lower herself down through the hatch and drop to the floor. However she had lost her nerve through fear of breaking something. It was either a limb or a large, blue pottery vase her mother had given her and she wasn't sure which would give her the most suffering. She couldn't risk breaking a leg and giving Shaun the excuse he was waiting for, which would allow him to have Amy move in with him. Sarah still wasn't convinced that he really wanted Amy full time and was positive that he only said it to upset her, but it was a risk she could not take.

At nine-thirty her despair and tearful stage was interrupted by the front-door bell.

"Use your key, you twat," she shouted through a watery sob. Pulling herself together, she realised having a go at Shaun from her current position probably wasn't wise, so she relented and applied the traditional call used in these situations. "HELP!" she wailed. Sarah's hollering was interrupted by a man's voice.

"Hello," he said, tentatively, through the letterbox.

"HELP!" Sarah repeated.

"Sarah, it's Andy. Are you okay?"

"No," she replied in resignation.

"What's wrong?"

"I'm stuck in the loft," she called back.

"Is Amy okay? Is she with you?"

"No. Her wanker of a father had her this afternoon and he was meant to bring her home at seven-thirty, but he didn't turn up, as per sodding usual."

"Right. So how did you get stuck in the loft?"

"Well I was looking for…. Andy, does that really matter? You are talking through a letterbox, like a desperate Jehovah's Witness. So can we stop the niceties and concentrate on you getting in the house and helping me down from here?" pleaded Sarah.

"Sorry. Sure. Okay. Back in a mo," he said and the letterbox sprung shut.

The sound of breaking glass was not the next noise Sarah had expected to hear and it made her squeal with fright. It was followed by the sound of the Yale lock being turned and the door opening.

"Hello!" called Andy rather too jovially, "I'm in."

"What the hell have you done to my front door?" screamed Sarah through the hatch as she leant through as far as she dared, to allow herself to see an upside-down Andy, who gave her a friendly wave in response.

"You studying for Mastermind?" he asked, gesturing at the assortment of books littering the stairs and hallway.

"Stop being a smart arse and help me down. First of all, you can take these," she said, handing down the Santa with parachute and pink tinsel, "Not a word, seriously, not a word," she instructed, as a huge grin spread across Andy's face.

When Andy had finally managed to coax Sarah out of the loft, having had to swear on Sebastian's grave that he would catch her, he stood watching her dial Shaun's number for the third time in succession. Her thin fingers turning white as she gripped the phone.

"Do you think, perhaps, he's not there?" Andy said gently.

"Not helping," pointed out Sarah. "If he's not at home and he's not here, then where the hell is he and, more importantly, where's my daughter?"

"There's probably a simple explanation."

"Yeah, like he's kidnapped her." The words hung in the air. It was a flippant remark, but it suddenly wasn't very funny as the sickening possibility of what she had said struck Sarah deep in her gut.

Chapter 4

Kate was in a world of her own when the doorbell rang. So was Marmalade, it would seem, as she was sound asleep on her lap and the intrusion caused her to sink her claws into Kate's knees. She discharged Marmalade from her comfortable spot and hobbled across the hall to open the front door. Still bent over and trying to rub away the stinging sensation, Kate was met by a friendly, if slightly perplexed, face.

"Don't tell me, it's a local version of the Haka, one that the elderly can master?" said the grey-haired, and marginally overweight, man in front of her.

"Hilarious, Marcus. No, it's claw wounds, thanks to her," she pointed at the disappearing fluffy ginger tail as the cat made her escape through the open door.

"Can I take your coat?" Kate offered as Marcus stepped into the hallway.

"No, thanks," replied Marcus wrapping it tightly around himself as he headed quickly into the living room and settled himself into an armchair.

"Are you keeping well?" he enquired. Kate thought for a moment as she sat down on the sofa opposite him and absentmindedly straightened a cushion.

"Yes, I am, thank you, Marcus. I'm fine. How are you and

Niamh?"

"Niamh is wonderful, as always, but I need your help, Kate," he looked serious and Kate moved forward in her seat.

"Of course, Marcus, what can I do?"

"I need you to help me write a script."

"A film script?" Marcus nodded, "Sorry, Marcus, I'm the wrong person, I'm afraid. I just do books."

"That's a real shame because I thought you'd have a head start, this being the film script for *Love.com*." He watched her expression change.

"Marcus! Is it really happening?"

Marcus nodded and produced a bottle of champagne he had kept well hidden under his coat. He and Niamh didn't have any children and, since James had died, Kate had rather become a little project for Marcus. She had been a vibrant young woman when he'd first met her at an agency luncheon and he was keen to see that side of Kate re-emerge. Marcus didn't need Kate's help for the screenplay – the author was rarely consulted usually – but he hoped this would be the distraction that Kate needed.

"There is more news…" Marcus left what he hoped was a dramatic pause, "you have a leading man, nothing signed as yet, but I'd tear his ears off if he backed out now."

"Who?" Kate felt like a child at Christmas; that moment just before the wrapping paper reveals the best toy ever.

"Timothy Calder!"

"Noooooo!" squealed Kate in delight, "He's a huge star! Who else?"

"No one, as yet. The casting director's sending out begging letters as we speak. They want this out there quickly. So we start the script now and we film in early summer," and with that the cork left the champagne bottle with a well-timed pop.

Sarah looked awful. Her mascara had run in all directions across her cheeks and her eyes were puffy and red. She held Amy's pineapple in her hands and tumbled it over and over, like the thoughts in her head. She stared at the mobile phone and house phone placed on the table in front of her, willing one of them to ring. Both reminded her that it was now 10:44pm.

"Should I call the police?" she asked Andy.

"I don't know," he replied honestly. "As far as they are concerned, Amy is with her father, who has permission to have her."

"But what if he has taken her? Oh Andy I'll, I'll…"

"Shhh, it's okay," soothed Andy.

"It's far from okay! I'll kill the bastard!" Sarah forced out through her tears. Andy was in a state of abject confusion. He didn't, for a moment, want to believe that Shaun was capable of kidnapping Amy. There had to be a reasonable explanation, but it was becoming increasingly hard to imagine what that could be.

"Shall I call Kate?" suggested Sarah, blowing her nose.

"I wouldn't. She would have called if he'd turned up there with Amy. If you call, you'll only worry her."

"But I'm worried," blurted out Sarah.

"I know."

"Let's drive around and see if we can see them, or we could go over to his place."

"Sarah, they could be anywhere. It's most likely that he will be in touch soon and if he does, it will be with you here. So here is where we should stay," Andy said.

"I need to be doing something. I can't just sit here and wait for him to get in touch. The next communication might be a ransom note!"

"Let's not get… you know," said Andy gesturing a calm-down sign with his hands. As Sarah made more failed attempts to track down Shaun, Andy made an excuse to leave the room. He sat on the stairs and sent a text message to Shaun's mobile, asking if he wanted to meet up for a pint. Within moments a reply came through. ALREADY HERE COME + JOIN ME. Andy stared at the screen and dialled Shaun's number as he walked back into the kitchen and handed his phone to Sarah.

"'Hiya, mate," answered Shaun, recognising the number that flashed up as Andy's.

"Where's Amy?" demanded Sarah.

"Shit! That's a cheap trick, using Andy's phone."

"Cheap trick! That's rich coming from you. Where's my daughter?"

"Our daughter," he emphasised "is with her Nanny and Granddad."

"What?"

"She asked if she could see them," Shaun said in slow, bored tones. "We went over there and she fell asleep. I didn't like to wake her, so they said they would bring her over to yours later. Have you just got in?"

"No" said Sarah completely deflated, "I've been home for hours."

Andy and Sarah sat on the sofa waiting for the car to pull up and return Amy. Sarah hated herself for turning it into a drama in front of Andy. The sound of something as agile as a refuse truck echoed down the quiet street and Sarah jumped to her feet. Andy looked slightly alarmed at the sound of tyres against curb and followed Sarah to the window. Outside sat a large, white transit van and from it emerged a tall, thin woman with hair the same orange as Heinz baked beans and a small, sleepy child in her arms.

"Amy!" exclaimed Sarah running to the front door and out into the street. "Are you okay?" Sarah asked her daughter, as she took her from the woman's arms.

"Of course she's bleedin' well okay. She's been wiv us, ain't she?" came the barked response from the orange-haired woman.

"Andy, this is Irene, Shaun's mother," said Sarah, by way of both introduction and apology, before whisking Amy upstairs to her bed. Irene was what Sarah's grandmother aptly described as "the fishwife". She was loud, brash and generally vile. A family trait, it would appear, she had passed onto her son in abundance.

"Pleased to meet you," said Andy automatically offering his hand for Irene to shake. Irene stared at him, sniffed and nodded. The silence was crippling, but the occasional shrug and forced smile was all Andy could muster during the next couple of deathly silent minutes as they stood in Sarah's hall. He could not think of a single thing to say to the woman. As it was the evening, he felt he couldn't even resort to his staple favourite in these situations and discuss the weather. Just as he was about to die of awkwardness, Irene spoke.

"You 'er latest are ya?" said Irene, in a broad Mockney accent.

"Sorry?" faltered Andy, taken aback by both the harsh voice and its volume.

"You and Sarah, shacked up togevver, are ya?"

"Oh no. No not all. We're just good friends." Irene's eyebrows danced at his response, "Well… I say friends, we don't see that much of each other, really. It's just that we have a mutual friend, a shared friend," Irene's eyebrows continued to tango as Andy searched in vain for the right words. "Kate is a mutual friend," Irene showed no recognition "Kate was Shaun and Sarah's bridesmaid."

"Oh 'er. Stuck up cow, she was. Wouldn't play any of the games at the wedding do." Andy's mouth opened to defend Kate just as Sarah walked back in.

"Andy is Kate's fiancé's brother, Irene. Kate didn't play any of the games at the wedding reception because they were drinking games involving drinking copious amounts of absinthe and cheap Blue Curacao or, as we discovered in Accident and Emergency later that evening, anti-freeze."

"Shauny didn't know they was playing a joke, did he? The Twerton side of the family are a righ' scream. Nobody meant any 'arm, I mean…"

"Irene, can I stop you there, lovely though it is to reminisce," winced Sarah. "Thank you for bringing Amy home."

"Tha' it?"

"Oh, did you want money for petrol?" said Sarah with more

than a hint of sarcasm in her voice.

"Nah… well if ya offerin', a fiver would see us clear. Ya can't just dump the kid on our Shauny when e's gotta go to work, ya know. It ain't on, luv. He had no choice but to drop 'er into ours. In a right fluster 'e was an all, poor fing."

"What?" said Sarah. Andy moved closer to her as an almost imperceptible shaking was visible in Sarah's hands, as she stopped searching her purse for notes.

"What d'ya mean 'what'?" mimicked Irene cruelly. "It's not right calling up all hours of the day and night and dropping tha' poor little scrap on him. You can't cope, so why don't you hand 'er over to Shauny before the Social take 'er away?" With one quick movement Andy stepped in front of Sarah and held a £10 note under Irene's red-veined nose, which grabbed her attention as intended.

"I think there's been a misunderstanding somewhere along the line, but no harm done and Sarah is very grateful to you for taking the trouble to bring Amy home," he said, hurriedly ushering Irene out of the hall and to the front door.

"Ain't no mis…"

"Thank you," said Andy loud enough to drown out Irene, as he propelled the monstrous woman out of the front door. Putting his back to the door he sighed in relief as it clicked shut. His relief was short-lived as he felt something sharp dig into his back and he lurched away from the door. A pointed fingernail attached to a bony finger receded and Irene's orange-trimmed face appeared in the shattered door panel.

"She's mental. Ain't fit ta be a muvver. You wanna leave 'er, but I expect you will, like all the ovvers av." This was followed by a laugh so evil it would have rivalled Cruella de Vil, but it thankfully ebbed away as she stomped back to her van. With the van revving wildly in the background, Andy returned to Sarah, who had passed the "too angry to speak" stage and was now, once more, in a crumpled heap of tears on the bottom step of the stairs.

Marcus emptied the last drop of champagne into Kate's glass, getting there a fraction quicker than her hand, which was intended to stop him.

"No more for me, thanks," she said, too late.

"You can't leave this stuff, it just goes flat. None of those little gadgets for keeping it fizzy ever work, you know."

"Tried them all, have you?"

"It's my line of work, you see. Champagne is almost an occupational hazard. Book launches, charity events, film premieres. The list is tiresome, really," he nodded gravely.

"It sounds terrible," said Kate, as she tucked her feet underneath her on the sofa and took another swig from her newly refilled champagne glass.

"You, too, could be a part of all that, you know."

"Not really my sort of thing." Kate screwed up her nose a little. "James and I went to one or two when the first couple of books were published. We did a few charity things, too, which were quite good fun, and my first book launch in Harrods's Food Hall was a laugh, with that celebrity chef what's-his-name?" Kate laughed at the memory. After a pause, she said, "Truth is, I don't really fancy it on my own".

"But you wouldn't *be* on your own," emphasised Marcus. "I would be there, Niamh would be there Tom, Chris, Percival, Sheila and lots of other people that you know, plus your friends and family."

Kate sighed. She knew Marcus was right, but London and these glittering social occasions just didn't interest her and, more than that, they made her anxious. She had lost the feeling of excitement and it had been replaced by trepidation. She used to worry that no one would talk to her or that they would check the guest list and realise it was a big mistake and throw her out. Now she was happy if people ignored her and, generally, she just felt tired at the thought of it all. James had loved those sorts of events and Kate had gone along for his sake. With him by her side everything was fine and she was relaxed. She also still didn't feel up to explaining why James wasn't with her. Marcus's voice cut into her thoughts.

"You know that there will be events associated with the film, don't you? Things you'll be expected to do."

"I know. I'll work up to it, though, Marcus. I'll start with increasing my champagne tolerance," she smiled, raising her glass to his.

"How about you get a little practice in sooner rather than later? The children's charity, PSDS, is having a Christmas Ball. You know the sort of thing – buy a table, celebrity guests, nice meal, charity auction. Please come," he finished, with his hands clasped together, as if sending up a small prayer.

"In London?"

"I'm afraid so. Some ghastly big hotel. Now, what's it called? Chipolata? No, that's not it." Kate knew he was teasing her, so gave him her best school-teacher look, but he continued, "Could be The Sausage. No, that's not it. The Savaloy, that's the one!" he said, with mock disgust.

"The Savoy," Kate corrected. "I'm a little tempted. I'll think about it. Okay?"

"Okay, darling girl. Let me know soon. Anyway, this script. First we do a rough-and- ready conversion from book to script. You know, the basics – Fred speaks blah blah, Gertrude speaks blah blah."

"Don't recall those characters in my book, Marcus, but perhaps I'll use them in a future novel."

"Yes, well, I'm just trying to explain that we have our work cut out. After the rough script, we need to get it to a full, usable state. What works in a book doesn't always work on the screen. Each scene has to be thought through – each setting, where the characters are, how they are standing. Showing their emotions and what they're feeling, that's a tricky one. Special effects."

"Let me stop you there," interrupted Kate. "The story is about two people getting in touch through the Internet after a number of years. There won't be much in the way of special effects, I'm afraid, Marcus. I think this might be a little different to what you're used to on Agent X."

"I think I'll be happier when we are locked away and can focus on it and start to bring it to life," said Marcus, leaning back in the armchair and resting his head against its back.

"Locked away," chuckled Kate. "You make it sound like a prison sentence."

"This isn't an afternoon's work, Kate. I suggest we go to my cottage in the Cotswolds for a couple of months until we have cracked this." This made Kate sit up and suddenly feel a little more sober than she had two minutes before. Marcus was right. She had not appreciated what sort of commitment he was asking from her or how much work was involved. She stared at Marcus as he relaxed in her armchair. He was a real gent. Even in this relaxed situation, having consumed a fair amount of champagne, his tie was still in place and his top shirt button firmly done up. For a man in his fifties, his neatly trimmed wavy hair was very grey, even white in places, but it somehow seemed to suit him. Kate couldn't imagine how odd he must have looked when it had had colour in it.

"A couple of months," she repeated slowly.

"Easily," nodded Marcus. "Let's set ourselves a first task of reading the book again so it's fresh in our minds."

"But I wrote it. So I know the story pretty well."

"You'll be surprised. You'll see it differently if you read it and try to picture every scene on the big screen," and he flung his arms out, narrowly missing his glass, which was perched precariously on the coffee table. "Think about the characters' expressions, how their faces change, how they react to news, how they run." He stopped himself as he saw that Kate was about to interject with another comment about it not being an action movie.

"Let's meet up next week and map out a plan. We'll aim to set off for the Cotswolds straight after the New Year," Marcus suggested enthusiastically. "To an exciting New Year!" said Marcus, as he raised his glass in a toast.

"An exciting New Year!" concurred Kate, and their glasses clinked once more.

Andy finished tapping the panel pins into the frame of the front door to hold the trimmed cover of the *Illustrated Atlas* in place. Sarah didn't have any odd bits of wood lying about and neither of them felt like venturing into the loft, so Andy made do with the book cover and pledged to replace it. He felt suddenly exhausted after the evening's turbulent events. Sarah, on the other hand, appeared still to be high on adrenalin and was busily wiping down kitchen surfaces in between running to the bottom of the stairs to listen out for Amy. As she ran into the hall for the second time within the space of two minutes, Andy stopped her.

"Sarah, she's fine. Amy is completely unaware of the drama that unfolded here tonight." Sarah looked at him doubtfully. "Honestly, she'll be fine. She'll wake up tomorrow full of beans. Trust me."

"I thought I heard her," said Sarah. Andy shook his head.

"I'd have heard her, too. She's not made a murmur since you put her up there."

"What have they said to her, though? Shaun and Irene – they could poison her against me," Sarah said with a sigh.

"Not likely. She's a bright little thing, that one, and she doesn't see that much of them. You know, Shaun might be a bit more reasonable, and you might worry less, if Shaun was more used to having her. If he was able to look after her a bit more often." Sarah's eyes flashed and Andy knew he was overstepping the line.

"How can you say that? He's irresponsible. Look at the fiasco tonight, all caused by Shaun."

"Not all caused by Sh…"

"Don't try to defend him, Andy," Sarah spat, in hushed tones so as not to wake Amy. "If you've finished, I think you'd better go," she said. Andy handed her the small hammer and left-over panel pins, picked up his jacket and mobile, and left without another word.

Chapter 5

"Ah, dear boy, glad I've caught you. I'd like you to meet someone," called Marcus as a tall, dark-haired, god-like creature came into view.

"Marcus!" exclaimed the god as he engulfed Marcus in a bear hug before moving on. "Niamh!" he almost sang her name as he kissed her lightly on each cheek, and then looked her up and down admiringly. "Beautiful as ever. I can't stop. I'm sitting down the front. Maybe I'll catch you two later, after the auction?"

"Tim, just two seconds. This is Kate," Marcus announced proudly, as he turned to Kate and gestured with an outstretched hand. Kate had been momentarily mesmerised by Tim's presence, which delayed her reactions. By the time she had stood up and thrust out her hand towards him, Tim was already receding.

"Sorry, I've got to dash," he called over his shoulder as he bounded off towards the stage, stopping only to kiss two tiny females in slinky dresses and skyscraper heels.

"Kate, I'm so sorry," Marcus said, clasping her still-outstretched hand and returning it to her side.

"It's okay, you don't have to apologise on his behalf," replied Kate feeling very self-conscious as she retook her seat next to Marcus and tucked a non-existent strand of hair behind her left ear. "So, that was the famous Timothy Calder."

"It was. He's not usually a complete arse. Just sometimes, you understand," said Marcus. Niamh leaned forward and linked her arm through Marcus's.

"Tim is deceptively lovely when you get to know him," offered Niamh, in her barely detectable American accent, as she gave a broad, knowing smile and hugged Marcus's arm, as if sensing his mixture of embarrassment and annoyance.

Kate had decided to be brave and go to the PSDS Christmas Ball, as Marcus had suggested. She had been persuaded by Niamh to make a weekend of it and was staying with them, which had made the whole thing seem a lot less daunting – Marcus had arranged transport and tickets. Dinner was served in an impressive fashion as 12 waiters and waitresses came to the table simultaneously to serve everyone together. A nod from one waiter was the cue for the ladies to be served their starters and on the second nod plates were swept into place in front of the men. Kate didn't manage to drink further than halfway down her champagne flute before someone refilled it. The talk on the table was general updates between those who already knew each other and general-interest questions between those who didn't. Marcus was very attentive and pointed out a selection of people to Kate during the evening. Niamh was chatty, too, and frequently made Kate giggle, mainly through her gentle teasing of Marcus.

After dinner there was lots of table-swapping as people started to mingle or network, depending on their intentions. Kate wandered through the sea of dinner suits feeling like the villain at a James Bond convention and found herself talking to the floor manager for the latest Sky dance show – a very friendly woman and also a reader of Kate's books. Marcus was keen to catch up with Tim, so when he saw that Kate was deep in conversation, he headed off towards the front tables. He spotted Tim with his arm draped casually around the shoulder of a slender female in impossible heels as he was showing her a photo of his Italian villa. Marcus strolled over to the pair and introduced himself.

"Good evening, I'm Marcus. Is this man bothering you?"

"Marcus, this is Lumina, my soon-to-be leading lady in *Love*," he gave a little pause, "*Dot Com*."

"Very pleased to meet you. I'm Marcus Leonard." Lumina shook his hand limply, but appeared to have no recognition of who he was.

"Marcus is a well-known script writer. He's the genius that turns it from a dull old book into a blockbuster film script," said Tim, his eyes wide and expressive.

"Tim's going to spank me if I don't learn my lines," Lumina purred as she swayed slightly, which could have been due to the height of her heels, the champagne, Tim's close proximity or a combination of all three.

"And if you do?" smiled Marcus, raising an eyebrow at Tim. Lumina looked puzzled, but was quickly distracted.

"I need to talk to Fritz. I'll see you later, Tim. Nice to meet you, Mark," and she tottered off.

"Bloody hell, Tim! We haven't even started filming and you've homed in on her. She's young, Tim, and we don't want her hating you for the duration of filming, so could you keep your trousers zipped for a couple of months? Please!"

"It pays to warm a few up. Don't worry! I wouldn't do anything to mess this up. I know it's important to you because of that author lady you're friendly with."

"Kate Marshall," Marcus said, to which Tim nodded distractedly.

"So, are you enjoying tonight?" asked Tim.

"Yes, you know me. I like a party, unlike you, you miserable sod."

"I just see them for what they are. Opportunities to schmooze and network and, in this rare case, make some much-needed cash for a very worthy cause."

"So, who are you here with tonight? Is it that lovely girl you were with last time I saw you? Sorry, I can't remember her name."

"Poppy?" suggested Tim.

"No, that wasn't her name."

"Kitty?"

"No, she was a blonde girl."

"Oh! Gemma Arterton. That was ages ago,"

"Blonde, not Bond!"

"Jemima?" Tim offered as he waved away the champagne-wielding waiter.

"No, that wasn't it. She was with you at that awards evening a couple of weeks ago."

"Oh, Katrina," Tim said with relief.

"Yes. Katrina!"

"That didn't last. She wanted to choose furniture together after the second date, that's never a good sign," flinched Tim. Marcus nodded and thought for a few seconds.

"Did you go out with those others in that short space of time?"

Tim smiled at the question. "It was two weeks ago, Marcus!"

"Are you ever going to settle down?"

"Don't rush me, I'm getting around to it," grinned Tim, patting Marcus affectionately on the back.

"Via a particularly scenic route, it would seem."

"Well 'it' has never happened to me."

"By 'it' do you mean love?" asked Marcus.

"Yeah, love, whatever it really is. You and Niamh have it, my friends Toby and Greg and my cousin Steph and her awful husband Ramsay have it, Posh and Becks, Elton and David, Barbie and Ken, I think, but that's about it. The rest are just getting by and I'm not going to spend my life getting by with one woman when I can have a bloody excellent time enjoying it with lots of women. It's not fair, not to share!"

"You are missing the point," said Marcus adjusting his bow tie.

"Anyway, I might have already had 'it'; I could have had 'it' lots of times. How do you really know if you have 'it' or not?" Marcus shook his head and waved Niamh over to them and, as if she'd been waiting for the signal, Niamh waved her acknowledgement and elegantly made her way through the tables and gave Tim a kiss on his cheek. Marcus put an arm around her waist and pulled her to his side "Help me, darling. What does being in love feel like and how do you know that it's the real thing?"

"Wow, now there's a question I wasn't expecting. Give me a minute, boys." Niamh thought for a moment then said thoughtfully, "For a woman, it's like your first orgasm." Tim stepped backwards and almost spat out his recent sip of water.

"Oh, please do explain," he encouraged, grinning from ear to ear like a schoolboy. Niamh ignored him and continued undeterred.

"You see, up until then, if someone asks you if you've had an orgasm you reply, 'I'm not sure. Probably. I might have done'. Then you have one and you realise, that's it! That's an orgasm; that's what all the fuss is about and it's everything you hoped it would be and more. And it's only then that you realise it's completely unmistakeable. And finding love is exactly the same." Tim looked puzzled and rolled his eyes at Marcus, who just nodded sagely.

"She's absolutely right, Tim. You will definitely know when it hits you."

"There are rather a few more people having orgasms than falling in love, I suspect. Well, definitely, where I'm involved." Tim winked and took another sip of water.

"I suspect most of the ladies in your company are doing both. Please be careful with them, Tim. Having your heart broken hurts," said Niamh, touching his arm.

"In other words, please don't be an arse," stated Marcus, with a smile.

"You've reminded me that I need to find the Corrie crew. There's a couple of ladies there I need to give my number to. Well, Pippa's number, obviously, not mine!"

"How is your overworked PA?" asked Niamh.

"She's fine, she loves it. We must do dinner soon," said Tim, indicating the three of them. And with that, he was gone.

When they announced the music was about to start Kate returned to her seat. Across on the Corrie table, Kate watched

Tim joking with two of the ladies, who were giggling excitedly like tickled hyenas. The music came from some very trendy group and someone who was third on a talent-singing show a couple of years ago. There was a break before the auction, so Kate and Niamh did the customary thing and went to the ladies together. Niamh was a kind soul wrapped in a vibrant personality, who seemed to worry just a little bit about everyone.

"You're not really enjoying it, are you?" asked Niamh gently as they made their way upstairs.

"Oh no, it's lovely. The food's lovely and everyone's..."

"Lovely?"

"Yes. Sorry, you'd think I'd have a wider vocabulary, being a writer." They stopped at the bottom of the first flight of stairs so that they could continue their conversation and stood back to let others pass.

"Kate, can I be honest with you?"

"Of course," said Kate, although she was hoping Niamh wasn't going to be too honest about Kate's dress. She knew now that the plain black would have been far better than the sparkly one she was wearing. She looked as though Amy had sprinkled glitter on her.

"When you are ready, you will enjoy things again. You just need to give yourself permission. You deserve to enjoy yourself, Kate."

Kate knew exactly what Niamh meant. Since James had gone there hadn't been many moments where Kate had found herself having fun and when she did, it was like a shutter coming down that suddenly made her stop. She didn't know if it was her own insecurities or sadness, but there was definitely something that kept moderating her happiness. Kate smiled at Niamh and nodded.

"You get things out of proportion in your head. I actually worried that there might be an empty seat next to me," said Kate. Niamh responded with a pained expression. "I know it's daft and it has been lovely tonight. Nobody has asked me about James and, in an odd way, that's a little sad. Like he's been forgotten. There's no pleasing me, is there?" said Kate, with a shrug and a small smile.

"We're women. Of course there's not," Niamh said, giving her a hug.

Niamh and Kate bypassed the nearest toilets to avoid a queue and found themselves in a quaint English oasis with an exotic garden mural on the wall and no queue. Niamh disappeared behind an ornate door painted a delicate shade of green and Kate clip-clopped her way down to a free cubicle at the other end of the room. Once inside, she could clearly hear the conversation from the cubicle next door, where someone was sniffing and someone, with an Irish accent and a slight slur, was comforting them.

"That's better, Jemima, he's not worth it. You're worth ten of him. You're better off without him, so you are. He's just a flashy bastard."

"But I love him," squeaked the sniffer, followed by a loud, unladylike nose-blow.

"He doesn't deserve your love. You save it for someone who does."

This is just like being eighteen again, thought Kate with a smile, but this time she wasn't the sniffer, which did make her feel better. She found herself ready to leave the cubicle, hand paused on the flush, but she couldn't quite bring herself to push down the handle because she wanted to hear more about the sniffer and the flashy bastard.

"When he came over, I thought he was going to join our table, but he just patted me on the back like footballers do and ..." more sniffing followed, "did you see him with her from *Daybreak*? And that Lumina, she was all over him like a rash."

"It'll be her with the rash come tomorrow, I wouldn't wonder," and with that they both laughed and Kate felt that was a good point to flush and leave.

Niamh was standing outside the toilets smoothing her deep-plum dress over her hips. She was a naturally elegant woman, always looked immaculate, but somehow made it seem as if it had all happened without any effort. As Kate emerged from the toilets, Niamh lit up like a beacon.

"Here you are. That's good. I was starting to wonder if you'd gone out of the window."

"There was no window, Niamh. Stop worrying, I'm fine." At least she was feeling better than the sniffer. When they got back to their table, Kate and Niamh were greeted by Marcus as if they'd just returned from a marathon.

"Ladies, you're back. Wonderful. Just in time for the auction."

"Marcus, who is Lumina?" asked Kate.

"She's your leading lady!" He swung around dramatically, to look her square in the eyes.

"Right. Okay. Still don't know who she is, sorry."

"Kate, have you been living in a cave? She is a starlet with huge potential. Bit of a diva, by all accounts, but very talked-about right now."

"Would I have seen her in anything?"

"Did you do Cannes this year?" he asked, but Kate didn't dignify that with an answer and Marcus was already shaking his head. "Obviously not. She played a gangster's moll in that Brit flick, the one that was half black and white apart from the machete scenes. She got terrific reviews."

Kate was thankful she'd missed the machete film – violence and horror were most definitely not her thing.

"Is she here tonight?"

"Yes. Do you want to meet her?"

"Maybe later."

"Do you see the five tables at the front? She's on the second one from the left and she's near the stage. Lots of blonde hair and a blue, off-the-shoulder dress."

"Yes, got her," replied Kate, as she spotted the back of her head. With its mass of back-combed hair on top of a very petite body she looked like a lollipop.

"So, leading lady, you said?"

"Yes! Do you not read your emails?"

The music built up and the host gyrated onto the stage to start the auction. It started off quite tamely with some pairs of tickets for dinner and overnight stays at the Savoy hotel. Next up was a bar stool from the Rovers' Return signed by the cast of Corrie, and a signed England football that caused a flurry of excitement, followed by a box for Ladies Day at Ascot, and designer diamond earrings, which really hotted up the bidding frenzy. Various other increasingly exotic items followed and the final amounts went higher and higher. Kate was pleased when the host announced the last item. It was a romantic weekend in Monaco in a top hotel, with helicopter flights and a party on a private yacht.

"Who'll start me at 10,000?" he asked.

"Not me," muttered Kate. She looked around the room to see if she could spot any more celebrities and do a bit of people-watching. When Kate pulled her attention back to the auction, the host was getting very overexcited and waving frantically between three tables at the front.

"I think Tim is after this one. He likes to go for the last lot of the night," Marcus said. Kate strained her neck and could see two men up on their feet, waving their arms about, at tables either side of Tim's. Tim was the complete opposite, as he was sitting looking very relaxed, with one foot resting on his knee. The man on the left shook his head and sat down, and the host wiped his forehead and turned back to Tim.

"Any advance on 100,000 pounds?" he said smoothly, and the man to his right shook his head and sat down too. Kate noticed that this man was sitting next to Lumina, although she was now sitting sideways on her chair, staring at Tim and clapping her hands. "Sold to Timothy Calder!" The whole room erupted into applause, hoots and whistles as Tim casually got up and sauntered through the tables shaking hands and nodding acknowledgements. It was the most impressive exit Kate had ever seen.

"Bravo, dear boy!" called Marcus as Tim walked past, and he received an exaggerated wink in return.

"Ooh, these look nice," said Didi with wide eyes as her fingers hovered over the H- shaped box of chocolates. Kate was already lounging in the armchair, letting an Eton Mess- flavoured one melt in her mouth.

"They are amazing," Kate managed to reply, without dribbling. Kate had done the tea round in record time and was now relaxing in Didi's room. Didi settled on a praline, leant back on her pillows and closed her eyes as she bit into the chocolate. There was silence for a few seconds whilst they savoured the moment of indulgence. Didi opened one eye.

"So, tell me tales of sex, drugs and rock and roll, or hip hop and street, or whatever it is these days. I've been dying to hear all about your charity evening with the stars," said Didi with a cheeky grin.

"Uh," groaned Kate, her eyes still closed.

"You can do better than that, and if you can't, just make it up!"

Kate shuffled herself into a more upright position and looked at Didi, who was excited and hopeful. "The food was excellent, there was plenty of champagne, the music was okay and the evening raised thousands of pounds for a very good cause."

"That's the party line. Now for the gossip. So, who did you meet? Anyone famous?"

"The host was that celebrity jungle winner from a few years ago – the tall one who screamed a lot."

"I think I know the one. Who else?"

"Our table was all authors and publishers. The table behind us was all from *Coronation Street*. They were a rowdy bunch."

"Now you're talking! I like a bit of Corrie. Which Corrie actors were there?" Didi leaned a little forward.

"Sorry, I don't watch it, so I don't know their names."

"Shame," said Didi, sinking back on her pillows with a small wince as a tube got snagged.

"Alan Rickman was there."

"Really? Did you speak to him?"

"No, but I saw him quite close up. He said goodbye to Marcus as he was leaving."

"What about that chap they've got lined up to play the lead in your film? Timothy what's-his-name?"

"Calder. I only saw him for a moment, but I can't deny he's completely gorgeous."

"I was having a good look at him the other day. He's in those magazines," Didi said, pointing to a pile on her bedside cabinet. "I'd only kick him out of bed to get me a cuppa!"

Kate pondered for a moment, "I'm not sure if it's his eyes or the smile, but he definitely has something. He's better in the flesh," said Kate, leaning over and picking up a random chocolate from the box.

"I bet he is," said Didi, with a mischievous smile. "Anyone sexy on your table?"

"No. Sorry to disappoint you. Any developments here?"

"Heck, no. I badger them on a daily basis to send me home, but they fob me off."

"Be patient. You've got weeks here yet. So, where's home?"

"A little flat just a stroll from the Downs. Huge buses pass by just outside all the time, so I can get into town as easy as having my own chauffeur." Didi adjusted her top sheet.

"By town, you mean London?"

"As the youth of today would say 'der'."

"Sounds nice."

"It's home and the local council are spending millions in the local area. Up and coming we are, don't you know," Didi said with a chuckle.

"They must have convalescent homes in London. Why come to deepest, darkest Northamptonshire?"

"Same level of care but cheaper."

Kate nodded her understanding, "Don't be in a rush to leave, Didi, it'll be different at home, having to do everything yourself. Make sure you're completely better."

"Stop fussing. I can look after myself. Always have, always will."

"Yes, I know, but humour me. When you're ready, I could take you home, settle you in. Okay?"

"If it's no trouble, I'd like that, thank you," smiled Didi, and for a brief moment there was a glimpse of a lonely old lady, but in a flash she was gone. "So definitely no chance of rampant sex at this do, then?"

Kate just rolled her eyes.

Chapter 6

Kate was feeling surprisingly bright when she woke up. Some nights she struggled to get to sleep, but last night she had fallen asleep quickly and slept soundly, until the birds had eased her to consciousness, and she felt all the better for it. The spluttering of Sarah's car signalled her timely arrival and Kate put the kettle on.

"Tea or coffee?" she called out, as Sarah shut the door behind her. Sarah was one of those people who drank both, depending on her mood.

"Brr, tea please," she shivered. "You could freeze your tail off out there today."

Sarah wore skinny jeans and furry boots, which highlighted her ridiculously thin thighs. She had two jumpers on under her jacket, which she had wrapped tightly around herself as she dashed inside.

"Are you picking up fashion tips from the oldies at the home?" chided Sarah, pointing at Kate's long, grey cardigan.

"It's warm. I'm only seeing you today and you're my friend, so shut up." They both sat down at the kitchen table and Sarah gave two envelopes to Kate.

"Happy Christmas!"

"Thank you," Kate said, as she ripped open the first envelope and removed the card. "Oh!" she said, studying the Christmas card that depicted a shiny red Christmas tree with antlers impaled in it. "Thank you. That has to be the scariest looking Christmas card I have ever seen," said Kate with a forced smile.

"I know," shrugged Sarah. "It's the thought that counts. Anyway, they were on sale."

"Where at? The Freddie Krueger gift shop?"

They both laughed and Kate opened the second card. As she did so, spoonfuls of glitter landed on the kitchen table. Kate smiled and studied the home-made card that had a triangular piece of white paper stuck on the front, with a pink head drawn on the top and lots of glitter all around it. At the bottom of the card, Amy had written in her neatest writing "James".

"It's an angel," Kate said at last.

"Spot on," replied Sarah, leaning over and giving her a hug. "You okay?"

"Yeah. I am, actually. That was really sweet of her." Kate shook a little more glitter off the card, which willingly obliged and added to the already well-decorated table.

"So, do we have a plan for attacking the shops today? I'd love to get it all finished if we could," Sarah said, as she cupped her mug with both hands in an attempt to warm herself up.

"I have a list," said Kate, pulling a piece of paper out of her cardigan pocket with an excited flourish. Kate made lots of lists. James hadn't been a fan; he'd made a few comments about it being her way of controlling things, but to Kate making a list and ticking things off was fun.

"You really are Little Miss Organised," mocked Sarah, who had absolutely no idea of what she would buy for anyone and even less idea as to how she would pay for it. As if sensing Sarah's dilemma, Kate opened a cupboard and produced four wicker baskets. "I found these and I thought I might make them into hampers for a couple of people. Pick out their favourite coffee and biscuits, add some of my special mince pies with maybe a bottle of fizz. What do you think?"

"Really great idea. I would love it if someone did that for me."

"I only need two, though, so would you like the others? Can you get some cellophane and bows from work to finish them off?" asked Kate.

"No problem. Tick. That's two presents sorted already. We are on a roll!"

Sarah had two jobs – there was the bar work for extra money since Shaun left, but her real love was floristry. Unfortunately, the small florist she worked for didn't need her full time, and didn't pay particularly well, but she loved it and her boss, Esme, was more like a friend than a boss, so it was a great place to escape to three times a week. The florist's had a great name too – it was called "Back to the Fuchsia", which brought a smile to a lot of faces, including Kate's.

"I've something to tell you," said Kate.

"You've won the super-duper, multi-rollover lottery?" said Sarah hopefully, to which Kate shook her head. "You're pregnant with triplets and it's a girl, a boy and a puppy?"

"Not very likely. I think you need to have sex with a magician for that to happen." Sarah took another sip of tea and scrunched up her face in thought.

"You're going to be the next prime minister and make chocolate free for women?"

"No, sorry, you're out of guesses. I'm going to stay with Marcus for a while so we can finish writing this script. He's got a place in the Cotswolds that he escapes to."

"When, how long for and can I borrow your clothes whilst you're gone?"

"Straight after New Year, for a couple of months and yes you can, but you'll look daft. My clothes are all size 10 to 12 and you're what now? Minus 4?"

"Yeah, something like that. What's happening to Marmalade?"

"I was thinking about a house-sitter. Do you fancy it?"

"I would really love to, but it's too far from Amy's school and work. Sorry."

"Never mind, I thought you'd say that, so I'm thinking of asking Andy."

"Good idea. From what he said, his house is a wreck and probably being used by film companies to double as a war zone, so I think he'd jump at the chance."

"Right, let's hit the shops!" said Kate emphatically, and they downed their drinks and headed out into the December madness.

"Er, yes, I'm sorry. I got caught up a bit…"

"Tim, are you kissing someone?" snapped Pippa into her mobile. Being a personal assistant to Timothy Calder was part-nanny, part-project manager and part-detective.

"Sorry. Bye," he whispered.

"Bye? Tim, I thought you wanted to sort out Christmas shopping before lunch? Lunch is booked and I can't move it if you want to get to the TV studio on time…. Are you still there?"

Tim stopped kissing and shut the hotel door behind him. "Sorry, Pips, I wasn't saying 'Bye' to you it was… ah, well, it wasn't you."

"No, some poor unfortunate soul, I suspect," replied Pippa crossly.

"Now, Pips. You're not jealous, are you?" Tim smiled into the phone.

"No," came the unequivocal reply.

"Are you sure?" he said slowly, teasing her.

"Yes, I am sure, thank you very much for asking. Tim, shall I just order what I think for Christmas presents, because you're clearly not going to meet me this morning, you've run out of time?"

"No, don't be over-dramatic, I'll make it. In fact, I'll be with you soon," he said, striding towards a lift as the doors were about to close. He beamed a smile at the scowling female occupant as he waved his free hand between the closing doors.

"How long is 'soon' exactly, Tim? I know what your idea of time-keeping is like – 'soon' could mean Tuesday," Pippa said, with a sigh.

As the woman in her mid-thirties registered who had just joined her in the lift, her demeanour completely changed. She went from ice queen to smitten school girl quicker than switching on a light. Tim stepped inside and his lift companion stared at him, totally mesmerised by his striking green eyes. Tim smiled back at her and mouthed "ground floor?" before leaning across and pressing the button to send them racing downwards. The woman mouthed back "please". This may have been because she was mimicking Tim, or more likely, because she'd lost the power of speech. Tim gave her another killer smile and made apologetic gestures at his phone before continuing his conversation.

"Pips, you really should trust me, you know. I've never really let you down, now have I?"

Pippa didn't need to think about this question.

"Talk show two weeks ago; you were playing drinking games with Bruce Willis so you were both late for filming. Last Agent X film, you slept with Winona what's-her-face so she burst into tears every time she saw you and I had to choreograph her movements to avoid her bumping into you for three weeks of filming. You promised to call my mum on her birthday, but despite me writing the number down on a piece of paper, a post-it note, your hand and texting it to you, you still never managed it. You called Eamonn Holmes a f…"

"Wow, that's a long list, Pips. What can I say except I'm truly sorry?" Ping went the lift and he blew a kiss to his lift partner, who visibly swooned and stayed in the lift, even when the doors closed again.

"So, where exactly are you?" said Pippa, looking at her watch.

"Here I am," said the husky voice just behind her left ear.

"Crap!" shouted Pippa, just a little too loud. "You really shouldn't do that," she scolded, as she felt her cheeks burn with the rush of blood and her neck tingled with the sensation of his warm breath. Tim ended the call on his mobile and jumped over the arms of the two large, green, high-back chairs and landed neatly in the one next to Pippa.

"Hi, Pips, here I am, just a little late."

Pippa had been waiting in the Thames Foyer at the Savoy, Tim's favourite London hotel, for her boss to arrive so that he could give her his instructions on what to buy for his family and friends for Christmas. Pippa was keen to do this earlier this year after the nightmare that saw her wrapping Tim's presents and delivering them herself last Christmas Eve.

Pippa pulled herself together and pushed the selection of Christmas gift guides across the low glass table to Tim. "I'll order drinks, whilst you look at these. Tea?"

"Lady Grey, no milk…"

"I know, speak to Alistair about your secret stash."

"Please and some madeleines." Tim perused the Tiffany brochure whilst Pippa discussed their order with a waitress.

"I'm so sorry, but we don't have Lady Grey. We do have Earl Grey," offered the impeccably uniformed waitress, who looked desolate that she wasn't able to provide what Pippa had requested.

"It's okay, I know you stock about 30 different teas but this awkward whatsit only likes Lady Grey. So if you speak to Alistair, he keeps a pot of the stuff just for Tim and he'll sort it out."

"I see," said the waitress, who still looked confused, but went off to fulfil the order all the same.

Tim was casually dressed in jeans, white t-shirt and light-grey jacket. As he leant forward, his dark hair fell onto his forehead; it was a little long at the moment and she made a mental note to book him a hair appointment. Tim's eyes fixed on the pages of the brochure and she watched him absent-mindedly lick his index finger and turn the page. Pippa wasn't sure how long it was that she'd been watching Tim, but Alistair appeared with a silver tray and set down the ornate silver tea pot in front of Tim with a wink, followed by two trays of three miniature madeleines and a cappuccino for Pippa. Pippa eyed the madeleines enviously before pulling herself together.

"Right, who's first? Your brother and his family?"

"Yep, okay. Bernie would like a large Christmas Hamper from Fortnum's and the boys would like those new remote-control helicopter things that shoot at each other," said Tim, opening up the Hamley's booklet to show Pippa. She moved in closer to look and took in a huge waft of his recently applied aftershave. Some days this was the best job in the world.

"Right. Good start. Who's next?"

"I need a couple of these necklaces, usual gift wrapping," said Tim, pointing out the diamond-encrusted necklaces.

"Is that two, then?" said Pippa harshly.

"Yes, two of those, please, and then two of those not so…"

"Expensive, gaudy, brash?" suggested Pippa with a forced smile, staring at the necklace Tim was pointing to.

"Sparkly," explained Tim with a tilt of his head.

"Okay," said Pippa, wondering who would be opening those on Christmas morning.

"Auntie Pam would love this bangle," said Tim, pausing to point at a heavily enamelled piece in Tiffany's brochure, "and also the wine hamper from Fortnum's."

"I bet she would," muttered Pippa as she jotted it all down. She couldn't help but enjoy herself, spending vast amounts of someone else's money was fun and quite therapeutic.

"Pips, you're a complete star. Right, job done." Tim said, twenty minutes later.

Pippa looked at her watch. They were still on schedule.

"Right, Terry should be bringing the car round any minute now. Okay?"

Tim's phone beeped into life. He checked the screen and jumped up.

"Got to take this. I'll meet you out the front." He strode out of earshot as he answered it. Pippa sat back and took in the beauty of her surroundings: the sumptuous furnishings, the indoor gazebo with piano to accompany afternoon tea, the stunningly crafted domed cupola above her, letting the light flood in. There was something special about the Thames Foyer. It was luxurious and yet comfortable and she loved that her job enabled her to spend time there and call it work.

Kate could barely feel her fingers. This sensation was partly due to the chill in the air, but mainly because of the many bags she was now carrying. Sarah was a woman on a mission and they had visited the market and countless shops and must have walked the equivalent of at least three marathons, Kate decided.

"Woman in need of a break here," said Kate, in desperation.

"Come on. Don't give up now, we've done really well. I just need to find something small and cheap that looks tasteful for Amy's teacher," said Sarah.

"No. I'll stage a sit-in here," said Kate, as she stopped walking. Sarah was aware that Kate was no longer next to her and spun around, her shopping making her nearly overbalance with the generated momentum.

"Really?"

"Really!"

"Come on then, lightweight, let's dump this load in the car first."

After depositing their hoards of treasure, they went to a coffee shop, where everyone looked slightly stressed and had multi-coloured bags at their feet.

"I saw you looking at that shirt earlier," said Sarah.

"The pin-stripe one was lovely," replied Kate, blowing onto her hot tea.

"Who were you thinking of getting it for, then?"

There was a pause before Kate said slowly, "James." Sarah smiled and reached across the table to take Kate's hand.

"I'm okay. Really I am," said Kate returning the squeeze. "What is odd is that last year I had a reference point 'how crap did I feel this time last year?' Nearly two years on, I can't remember exactly how I felt or what I was doing. People have stopped asking me how I'm coping, too."

"Because they can see for themselves," replied Sarah, nodding wisely.

"So, how am I coping, Sarah?"

"Oh, you're doing just fine."

Sarah gave her a big hug. James had often hugged Kate, of course, and so many times he had made her jump and laugh by sneaking up behind her and enveloping her in a hug. She was sad that she would never feel that again and she added hugs to her mental list of things she missed.

"It will keep getting better. Amy is completely over Sebastian," said Sarah helpfully.

"That's because she's got another hamster."

"Perhaps that's the answer?" shrugged Sarah, with a wry smile.

"I don't think furry rodents are for me…or men. Not right now, anyway."

"Okay, not right now, but you know you shouldn't rule it out. One day maybe?" ventured Sarah.

"One day. Maybe. Anyway, talking of furry rodents, how is Shaun?"

"Oh, don't put poor Sebastian in the same category as that turd! He makes my blood boil just thinking about him." Sarah raked her hands through her short hair as she felt the familiar feelings surge inside her.

"He goes to a lot of trouble to wind you up," said Kate.

"I wish he wouldn't. I feel like I can never be rid of him because of Amy. He's a mistake I made years ago, but I'm always going to be paying for it and that seems so unfair."

"It is unfair. You need to find a way of minimising the impact he has on you because I don't think he'll ever change."

"Hit man?" suggested Sarah, with a hopeful look in her eyes.

"Too expensive."

"Kill him myself with the tin opener?"

"Too messy."

"Run away and live in a cave?" offered Sarah.

"Bit short on caves around here. Come on, chin up. You're made of sterner stuff. Anyway, don't let him spoil our shopping day. Where to next?" said Kate, in a poor attempt to jolly her out of the hole she was in.

"Back to the market, I think, to get one of those key ring and pen sets for Amy's teacher, and the cheap bookshop for my little bookworm."

"Then we'll finish at the posh chocolate shop and treat ourselves. My treat," reassured Kate before Sarah could protest about the cost.

Sarah almost fell through the door as it swung open with a huge bang. She struggled up the hall, looking like a kangaroo with six bowling balls in its pouch, as she clung on to all her bags. Just past the stairs, she stopped as something caught her eye. She shuffled backwards and looked up the stairs. On the landing was a step-ladder reaching up into her loft.

"Thanks for bringing the ladder back, Shaun." There was a long pause and then Shaun, who was a wiry man with closely cropped gingery-brown hair and matching chin stubble, appeared at the loft hatch, tucked something into his inside jacket pocket and reversed down the ladder. He took down the ladder and carried it downstairs. Sarah and her bundle of bags shuffled backwards to the front door to block his way.

"Did someone leave your cage open again?"

"Been spending my money, have ya," he said, nodding at the bags. "Got yourself some more luxuries?"

Sarah did her best to ignore him, but it was really hard not to take the bait.

"It's presents for our daughter."

"Yeah, she'll love Radox," he snarled, peering into one of the bags.

"Why are you in my loft?"

"I was in *our* loft! Because I was hiding Amy's Christmas

65

present."

"Why?" said Sarah, suspiciously.

"Because of all the break-ins around here. Dodgy area this is. People stealing little kids' Christmas presents; awful business. So, because I'm a good dad, I've put our Amy's present safe in the loft."

"What did you get her?"

"Surprise."

"So, not what she asked for, then. You can leave the ladder. Thanks."

"No can do. No ladder means nobody can nick Amy's present," he said, tapping the ladder.

"Don't be an arse, Shaun. Just leave it out the back."

"That's not safe. Like asking for someone to come in the night and kidnap her."

Sarah took a deep breath to control her temper.

"I'm not having a battle of wits with you, Shaun. I'll not fight with an unarmed man," she said, dropping all the bags at her feet and blocking the way. The relief in her fingers was immense as the blood began to flow back into them.

"Dear Sarah," smiled Shaun, as he reached across as if to stroke her face. For a moment they just looked at each other. Sarah thought he was going to kiss her. He paused, put his arms around her and lifted her out of the way, then yanked open the door, walked across the bags and left, taking the ladder with him.

"I really don't know what makes you such an arsehole, but it works!" shouted Sarah.

Chapter 7

"Come on, Lumina, don't be a bore. You have to come out and play," said Tim.

"I can't, what about Horse?"

"What horse?"

"My chihuahua. He's called Horse. I can't leave him."

"Could a neighbour look after him?" suggested Tim, who was now a little bored and beginning to thumb through names on his mobile phone.

"I guess so, but I'm still not sure about going out with you."

"It's traditional," said Tim, trying to sound convincing.

"Traditional?"

"Every good leading man takes his leading lady out for a meal before rehearsals start."

"But they don't start for weeks."

"I'm a forward planner and, besides, it's good luck for the film."

"In that case, okay. What time?"

"Seven o'clock."

"Okay, see you then," squeaked Lumina excitedly. She knew she wasn't going to be able to resist Timothy Calder much longer, but what girl could? One dinner with him and she'd be on the cover of every magazine and filling lots of pages inside them, too. At precisely seven o'clock, a black stretch limousine pulled up outside

Lumina's apartment building and the driver opened a rear door to reveal Tim holding a bottle of champagne. Lumina knew she looked fabulous as she walked towards the car in a short, tight, black designer dress and slid into the seat next to Tim.

"Wow, you look out of this world!" Tim said, handing her a glass.

"Thank you," she said, trying to keep her excitement under wraps. "Where are we going?"

"Do you like French food?" asked Tim, with a tilt of his head.

"My favourite," lied Lumina.

"Excellent. London City Airport, please, Terry," said Tim to the driver as he reached into his inside pocket and produced two passports. "Aren't PAs wonderful?" he laughed, and Lumina joined in.

In less than two hours, they were in the heart of Paris. As they sat on the private boat, with candles flickering around them, Lumina felt she'd probably had enough champagne to ask a few more searching questions.

"Does your bad reputation bother you?" she asked.

"What bad reputation?"

"You know, for all the over-the-top gestures you perform to lure women into bed."

"That's completely untrue. I don't know where they drum up this nonsense," he said, as he leaned back on his chair to get the waiter's attention, "Garçon, another bottle of Dom Perignon, s'il vous plait."

Lumina smiled and tried a different questioning route. "Do you believe in true love?" she asked, twirling her bright-blonde hair around her finger.

"Yes, of course," said Tim, keeping his gaze on Lumina. "To us," he said, raising his glass and clinking it gently against hers, "and to Paris," he added, raising his glass to the Eiffel Tower that, perfectly on cue, burst into a mass of sparkling white lights.

"Hi," said Andy, very unoriginally, as Sarah, with a finger over her lips in a 'shush' sign, opened the front door.

"She's asleep on the sofa," whispered Sarah, as she reached for her coat. "You're a life-saver, Andy."

"Not a problem, I'm happy to help out. How's the mumps?"

"Not too bad. She's all dosed-up. Just let her sleep."

"Okay. Now go. She'll be fine."

"Did you bring a ladder?"

"Yes, it's on the van. I'll sort it out," he whispered as he shooed her out of the door.

Andy walked into the cosy room with its gas fire on full. There was a tiny Christmas tree, most of which was barely visible under all the homemade decorations. Amy was fast asleep on the sofa, so he gently lifted her into his arms and carried her and her duvet up to bed. He stood and watched her for a while, just to check she was okay, but he wasn't really sure what he was looking for. He then popped to the van to get his ladder. In no time at all, the presents that Shaun had insisted must stay in the loft until Christmas Eve were arranged neatly under the tree. He stood the beautifully wrapped, ladder-shaped parcel behind the small tree, chuckled to himself and went to get a coffee.

The evening dragged. There was only so much C.S.I. with subtitles you could watch and Andy daren't put the sound on for fear of waking Amy. So, when there was the click of the key in the lock it made him jump. He got to his feet and walked into the hall. He was very surprised to see Shaun, with a ladder under his arm, halfway up the stairs.

"Mate, Amy's asleep up there," he called to him. Shaun stopped abruptly and peered through the slats of the banister. Clearly, Andy was one of the last people he had expected to see.

"Andy, what you doing here? Sarah putting on you again?"

"No, her usual babysitter's pregnant and, as Amy has mumps, she can't look after her, so, what with you being busy tonight…"

"I've just come to help Sarah by getting the presents out of the loft. They had to be put up there because of all the burglaries."

"There's no need, mate, I've got them down already," said Andy gesturing towards the living room.

"Bloody hell, Andy!" said Shaun raising his voice and going a bit pink, "You had no right to go in my loft and snoop about. What the hell d'you think you were doing?"

"Can you keep your voice down or you'll wake Amy up? And it's Christmas Eve, mate. Come on."

"I know it's pissing Christmas Eve. That's why I'm here, getting the presents out of *my* loft."

"Right. Well that job's been done, so shall I make you a coffee?" offered Andy, in an attempt to calm things down. Shaun began awkwardly reversing down the stairs with the ladder, which he propped up in the hall. He stalked past Andy into the living room, bumping him slightly. Shaun rooted through a couple of Christmas bags and then picked up a silver one and marched back to get the ladder. Andy put a hand on his shoulder.

"Sorry, mate, why are you taking one of Amy's presents?"

"Look, it says 'love from the Best Daddy in the World'. See it's from me." He jabbed his finger at the label.

"But won't she want to open that tomorrow?" Andy's hand was still resting on Shaun's shoulder.

"I'm embarrassed, mate. It's not much. I'll be back with something better. Okay?" He beamed his best smile at Andy, showing off his crooked teeth.

"Okay," said Andy, although it didn't feel okay at all. Shaun slapped him on the back and, still beaming, he left with his ladder and the small, silver Christmas bag.

Christmas had been good. Kate had spent Christmas day with Andy and his parents, and it had been a much jollier affair than the previous year, although James's mum did have a little weep after lunch. Kate and Andy had then gone to Sarah's for the evening. Kate had even had a couple of well-timed phone calls from her parents, who were now established in the Australian traditional Christmas, spending most of the day on the beach with friends and tucking into a seafood platter and barbecue. Kate realised how much she missed them when Christmas came around.

Kate had had a quiet New Year's Eve, going out and being surrounded by hoards of revellers was way outside her comfort zone, and the lack of a late night had enabled her to drive down to Marcus's cottage first thing on New Year's Day. She was keen to kick off the year with a new sense of purpose and a resolution to rebuild her confidence brick by brick.

But here she was on New Year's Day pulling up outside Sunset Cottage and starting a whole new chapter in her life. Niamh had flown out to America to have an extended holiday with family and friends whilst Marcus was writing, so he had already got himself settled in at the cottage. The front door opened and he was already waving at her to get inside.

"It's for you," called Marcus from the hall, as he held up the old-style telephone. Kate left the car and hurried inside.

"Hello?" said Kate tentatively taking the phone.

"Happy New Year!" shouted Sarah and Amy together.

"Happy New Year to you, too! Is everything okay?"

"Yes, we're all fine. Still recovering from last night. It was packed at the pub."

"Did Shaun have Amy?"

"Yes, but not without a ruck. Apparently I've imagined the mumps. When I got in, Amy was still up and he was asleep on the sofa."

"He is useless."

"Oh, and he bought her Christmas present round at last, it's a giant stuffed clown, which I will be having nightmares about."

"A clown?"

"Yep, it's bigger than Amy. He says it's to make up for the embarrassingly small gift he had to confiscate on Christmas Eve. God knows what that was, if it was worse than the psycho clown!"

"Shaun's the psycho, keep the door bolted!"

"So, are you getting down to work, then? Are you weaving in any new sexy scenes now that you know it's Timothy Calder playing the lead and you can make him take his kit off?"

"No! That wouldn't be true to the book. Although that is a very good idea! Anyway I've barely unpacked, so give me a chance."

"Did you take the turquoise bath robe I got you for Chrimble?"

"Yes, it'll be ideal here. It's a bit chilly. I really should go."

"Okay, call me lots, though, I'm missing you already," said Sarah, in a small voice,

"Wimp! Please make sure Andy feeds Marmalade."

"Stop worrying. It'll be fine," Sarah said in her best reassuring-mum voice.

"Okay. Speak soon. Bye."

By the end of the afternoon, Kate already found herself getting into the script-writing with Marcus's help. It was like returning to old friends as she talked about the characters and helped to bring them to life for Marcus. Over the following few days, they found that they quickly got into a routine of writing, walking, writing and eating, which seemed to work well. Marcus helped her visualise scenes by role-playing some of them, which had made Kate very self-conscious and giggly to start with, but once she got a feel for it, she could see how it helped. She even found she was enjoying herself and, for now, no shutters were coming down to stop it.

Kate received regular calls and texts from Sarah and Amy, which always brightened her day. Shaun appeared to be behaving himself, which made Sarah's life easier and gave Kate less to worry about. It sounded as if he was trying to worm his way back into Sarah's good books with flowers and cheap wine, but Kate knew Sarah was smarter than that. Kate called Andy once a week to check that the house was still standing, that he and Concetta weren't holding mad parties, and that someone had remembered to feed Marmalade. Didi wrote her the most beautiful and funny letters, which had Kate laughing out loud.

One morning in February, the daily paper arrived and Marcus heaved a sigh as he came back to the kitchen.

"Stupid boy," muttered Marcus, as he put the paper on the table and returned to his boiled egg. Kate came into the kitchen, gave Marcus a peck on the cheek as she did every morning and went to put the kettle on. She read the headline upside down 'Timothy COLDer – read exclusive with devastated Lumina!'

"Oh dear, is there going to be a problem for filming?" asked Kate, making herself a cup of black tea.

"They've both signed quite rigid contracts, so they'll just have to be adult about it and work together, but I can't deny it worries me. I doubt we'll get the best chemistry between our two screen lovers if the actors playing them hate each other."

"Ah, I see how that could be a problem. Can I read it?" asked Kate, reaching for the paper, which had a stunning front-page picture of Tim wearing dark glasses.

"You can, but don't believe a word of it. I'll call Tim later to find out what's really gone on."

They had a very productive day, so they were both quite pleased with themselves as they sat in the pub at the end of the village perusing the now-familiar dessert menu. It was a very old pub that had been recently renovated and they had made every effort to retain its original features. It was part-thatched and part-tiled due to extensions over its history. It was perfectly placed, with the village on one side and beautiful rolling countryside on the other, revealing the most stunning sunsets – if you knew the best place to sit. It was starting to feel like a home from home to Kate, but it was having an impact on her waistline. For some reason it was difficult to not have a dessert if you were having a pub meal. Kate settled on the crème brûlée for the second night in a row, put down her menu and surveyed Marcus's furrowed brow as he checked his phone again to see if Tim had called him back.

"So, is Timothy Calder really horrid?" asked Kate sipping her wine and watching Marcus's already-lined face wrinkle like a discarded sweet wrapper.

"I know it's a cliché, but you shouldn't believe everything you read, you know."

"So, how much of it is true?" asked Kate. Marcus pondered for a moment.

"About 80 per cent of it is true, I admit. You see, people usually want something from Tim. There are a lot of women who have decided that they are going to marry him and then there are the ones who just want the publicity. There's a lot of kudos in just being photographed with him. It creates instant media attention."

"So, you're saying that people use *him* rather than the other way around," mused Kate sceptically.

"Actually, I think it's mutual. People use him to further their career, make contacts, get seen in the right places, and Tim gets whatever it is he wants."

"Sex," said Kate, in a matter-of-fact tone.

"Well, yes," conceded Marcus.

"So, what is there to like about him?"

"You'll see for yourself when you meet him at rehearsals, but he is charming and, deep down, he is a nice guy. He does have a caring side. Honest," added Marcus, noting Kate's disbelieving look.

"Not exactly husband-and-father material, though, is he?"

"He's not your traditional father-figure, no," smiled Marcus.

"Try not to worry about him. He'll call you back when he's ready," said Kate, in an attempt to ease Marcus's worrying.

Dessert was fabulous, as always, and Kate was now feeling just a little bit like an overstuffed turkey as they headed back through the village to Marcus's chocolate-box cottage. Marcus linked his arm through Kate's as they walked companionably along.

"I have a rather nice St Emilion I've been saving. Shall we be naughty and crack it open?" said Marcus, giving a little pretend shudder of excitement.

"You know, I'm a bit of a heathen with wine, so it'll be wasted on me. Why not save it for when Niamh comes to stay?"

"Good idea! We'll open the Rioja. You're not worth anything better."

"Thanks!" said Kate digging him playfully in the ribs. As they approached the cottage, with the streetlights behind them, Kate gripped Marcus's arm and stopped him walking any further. "There's someone there," she whispered, as she pointed to the side of the house. "They've just disappeared around the back."

"Are you certain?" asked Marcus, as he strained to see. Kate inched up to the front window and peered through. She couldn't see anyone inside and the front door still looked secure. As she peered through the window, she could see a shadow moving across the back of the house. Suddenly feeling brave, she beckoned Marcus over.

"There's someone in the back garden," she whispered.

"Could be kids?" suggested Marcus, looking hopeful.

"Too tall," said Kate, shaking her head. "Here, take this and go that way," she instructed, as she handed Marcus a decorative stone from the front garden and sent him to the other side of the cottage. Kate picked up a heavy watering can, held it up to chest height and inched her way to the corner of the cottage. She could just hear the footsteps coming creeping in her direction, but they were barely audible over the thumping of her heart. As the hooded, tall figure turned the corner, both screamed and Kate threw the watering can, which hit the intruder square in the chest and sent him backwards into the rhododendron bush.

"Kate! Are you alright?" called Marcus through the darkness as he hurried to where the screams had come from, his decorative stone held aloft.

"Yes, I'm fine, I've got him," called Kate, although she hadn't technically got him, whoever he was – he was lying inelegantly in the rhododendron bush. It was a scene very similar to what happens when a deckchair collapses and the intruder was now struggling to stand up. Kate looked around for something heavier to throw as Marcus appeared protectively at her side, his face grim.

"Tim?" said Marcus, peering at the hooded figure flailing in the bush.

"Bloody hell, Marcus! Thank God it's you. I thought I was being attacked. I'm bloody soaked!" said Tim crossly, as he dragged himself upright, took off his hood and tried to brush the water off his clothes. Kate just stood next to Marcus without saying a word. The option of running away had crossed her mind, but who was she kidding? She wouldn't be running very far after the crème brûlée, so she just followed Marcus and a very wet and grumpy Timothy Calder into the cottage in silence as Marcus chatted away, finishing every sentence with "dear boy".

Kate tried to think of something appropriate to say, but words failed her. The moment for "sorry" seemed to have passed and her heart was still racing quite fast. Kate took off her coat, walked past Tim and Marcus, and went to put the kettle on. At least she could offer hot drinks once she'd found her tongue.

"He's gone to have a shower. No harm done, just dented pride. He'll be fine," said Marcus with a shrug as he entered the kitchen.

"I was just doing hot drinks."

"I think he might want something stronger. I know I do," smiled Marcus.

"Sorry," said Kate.

"My darling girl, don't apologise. You were tremendously brave. Goodness, it's his own bally fault if he sneaks about in the dark," said Marcus, striding over and giving her shoulders a squeeze.

"Thanks, Marcus." Kate made herself a black Lady Grey tea and headed into the living room, where Marcus had got the wood burner going and was pouring out two whiskies. Kate put down her tea next to her favourite chair and watched Marcus fussing over the fire for a couple of minutes before deciding she needed to go to the loo.

In the cottage the toilet was separate from the bathroom and, once inside, she found herself listening at the wall. What was she expecting to hear? A Hollywood theme tune that accompanied Timothy Calder's every action? She heard the bathroom door slam shut as Tim exited. Kate gave herself a mental shake, ran a brush through her hair, applied some Vaseline to her lips and straightened her shirt. She was about to meet Timothy Calder and wanted to make an impression, although she did fear she might already have done that with the watering can.

As she came downstairs, she could hear friendly chatter, which made her feel a little better as she was feeling ridiculously nervous. Was it the fact that she was about to properly meet a world-famous and extremely handsome actor, or the fact that she'd just tried to impale him with a watering can? She couldn't be sure. As she walked in, both men hushed and stood up, which took her a little by surprise and reminded her of period dramas and the lost art of manners. She thrust out her hand to Tim.

"I'm Kate, how do you do?" She winced at the formality of her words.

"Well, I'm dryer than I was. Very pleased to meet you, Kate. I'm Tim," grinned Tim, as he took her hand and they shook firmly. Tim sat back down in Kate's favourite chair, picked up her cup of tea and started to drink it. She was waiting for him to spit it out in disgust, but he didn't. Marcus surveyed the situation.

"Ah, Tim. Here's a whisky for you, when you're ready. I'll put the kettle on and get Kate a cuppa. You two chat," he instructed, waving his hands between the two of them as he left.

Kate tried not to stare at Tim, but it was hard not to in such a small space. She felt the blood rush to her cheeks as her heart thumped away. After an awkward pause Kate swallowed hard and started to speak. "I'm really sorry about the whole watering-can episode," she said, feeling very uncomfortable as she stood in the middle of the room, looking out of place.

"No need for an apology. My fault entirely. I knew Marcus was here, so I thought I would just wait until he returned. I guessed he was either at the pub or out for a walk. I hadn't realised you were here…"

"I had told him!" shouted Marcus, who was clearly eavesdropping in the kitchen.

"So, when I heard voices I ducked around the back. I'm also a bit twitchy, as I have the press on my tail."

Kate felt the warmth ebb away from her cheeks, which was a huge relief. "We saw the paper today. So have you and Lumina… um fallen out?" Kate cringed again at her choice of words. They weren't at primary school.

"Fallen out?" Tim mulled this over. "You could say that. She booked for us to do an 'At Home' spread with *OK* Magazine and had asked them about wedding exclusives. So I thought it was best to put a halt to things."

"And now she's gone to the papers saying you've broken her heart and given her dog depression," said Kate, reversing into the armchair to sit down.

"Yes, apparently so. I only met the dog twice. Once, she brought it to dinner and it snarled and yapped at me the whole time. The second time, I put things in Lumina's bag without realising the dog was in there, asleep, and he didn't take kindly to a hairbrush up his bum. So I doubt he's missing me too much, let alone depressed as a result." Kate smiled, but she didn't know what else to say. She was quite proud of herself for the conversation she'd managed so far. Kate was not confident at the best of times – but this was different. It was the weirdest thing talking to someone you've only ever seen in films or magazines and she was really struggling with the whole "not staring" thing.

"So, rehearsals in a few weeks. That'll be fun," said Marcus, as he returned to the room and handed Kate another cup of tea.

"Do you know what crew we've got yet?" Tim asked Marcus and the conversation drifted away from Kate. She shuffled back in the armchair so her body was angled towards the fire, but she was still able to have a sneaky stare at Timothy Calder without it being too obvious.

Chapter 8

The next morning Kate was woken by the sound of the radio and laughter, which she thought was probably one of the nicest ways to wake up. As she came downstairs in her jeans and an oversized Arran jumper she could hear the conversation as she approached.

"I don't care what you say, Marcus, if I was Niamh I would not be on a different continent while you were here with another woman. That's all," laughed Tim.

"I'm not having this ridiculous conversation with you. Now, out of the way, you're neither use nor ornament."

Kate felt a little guilty for eavesdropping as she wandered into the kitchen trying to look nonchalant and failing badly as she pulled the sleeves of her jumper down to cover her hands. Kate decided, after what she'd just overheard, not to give Marcus the usual peck on the cheek. She walked in and even though she knew he was there, she was still excited and slightly phased to see Timothy Calder in the kitchen, his hair still damp from the shower.

"Ah, good morning. Tea and toast?" asked Marcus, as he danced around the country-style kitchen with an elegance all of his own.

"Yes, please," Kate nodded. Tim already had a mug in his hand and he was leaning against the Aga, which at this time in the morning was the warmest spot in the kitchen, so Kate hesitantly went to join him. He gave a brief nod as she came to stand next to him. She checked the distance between them and decided that maybe she was a bit close, so she shuffled away slightly. When she looked up Tim was staring at her and her face went into instant-blush mode.

"Are you staying for a few days or do you need to keep moving?" she gabbled.

"No sign of the paps as yet, so I'll stay until I'm rumbled. I've got Terry driving the car around town on a random basis and Pip is booking me into hotels and restaurants I won't be going near, so that appears to be keeping them occupied for now."

"Around London, then," she said, feeling pleased that she at least knew that, thanks to Didi.

"Er, yeah," said Tim, with a brief twitch of his eyebrows.

"Who are Terry and Pip?" asked Kate, relaxing a fraction and leaning her side against the Aga.

"Driver and PA," said Tim.

Marcus brought Kate a mug of tea, removed hot toast from the toaster, and set it off again with another four slices safely on board.

Tim had gone quiet again and every time she glanced at him he was looking her way. The awkwardness was enough to make her try again with the conversation. "What are you going to do whilst we're working on the script?" asked Kate, hugging her mug with both hands.

"Huh, good question. I have absolutely no idea."

"I guess you're busy a lot of the time. What do you usually do when you have a free day or two?" Tim blinked hard. Perhaps he didn't really want to tell Kate what he usually did. The toaster went ping in the background.

"Waste it," said Marcus, as he ferried jams from the pantry cupboard to the large wooden table.

"Yes, you're spot on, Marcus, but I won't waste it whilst I'm here."

"You could go for a walk," suggested Kate. "It's really very pretty, especially down by the river and the woods and the sunset is simply stunning."

"Thanks, but I don't really want to get spotted, so I'll probably stay in and… read," said Tim, keeping his eyes focused on his tea. Marcus couldn't contain his laughter.

"You're going to read an actual book?" chuckled Marcus.

"I have books," said Tim. "Quite a collection, actually," he said turning back to Kate.

"Yes, you have," said Marcus, as he turned to Kate. "He even has some he hasn't finished colouring in yet!" Kate couldn't help but laugh. Tim smiled good-naturedly, but did look a little put out. "Come on, eat, eat!" said Marcus, as the three of them sat down to the mountain of toast.

Over breakfast, Tim and Marcus chatted about a mutual friend who was in and out of rehab, and Kate just concentrated on buttering her toast into the corners. When there was a pause in conversation, she leaned forward to speak and narrowly missed dragging her hair through her buttered toast. She swept it quickly out of the way and tucked it behind her ear.

"I'm guessing we're eating dinner in tonight. Shall I cook?" she offered. She liked to cook and she and Marcus really needed to break their pub-meal habit.

"That would be lovely," said Marcus.

"We could always get a takeaway," suggested Tim.

"Why, what have you heard about my cooking?" Kate was so used to Sarah's sharp tongue she reacted before she thought. Tim looked a little taken aback.

"No, nothing. I just don't want to put you to any trouble."

"It's no trouble, unless you're on some weird celebrity diet. I can cope with vegetarian, but I don't have the widest repertoire of recipes," she said grabbing a nearby pad and starting to make a list.

"We should be okay, then. I don't do diets and I'm a committed carnivore,"

"Then we'll all get along just fine," smiled Marcus, as he surveyed two of his favourite people.

After breakfast, Tim pottered about upstairs and made a few

phone calls. When he came bounding into the living room he wasn't expecting to be met at the door by Marcus's outstretched arm.

"Sorry, out of bounds. We're working. You can have the rest of the place."

"I'm not a puppy," Tim said, now feeling very left out, especially as he could glimpse Kate, who was sitting cross-legged on the floor surrounded by paper and a corkboard with lots of different-coloured pins on it. He was intrigued. "I'll be quiet."

"You'll be silent and you'll do it somewhere else in the house. Go on, away with you. We'll see you for lunch if we take a break then." Marcus regarded Tim over the top of his reading glasses, as he still stood there half-looking at Marcus and half-watching Kate. "Here, read this," said Marcus, handing Tim a well-thumbed copy of *Love.com*.

"Right. Okay, then. I'll see you both for lunch," Tim said, half to Marcus and half over his shoulder to Kate, who looked up for a moment and smiled before returning her gaze to the paper in front of her. Marcus shut the door and Tim found himself staring at the wood grain, with a book in his hands.

When they broke for lunch, Kate gave Sarah a quick ring as she was dying to tell her about Tim and the unfortunate watering-can incident. Kate went to her room to make the call and she barrelled through the story in a hushed voice.

"No, you didn't!" shouted Sarah after hearing the abridged version of last night's events.

"I did! He was okay, just very wet," giggled Kate, as she lay on her bed.

"Hang on, I've already seen the headline. I made Timothy Calder wet. No hang on, it was the other way round – Timothy Calder made me…"

"Behave yourself!"

"So, is he just as pant-wettingly gorgeous in real life?" asked Sarah.

"He is gorgeous, but no Tena Lady required."

"Does he have loads of Hollywood stories to impress the pants off you?"

"He hasn't said a lot to me, really. He's not like he is in the films. He's quieter. To be honest, he's not even like he was at the charity ball."

"Ooh, is he broken-hearted about Lumina? Are they going to get back together?"

"I met him a few hours ago, and Marcus and I have been working all morning, so I don't think my relationship with Tim has got to a point where I can discuss his deepest feelings and love life!"

"Maybe after lunch, then?"

"Maybe," Kate said, shaking her head.

"Are you going to hover outside the bathroom in case he makes a naked dash to his room?"

"No!" Sarah did brighten things up, and she was good at brightening Kate up. "Is Shaun still behaving?"

"Yes, I saw him yesterday and he wasn't himself."

"Well, that's an instant improvement!"

"Yeah, I guess so. He's taking us to the zoo on Sunday," Sarah said, with a little hesitation in her voice.

"You mean, he's taking Amy to the zoo. That's good. Are you working?"

"Er, actually no. Shaun's offered to take me and Amy out for the day and Amy chose the zoo. She wants to know if we could repopulate the rainforest if all the animals died out. You know how she gets into stuff,"

"Yes," agreed Kate trying to suppress the millions of alarm bells going off in her head. "Are you looking forward to a whole day with Shaun, then?"

"I wouldn't have used those words exactly, but it'll be okay. It'll be nice for Amy to have time with both of us together."

"You make sure you take good care of yourself."

"Oh, I will. Don't worry about me. And you lock your bedroom door. I don't want you being seduced by Timothy Calder and ending up like that poor Lumina. Every day, she's in some magazine weeping and wailing about him."

"I'll be fine. He's not going to be interested in someone ordinary like me and I'm afraid I'm not interested in men at all."

"That's good news, as it leaves more for me. Gotta go. Love you. Bye."

"Love you too. Bye."

As Sarah put the phone down she found she was biting her lip. She sensed that Kate was worried about her and, to be honest, she was a bit worried herself. Since Christmas, Shaun had kept to all the agreed days for seeing Amy and had only been late for pick-up or drop-off twice, which was quite remarkable for him. He had been increasingly less of a bully and a few times Sarah had seen a glimpse of a Shaun she remembered: cocky and carefree. She didn't want to hate Shaun, he was Amy's father and, for her sake, it was much better if they could put the past behind them and get along.

Andy ached all over; it felt as if even his aches had aches. He'd been working flat out renovating his house and, with his day job picking up, he'd found himself working until late every evening since the New Year. Now his body was protesting. He thought putting in the supporting RSJ today had probably been the last straw and his body was now fighting back.

Andy wandered into the bathroom and started taking off his dusty clothes. He went to switch on the shower, but then a thought struck him. Weren't baths meant to be good for aches and pains? He thought. At least that's what his grandparents frequently told him. He looked at the bath; he looked at the shower. Andy couldn't remember the last time he'd had a bath. He always just dived into the shower, it was quicker. He picked up the lone bottle of golden liquid on the edge of the bath – Gel Moussant, read the label in neat capitals. Andy guessed that was the posh name for bubble bath.

As he was all alone at Kate's house, Andy decided he would treat himself to a good old-fashioned soak. Nobody would know, so why not? He filled the bath, poured in a good slug of Gel Moussant and watched the bubbles mount up. He couldn't help feel a little bit excited at the prospect of sinking into the hot water. Andy got in and, despite that initial feeling of burning in his toes and other sensitive parts of his body, he soon settled down with an involuntary "Ahhhhhh".

He lay in the bath surrounded by a beautifully delicate scent of orange blossom and more foam than an Ibiza nightclub. He lay still, with his eyes closed, for some time, being engulfed in the warmth of the water and the blanket of sweet-smelling bubbles. The experience was immensely enjoyable and his tired muscles were enjoying it too. It was a big bath and he was able to stretch out his six-foot-four frame in it comfortably. He made a mental note to get a similar bath himself when he eventually made it to the fixtures-and-fittings stage with his own house.

The peace and relaxation was suddenly shattered by a bang and the bathroom door swung open. Andy jumped and foam and water went flying in all directions as he spun around to take on whoever had just burst in. He was rather surprised to see Marmalade the cat swinging from the door handle. As the door swung into the bathroom she gracefully alighted to the floor, where she flicked her paws in disgust at the wet tiles they'd encountered. The fluffy ginger cat sauntered over to a dry patch, sat down and stared at Andy.

"You gave me a hell of a fright," he said to the cat, who was staring at him with big amber, unblinking eyes. "Okay, time to get out and get you some food, I guess," he said, as he pulled the plug out and stood up. As the water quickly swirled away Andy realised that the towel was on the rail on the opposite wall, but before he could even step out of the bath he heard a blood-curdling scream.

"Madre de Dios…! Ave María Purísima," said a very startled Concetta, as she stared open-mouthed at one particular part of Andy's anatomy. Andy thought the rough translation was something like Mother of God and the start of a Hail Mary, neither of which was good. Andy put his hands up in apology, then quickly decided they were better placed somewhere else and tried to cover his modesty but, what with the gentle lapping of the warm water, that was not that easy to do… Andy looked around for something he could cover himself with and he reached for the Gel Moussant bottle and held that over the offending area. Concetta gasped, as all that had done was provide a magnifying effect!

At this point, Concetta spotted the cat. She shrieked again and clamped her hand to her already-open mouth. She turned her back on Andy and side-shuffled into the bathroom, her flamboyant dress swaying to the rhythm of the shuffle. She scooped up Marmalade and then side-shuffled back again whilst muttering the same Hail Mary under her breath. As Concetta reached the door, she paused for a second to have one last look at Andy and a quick glance at what he was trying to cover. Concetta shook her head, turned Marmalade away from the shocking sight and scuttled off.

"Lo siento!" called Andy to her retreating back. He didn't know much Spanish but he thought that that meant "sorry".

Sarah was surprised to find herself standing by the window with Amy on Sunday morning, peering out as they waited for Shaun to arrive. When they heard a distant rumbling and spluttering heading in their direction, they both looked at each other.

"Nanny Irene's van?" asked Sarah, and Amy nodded. Sarah sent up a little prayer, to a God she didn't believe in, that it wouldn't be Irene driving it. But as she heard tyres screech against curb she knew her worst fears were realised and pledged to find a religion she could believe in so that maybe she'd get better results.

Amy was already in the hall, excitedly layering on scarf, coat, hat and gloves whilst Sarah was desperately thinking of a way out without Amy knowing she was lying. Sadly, nothing came to mind before she saw two silhouettes at the front door. She pasted on a smile and opened the door. Shaun was wearing his usual battered black-leather jacket, but with a thick, black woolly hat. Next to him stood the dramatic and breathtaking sight (but not in a good way) of Irene, who had a cigarette drooping out of her thin lips and appeared to be wearing a red sleeping bag that doubled as a full-length coat and clashed wondrously with her orange hair. Her hair was escaping from underneath a magenta-pink crocheted hat with a crocheted flower on top. A matching magenta scarf was wrapped a number of times around her scrawny neck, making her look like the meanest cupcake in the shop.

"Daddy! Nanny!" shouted Amy. Thank goodness for small children to break the silence, thought Sarah.

"Hiya, Amy, Sarah," said Shaun.

"Hi," said Sarah, whilst she tried to unpeel her eyes from the horror that was Irene dressed for cold weather.

"I thought we'd make it a family day out," explained Shaun. "My van can't take all of us, so Mum's kindly brought hers."

"Are you going to drive, Shaun?"

"Nar, he ain't used to its ways like me. I'm drivin," answered Irene, her estuary English echoing up the street.

"Um, doesn't it have just three seats in the front?"

"Yeah. But I've got two fold d'arn seats in the back. That's where you're goin." Irene let out a plume of smoke and a short burst of a hacking cough. Shaun smiled at Sarah.

"We could take mine," said Sarah hopefully.

"Nah, yours is unreliable. The van's fine. Come on then, my girls, I'm buying the ice creams. Let's go!" Irene rolled her eyes like a shark does just before it bites. Sarah reluctantly put on her winter apparel before taking her daughter's hand and resigning herself to a day of torture with Irene. "I don't think there will be any ice cream today as it's winter," Sarah pointed out, for Amy's benefit.

"If Daddy says he'll get you an ice cream then he will," said Irene with a barely disguised scowl.

The journey to the zoo was the hour of interminable hell Sarah thought it would be. It turned out that the fold-down seats in the back were just that. Irene had somehow managed to fit two ex-cinema seats into the back of the van. As she pointed out, with a very yellowing pointy finger, they were bolted in and had seatbelts, although the seatbelts were, in fact, bolted to the side of the van so, should there be an emergency, Sarah suspected she would be garrotted before anyone found her. Whilst there were many downsides of the cinema seats, the main ones that came to mind throughout the hellish journey were that Sarah was alone in the back, there was no heating, the seats faced backwards, which made her more than a bit queasy, and, best of all, it was a van, so there were no windows. Therefore she'd spent the entire time in the dark. So, when the van finally stopped and the sliding door was opened, she was blinded by the daylight and she had no clean answer for the question Shaun asked her.

"That was alright, wasn't it?" At least now she knew what it would be like to be kidnapped.

The next few hours were spent trudging around a zoo full of animals that were all huddled up in their respective homes, as most of them were traditionally from warmer climes, which was exactly where Sarah wished she was. Although pretty much anywhere without Irene would have been fine. Amy was on good form and was engrossed in ticking off the animals on the list she'd made. She really came into her own at the "Ask a Keeper" session, where she grilled the poor man mercilessly about their captive breeding programme.

"Don' she take after our Shauny?" said Irene, leaning a little too close to Sarah, her ashtray breath stinging Sarah's eyes.

"Because she's good at torturing people with words?" replied Sarah, under her breath.

"Eh?"

They left the "Ask a Keeper" session and ventured into the frosty air outside.

They bought hot drinks and sat in the corner of the restaurant, eating the sandwiches that Sarah had made.

"Was this?" asked Irene peering inside the sandwich she'd chosen.

"It's pâté," explained Amy, as she munched happily on hers.

"Looks like road kill to me," sniffed Irene. "Ain't you done nuffin better? There's not many of 'em 'iver."

"No, Irene, sorry. I didn't know you and your delicate palate would be coming along today." Irene sniffed again, put her crocheted hat and scarf back on, and sloped off for another cigarette.

"Hope you don't mind me mum coming. She was really excited when I said it was a family day out – and she is family," said Shaun, making Sarah almost feel sorry for him.

"It's okay. I'm not looking forward to the ride home, though."

"I'll go in the back, if you like," offered Shaun. Sarah had already considered this option, but that would then put her in the front with Irene and she'd have to witness the treacherous driving, rather than just feel it. So she opted for nausea in the dark instead.

"No, it's okay, but thanks for offering." She smiled at Shaun and he smiled back. Just for a moment there was a glimpse of something between them and then it was gone.

"I'll buy us all ice creams later," said Shaun.

"Yay!" cheered Amy.

"I don't think anywhere will be selling them, though," said Sarah giving Shaun a stern look. She hated it when he built up Amy's hopes and then dashed them, even if it was just an ice cream.

"You need to trust me, Sarah," said Shaun, reaching out a hand that stopped just short of her own. But look where that's got me, thought Sarah.

Amy had studied the zoo map and instructed them that the next animals to be visited would be macaws and penguins. The latter were obviously not from the rainforest, but they were Sarah and Amy's favourite because they never failed to make them laugh. So, when Irene returned, the odd little party headed off on the next leg of their exploration. Sarah found the afternoon bearable, and was pleased when Shaun gave Amy some money to buy a toy penguin and a book about the rainforest.

Before too long Sarah found herself back in the dark van, lurching around whilst she tried to sing songs to herself to take her mind off the torture. The van suddenly stopped and she was thrown back into her cinema chair (with handy cup holder) and then forwards, to be half strangled by the seatbelt, exactly as she had predicted. The van door slid open and the light hit her eyes once again.

"Ice-cream stop," said Shaun triumphantly. Sarah unbuckled her seat belt and stepped out of the van and discovered that they were in a lay-by, where, of all things, there was an ice- cream van. Shaun put something in his coat pocket and then took four large, swirly ice creams from the large, unshaven vendor before coming back. Amy opened the passenger door and eagerly took her ice cream as he handed them all out.

"Thanks, Daddy. What did the man in the ice-cream van give you?" asked Amy

"What? My change?" said Shaun, zipping up his jacket to the top.

"No, something else, you put it in your pocket. Is it for me?"

"Oh, yes, it is for you. It's serviettes!" said Shaun, pulling one from his trouser pocket.

Sarah sat half in the van, her frozen fingers holding the cone in a death grip. She was already so cold and she wondered why on earth someone would be selling bloody ice cream in the middle of winter and why she was fool enough to eat it. She watched the ice-cream van drive away.

Chapter 9

Another cold February day passed at Sunset Cottage and Kate found she was a little more relaxed in Timothy Calder's company; he was just 'Tim' now. He was not like his Agent X character or the person she'd read about in the press. She had known that was just acting and journalism, but it was odd when all your assumptions crumbled.

Kate came out of the bathroom in her turquoise bathrobe and a white towel in a turban on her head as Tim was coming out of his bedroom.

"Bugger me, it's a giant smurf!" he laughed, and Kate smirked, but tried to give him a stern look. "Sorry, can I make it up to you?"

"Yes, you can. I'll have a tea and a walnut whip please. I'm going to get dressed so I'll be down in five minutes."

"I didn't know there were walnut whips in the house. I love those things!" and he hurtled downstairs like a child on Christmas morning.

Kate did a sweep of the ground floor and found it empty. She knew Marcus had gone out in search of a bottle of quaffable red, but had expected to find Tim. As she walked into the kitchen she saw a shadow in the garden, so wrapping her cardigan tightly around herself she went to investigate. Tim was sitting on the garden bench surrounded by a randomly heaped collection of blankets and throws. He didn't hear Kate approach until she was sitting on the bench next to him dragging blankets around herself.

"Here, let me help," he said, wrapping a tartan throw around her shoulders and inadvertently giving her a fleeting squeeze as he did so. Kate shuddered, either from the chill in the air or because of the contact.

"I bet you've seen sunsets all over the world."

"I have, but it's rare that I actually have time to watch a sunset develop. It's often a quick glance out of taxi or hotel window."

"What better place to watch it than Sunset Cottage? I can see why Marcus bought this place."

"Huh," snorted Tim, "He bought it because he'd just sold a script to Hollywood and Niamh thought it was a good omen with its tenuous link to Sunset Strip. It was weeks before they realised it was a prime location for watching the sun set over the Cotswold countryside."

Kate chuckled. This was one story Marcus had failed to share with her. Tim handed her a mug and a walnut whip.

"Wow, I didn't know you could make tea," said Kate.

"I can. I just don't get much opportunity."

"No, I hear kettles are very rare in Hollywood." She sipped her tea and nodded her approval.

"You really can't do the normal stuff, you know, you would need a team of bodyguards to go to the supermarket. I find hotels are the easiest option."

"When was the last time you cooked for yourself?"

"Ooh, let me think," Tim pondered for a while. "That would be about eight years ago."

"Eight years?" Kate nearly spat her tea out.

"I don't need to, there's always someone to do it for me..." Kate shook her head and Tim continued "They make you like this. You become dependent, and that's how divas are made. Dirk Bogarde couldn't write a cheque."

"Can you?"

"Don't need to, I've got cards," and he stuck his tongue out at her.

"Do you do any normal stuff?"

"Not often, but I'm still just Tim."

"I still find that odd, because I know you as Timothy Calder," said Kate.

"I don't follow," he said shuffling around so that he was half facing Kate but keeping a tight hold on a rather floral blanket.

"Colin Firth is always Colin Firth, it's always his full name, right?"

"Yes, I know Colin very well."

"That's my point. You know a man called Colin, but the rest of the world knows a film star named Colin Firth."

Tim was eyeing her speculatively. "You're not convinced, are you?" said Kate.

"Not really."

"Maybe Colin was a bad example. What about Marlon Brando?"

"One of the greats. I never met him."

"So, if you were introduced to him and he says, 'Hi, I'm Marlon.'"

"Oh, God, I see what you mean. He's not just a Marlon, he's the great Marlon Brando. Marlon is some character from Emmerdale."

"Exactly," ended Kate, taking a bite off the top of her walnut whip to emphasise her victory. They both sipped tea in silence for a bit, watching as the sun drifted south, taking the day with it and leaving behind a chaos of colour strewn lazily across the early evening sky.

"I like really bad knock, knock jokes; that's normal isn't it?" said Tim.

"Well, it's not celebrity, but I'm not sure it's normal," said Kate, with a shake of her head.

"What's not to like about knock, knock jokes?"

"They're silly and not very funny."

"But that's the point, they make you groan, rather than belly-laugh. Oh come on, they're great. Knock knock," Tim swivelled himself around a bit more to face Kate directly, looking eager for her to participate. Kate sighed.

"Who's there?"

"I smelp."

"I smelp who?"

"See! How is that not hilarious?" said Tim, in between chuckles.

"You got me to say 'I smell poo'. You are an evil genius." Kate rolled her eyes.

"Okay, okay, better one. Knock, knock."

"Who's there?" Kate sighed heavily.

"Interrupting muppet."

"Interrupting m…"

"Mahna Mahna, do doo do do-do." Tim grinned at her.

"I'm going to start dinner, as I fear you have a very long list of these."

"I have!" Tim said looking quite proud and he smiled to himself as he watched her go back inside. He turned back to watch the end of the sunset; reds and oranges diminishing into shades of purple as night claimed the colourful display. Tim stared into the night sky and pulled the tartan throw closer to him.

Over the last couple of days, Kate had found herself much more of an even contributor to conversations. Marcus and Tim had both given her some useful tips about how to work with the various crew members and Kate was very glad of the advice. Tim had read *Love.com* and Marcus had made him a sticker saying "Good Reader", which Tim good-naturedly had worn all through dinner. He had been complimentary about the *Love.com* story and had asked some good questions about the characters, their backgrounds and motivations.

Kate got off the phone from Didi and saw that Tim had joined her in the kitchen and was watching her as she updated one of the lists stuck on the fridge door.

"Tea?" she asked instinctively.

"Please," he replied.

Kate now knew that Tim took his tea in exactly the same way as her; Lady Grey, black with no sugar. Kate found herself still grinning and she felt she should explain.

"That was Didi, a friend of mine. She's recovering from an operation and being nursed is driving her barmy. She's very funny."

"I could hear that. I had to come and investigate what was making you laugh so much."

"You can't fail to enjoy yourself with Didi." This piqued Tim's interest, but he kept it to himself. "She's looking for a man. She thinks she might have found one, but he's on a different floor, so she's bribing everyone to wheel her down to him. He's had an eye operation, which Didi thinks is a bonus because he'll see her in soft focus!" laughed Kate. "Do you have any mad friends?" she asked.

"Ah, now there's a question, but the tricky word in the sentence is 'friends'," said Tim. Kate looked puzzled, but listened intently. "In my business, you have hundreds of 'friends', most of them you have only ever air-kissed at parties, some you may have exchanged a couple of sentences with. Then you have the next layer down, who are 'friends' you made on a film set, so you do know them well for a short amount of time but haven't heard from them since."

"No proper friends?"

"Bernie is a good friend, but he's also my brother. Rarely do you have true friends; I can count mine on one hand."

"Wow, there was an answer I wasn't expecting. It's a very different life, isn't it?"

"Sometimes I feel like Mickey Mouse."

"Recognised everywhere and loved by millions of screaming girls?" grinned Kate.

"Not just that. People want your autograph and a photo with you, but that's it. It's very transactional, most never speak or even say thanks."

"That is just like being Mickey." Kate thought of her trips to Disney World as a child.

"Except, unlike Mickey, I can never take the costume off."

Tim's phone sprang to life and he waved his apologies and left the room quickly, leaving Kate sipping her tea. Tim was very attached to his mobile phone; he never actually put it down. He frequently disappeared to take or answer calls and someone called Jackie was a regular caller.

That night, over homemade beef casserole, which Kate had left simmering gently in the traditional Aga for most of the day, talk turned to read-throughs, rehearsals and filming, which were now looming as most of the script had gone for storyboarding.

"Max says the storyboards are coming together and we have a draft crew list, but that will change," said Marcus, and Tim nodded as he dipped some bread into his sauce.

"I'm surprised by all the steps in the process and how long it takes," said Kate.

"This is moving very quickly; I think my schedule is the only thing slowing it down," said Tim, spearing a mushroom, "I'm flying out to Canada this weekend for three weeks of filming. I'm playing a gangland boss."

"Only three weeks?" queried Kate, a little shocked at him having taken what was clearly only a small part in the film. As if reading her thoughts he said, "It's a key role. You see, I cost lots of money," said Tim, "so they will film all my scenes back to back over the three weeks, just to get them done quickly. So it will be the usual madness. The rest of the film will be a few months being filmed. I've also already done a couple of weeks on location in London for it, too, but it's a Canadian film company so the main set is in Canada and my character is in his office most of the time, until he gets shot."

"You need to be doing less of the action stuff. It's time you grew up," chuckled Marcus. Kate smirked. She guessed Tim was over 30, but he certainly looked a lot younger.

"It's knackering, all that running and fighting. It is!" protested Tim as Kate and Marcus were exchanging looks and smiling to each other. "I do most of my own stunts… maybe not as many as

I used to, but that's more to do with Health and Safety than with me. You try jumping off a building onto a moving car!"

"Must be terribly hard," said Marcus, nodding earnestly.

"Bog off. The pair of you," Tim said, as he leant back in his chair and savoured a mouthful of St Emillion. He looked across at Kate, who was meticulously rounding up peas with her fork. Her long hair was loosely clipped back off her face and he took in her neat eyebrows, pale-blue eyes and heart-shaped face. She wasn't wearing any make-up. All he'd seen her apply since he'd been there was a little Vaseline to her lips using her finger. Something he'd found strangely erotic, but he had put it down to his unplanned couple of days of celibacy. Kate looked up and met Tim's gaze and gave a little smile.

"Who has room for butterscotch tart?" she asked.

"Always," said Marcus, raising his glass as if in a toast to butterscotch tart.

"Just a little," said Tim. "A few days away from the gym is a dangerous thing in my business," he said, patting his smooth stomach.

Kate remembered a few topless scenes from the Agent X films and smiled to herself as she sliced up the butterscotch tart. After dinner, Kate and Marcus cleared away the dinner things and loaded the dishwasher while Tim went to relax in the living room. This had become their little routine. Kate and Marcus joined Tim, and Marcus dutifully refilled their wine glasses.

"Look, it's starting to snow," said Kate, as she saw the first few wispy flakes swirl outside the window. As the flakes grew fatter and started to settle, the three of them found themselves staring out of the window. Tim's arm brushed against Kate's and they both jumped slightly at the sensation. Tim smiled awkwardly at Kate and she pulled her long grey cardy around herself and folded her arms. They stood bewitched by the white blur that fell rapidly, with flakes so clearly visible, but each one then instantly vanished as they met the already lain snow. A breeze picked up and hurled a flurry of snow along the lane outside and all three heads followed its journey as it sailed over a parked car and the windscreen wipers swished across the screen.

"Pap!" blurted out Tim, as he quickly stepped to the side of the window.

"Bugger," said Marcus, straining to see the occupant of the car.

"Are you sure? I think they might be drinking something," said Kate, noticing that they were lifting something dark-coloured up to their face.

"You're right, they've got a long lens in there. Bugger," Marcus repeated. Tim was already on his phone talking to Terry, his driver, and then to Pippa.

"Pips, you're an angel. No, it's okay, I've spoken to Terry. He's leaving now. Great. Bye." He ended the call and addressed the two concerned faces. "It's okay, Terry is on his way. He was the right side of town, so he'll be here within the hour. The apartment and my hotel are still surrounded, so Pip will book me into Browns. Right, I'd best gather my things together," he said, trying to sound bright. Marcus stepped forward and patted his arm.

"Ah well, they were bound to track you down eventually."

Marcus drew the curtains and went to give the fire a prod. Kate fidgeted about, not really knowing what to do. A few days ago she struggled to not blush every time she spoke to Tim, but now they had an easy way between them. Perhaps being trapped in a small cottage together was an accelerant and speeded up the process of getting on with people. She went upstairs and knocked tentatively at his open door, before pushing it slowly open. Tim was sitting on the bed looking forlorn as he fiddled with his phone. An open holdall lay on the bed next to him.

"You okay?" asked Kate.

"Yeah," said Tim, letting out a lungful of air. "I only came here to escape, but I guess I've surprised myself by really enjoying it."

"Sometimes you just need to recharge the batteries. Look

at things from a different perspective. Or write a list," she paused and he snorted a laugh. "Maybe the list thing is just me, then, anyway… a little something for the journey," she said, as she put the last of the Walnut Whips into the holdall.

Tim stared at his feet for a bit before turning to look at Kate, "You are a really lovely person, Kate," said Tim his eyes scanning her face, as if looking at her properly for the first time.

"You're not so bad yourself," she said getting up to leave.

"Thanks, Kate," said Tim, and he opened his mouth, as if he was about to add something, but he seemed to change his mind.

"Right, well, I'll leave you to your packing," said Kate and she left the room wondering why she unexpectedly felt a little down. Maybe it was the suddenness of Tim's departure, she wasn't sure.

When he came downstairs, Tim was dressed in black and wearing the hoody that she'd thrown the watering can at. He was also wearing his dark glasses, which somehow made his perfect cheekbones and jaw line more noticeable. He dropped the leather holdall at his feet and chatted conspiratorially with Marcus. Tim's phone rang.

"Okay, Terry, great. Plan is for you to meet me up the hill. Yep, that's it. About ten minutes. Great I'll set off in five. Bye."

"Right, darling girl, we have a situation. You'll need your coat and wellies on," said Marcus. Kate couldn't help feeling a sudden twinge of excitement at the unfolding events and the glimpse into the craziness of Tim's life. There was something different about Tim and it wasn't just the sunglasses. His manner had changed, the self confidence she'd seen at the charity ball was back and he was pacing like a boxer before a big fight. Her new friend, Tim, had disappeared and Timothy Calder was back and she felt a little sad. The feeling was soon overridden as Kate piled on the outdoor wear and dug out the sunglasses, which made her giggle a little childishly as the three figures stood looking at each other in the dim light.

"We had best say our goodbyes here," said Marcus, engulfing Tim in a bear hug. They slapped each other on the back. "Loved it, dear boy, wonderful to have you here. Niamh will be devastated that she's missed you."

"Thank you, Marcus. You're a true friend. Give Niamh my love. I promise we'll catch up before filming." Tim turned to stand square in front of Kate and she realised she was glued to the spot and she was her fifteen-year-old self again: shy, unsure and very awkward. She decided to go for the hug at the same time that Tim had decided on an air kiss, so he ended up kissing her ear, which sent a lightning bolt somewhere she didn't care to mention. Kate was mentally kicking herself; really what was she thinking by hugging Timothy Calder? Had she gone mad? They pulled apart and for reasons she could not explain, she thrust out her hand to shake Tim's. He stared at it for a second and then took it in both hands. There was that shudder again.

"Bye, Kate. It's been an absolute pleasure. I really can't wait to work with you. Look after the old boy for me, won't you?"

"I will. Bye, Tim, take care of yourself," she said feeling herself blush. What was going on?

"Right, action stations," said Marcus, taking Kate's arm and leading her out the front door, which he locked behind them. The snow was coming down hard now and it was complete madness to be out walking in it. Against Marcus's better judgement Kate was roadside so that the photographer couldn't get a good look at the man she was walking with. They kept up a good pace and strode past the parked car. Kate had to concentrate really hard to neither look at the parked car nor turn around to see if she could catch a glimpse of Tim sneaking out of the back garden and then making his way up the hill to where Terry would meet him. The snow was now near blizzard conditions and was stinging Kate's face as they ploughed on through the village. She could barely see anything now that the sunglasses were covered in snow, so she was grateful to at last hear Marcus's phone ring. They stopped for him to answer it.

"Excellent. Well done." He turned to look over his shoulder at the car, barely visible in the distance. "No, you're okay, the pap is still there. Right. Okay. Bye now." Marcus gave Kate's arm a squeeze. "Plan executed beautifully. Agent X has made his escape. Let's head back." Kate felt a sense of relief and realised the adrenalin had been pumping around her system. As they walked back through the Christmas-card picture of a village, all covered in snow, albeit currently whipping quite violently at her back, she resisted the temptation to stick her tongue out at the photographer as they passed. As they reached the cottage, Kate felt there was something sad about the set of lone footprints that made their way behind the bushes and up the hill.

Sarah jumped happily out of her rust bucket of a car and crunched along the gravel drive to Kate's front door, where she met Marmalade, who was sat staring up at the door handle.

"Oh dear, has Andy shut you out again? Come on," Sarah said as she unlocked the door and the cat shot inside. "Helloooo! Anybody home?" she called as she placed the lasagne, with instructions on a post-it note, in the fridge. She headed back into the hall and nearly fell over a cardboard box that looked as though it contained rubbish. She was about to browse through the papers when Andy appeared at the top of the stairs. He looked a little alarmed when he saw what Sarah was doing.

"Hey, it's the dinner fairy!" he said, running down the stairs to give her a hug.

"Lasagne. It's in the fridge. Read the instructions!" she scolded. "I see you've got some salad in there that'll go nicely with it," she reached up and flattened down his fringe, which was looking as though a cow had licked him. As soon as she'd done it, she realised it was actually quite an intimate thing to have done and apologised straight away, making them both a little uncomfortable.

"Sorry, Andy. I just saw the sticky-up bit and… sorry."

"No, it's fine. I don't want to walk around looking like a dork. Thanks."

"So you're being evicted, then?"

"Yes, Kate's back on Friday. To be honest, she did say I'm welcome to stay, but my little house is liveable now, so it'll be nice to move in properly and call it home. Still a lot to do, including all the decorating, but apart from that it's fine. You'll have to come over and have a look around."

"I'd love to, thanks. I can't stop. Did you want me to dump this in the recycling?" she gestured to the box on the floor.

"Ah, no. Thanks for the offer. No, it's stuff I need to sort out."

"Is that James's stuff?" questioned Sarah, recognising that the letter on top was addressed to James.

"Uh, yeah, it is," winced Andy.

"Where from?" asked Sarah.

"It's his office stuff," said Andy running his fingers through his damp hair and making it stick up again.

"But you said you'd done all that yonks ago."

"I know. Look, I'm sorry, I just bundled it into a box and then I just didn't get around to sorting it out. It'll be my first job when I move in. Promise," he said running his fingers in a cross your heart motion across his chest.

"Don't worry, Waster. I'll do it," Sarah said good-naturedly picking up the box.

"No," said Andy, a little firmer than he'd meant to, "it's fine. I will do it. I promise." He repeated the cross your heart gesture.

There was no fooling Sarah, something was clearly up and she was like a dog with a bone, so she stood there gripping the box as Andy now had his outstretched arms waiting for her to pass it to him.

"Actually," she said with a smirk, "I'm not in that much of a rush. Let's go through it now, shall we?"

"Oh no, sorry, I can't. I need to be… Um, I have to…"

"What's up?" asked Sarah. "Don't try to lie, it's pointless. Just tell me what's going on."

Andy stood for a moment and stared at Sarah. She was gorgeous when she was being bossy and for the life of him he couldn't think of a valid reason not to tell her.

"Put the box in the living room. I'll make drinks and I'll show you what I've found. It's probably nothing and it was all a long time ago, so I think we should just shred the stuff and say nothing to Kate."

"Oh, my God, Andy, you are worrying me now. Sod the drink and just show me, whatever it is," said Sarah, starting to get scratchy with him. They went through to the living room, Andy rummaged down the box and produced a large, brown envelope, which he handed to Sarah. Before she could take it he added, "It was two years ago. It probably means nothing and Kate most likely knew all about it."

"She can tell us what she did and didn't know. Now give me the sodding envelope," she said, snatching it from him. Sarah pulled out the two bulky documents inside and read the solicitors' slip that was stuck on the front; it read, "Docs enclosed as discussed. Return to me once signed and witnessed. Regards, Becky". Sarah leafed through the documents, taking what seemed to Andy like forever. The silence was crippling him.

"How's Shaun?" he asked, for something to say.

"He's fine," mumbled Sarah, as she continued to read and flick back between the two documents. When she'd finished, she turned to Andy and he saw a flash of something in her eyes. "So *your* brother was going to get Kate to sign over *her* house and then he was going to mortgage it?"

"I don't know," he said, putting his hands in the air. "It's probably not unreasonable to put the house into joint names. I didn't realise it was Kate's house until I read this. I thought it belonged to her mum and dad."

"Her grandparents left it to her, something to do with avoiding inheritance tax. I don't know," said Sarah waving what she felt was irrelevant away, "but I do know it's hers and she wouldn't go signing half of it over to anyone. And this is already signed by James and dated for their wedding day. He's signed the mortgage agreement, too. She definitely wouldn't have agreed to mortgage it!" Sarah was on a roll and she was directing all of her sudden anger towards to Andy. "What the hell was he going to do with all that money? Oh, my God, was he going to leave her? Was it all a scam?"

"No! No I'm sure it wasn't! Christ, Sarah, calm down. This has nothing to do with me. I'm as confused as you are and have just as many questions. He was my brother and he didn't mention any of this to me."

"When did you know about this? Have you known all this time?"

"God no, of course not. I came across the box when I was sorting things out for the new house and realised I had never got around to going through it. So one night when I was here I settled down with a beer and started looking. Most of it was statements, printed-off emails, receipts for stuff – you know the sort of thing," he said, "then I came across this." He pointed to the envelope. "I must have read it a dozen times and I'm still confused. I was just going to shred it."

"You can't do that!"

"Why not?"

"Kate has a right to know what was going on behind her back!" said Sarah vehemently.

"Sarah, it was two years ago. James is dead. What good can that possibly do? It will only cause upset. You can't do that to her so near to the anniversary."

"Don't you go making me into the guilty party. I'm not the bad guy here."

"And you don't know that James was, either. Kate might know all about this. It's really nothing to do with us. It will do no good to tell her."

"The good it will do is that Kate has spent two years with a broken heart over a man who was about to rip her off." Andy opened his mouth so Sarah amended her statement, "who *could* have been about to rip her off."

"We can't take away her faith in James. Even if he was, and I'm not saying he was, but even if he was, he didn't actually do it."

"Only because he died!"

"Right, okay, but my point is she still has the house, everything is in order and she's getting over losing him. I wondered at times, in the early days, if she would ever get over it, but she is. Before Christmas, she was laughing about that time James and I trashed the bouncy castle at Amy's birthday party, and she did it without that pause at the end where you see the sadness hit her. It didn't happen. She is coping and maybe she's even moving on. She's got the film coming up. This is her time. This would just make her question her memories of James and I can't see how that would help her."

Sarah hated it when other people were right. She was still boiling mad, but Andy was also right that this wasn't his fault. It was James's and he was no longer here, so unfortunately she couldn't interrogate him. Sarah slumped back against the cushions.

"Oh, crap. Get me a cuppa, please," she sighed, kicking off her shoes and pulling her legs up underneath herself.

"I thought you were in a hurry."

"I was only going food-shopping. Where's my tea?"

"Coming right up." Andy smiled at Sarah as she slumped into the sofa and picked up the documents to have another read. When Andy returned with the tea, they sat in silence for a bit.

"Do you think he really loved her?" asked Sarah.

"Kate is a very easy person to love. She's beautiful, kind, generous, funny, loving."

"Okay, I get the picture! What does that make me? The quirky, ugly one?"

Andy put his arm around Sarah and gave her a friendly squeeze.

"Don't be silly, Quasimodo."

Marcus and Kate had a few changes sent through for the script as the storyboard was coming to life, but they were all things they could accommodate with ease. A week had passed and the work rate had reduced considerably, so Kate turned her attention and free time to finishing her latest novel, which was now embarrassingly overdue. Eventually, they got the call that the script and storyboard were agreed and, once crew and finances were approved, they were set to go to production, which Marcus explained to Kate comprised rehearsals, set design and production and, ultimately, filming. Tim had called a few times to speak to Marcus from some exotic location, a top hotel or a celeb-ridden party and each time Marcus had passed on Tim's regards, but she wasn't sure if Marcus was just saying it to be kind.

"It's our last night tonight. I think that calls for a trip to the pub!"

"Here, here!" agreed Kate. She would be very sorry to leave the cottage, and Marcus's company for that matter. It was early March and spring was just around the corner. The pub was busier than it had been, as people were clearly coming out of hibernation. Despite their recent reduction in visits, they got their favourite table and Kate settled on the duck breast followed, obviously, by the crème brûlée. After their meal, they were lucky enough to grab the pole-position sofa in front of the open fire. Kate sank into it and nursed her tumbler of Baileys, her last-night treat.

"It's been nearly two years, hasn't it?" asked Marcus. Kate knew exactly what Marcus was referring to.

"Yes. On 15th March it'll be two years since James died."

"I thought it was soon. Does it feel like two years?"

Kate thought for a moment and sipped her drink. Time was a funny thing; it had a way of confusing things.

"It feels like a long time since James was here, but not that long ago since the police were standing at my door. It's odd when you think about it – James and I were only together for 26 months."

"Were you?" quizzed Marcus. "I didn't realise."

"We were a bit of a whirlwind, really, but it's odd to think that he will soon have been gone longer than the time we had together."

Marcus put an arm around her shoulder. He was like a second dad and being close to him helped when her own father was so far away.

"I'm okay. I miss him, but my life is plodding on and, shhh don't tell anyone, but I'm enjoying it. Just a little bit."

"Well done, darling girl, I'm proud of you. James would be proud too." And he kissed the top of Kate's head.

Chapter 10

Kate came home to an empty house. There was a lovely feeling about stepping inside her own home again and she hadn't realised how much she'd missed it while she'd been away. It was definitely good to be back. Marmalade came to greet her and danced excitedly around her legs.

Kate dumped her case in her bedroom and peeked around the guest bedroom door; she could see that Andy had clearly moved out as there was no trace of him upstairs. She discovered that he had been at work in the kitchen as the wobbly kitchen cupboard and sticking kitchen drawer had both been fixed. She looked in the fridge and was pleased to find milk, eggs and a key lime pie with a note on it from Sarah: "Be over lunchtime to help you out with this! Missed you, love Sarah X".

Kate sent a text to Sarah before she gathered up the mountain of post and went to sit in the conservatory to read through it. As she looked out across the garden she was pleased to see the splashes of colour from daffodils and tulips in every flower bed, as if a child had been busy with a paint pot. She decided she would sort out the post, unpack and then visit James's grave. The post was fairly dull, as she had expected – mainly brochures for things she didn't want, vouchers for things she didn't need and bank statements. She put on her coat and gloves and, looking out of the window, decided she didn't need a scarf as it was clear and bright and only a little chilly.

Her car had just turned the corner into the neighbouring street when Sarah's car appeared at the other end of the road, drove along and then pulled into Kate's driveway. Sarah was a bit surprised that Kate's car wasn't there because she knew she was home from the text she'd received. Sarah let herself in, took off her coat and felt the kettle; it was still warm, so she guessed that Kate had just popped out for something. Sarah wandered through to the conservatory and looked out across the garden and wondered how long Kate would be when it hit her.

"SHIT!" she said out loud and ran for the door, slinging her coat on as she went. The gravel flew up behind her as she sped out of the driveway in the same direction that Kate had gone. It was only a short journey, but Sarah spent all of it repeating the same word over and over again.

"SHIT. SHIT. SHIT." She could not believe that she had completely forgotten. Maybe she could believe it just a little bit; she really did need to get a big calendar and large day-glo marker pen. More importantly, she now couldn't believe that she hadn't thought this through properly. She felt like such an idiot.

Sarah parked the car in the first two parking spaces she could see and ignored the neat signs saying, "Please keep off the grass". Wrapping her flapping coat around her, she sprinted across the lawn area, dodged around some rose bushes and then joined a path. In the distance she could see Kate standing alone at the foot of James's grave. Sarah ran to join her and Kate turned as she approached. Sarah threw her arms around and her and hugged her hard. They both stood and stared at the grave. The whole grave was crammed full of daffodils, their big yellow faces bobbing gently in the breeze.

"I'm so very sorry. You weren't meant to find out like this. I was going to explain. It was one of my impulsive moments. You see, it seemed like such a good idea when Amy had said it and she'd been

109

getting puzzled that he wasn't a flower yet and I thought it would be nice and I was going to tell you, but then you went away...."

Kate interrupted "Shut up you daft tart. They're beautiful."

"Really?"

"Yes, really. James would have loved that he was a daffodil for Amy. Well, about a hundred daffodils!" Kate linked her arm through Sarah's and the two women stood and stared at the sea of yellow. It really was a glorious sight that covered the entire grave like a blanket of sunshine.

"It was the spare bulbs at Back to the Fuschia that swung it. We'd been making up pots and Esme had seriously over-ordered the daffodil bulbs and she asked if I wanted some. So I took the lot."

"And that's where the ones you gave me came from, too."

"Yep. You really don't mind?"

"I said I love it. Come on. Let's get home and have a natter. I've done what I needed to do here." Kate bent down and snapped off a few daffodils and they walked back arm in arm to the car park.

Back at home, Kate arranged the daffodils in a small vase and put them on the kitchen table. Despite having spoken on the phone every week, they found they had loads to tell each other and barely came up for air for the first hour.

"So, you didn't give Tim my photo and phone number and he isn't a tosser," said Sarah, finally coming to the end of her long list of questions to ask Kate about him.

"No, he's kind of normal. Well, he starts off as a bit arrogant and he sort of slips back into the über-confident style, but in between, he's fine."

"In between he's dull?"

"No, he's not dull, don't be unkind!"

"Very hot, but a bit dull?" persisted Sarah.

"No, he's hot, obviously, but, no, he's not dull." And she threw a cushion at her, which Sarah adeptly caught and snuggled behind her head for extra comfort. "So, is Shaun still behaving himself?"

Sarah tensed and instantly looked less comfortable, despite the extra cushion. "Yep, he's er, he's okay."

"Not let Amy down recently?"

"No, he's been fine and he's been spending more time with her." Sarah stared at her chipped nail polish.

"That's good, then," said Kate, in a very perfunctory manner.

"I wanted to ask you what you honestly thought of Shaun. You didn't really hate him, did you?" asked Sarah leaning forward and studying Kate closely.

"Hate is a strong word,"

"He has some good points. Don't look like that," said Sarah, registering Kate rolling her eyes. "What did you think? Honestly?"

"Honestly?" asked Kate. Sarah nodded in response, biting her bottom lip.

Kate took a deep breath.

"I didn't like him. I tried to like him, but he was just generally unpleasant to me most of the time. He frequently made snide comments to me, but he was always careful to make sure they were out of earshot of anyone else."

Sarah looked shocked, "You never said."

"It was never the right time. And it seemed childish to tell you that Shaun was saying mean things to me. You know, he even congratulated me on my inheritance at James's funeral."

"Kate, I'm sorry." Sarah shook her head, "That's an awful thing to do."

"Sarah, that was just one of many nasty comments. Please don't beat yourself up. He was such a good actor and he acted his best scenes with you."

"I'm a fool," said Sarah, leaning back on the cushions.

"It wasn't that you were a fool, it was more that he played the loyal husband role so well he should have got a bloody Oscar for it. I often wondered what it was that attracted you to him. I just couldn't see it."

"He poked me in the back with a ruler in biology class."

"Nice pick-up approach. As you got older, I thought you'd see him for what he was, but you didn't."

"Beauty is in the eye of the beer-holder?" Sarah offered and she went to carry on, but Kate was feeling as if she was on a roll.

"I thought he was having an affair when you were pregnant with Amy and then again just before James's accident."

"Who with?"

"The first time I wasn't sure, but the second time I thought it was a barmaid." She paused as she tried to recall the name. "Melissa or something like that."

"Melanie," said Sarah quietly.

"Yes, Melanie," nodded Kate in recognition. "I couldn't prove it and I wasn't about to play sleuth. You kicked him out shortly afterwards anyway."

In the pause that followed, Sarah spoke with a quiet voice "But he wasn't... having an affair?"

"Well, it doesn't really matter now, I suppose. But as it turns out, he was." Registering the shock on Sarah's face, she added, "Sorry, Sarah. Shaun and Melanie had been going on for a while. Phil told me after that pub cricket and barbecue night in the summer when he'd overdone the Pimm's." Kate stopped talking and noted that Sarah still held an awfully shocked expression, "Goodness, that feels better. That must be what confession feels like. I've not upset you, have I? I have, I'm sorry, I shouldn't have said anything."

"Um. I guess it's a bit of a shock," said Sarah slowly, thinking that that was the understatement of the decade, up there with Custer's "It's just a minor problem with a few Indians".

"I am sorry, Sarah. I know he's still Amy's dad, but the bottom line is he's a bad lot and you deserve far better and, like you said, he's in the past." There was a long silence.

"I didn't," said Sarah meekly, biting her bottom lip again, harder this time.

"You didn't what?"

"I didn't say he was in the past." Slowly, realisation dawned on

112

Kate and her expression changed at least five times in the space of the same number of seconds.

"Oh, God! No, you're not. You haven't. Have you?"

"Got back together? Yes we have," said Sarah, with a grimace.

"Sarah!"

"I know, I know. I'm clearly an idiot. He's just been so nice lately; he's paid off my credit card and Amy likes having him around and you were away and…"

"Has he really changed? Has he stopped seeing Melanie?"

"I don't know. I want to think he's changed but… I don't know where he is half the time."

"And the other half of the time you do know, because?" said Kate her unease growing.

"He moved back in. Sorry!" said Sarah, covering her face with her hands. Kate raised her eyebrows.

"Okay, so what are you going to do now?"

"Question too difficult…" sighed Sarah.

"I'll get the key lime pie and then we need a plan."

"A plan for what?"

"We need to know if he is being faithful to you now. I take it that's the key thing?"

"Yep. If he's shagging around, he's definitely out."

"Any other criteria we need in order for you to kick him out?"

"I should just kick him out anyway, shouldn't I?" said Sarah "You would, wouldn't you?"

"I don't know. I like to think I would, but if you're kicking out your daughter's father you need to be sure of your reasons why, because you have someone else you need to be able to justify it to."

The women sighed in unison. Kate silently got up and went to the kitchen. As she passed the front door, it opened and made her jump. Concetta came marching into the house.

"Senora Kay, you hom!" said Concetta and she hugged her. The shock of a friendly welcome from Concetta and her attempt at English were a lot to take in. Kate nearly fell over and, once she was balanced back on two feet, she stared at Concetta but had no words, so she nodded and smiled in a strange sort of role reversal.

"Endy 'as gonna, si?" said Concetta very slowly.

"Si. You've learnt some English," said Kate, who was mightily impressed that they could exchange words, even if it wasn't very many and they weren't grammatically correct or in the right order.

"Endy help me," grinned Concetta, showing teeth Kate never knew she had. It was a bit disconcerting having Concetta smile at her.

"Well done Andy, then. He's a nice man." At this Concetta started giggling like a four-year-old and waved her headscarf at Kate as she went to hang up her coat. Kate cut three slices of pie and took them into the living room.

"Was that Concetta?"

"Yes, it was. Did you know Andy was teaching her English?"

"Those two have been thick as thieves, laughing and joking together. I think aliens came and swapped her," said Sarah, thrusting a fork into the pie. She sat there savouring the mouthful. Sarah had been doing lots of cooking lately, which she knew she only did when she had something on her mind. She'd been fretting for the last three weeks, ever since she'd had a drunken fumble with Shaun and the next day he'd turned up with his things, as a surprise, and announced to Amy he was moving back home. She knew she should have said no immediately, but there was a tiny part of her that wanted him back. Right now, she hated that part of her. It was clearly a defective gene from her father's side. Sarah wished that, just sometimes, she would take time out to think things through instead of leaping in with both feet. They heard footsteps in the hall again.

"Concetta, we're in here," called Kate. Concetta appeared in the doorway and repeated the scary smile, which made Sarah nearly choke on her pie. "Would you like to join us?" asked Kate, proffering the pie.

"Si, Senora. I like vherry much." Concetta smoothed down

her apron and flamboyant skirt and sat gingerly on the edge of the sofa. She looked a little uncomfortable, but then started to eat. Andy clearly hadn't covered food in his English lessons as all Concetta could manage was an exaggerated rub of her stomach, which they recognised as a positive thing. The three women sat in silence and ate.

"Nice pie, Sarah, thank you. Now have you had a think about Shaun?" asked Kate, putting down her plate.

"He bad man. He no love you," stated Concetta, jabbing towards Sarah with her fork and sending a few crumbs into the air. Sarah was more than a bit taken aback.

"Do you know Shaun, Concetta?" asked Sarah.

"Endy tell me. Shwarn is bad man, he no love Sarah."

Kate and Sarah exchanged looks. This was news to both of them that Andy had a view on Shaun and Sarah's relationship, and one which he was prepared to discuss with Concetta.

"Thanks, Concetta, that's good to know," said Sarah.

"Well come, lady," said Concetta, who was now looking very satisfied that she'd managed to get her point across. She polished off the pie in record time and cleared away the plates. "I work." And she smiled at them both and disappeared.

"Did you see her legs?" whispered Sarah, as soon as Concetta was out of earshot.

"No, why?" said Kate.

"They were so hairy a yeti would take photos!"

"They do things differently in Spain. Anyway, ring Andy. See what he knows." Kate leaned over and passed the phone to Sarah.

"I don't know what to say."

"Make out you know something and see if he confirms it."

"Mmm, okay," said Sarah, perking up a little. Andy answered on the second ring.

"The wanderer returns! Welcome home, Kate. If the house fell down it wasn't me. Honest!"

"Hi Andy, it's me."

"Oh, hi Sarah. Is Kate okay?"

"She's fine, you can speak to her in a mo. I just need to ask you something."

"Fire away."

"I know Shaun is seeing Melanie and I wanted your help in chucking him out," she said, as convincingly as she could.

"What time shall I come over?"

"So you knew?!"

"Er, yes. Look you're never quite sure with those two, though, because they split up and then make it up all the time."

"You didn't tell me," said Sarah, her voice suddenly a lot softer. She felt as if she'd been punched. She was getting an emotional battering this afternoon.

"How could I when you seemed so pleased that Shaun was back? I did tell Shaun I'd kill him if he cheated on you again."

Sarah was looking at Kate, but was speaking into the phone. "You must despise me for being so weak."

"No!" replied Kate and Andy together, and Kate came over to put her arms around her. She took the phone from her.

"Hi, Andy. Can you meet us at Sarah's in about an hour?"

"No problem. I'm sorry, Kate. Please tell Sarah that I'm really sorry."

"I will. Don't worry, she'll be fine."

Kate and Sarah jumped out of Kate's car as soon as they caught sight of Andy's van. They took it in turns to hug each other and there was a quiet determination amongst the three of them. Sarah unlocked the door and was relieved that Shaun wasn't home. Kate handed her a bin bag.

"Here, put his clothes in this. I'll do shoes and bathroom," instructed Kate, as Andy appeared at the front door with his tool box. Sarah looked at him with a puzzled expression.

"Changing the lock," said Andy, as he threw a new key to Sarah. Kate and Sarah worked quickly and swept through the house collecting up anything that was Shaun's. When they deposited the two full bags on the front-door step, Andy was already working on the back-door lock.

"Shaun's going to flip," said Kate, looking worried.

"Yep, and I'm going to flip out when I see that sodding Melanie," said Sarah.

"Be careful. You want to keep your job and, if you lose it with her, Phil won't have a choice, he'll have to sack you. Don't give her the satisfaction," exhorted Kate.

Sarah knew that Kate was right, but she also knew how good it would feel to let out all her anger in Melanie's direction. At least now she understood why Melanie was always so off with her and why every attempt of hers to be friends had been met with a frosty reception.

"Right, job done," said Andy, smoothing his thumb over the edge of the door. "I've also added two new bolts top and bottom on both doors, just in case he… well, just in case."

"How about you fetch Amy from school and we'll wait here for Shaun?" suggested Kate.

"No, I want to tell him what I think of him," said Sarah.

"I think I may have a better idea," said Andy. "Why don't you both get Amy from school and go back to Kate's. We can tell Amy it's a sleepover. I'll stay here and wait for Shaun."

"What am I going to tell Amy? She'll be upset," said Sarah, as if realising for the first time the implications for Amy.

"Come on, we'll think of something," said Kate. "Grab some things for Amy and let's go."

"Dear boy, not a good time. Niamh and I are at the theatre," said Marcus into his mobile, as he ignored the glares from those around him, Niamh included.

"Which theatre?"

"New Wimbledon, why?"

"I'll be there in less than five minutes. I was on the way

117

to yours anyway," said Tim before the line went dead.

"Tim, no, the bloody show is about to start," said Marcus, in vain.

"Marcus, the band is setting up. Look!" Niamh pointed to the front of the stage, where the band members were shuffling about below.

"I'll have to speak to him outside or he'll come barrelling in here. He sounds in a tizz."

"Okay, but please be back before it starts."

Marcus apologised to the rest of the row in turn as he shuffled along the seats and made his escape. He hadn't been outside long when Tim's car pulled up and the rear door opened to reveal Tim looking pale and wearing his trademark sunglasses.

"Get in," he instructed firmly.

"No, the show's about to start. What's so blathering urgent? Are you all right?"

"No, I'm not well." He saw Terry's eyes flick to the rear-view mirror and decided that perhaps this was a conversation better had outside the car. "I'll be ten minutes, Terry, okay?"

"Thank you, Terence," added Marcus. Terry saluted to them both. Marcus ushered Tim up to the top of the theatre's cream steps, where they sat down. "What do you mean by 'not well'. Is it serious?"

"I don't know. I haven't slept properly for two or three weeks. I can't face food and I've had time off the set," said Tim. Marcus looked suitably shocked.

"Good heavens. What does your doctor say it is?"

"I've been to a couple and they've done tests but can't find anything physically wrong."

"This needs referring to a specialist."

"He referred me to some counsellor and I've just come from a session." Tim looked agitated, stood up and started to pace up and down along the step that Marcus was sitting on.

"And what was his conclusion?"

"That's the thing, it makes no sense," Tim snorted uncomfortably.

"What doesn't?" Marcus was momentarily distracted as he heard the band tuning up inside. Tim spun on his heel to face Marcus, his hands clasped together under his chin.

"The counsellor thinks… he suggested that it might be… that I'm in love," said Tim slowly, his pale forehead slightly creased.

"Good Lord! And are you, dear boy? Are you in love?"

"I'm not sleeping, I'm not eating and generally I feel like shit, so I'm thinking 'no', because everyone tells me how wonderful being in love is."

"So what did you tell the counsellor that led him to this conclusion?"

"That she occupies all my thoughts. I can't concentrate on anything. The more I try not to think about her, the more I go over every conversation, every touch and relive it. It's like some weird obsessive thing." The band struck up into an intro and Marcus got to his feet.

"It sounds like love to me, too, so my hearty congratulations, dear boy, I'm thrilled for you and Lumina. We must do dinner, but right now I need to go or I'll be getting a divorce," and he turned to leave.

"Kate," said Tim quietly to Marcus's back. "Not Lumina. It's Kate."

Chapter 11

When they got back to Kate's house, Sarah took Amy into the living room to talk to her. She tried her best to explain the situation with Shaun in a way she hoped Amy understood. Amy sat quietly looking at her mother.

"We'll be fine, just the two of us, and you can still see Daddy. It'll be just like it was before. Okay?" Sarah studied her daughter's face for some clue as to how she was feeling about this sudden change of events.

"Is Daddy going to get cross?" asked Amy, her face now showing concern.

"I think he will, a bit. That's why Andy is going to talk to him and we're going to stay here. Just until he's stopped being cross."

"Can I always stay with you? I don't like it when Daddy gets cross. He says bad things."

"Of course you can always stay with me. That's what mummies are for. I'll always keep you safe, Amy. It's up to you when you want to see Daddy." Sarah brushed the soft ringlets behind Amy's ear and stroked her smooth cheek. She didn't know if Amy was okay with what was happening, but she knew in her heart that it would be best for both of them.

"Can we make pancakes?" asked Amy, suddenly perking

up.

"Yes, I'm sure we can."

"Yay!" cheered Amy, giving her mother a quick hug before skipping off into the kitchen, leaving Sarah slumped on her knees in front of the sofa. Sarah's phone started to ring in her pocket and, as she pulled it out, she could see it was Shaun. Her stomach lurched but she pressed the button to answer it anyway.

"Sarah, what's going on?"

"It's over, Shaun, it always was."

"Come on. Can't we stay friends?"

"That's like Amy asking if we can keep the hamster even though it's dead. So, no."

"You never look at things from my point of view," said Shaun, anger bubbling in his words.

"That's because I can't get my head that far up my own arse!"

"You bitch! You can't lock me out of my own house and kidnap my daughter. You've really lost it this time. I'll have the police and social services onto you. You stupid cow, did you really think you could get me out of your life that easily by just changing the locks? I'll always be here."

"Thanks for the call, Shaun. Now go and play happy families with Melanie. Don't bother calling social services, I've already made them aware as I guessed you'd be making threats."

"You think you're so superior. You won't win, you know. I'll see you in court!"

"I'd like to see you inside a chalk outline! But I'm not that lucky!"

"You won't win Sarah, the cream always rises to the top."

"So does scum!" With that, Sarah poked the red "off" key and threw the mobile onto the sofa. It just wasn't the same as slamming down a receiver on someone. Almost instantly, Kate's mobile sprang into life and she bounded in from the kitchen to answer it.

"It's Andy," she said to a worried-looking Sarah before

she answered the call. "Hi, how did it go?"

"He shouted a lot but I stepped outside as soon as he arrived and pulled the door shut, so I couldn't have let him in even if I'd wanted to as Sarah has the keys. He kicked the door a few times and now he's gone off with his bin bags. So, I'm coming over now."

"He just called Sarah and I'm guessing by her face he's had a bit of a go at her, but she's okay," said Kate as she joined Sarah on the floor and gave her a hug. Sarah rested her head on Kate's shoulder. "I'm doing spag bol and pancakes by request. See you soon."

"Great, bye."

As Kate ended the call her mobile flashed into life again, this time it was an unknown number so she hit the "reject" button and gave Sarah a proper hug.

"For what it's worth, I think you've done a brave thing today, and the right thing for you and Amy," said Kate.

"Thanks. I can't help thinking that if I hadn't let him wheedle his way back in again we wouldn't be in this position, which is definitely a worse one. He'll be even more of an arsehole now. If that's possible."

"You'll get through it. Amy seems okay. She's certainly not bereft at the thought of not living with Shaun. You'll both be fine. Come on, Andy's on his way, let's get the dinner on."

Andy had perfect timing as he arrived just as dinner was being piled onto plates. The meal was surprisingly jolly, with Amy updating them on what had happened at school. This was a lot about a game of fairies and a bit about counting. They all had a go at tossing a pancake and the adults all tried to get away with as many innuendos as possible without Amy wondering what was so funny. The general conclusion was that the biggest tosser wasn't there!

Kate and Sarah were in the kitchen verbally pulling Shaun apart in whispers, which they both found therapeutic, while Andy was getting slaughtered at junior monopoly, when they heard the van pull onto the gravel outside. Sarah went to the window, her heart racing. Andy was up on his feet and out of the front door before Shaun had turned the engine off. Shaun swung open the driver's door in an exaggerated motion and dragged himself out of the car. He swayed slightly as he came towards Andy, fist first. Andy simply dodged to one side and let Shaun fall face down on the gravel.

"Come on, Shaun. Let's not do this," said Andy, as he bent down to help him up. The smell of whisky was overpowering. "Bloody hell, mate, how many have you had?"

"Fuck you, you're no mate of mine," he slurred, as he pushed away Andy's offer of help. Shaun sat himself up on the gravel and put his hand to his face, which was bleeding from two small cuts on his chin and cheek, inflicted by the gravel. "That's actual bodily harm! That's a few month's inside, mate!" Shaun spat the words at Andy.

"I don't think so," shouted Kate from the now-open kitchen window, holding up her mobile phone. "I've got it all on video. Shall I upload it on YouTube or just email it to the police?"

Shaun started to laugh and held his hands up, as if in surrender.

"Any chance of a coffee and a plaster before I go?" He grinned at Sarah and Kate, who were both peering out of the window at him.

"No!" shouted both women at once and then high-fived each other. Sarah really liked the feeling of being on the winning team for once. Andy piped up from outside.

"I think we should call him a taxi."

"I've got a huge list of things I'd like to call him but there are little ears listening. Let me tell you, there are lots of four-letter words on that list and 'taxi' isn't one of them!" shouted Sarah triumphantly. Andy gave her a look that said he'd hoped for a more adult response. He bent down and hauled Shaun onto his feet and guided him over, so he could lean on the bonnet.

"Wait there," he instructed, before marching back inside

the house. Both Sarah and Kate turned as he strode into the kitchen. "Look, he is an arsehole, but he's in a state. We can't just leave him like this." Kate's mobile started to ring again. She glanced at it and saw that it was the same unknown number from earlier and rejected the call again.

"He's not coming in," said Kate, switching off her mobile, "Amy's in there. You don't know what he might say or do."

"She's right," agreed Sarah. Kate opened a cupboard and pulled down a first-aid kit. She got out a strip of plaster, cut off two pieces and handed them, with a couple of squares of kitchen roll, to Andy.

"Here, he can patch himself up and I'll call a taxi."

"Thanks," said Andy, taking the things from Kate. Kate headed into the living room and ruffled Amy's hair as she passed.

While Kate was calling the local taxi company she could hear raised voices outside again, so she walked back to the kitchen to see what was happening. Shaun had got inside the van, had locked the door, and was shouting at Andy through the part-wound-down window. Sarah was also pitching in from the kitchen.

"Do you have to leave so soon? I was about to poison your coffee!" she called. It really was making her feel so much better about her decision, to see Shaun for the vile and hateful individual he really was. Andy passed Shaun the plasters and kitchen roll through the gap and made an attempt to grab the car keys through the window, but the gap wasn't big enough. He managed to retrieve his hand just before Shaun wound the window right up. He stuck his fingers up at Andy and started the engine. Andy was getting frustrated with him now, his usual relaxed manner was gone and his jaw was tight as he went and stood behind Shaun's car. As Shaun had driven in he was going to have to reverse out and Andy hoped he wasn't about to add attempted murder to his list of misdemeanours. Shaun put the van in reverse and revved the engine threateningly.

"Christ!" said Sarah, "He's going to run Andy over," and

she ran to the front door.

"I'm really sorry about this. Can you hold? We might not need that cab after all," said Kate to the patient operator from the taxi firm. Sarah stepped onto the gravel and Shaun slammed the car into first gear and it lurched towards Sarah. At the last second, he yanked the steering wheel around; the van narrowly missed Sarah but ploughed into one of Kate's pots, careered across the front garden and swerved out of the drive, only missing Andy by a fraction. Kate cancelled the cab and dialled 999 as Andy ran out onto the street just as a perfectly timed police car glided around the corner and blocked Shaun's exit.

The next day was Friday and Kate dropped Amy off at school, saw her safely inside and headed off to the convalescent home. Didi was utterly thrilled to see Kate and told her so about five times. Kate was equally pleased to see Didi. Whilst they had exchanged letters and had a few chats on the phone, it really hadn't been the same. Kate was amazed by how well Didi was looking, and the fact that she was out of bed, fully dressed and walking about had taken Kate quite by surprise. They settled themselves down in a nice corner of one of the lounges and Kate went and got the drinks.

"So how was my replacement?" asked Kate, with a smile.

"Worse than useless. Dull as a party political broadcast, but with less smiling. I think she was stealing the biscuits, too. We all started to get rationed. Anyway, she's gone now and they're just muddling along. I'm okay. I can get my own drinks. I'm allowed now that I'm mobile."

"I can see that. You look terrific. So have they talked to you about when you can go home?"

"I've told them a couple of weeks and then I'm digging a tunnel," said Didi with a wink.

"You need to get the okay from the doctor, Didi. You've stuck it out this long and it's clearly done you good."

"We'll see," smiled Didi.

125

"Don't forget, I'll take you home and settle you in. I don't mind sleeping on your sofa for a couple of nights, if you like," offered Kate.

"That's really kind and I'll say yes to the offer of a lift and no thank you to the babysitting."

"Deal. So any other news, like how are things going with your man with the eye operation?"

"Feeble Kneevil? He fell off his zimmer frame and ended up back in hospital. I think I may have scared him. I can't think why," Didi chuckled. "More importantly, tell me about Timothy Calder," Didi sat forward in her seat and cupped her coffee mug as she listened intently to Kate's update.

"So, no sex then?" asked Didi when Kate had finished.

"No! You are so naughty," laughed Kate.

"And you've not heard from him since?"

"There were a couple of calls to the cottage when he rang to speak to Marcus but that was all. I'll see him again next week when we start rehearsals."

"Did you not swap mobile numbers? Isn't that what you young people do these days?"

"He didn't ask for mine and I wasn't going to offer it. He'd just think I was being a pushy fan."

"Never mind. Perhaps we can fix you up with someone in the film crew. There will be loads of people working on the film set. There must be someone you could take a fancy to."

"Really, you're incorrigible! I'm fine being single, thanks. It's been two years since James died and ..." Kate wasn't entirely sure what was meant to come next in that sentence, so she sipped her tea instead. Didi leaned forward and patted her knee.

"You're doing fine. Just fine."

I am, thought Kate. I really am.

Kate came home to find Andy and Concetta dancing in the kitchen and Sarah rolling about laughing. Concetta was dressed in one of her many amazingly colourful dresses and this one appeared to have extra layers of turquoise and orange underneath that were visible when Andy twirled her around. They came to a finale and Sarah paused the music as Andy and Concetta slumped onto kitchen chairs. Concetta's breathing sounded reminiscent of an ageing steam train going at full tilt, her rather ample bosom heaving with every breath.

"Endy, you make me girl again." She slapped him playfully on the arm and danced out of the kitchen. "Senora," she nodded and smiled at Kate as she went past. Kate was still standing in the doorway, taking in the bizarre spectacle.

"You forgot your mobile," said Andy, handing the phone to Kate.

"Any update from the police?"

"Shaun was released on bail this morning, pending a court date. I've let the school know that he's not to pick Amy up because of the drink-driving charge and they were fine about it," said Sarah.

"Bugger, I was hoping they'd lock him up, but I guess he's just looking at a fine," sighed Kate. "I don't need to say it, but I will anyway, you and Amy can stay here as long as you like. I love having you both."

"Thanks, Kate, you're a star. Definitely a couple more nights, I think. Maybe we'll go back on Monday. I'm working at the pub for a long shift this evening, so can you pick her up from school and feed her, please?"

"I'm working over that way this afternoon. I'll get Amy, if you let the school know," suggested Andy.

"Okay, great. Thanks, guys. I would be a mess without you two."

"We know," said Andy

"Shut up!" said Sarah, making a fist at him and pretending to punch him.

"That's actual bodily harm, that is, mate!" joked Andy.

"Right, I have to go. Concetta, me voy en mi coche ahora!"

"Si, Endy estoy listo," came the reply.

"Er, translation please?" asked Sarah, with a quizzical expression.

"I hope that I said: I'm leaving in my car now, or something similar and Concetta said she was ready to go too." Andy went a little pink and nervously brushed his fingers through his hair. "I sometimes give her a lift, otherwise it's a long walk for her."

"Oh, okay," grinned Sarah, as Andy zipped up his coat and held the door open. Concetta waved goodbye as she bustled through it in a blur of turquoise and orange, only partially covered by a zebra-print jacket.

"Where is she going dressed like that?" asked Kate, once the front door had closed with both Andy and Concetta safely on the other side.

"In that outfit, my guess would be the Rio carnival!" said Sarah.

Sarah went to get herself ready for her shift at the pub and emerged looking very smart in black trousers, white shirt and full make-up, with her hair clipped at one side, making her look particularly young.

"You don't look old enough to be served, let alone serve customers," said Kate.

"You see, that's why you're my friend. You make me feel so much better!" They hugged and Sarah left. Kate watched her drive off and then turned around to look at the kitchen. She noticed her mobile on the table and switched it on. There were two messages. The first one was virtually blank, just someone huffing and clicking their phone off. The second one had been left at nine-thirty the night before and it was Tim. Kate pulled out a chair quickly and sat down to listen.

"Hi Kate… it's Tim. I was hoping to speak to you but,

anyway, I hope this is your number. Marcus gave it to me. I hope that was okay. I was ringing to see if you wanted to catch up this weekend before rehearsals start. Just in case you had any questions about filming. So… that was all. I've texted you, so you'll have my phone number. Bye." Kate pulled up the text message, which just said, "Tried to call, left a message, please call back on this number. Tim". Kate stared at it for a little bit and realised that she was smiling. She was a little suspicious as to why Tim would want to catch up with her, especially on a weekend when he could be jetting away anywhere in the world, but she couldn't help but feel pleased about it, too. She rang the mobile number and it went to an anonymous voicemail much like her own.

"Hi Tim, it's Kate. Thanks for the invite. Sorry I didn't get back to you sooner, but we had a bit of a drama here. Anyway, you don't need to know about that. So, my mobile is now on and I'm free all weekend, so let me know. Bye." She hoped the message had sounded relaxed. She was starting to realise that she cared what Tim thought about her, and she was keener than she'd realised to see him again. Kate busied herself with emails and collating things she thought she might need for rehearsals on Monday. Her phone rang and she saw it was Andy, which made her give a little disappointed sigh.

"Hi, Andy, is everything okay?"

"Hi, Kate. You're on loudspeaker in the car," he said.

"Hi, Kate," chimed in Amy.

"Hi, Amy."

"We've had an idea. Do you fancy bowling, then a film and pizza as Sarah is working?"

"Have you two been plotting?" asked Kate.

"Nooooo!" they both insisted.

"Sounds like a good plan to me. Count me in!"

"Great! We'll be there in ten minutes."

Kate really enjoyed herself with Andy and Amy. The bowling had been lots of fun and she hadn't been for ages. Andy was fiercely competitive, but had absolutely no competition from Kate and Amy. They then watched the latest Disney offering, which they all enjoyed, even if the 3-D glasses did give you a bit of a headache. They picked up pizza on the way home and were dividing it up in the kitchen when Kate's mobile rang. As she had now programmed in Tim's number, she could see it was him calling. She walked quickly out of the kitchen and headed upstairs, took a deep breath and answered it.

"Hi, Tim."

"Hello, Kate, is that you?" Kate resisted the desire to go "yes, obviously it's me, you called my mobile", but instead opted for:

"Yes, it's me. Hi, Tim."

"Kate, I'm really sorry, something has come up. Er, someone I know is in hospital, so I'm sorry I won't be about this weekend now. I should be okay for rehearsals, but if not, Pip will keep everyone updated. Okay?"

"Of course, I'm sorry to hear that. I hope everything is okay."

"Sorry, Kate. Bye," and he was gone. Kate sat down on the end of her bed and stared at the mobile. He had sounded preoccupied, quite different to how he had sounded in his message. Perhaps he had been at a loose end last night and tonight he'd had a better offer. Or perhaps she should stop jumping to conclusions and believe what he'd told her, that someone was in hospital. He hadn't given any clue as to who was in hospital, which struck her as odd. Usually you'd say who they were if they were a relative; you'd say my cousin, my sister, whoever it was, or for anyone else you'd just say a friend. But then Tim had been a bit deep when they'd talked about friends before. She listened to the laughter and squeals coming from downstairs and decided to pull herself together and go and join in before all the pizza disappeared. She also decided to forget about Tim and look forward to the excitement of the

130

film industry on Monday.

Kate had put Amy to bed and was pleased that she went straight off to sleep despite Sarah not being in the house. Nobody had really questioned why Andy was still staying there. He had just assumed the role of protector and both women were quite happy to let him, given that Shaun was still out there somewhere.

Kate and Andy watched a documentary before deciding they should go to bed. Sarah had her own key, so there was no need to wait up. Kate was just writing down a couple of things on the shopping list, as they were using things up quite quickly with four people in the house, when the phone rang.

"Kate, it's me," said Sarah. "I'm in A&E."

"Oh, God, what's happened? What's he done?" asked Kate, fearing the worst.

"It's not me, it's Melanie. I found her as I was leaving the pub. She's been mugged and they've made a mess of her. Phil helped me to get her into the car and I drove her straight here. I'm waiting until her mum gets here."

"That's good of you, considering the trouble she's caused."

"It was Melanie who told the police that Shaun was over the limit last night."

"Did he beat her up?"

"No, he's smarter than that. There were two thugs, apparently. They took her purse, but they knew her name and they have concentrated on punching her face. She looks awful, Kate. I'm sure Shaun's behind it. I was ringing you to say you should go to bed. I've got a key and I'll see you in the morning."

"Sarah, be really careful. Please."

Chapter 12

Kate was first up on Monday morning. She felt like a child on their first day at school; very excited, a bit worried and completely unsure what to expect. Marcus had explained that most directors don't have the screenwriter on set, let alone the author, but Che was different and he liked to change things on the hoof, so he wanted Marcus on hand most of the time. Marcus wanted Kate there in the hope that she would get caught up in the excitement and enjoy herself.

Kate put on the dress she had got out the night before, but she was now trying on different cardigans and jackets to see what went with it best. She was just adjusting the sleeves on a cream cardigan as a dishevelled-looking Sarah put her head around the bedroom door.

"Hey, gorgeous, fancy a shag?" grinned Sarah.

"Delightful! You look as though an inexperienced bird has made a nest in your hair."

"They do that, the little sods," Sarah said, smoothing it down with both hands, but to no avail. "I was just trying to get you acclimatised to the film industry. They're all at it, you know. You're bound to get offered sex or drugs – or both!" exclaimed Sarah excitedly.

Kate turned away from the mirror to give Sarah a hard stare.

"I was just saying." Sarah plonked herself down on Kate's bed and had another attempt at her hair before giving up and straightening Kate's cardigan.

"What is it with you and cardigans?"

"I like them! They stop you getting cold."

"You're not 90!" Sarah protested and straightened Kate's necklace. "I'm really proud of you. I know I don't really have any right to be and that it's all down to you, but I am proud of you." Kate knew that Sarah wasn't just talking about the film.

"I know. I wouldn't be here, in this cardigan, if it wasn't for you," she said, and Sarah stuck her tongue out at her.

At the rehearsal hall, Kate was ushered into a meeting room to wait. A short woman with dark-brown hair in a neat bob cut popped her head around the door. Kate guessed she was in her early thirties. She wore a smart grey skirt and a pink cardigan and Kate took an instant liking to her.

"Sorry, I didn't know anyone was here yet. I'm Pippa, Timothy Calder's PA. Have you seen Che Beynon?"

"Sorry, I don't know who he is," said Kate, wishing she'd written down the names Marcus had reeled off.

"He's the director. Sorry, I didn't catch your name?" said Pippa, diplomatically, as she came into the room.

"I'm Kate Marshall." Kate offered a hand and Pippa shook it warmly.

"Very pleased to meet you, Kate. I'm a big fan. When's your next book out?" gushed Pippa, looking genuinely starstruck.

"I've been a bit slack on the novel front, what with the script," said Kate, feeling rather guilty that there might be more people waiting for her next book, which she'd failed to deliver.

"Of course, of course." Pippa sat down next to Kate, "I think *Love.com* is brilliant. Tim is going to be amazing as Patrick."

"You think?" said Kate.

"Definitely. Once I knew about the film, I read the book

a second time and I could picture him as Patrick."

"That's nice to know. Thanks," said Kate "Is Tim going to make it today? What with being called away to hospital."

"He's on a flight now – should be landing soon. He'll be later than planned. Hopefully he will have slept on the flight, so he shouldn't be too grumpy," she laughed. Kate gleaned from this that he must be flying long-haul from somewhere.

"That's good. Do you know if they're okay… the person in hospital," asked Kate, knowing she was being a bit cheeky, but curiosity was getting the better of her.

"As far as I know. Right! Can't sit here gossiping. Do you want to come and meet a few people? We won't be in here until everyone's arrived; then we'll agree the plans for the day and then off we go!"

Kate picked up her handbag and followed Pippa. In between answering calls she gave Kate a full, guided tour and a run-through of how the day would most likely pan out.

"This is where we'll be doing the run-throughs," said Pippa, as they entered something that resembled a school hall. There were a couple of cameras set up, some chairs in rows and quite a few people milling about.

"Darling girl, here you are!" boomed Marcus, as he kissed her cheek. "Tim's late, Lumina's having some pooch crisis, Che's gone AWOL and we've got a lighting engineer down with flu. Other than that, welcome to the film industry!" he said, giving her another hug and appraising her. "You look terrific! It's lovely to see, really lovely." Marcus had a way of making you feel good about yourself with just a few kind words.

"Right, let's do the guided tour!"

"It's okay, Pippa showed me around earlier."

"Righto! I'll talk you through what usually happens on a rehearsal day." Kate didn't have the heart to tell him that Pippa had done that too, so she picked up her drink and followed him dutifully. Marcus was more thorough than Pippa and also had a writer's view of what would be happening, when they would be needed and what would be interesting to them.

Marcus introduced Kate to an older man called Dennis, who was the assistant cameraman. He was very happy to chat to Kate and explained the differing roles of key grips, dolly grips and other sorts of grips. Kate spotted Tim out of the corner of her eye. He was striding across the rehearsal room with Pippa at his side – she was passing him pieces of paper and talking very fast. Kate tuned out of what Dennis was saying and found herself checking her hair. Dennis was still talking, so she nodded earnestly at him.

"Thank you. Would you mind if we caught up again later, so that I could ask you some questions?"

"Of course, anytime," smiled Dennis, which made her feel a little guilty, as he was clearly a kind person. Tim was now heading straight in her direction, looking lightly tanned and completely gorgeous. He was wearing dark-blue jeans and a crisp, white shirt and all Kate could do was stare, the easy relationship they had at the cottage forgotten as Timothy Calder, the film star, headed her way. As he got to within a couple of metres of her, she smiled at him and opened her mouth to speak, just as someone yelled. "Tim!" Tim completely diverted off and walked straight past Kate, without appearing to notice her at all. She closed her mouth, took a deep breath and went in search of Marcus.

Pippa came scurrying round and herded everyone into the overcrowded meeting room. The director, Che, stood up, introduced himself briefly and then asked everyone else to do the same in turn. It was a slow, creeping death of introductions that was getting closer and closer to Kate and she could feel her palms starting to sweat. Marcus was next.

"I'm Marcus Leonard, script writer," and he turned and looked at Kate. Kate had been expecting him to say more, so was taken by surprise.

"Oh, I'm Kate Marshall, I'm a writer. I wrote the book

that the film is based on and I helped out with the script, too." She received lots of smiles and nods in response, which made her start to relax. Tim had entered the meeting late and was standing near the door. When it came to him he stepped forward, giving a warm smile before speaking.

"Hi, I'm Timothy Calder, male lead. I'm excited about this project and to be working with you." And just for a second Kate thought he was speaking just to her.

There were some finance people and quite a few actors for the other key roles, but there was no sign of Lumina. Che then gave a speech about what he felt he brought to the film, a bit about his style and how he liked to work. He then ran through the plans for the next couple of days, reminded them of the date for the start of filming and handed out a draft schedule.

The meeting went well and Kate felt that she understood more than half of what was said, which she thought was good for day one. They were now all grouped in the rehearsal room and Pippa was animatedly explaining the *Love.com* story to a lighting technician.

"It's about Patrick and Marianna; they were childhood sweethearts. They lose touch when Marianna emigrates to New Zealand. She contacts him through a website when she hits 30, to find that he's a very successful man with a string of companies and an equal number of failed relationships. But the other reason she gets in touch is because she's dying, but she doesn't tell him that. After she dies, her sister Marcie carries on emailing Patrick, signing off as 'M', and they fall in love. Marcie keeps putting off meeting Patrick, for obvious reasons. Eventually Marcie meets him as herself and there's a connection, but Patrick is confused because he thinks he loves Marianna. Then Marcie has to face him and tell him the truth, for fear of losing him, because he's being faithful to Marianna. Patrick's furious when he realises what she's done. He's also sad about Marianna's death. Anyway, eventually he realises that it was really Marcie and her emails that he fell in love with and then they get together at the end. It's brilliant really."

The lighting technician looked slightly confused and just nodded. Kate was quite pleased with Pippa's summary of the story; she would have struggled to have been that succinct herself – she'd never been very good at perfecting a synopsis.

A door slammed and in walked Lumina. Everyone turned to watch her as she walked confidently across the room carrying a large, red designer bag in the crook of her arm, with a small dog's head poking over the top. Kate assumed both were real. Lumina had impossibly high-heeled shoes on in a matching shade of red, skin-tight trousers and the biggest sunglasses Kate had ever seen. Her blonde hair was professionally curled and it bounced around her shoulders as she walked. Pippa ran from person to person like a human pinball, then took Lumina's bag containing the dog and went off again. Kate settled herself down next to Marcus and waited excitedly for rehearsals to start. After a bit of a discussion, the scene and line numbers were announced and Kate turned to that page in her own pristine copy of the script. The room fell silent and the lights beamed on to a spot on the floor.

Tim took a sip of water and strode into the middle of the puddle of light. Lumina joined him, still wearing her sunglasses and clutching her script tightly. Tim went to air-kiss her and she turned away. He leaned forward and quietly said something that made her scowl in his ear. Someone called "Quiet on set, rolling, action" and, as Tim started to speak, Kate found herself transfixed. She was looking at Patrick. Lumina started off okay and then fumbled her second line, even though she was reading directly from the script. Tim tensed and glared at her, but she carried on. After two more attempts and two more fumbles from Lumina, Tim was turning red and jerking his hands about in frustration.

"Just stop!" said Tim. He turned to Che. "This is pointless, she has no change of pace to her words, there's no character!"

"It's a cold read, for Christ's sake, Tim!" screeched Lumina. Che quickly corralled Tim and Lumina into a corner to talk it through.

"What does she mean by a 'cold read'?" Kate whispered to

Marcus, a little concerned that it was an insult to the writing.

"She means that at run-throughs you just have to read, you don't have to act. It's just that different actors approach a read differently."

"Okay, so she is kind of right, then?"

"Yes, but Tim won't see it like that." After more discussion and arm-waving from the actors they all retook their places and started the scene for the third time. This time, Tim was stronger with his delivery and Kate found she was staring at him without blinking, which probably wasn't good for her eyes. She'd only seen a couple of the Agent X films, but she decided she was going to order them all when she got home. Lumina stumbled again on her lines and Tim stepped in front of her and splayed out his arms.

"What's going on, Mina?" he said. Lumina threw her script on the floor and ran out as best she could in her skyscraper heels. Tim then turned and did a theatrical style bow to Che as if he was doing a curtain call before walking off in a different direction.

"Great start," grumbled Marcus. "I knew there would be a problem. Why can't Tim just keep it in his pants?" And he went off after Tim, leaving Kate on her own, thinking that it was probably going to take years to complete filming if every piece of dialogue was going to take this long to perfect.

"There you go," said Sarah, standing back to admire the flowers she'd arranged in a jug. She'd failed to find a vase in Melanie's tiny kitchen.

"Thanks, Sarah, they're lovely, but I'm not sure about putting vinegar in with them," said Melanie, who was curled up on the sofa, huddled up under her duvet.

"Vinegar is a florist's secret tip; it kills the bacteria." And hopefully it would make these fading flowers last a few more days, thought Sarah, who'd got them free from Back to the Fuschia.

"It's kind of you to come round." Melanie pulled the bright-red duvet nearer to her chin. Sarah wondered if the rest of her bedroom matched the bright duvet, but sadly the door was closed.

"Your eyes are turning wonderful colours," said Sarah, with a twitch of her eyebrows. "Have you heard from Shaun?"

"No, but I didn't expect to," Melanie said, looking at Sarah, "I'm so sorry for everything. I know I was never that nice to you."

"Never mind that now," said Sarah patting the duvet. "What was it that made you change your mind about Shaun? Was it the drink-driving?"

"No, that was me getting my revenge, really, but that back-fired," she said, pointing to her own face. "He spun me some story about you being a mess and that was why he'd moved back in with you. I wasn't happy about it. He promised me that you weren't back together; he made out he was worried for Amy's safety." Sarah bristled but kept quiet because she wanted to hear more. "But each time I saw you at work, I struggled to believe that you could be so completely normal there and yet such a mess at home. Sorry."

"It's okay, carry on," said Sarah forcing a smile.

"So I started following you and the more I watched the more I saw someone very much in control who loved and cared for her daughter. Then I saw you and Shaun together, just for a moment. He was leaving one night as you came home from work." She paused and hung her head for a second before taking a breath and continuing. "He was due to meet me that night. As you passed in the doorway he kissed you and you pinched his bum and he… he promised you a good time when he got in."

"Ever the romantic is Shaun!"

"I felt sick. He was sleeping with both of us, Sarah. Taking us both for fools."

After Sarah and Melanie had bad-mouthed Shaun a bit more, they ran out of things to talk about, so Sarah made her apologies and headed home.

Sarah was dismayed to see the familiar sight of the dirty-white transit van outside the house. And what, from a distance, looked a lot like Ronald MacDonald's mum sitting at the wheel. Sarah sighed and prepared to face the inevitable, as Irene clambered out of the van and stormed along the pavement to meet her.

"Where is he? Where's my Shauny?"

"Hello, Irene, lovely to see you, as always. Can I help?"

"You deaf? Where's Shaun?"

"No, but thank you for enquiring about my health. I have absolutely no idea where Shaun is, as I have had the good fortune not to have seen him for quite some time."

"If you see him or you 'ear from him, you call me. Got it?"

"So did you let him off his leash and he ran off? Tut, tut."

"If he did, he's runnin' away from you!"

"I'll give you that one, Irene. Safe journey now, you take care." And, with that, Sarah walked past her and headed inside.

As she heard the sound of Irene's van revving furiously away, Sarah decided she'd make an impromptu picnic and call round to see how Andy was getting on with his house. She also had an ulterior motive as she was on the cadge for a babysitter. Amy really liked Andy and with the Shaun situation as it was, Sarah felt that Amy was safer with him than with a local teenage girl, however responsible she might be.

Andy was standing at the front door in his dusty work clothes, smiling at her as she pulled up outside. His hair looked as if he'd turned grey overnight, from all the dust. His white t-shirt was no longer white, but fitted him snugly and gave a good outline of the solid body underneath. Sarah bounded over and gave him a kiss on the cheek.

"Yuk, dust!"

"Sorry, it's everywhere. The plasterer was working upstairs and I've been sanding downstairs. There's dust on everything, but I've had a wipe round, so the kitchen should be okay."

Andy led her into the small hallway, past a bare wooden staircase and into a show-home kitchen. The room was vast, as Andy had knocked through two of the downstairs rooms into one. There was a big window onto the garden and every other piece of wall space had a cupboard on it. She spun around a couple of times to take it all in; the gleaming black-granite worktops, the cupboards, the six-ring hob and the big oven, but, above all, the vast quantities of wood.

"Did you do all this?"

"Yeah, it's what I do." He gave a cheeky smile and hopped up to sit on the granite worktop. "This'll be a breakfast bar once I get some bar stools, but I haven't got around to that yet. Have a seat." He indicated the shiny space next to him. But Sarah was still transfixed by the dream kitchen.

"Did you make all this?"

"Yeah, every door, every drawer, every knob. All my own work."

"What's this wood?" Sarah said, as she ran her fingers across the very dark, wooden worktop until it joined the cool, shiny granite.

"Everything is oak apart from the tops, which are wenge. It's African rosewood; closest thing to ebony without the hefty price tag," he explained, as he watched Sarah closely.

"Andy, it's all amazing. No wonder you make a living doing this. I'd buy this house right now, even in this state, just to have this kitchen."

"Thanks, Sarah. I'm glad you like it. So what's for lunch?"

"A smorgasbord of taste and texture from the supermarket discounted section – with some crusty bread!"

They sat on the worktop, with the pots and bowls between them, so that they could pick at the food and natter at the same time. They talked and laughed and the time soon sped past.

"I had better get going as I have to track down Esme's cousin and see if he's free for Amy's party. Apparently, he's got

141

some exotic pets." Andy raised his eyebrows at this. "Not Playboy pets, animal pets! And he's willing to bring them round, so I'm doing an animal- theme party."

"She'll love that. Before you go, have a look at the patio."

"You've laid a patio?"

"Yeah, I was fed up of all the inside work." Sarah gathered up her things and followed Andy out to the back of the house, where they stepped onto what Sarah thought was the prettiest patio she'd ever seen. In front of her was a circle of marbled yellow stones spiralling out into a large, circular patio, with a path looping around the garden and another smaller circle the other side, which Sarah thought would be a fabulous barbecue area.

"Wow, Andy, this is gorgeous!"

"The stones are a type of Indian sandstone, so you get all these colour variations from the yellow through to that pinky colour like that one there," he said, pointing out a pinker one with his dusty boot.

"I bet it was expensive."

"Not bad, really. I have a couple of friends in landscape gardening and this is popular right now, so they've bought huge quantities of the stuff. I've done them both good prices on kitchens in the past, so they do me virtually trade price on the stone. I've got loads left over, too. I majorly miscalculated!" Andy said, pointing down the side of the house to the stacks of stones piled up in neat rows.

"Ooh, are those going begging? I'd pay you for them, of course."

"What do you want them for?"

"A hot-air balloon!" Sarah pulled a silly face. "A patio, like this one. I'd need you to help me, obviously," said Sarah, screwing up her face in anticipation.

"There's enough for a small patio," he sighed, good-naturedly.

"Brilliant. Thank you!" and she flung her arms round his

neck.

The rest of the day of rehearsals had seemed to whizz by in a blur. Kate's head was spinning with all the advice and explanations from Marcus, and excitement from watching the actors run through the scripts.

"Have Tim and Lumina made up?" asked Kate, after the pair had done another read- through where Lumina had held her own and Tim had been utterly brilliant.

"I hope so. I told him to do whatever it took to achieve an agreeable working relationship."

As they were talking, Tim came striding past, still speaking into his mobile. "I'm just glad the op went well. Just let me know if you need anything else." And then he was past them. Clearly, Kate wasn't the only one who had heard, as one of the crew said snidely, "Probably an abortion he's paying for." And another responded with, "More likely to be a boob job!" and they all cackled with laughter. Marcus coughed loudly and the crew dispersed.

Kate was keen not to get in the way, so she set herself up in a corner with her laptop. She was just opening up a file when Pippa appeared at her shoulder.

"Are you a dog person, Kate?" she asked, looking frazzled.

"I like all animals, but I'm probably more cat than dog. Why? Is there a problem?"

"It's Horse." Kate was about to ask the obvious question, so Pippa continued. "That's the bloody stupid name that Lumina has for her horrible little dog. He hates me; he'll bite me if he gets half a chance. I need someone to babysit him so I can get some work done. It's driving me mad!" Oh, great sales pitch, thought Kate, I really want the job now!

"Could Lumina's PA not look after him?"

"What PA? She's had two and they lasted all of five minutes each. Since then she's conducted an endless round of interviews

143

but can't find anyone she connects with, darling," mimicked Pippa.

"You could leave him with me, if you like," offered Kate, trying not to sound as reluctant as she felt. Maybe one day she would say no to someone, but that clearly wasn't going to be today.

"You're a life-saver!"

Pippa returned a short while later with a small pink-and-white bag and plonked it on the table next to Kate's laptop.

"There you go. He's been fed and watered so shouldn't need anything for an hour or so. Thanks again," Pippa said and she disappeared before Kate could get any words out. The end of the bag was made of mesh and inside sat a very sad-looking chihuahua. He was a creamy-beige colour with a white stripe down his face and chest. He had some fluffy patches by his ears that made him look cute and puppy-like. His big, dark eyes met Kate's.

"Hello, you must be Horse," she whispered, leaning her face in closer.

"Grrrr" grumbled Horse, with more menace than you would think possible from a very small dog zipped into a bag.

"Right, okay. You can stay in there, then," and Kate gently moved the bag further onto the table. He soon went off to sleep, which made for easy dog-sitting. Kate gave the occasional look over the top of the laptop to check on Horse. Before long, people were packing up around her and it was the end of day one. She sat back in her chair as a rhythmic tap of heels announced that Lumina was approaching. Kate turned to see her scowling face half hidden by sunglasses.

"You've got my dog!" Lumina said, snatching the bag off the table and sending poor Horse into a spin inside.

"Yes, I was dog-sitting for Pippa. Well, for you, actually," said Kate, with a smile. "We didn't really get a chance to meet. I'm Kate," she said, offering a hand to shake.

"Horse is delicate. I don't like him being left with just anyone."

"I was just trying to help," stated Kate, feeling quite put out by Lumina's rudeness.

"Has he been sprinkles?"

"Sorry?"

"Tinkles, sprinkles?"

"He's just been sleeping for the last couple of hours. He's been fine."

Lumina gave a huff and waltzed off, slung the bag over her shoulder and started speaking into her mobile. Kate couldn't help but feel a bit sorry for Horse – she'd be grumpy, too, if she spent half her life under Lumina's armpit, however silky-smooth and deodorised it most probably was.

Kate packed up and headed down to join the small remaining group. Pippa began ushering Tim and Lumina out of the building and Kate and Marcus followed on behind. Pippa opened a door and Tim and Lumina stepped out. They were all momentarily blinded by flashes of light. Kate hadn't realised that it had grown dark outside and for a moment she was stunned as the flashbulbs went off around her. There were about a dozen or so paparazzi waiting next to the exit. Tim raced to the waiting car, cursing as he went, whilst Lumina flicked her hair back and trotted after him, making a half-hearted attempt to cover her face with one hand. Horse started yapping as if throwing insults at everyone. Kate felt an arm around her shoulders and Marcus guided her back inside and shut the door. Kate found she was trying to catch her breath. She had no idea how famous people coped with that all the time.

"But, nobody's meant to know we're rehearsing here," puzzled Pippa with a frown. "If they do get a tip-off, they usually wait at the front, not at this exit," she said, clearly confused. "There's been no press here all day, so why now?" she asked nobody in particular.

When Tim finally calmed down, he sat quietly in the limo sipping some bottled water. Lumina was studying her own reflection in the dark glass of the windows and smiling to herself.

"Are we going out this evening?" Lumina asked. Tim closed his eyes and slowly drew in a deep breath. "Tim, you promised, we have a deal, remember?"

"And I am a man of my word. So, yes, we can go out this evening. How does the cinema sound?" to which Lumina sat up straight and stared at him.

"I hope you're not serious!"

Chapter 13

A few days later, Kate found herself exhausted and crashed out in her garden, as it was an unexpectedly warm April day. Amy was busying herself looking for mini beasts with lots of help from Marmalade, who was keen to round up anything that scurried out from underneath the pots and rocks that Amy was lifting up. Kate and Sarah were sitting lazily in the steamer chairs, taking in the much-needed warmth. Sarah handed a newspaper to Kate.

"Newspaper? You?"

"Look who is on the front," Sarah said, adjusting her lounger awkwardly in an attempt to get it to lie flat. Kate unfolded the newspaper and looked at the picture on the front. It wasn't the main story, but it took up a good quarter of the page and the heading of "Tim Called Her" and a subheading "We're back together, says Tumina".

"Please tell me that's a typo. Tumina! Seriously?"

"Yep, you had Brangelina now you've got Tumina; they do look quite sweet together don't you th… Ahh!" yelled Sarah, as she finally moved the right lever and found herself crashing down into the flat position. "Bloody silly thing."

"I agree," Kate said, studying the photograph. Tim was wearing full evening dress and Lumina was in a floor-length magenta gown with some sort of fishtail detail.

"Lumina looks fabulous in that dress, doesn't she?" said Sarah, moving the lounger up a notch.

"Looks a bit like a sunburnt mermaid to me."

"Oh my goodness," said Sarah, in shock as she turned to face Kate. "You never bad- mouth anyone," to which Kate raised an eyebrow. "Well, hardly ever. But now you mention it, she does look a bit fishlike."

"This explains the truce at rehearsals, then, if they've got back together. I'm surprised nobody said anything." Kate read a few more details about the event, which had been a film premiere in Leicester Square. Kate felt a pang of disappointment. She folded the newspaper back up and slapped it on Sarah's chest, making her jump.

"Thanks, mate!" Sarah said, removing the newspaper. "Lovely Andy is ripping up tree roots and laying me a patio."

"That'll be good. You need somewhere to sit outside at yours,"

"Exactly. I'm hoping it'll be done for Amy's party. It's just a hole with plastic over it at the moment."

"Baby-sitting, patio, what next, I wonder?" Kate said.

"What are you insinuating?" said Sarah, leaning up on one elbow.

"Just that you are spending more and more time together and that's nice," said Kate, who had her eyes closed.

"I do like him, but he's just a friend," said Sarah.

"And friends make bad partners because… they know that you're really a horrid old tart?" said Kate.

"There is that," said Sarah, taking a half-hearted swipe at her friend and missing. "The thing is, I value his friendship more than anything. And he's nice. He's not what I'd usually go for."

"So that would be a huge improvement."

"I don't know. What if he doesn't like me like that. Not that I'm saying I like him like that!" Sarah said quickly, to get her message across.

"Of course not. Andy is a decent guy; he'd let you down gently.

148

He'd explain that you have legs like a flamingo, the body of a twiglet and you clap like a retarded sea lion when something's funny."

"Arp, arp, arp!" mimicked Sarah, before whacking Kate with the newspaper and this time scoring a direct hit.

"Mummy, what are you doing," asked Amy, looking quizzically at her mother, who was having another go at her sea-lion impression. Sarah and Kate started laughing.

"Mummy was being a sea lion. How are you getting on?"

"Very good. I found some spiders, earwigs and woodlice!"

"How lovely!" exclaimed Sarah, giving Amy a hug. Amy skipped off back down the garden. "I was into Barbie at her age not creepy crawlies!"

"She's her own little person. No stereotypes for our Amy. That's one of many things I love about her," Kate said, watching her disappear behind the rosemary bush.

"Like you and your cardigans," laughed Sarah.

"I'll close up that steamer with you in it, if you're not careful."

"You need a mini makeover, then Timothy Calder will whisk *you* off to a film premiere!"

"Hang on! Who said I wanted to be whisked off ?" Kate was now feeling affronted.

"Are you female?" to which Kate nodded. "Then of course you do!"

"You're as bad as Didi!"

"Oh, how is Didi?" asked Sarah, who was very easily distracted.

"She's causing mischief. I think they'll let her go home in the next couple of weeks," said Kate.

"That's good news, but don't sidestep the matter in hand. You would, wouldn't you?"

"You lost me," said Kate, "I would what?"

"You know. Timothy Calder. You would?"

"I would?"

"Shag him," stated Sarah.

"Sarah!"

149

"I would, defo," said Sarah with a wicked little grin.

Kate offered Sarah first dibs on house-sitting again but Sarah declined for the same reasons as before, and Andy jumped at the chance of a dust-free home, even if it was only going to be Monday to Friday this time. When Monday came round, Kate found she had those same excited butterflies tumbling around as she'd had before, but this time she was also looking forward to catching up with the people she'd met. Filming was at a big London studio and Kate had felt such glee when she had proudly announced her destination to the taxi driver, who very disappointingly hadn't responded with matching excitement, he'd just said, "Okay, love," and set off.

Once safely inside with a lanyard and name badge, Kate was free to wander, but she headed off in the direction she'd been told in the hope of quickly finding a familiar face. There was a series of huge warehouse-type buildings and signs everywhere, most of which made little sense to her. She was totally amazed by the scale of the site, or the "lot", as Marcus had called it. Kate was just starting to fear that she had been given incorrect directions when she saw a sign for "C Stage" and lots of activity going on outside. People were carrying things inside and there were vans parked nearby with their rear doors open. Groups of men, mostly in black t-shirts despite the April breeze, were milling about either on mobile phones or studying pieces of paper. She spotted Dennis.

"Hello, Dennis, this looks exciting," said Kate.

"Morning, Kate. I don't know about exciting – there's loads of issues with the set build, the rig and dolly, but you don't need to worry about that. Marcus is inside. They've made a home for you next to the green room – go straight through past the set, then through the elephant doors into D Studio." He nodded his head, obviously thinking the instructions he'd just given were quite clear. Kate was not as sure, but thanked him and strode inside.

Kate hadn't really known what to expect but was amazed by

what greeted her. The huge space had been divided up into smaller sets, and the first that she saw was Marcie's apartment, which looked like a real home apart from being open on two sides and with no ceiling. Patrick's office was next, complete with large, green window into which Kate assumed they would add a scene in post-production. Then there was Patrick's car – a vintage Jaguar, surrounded by green boards, again ready for post-production wizardry to make it look as if it was speeding up a motorway or through the countryside. Patrick's apartment was a smart and stylish bachelor pad and Kate found that she had slowed to a shuffle as she wandered past open-mouthed.

"Darling girl, over here!" came a call she recognised, and she turned to see Marcus waving enthusiastically.

"So, here we are. It's not perfect but it's a good start. Excited?"

"Very," nodded Kate, who wanted to run and play in the giant doll's house they had created next door. Marcus was wearing what looked very much like a golf jumper with a diamond pattern on it, and a pink shirt underneath.

"So, any sign of the actors?" asked Kate.

"Briefing, then hair and make-up, followed by wardrobe," said Marcus.

"Of course," said Kate feeling like the rookie she was.

Pippa came scurrying in with what looked, for a second, like a baby harness strapped across her chest. Once Kate's eyes had a chance to process the sight before her, she realised that it wasn't a baby, but a dog. In fact, it was Horse. He was suspended in a pink-and-black harness, which clashed wonderfully with the lime of Pippa's shirt, with his little legs dangling in front of him. Kate failed to stifle her laughter, which made Pippa's already unhappy face turn even sourer.

"I'm sorry, Pippa, but what are you wearing?" asked Kate.

"It's a luxury dog-carrying harness. Lumina bought it for me so I wouldn't have to leave Horse anywhere. You know, the sooner that woman gets a PA the better. I've a good mind to find her one myself," said Pippa, with passion.

"You don't think you might put them off at interview, dressed like that?" asked Kate.

Pippa sat down opposite Kate, so it now looked as if Horse was sitting on her lap. This made it even harder for Kate not to laugh, as Horse was staring straight at her; he didn't look particularly happy with the set-up either.

"I used to love my job," confided Pippa, "but this is pushing me to the edge," she said, pointing a finger firmly at Horse, who was momentarily distracted by it, but soon returned to staring at Kate.

"Then you need to tell Tim you're *his* PA. Maybe if you fail to do a couple of things for him, he'll realise you're overworked and he'll encourage Lumina to get her own assistant?"

"My pride won't let me drop any spinning plates," she said with a sad smile. All of a sudden Horse began a shrill ear-splitting yap that made them both recoil. Unfortunately for Pippa, she had nowhere to recoil to.

"Hello, dear boy," they heard Marcus say behind them. So Horse was just signalling the arrival of Tim, his arch nemesis.

"Pip, I've told Mina that bloody dog is not coming on set!" said Tim in a voice raised enough to be just audible over the yapping.

"But, she said you said that it was okay," said Pippa.

"That's just... wrong. Sorry, can you take it somewhere. Cage it, drown it, whatever, I don't care, but it does not come back on set," he said firmly. Then seeing Pippa's look of dismay, he said, "Unless it's in the catering van," to try to lighten the situation, which was very hard over the incessant yapping. Pippa got up.

"Come on, Horse, it's time for sprinkles, anyway." Pippa nodded at Tim and trudged off full of despondence. As she left they heard the yapping fade away.

"That bloody dog hates me." said Tim, "Any tea going in here?"

"In the corner," pointed out Marcus. Tim had clearly been to hair and wardrobe; his hair was neat and he was wearing a perfectly fitted suit with an open-neck shirt. Kate found herself staring, but didn't look away until the last possible moment. He was even starting to look like the Patrick she'd imagined in her head. Kate didn't want to appear paranoid but she was getting a definite sense that Tim was ignoring her, as all of the conversation so far had been with either Pippa or Marcus, not even a hello or nod in her direction.

"Uh, Tim, could I have a word please?" said Kate.

"Not now, sorry. We'll be filming soon and…"

"It's a one-minute chat about Pippa," she cut in.

"What's the problem?"

"Pippa is really unhappy, she's doing the job of two PAs, which isn't very fair. I just thought you ought to know, because I know you'd hate to lose her." Tim pondered this for a moment as he stirred his tea. She saw his shoulders relax a little.

"Do you want a tea?"

"Yes, usual please," said Kate softly. Tim handed the tea he'd just made to Kate and got to work on a second one for himself.

"I know you're right. I'm just in a difficult place right now," he sighed. "Lumina's a very demanding lady." Kate felt her eyebrows twitch at this. "I'll see Pip right, I promise," he said, as he finally turned to look Kate in the eye. He looked at her for a few moments before smiling just a brief smile.

Kate felt like she was on a Wurlitzer all morning, being spun in all sorts of directions. Che was high on the buzz of filming and was shouting and laughing in equal measure. There were frequent shout-outs for make-up, wardrobe, lighting, rigging and a multitude of people, but only one call for script. Kate made the changes, Marcus concurred and they were back in the actors' hands within minutes. Kate was very charged-up by the whole process. Tim hadn't been on set much so she had only seen him deliver a few lines. They had retaken him entering a room four times because the set wasn't right, and she was amazed by his patience, which on other occasions had been lacking. Tim and Lumina had done one scene together and it had gone well. Kate was pleased with the huge difference in Lumina, as she now seemed to have a better grasp of Marcie's character and situation than she had had a few days ago in read- through.

Kate was enjoying her lunch and chatting animatedly to Marcus about the morning's filming when Tim swooped in and sat next to her.

"How are things with you two?"

"We're tickety-boo thanks."

"Yes, we're fine. I'm thoroughly enjoying myself. Whole new experience for me," said Kate, her enthusiasm overflowing.

"That's good. Kate, do you want to meet up tonight for a drink?"

"Oh, that would be lovely," she said, feeling awkward but not sure why.

"Yes, that would be lovely," echoed Marcus. "Shall we say after dinner? Ten-ish?" Tim sighed and straightened up to look at Marcus. He regarded him a little scornfully.

"Now, Marcus, you know you'll be tucked up with a hot-water bottle by then, won't you?" he encouraged.

"No, definitely not. I'll be wherever you are," Marcus said flatly as he pushed his plate to one side. "Thanks for the invite, we'll see you later. I take it Lumina will be joining us?"

"I'm afraid not. She's helicoptering in each day; she can't bear to sleep in strange beds, all of a sudden."

"That explains a lot. Righto, see you anon. Come on, Kate," said Marcus standing up, taking Kate reluctantly with him. She had to admit she was a little narked at Marcus playing the overprotective parent, but she knew it was only because he cared. Tim was obviously going to be at a loose end with Lumina not staying and was looking for company, but even so, Kate was a little flattered that he'd asked her.

When there was a natural break in the afternoon, Dennis took her over to show her how it looked on playback on the screen. It was all she could do to stop herself from jumping up and down like a five-year-old. Che caught up with Marcus towards the end of the day and went through some things he disliked with the dialogue in the scenes planned for the following day. He also dropped what could have been a bombshell about his decision to move the location filming to Bath instead of London. It was both an artistic call and a practical one, as all the London locations he had hoped for were either being filmed in or having work done; Che also felt that Bath would add a different dimension, both to the story and to Patrick, by highlighting evidence of his single-mindedness. Kate was not happy about the change but it was no longer her decision to make – she had signed away her story.

As she left, Kate spotted Pippa on a patch of grass and was keen to know if her word with Tim had had any effect.

"Hi, Pippa, how's it going?" Kate asked and, as she said it, she spotted the small dog sniffing the grass by her feet. So, apparently Tim was not quick to act on his promises.

"I'm okay. We're just going sprinkles." She turned back to address Horse, "Come on, Horse, go sprinkles for Pippa, there's a good boy."

"You've got the patience of a saint," said Kate.

Once she and Marcus had checked into the rather nice hotel and she'd unpacked, she soon found herself sitting at the bar, nursing what she felt was a well-earned gin and tonic. She was surprised to hear Niamh's voice behind her. She swivelled as elegantly as she could on her twirly bar stool to watch Marcus and Niamh enter the bar arm in arm, giggling like teenagers. Kate hopped off the stool to greet them.

"Hello, Niamh, this is a nice surprise."

"Good evening, Kate. I'm only staying tonight, then I'll leave you in peace."

"It'll be nice to catch up." Kate looked at Marcus, who was watching Niamh as if he hadn't seen her in weeks rather than just a few hours ago at breakfast. After the pleasantries, they went through to dinner. Towards the end of the meal, Kate was starting to feel a touch gooseberry-like, so she offered to finish off the script amendments on her own and Marcus gladly accepted. Kate texted Tim to say that she couldn't meet for a drink as she was working, and also to let him know that Niamh was there, in case he wanted to take the gooseberry slot she'd just vacated. She didn't get a reply.

Chapter 14

It was a cool and dry evening, so Andy decided he'd kill two birds with one stone and whilst he was babysitting, he would finish off the patio for Sarah. He had let Amy in on the secret and she was very excited when he arrived, especially when he produced a small spade for her to work with. He also found himself giving her a long lecture on safety when using it, but realising he was starting to sound like his own father, he stopped. Andy answered a few questions about the CO_2 footprint of the patio slabs before they donned their wellies and headed outside. Amy was very keen to get started. Andy was just moving the plastic, which was covering the hole, when the phone rang, so he left Amy to it. He went inside, hastily removed his wellies, and padded into the living room to answer it.

"Hello," he said, as he picked it up

"'Ooze tha'?" snarled the not-completely-unfamiliar voice.

"I'm Andy. I'm the babysitter,"

"A bloke babysittin', that ain't right in my book. So she's out again, is she?"

"Yes, Sarah is at work. Is that Irene?"

"Yeah, it is. Do I know you?"

"We've met a couple of times. Can I help, as Sarah isn't here?" He glanced over his shoulder as he thought he saw movement in the hall, but when he looked again there was nothing there and he was quickly drawn back to the conversation.

"'Ave you seen my Shauny?"

"Shaun? No not er… not since he was arrested," hesitated Andy, and he held his breath and waited for the explosive reaction from Irene, which surprisingly didn't come.

"'E's gone missin'. Ain't no one seen him for two weeks. I'm worrying meself sick."

"I'm sorry to hear that, but Shaun can take care of himself."

"It's all 'er doin', you mark my words. She's mad that one!"

"I don't think Sarah's seen him, but I'll ask her when she gets in and I'm sure she'll call you if she hears anything."

"Huh, I doubt it. 'E said he was going to see Amy and nobody's seen or heard from him since."

"If you're worried, Irene, you should register him as a missing person with the police."

"I 'ave done, but they're no bleedin use iver!" and, with that, there was a thud and the line went dead. Andy looked at the phone.

"Bye, Irene, lovely to catch up with you, too." Once he'd pulled his wellies back on, he re-joined Amy in the garden.

"Sorry about that. My word, you're doing well," he said, as he looked at the almost- full trench that he'd previously dug out to remove the tree roots. "Great job. I'll help you finish that, then we can spread out all the sand,"

"What sand?" asked Amy, looking confused.

"This sand!" said Andy, in a ta-dah moment as he opened the side gate and revealed a pile of sand he had deposited there earlier. He hadn't dared leave the slabs in case someone had stolen them, so those he would have to lug in from the van.

"Right, keep going; we've loads to do before Mum gets home," said Andy, picking up his spade. Amy grinned back at him and dug her spade happily into the earth too.

Amy was surprisingly helpful. When he could see that she was starting to flag, he ushered her inside. Andy hovered around outside the bathroom door while she had a bath, talking to her all the time to make sure she wasn't drowning. He knew this was a bit paranoid, but he cared about Amy and wanted to make sure she was safe all the time. He brushed her hair with difficulty then put her to bed. Once he was happy that she was fast asleep, he went back to the garden to start laying the slabs.

When Sarah came in, Andy was asleep on the sofa. Sarah looked at him for a moment. She'd never really studied his face before. His hair was a mess, but she liked that he wasn't bothered about how he looked or what people thought. He had surprisingly neat eyebrows and very pink lips that pouted slightly as he slept. He had a scar on his nose and his five o'clock shadow was now definite stubble. Sarah pulled herself away from her thoughts and gently touched Andy's shoulder to wake him. Andy jumped violently, kicked out his right leg and promptly fell off the sofa.

"I'm sorry, I didn't mean to make you jump," said Sarah, before bursting into hysterical laughter once she realised he was okay.

"I must have nodded off. Is Amy okay?"

"Don't fret, I'm sure she's fine. It's okay to have a nap. I expect you'll want to go to bed now?" said Sarah, picking up a cushion that had jumped off the sofa with Andy. As soon as the words were out of her mouth, she realised her double entendre. "Er, sorry. What I meant was, you'll want to go to *your* bed now, not my bed. Well, obviously, not my bed," she rambled.

"I'd better get going," he mumbled, as he ran his hands nervously through his hair and went a little pink in the cheeks. "Oh, before I do, Amy has a surprise for you. She'll show you in the morning. You need to promise not to go in the garden until she gets up, okay?"

"Okay, I promise," she said, still feeling awkward about the bed comment.

"Right. Night then," said Andy, picking up his coat.

"Yes. Thanks for babysitting and for the surprise," and

she kissed his cheek. Andy paused for a moment, as if making a decision.

"Night, Sarah. I'll probably see you tomorrow," and he left.

The days on set all started to jumble into one another. Kate was amazed how quickly the time had gone and also by how much she'd learnt. Dennis had explained a multitude of things to her and this had really helped. She loved seeing the playback on his monitor, as she felt as if she was actually watching little snippets of the film. Pippa's life had got a little better as she'd managed to find a personal assistant for Lumina and although Lumina had originally said that the young woman wasn't suitable, after a chat with Tim she had accepted her and Pippa was relieved of her Horse duties.

When Kate came back from lunch, Marcus and Tim were huddled in a corner looking very conspiratorial. She smiled at them and went to make herself a drink. A click clack of heels announced Lumina's arrival and she strode in with Horse under her arm. As soon as he caught sight of Tim he started to yap. Tim stopped his conversation with Marcus and looked impatiently at Lumina.

"Sorry," she said sweetly, as she started to coax Horse. "Sh, baby boy, it's only Uncle Timmy. Sh, there's a good boy." Horse stopped the yapping but was now emitting a low, grumbling growl, and every now and then you could see him bare his teeth.

"Would you like a drink, Lumina?" asked Kate.

"Sparkling mineral, please," Lumina replied, as she went to join Tim and Marcus. The growl from Horse got louder the closer she got to Tim. They were then all three in a huddle until Tim's phone rang and he raced away to answer it. As he stepped away he mouthed to Marcus, but out of sight of Lumina, "It's Jackie", and the two men smiled at each at other. Lumina and a calmer-looking Horse came to join Kate on the comfy seating, and Lumina sat down and popped Horse onto her lap, where he settled down and closed his eyes.

"I wanted to talk to you about my character," said Lumina. "I've been thinking about an angle that I think would work better."

"Oh, okay. What was your idea?" Kate said, trying very hard to look as if she was keen to hear the suggestion, rather than betraying the screaming voice in her head that was shouting, "Don't mess with my characters!"

"I'm thinking that as Marcie and Marianne were so close…"

"Marianna," corrected Kate.

"Oh, yes, Marianna. As they were close and Marianna died before her time, I thought, what if Marcie had been possessed by Marianna's spirit?" said Lumina, and swirled her hands over her head for emphasis. Kate heard Marcus stifle a laugh behind her and try to turn it into a cough. She thought for a moment about how best to respond.

"I like it, it's an interesting idea," to which Lumina nodded vigorously, "and whilst I think you could act out that scenario brilliantly, I think we might struggle to get that across to the audience."

"Really? I disagree. I think they'd get it if I did different mannerisms or a different voice," said Lumina as she got carried away with the idea.

"Also," said Kate, cutting her off a little, "the key to the story is that Patrick has fallen in love with Marcie, through the emails. It never was Marianna who he fell in love with." This hung in the air for a moment and Kate could feel that her palms were getting a little sweaty. Eventually, Lumina gave a little nod. Kate continued, "Thanks for coming to talk to me about it, and I think it's a great idea, but perhaps for a whole other story."

"Oh, okay," smiled Lumina. "There was something else." Dear God, preserve me, thought Kate. "You've been looking at the rushes, haven't you?"

"Sorry, not sure what you mean by rushes?" said Kate.

"The playback, the raw cut of the film," explained Lumina.

"I'm sorry. Yes, I have. You look terrific. I'm really excited about it," said Kate, honestly.

"Can you see the spark between me and Tim?" Kate was stumped for the second time in two minutes.

"I've not seen that much of it, to be honest," she said feeling uncomfortable.

"But you must be able to tell that we are lovers, me and Tim? The magazines will love it, and everyone will want to see the film so that they can glimpse what we are like as a couple," Lumina persisted.

"You do work very well together, I believe I'm watching Patrick and Marcie, so I'm sure the audience will too," said Kate. Lumina looked a bit dejected by this.

"Can't you see Tumina? That's what they call us," simpered Lumina.

"I guess I'm too focused on my characters, but you and Tim do have something together on screen."

Sensing Kate's reluctance, Lumina said, "Well it will be good for you, too, if Tumina makes people come and see it. Films like this don't come along that often. You might get asked back to work on another one if it goes well," Lumina said, as a little coldness crept into her voice and she swept up the sleeping Horse and left.

Once Lumina had trotted off, Marcus came over and gave Kate a hug.

"Bravo. Beautifully sidestepped!"

"Thanks. You were no help whatsoever," said Kate, giving him a playful thump on the arm. Kate swivelled around for no apparent reason and made eye contact with Tim, who was leaning against the doorway watching Kate and Marcus. There was a brief moment where they both looked embarrassed, smiled at each other and then looked away. Marcus looked from one to the other and smiled to himself.

"Tim, I meant to say, thanks for sorting things out for

162

Pippa," said Kate praying for the colour in her cheeks to subside.

"No problem. You shouldn't have had to ask me."

"She seems happier," said Kate, starting to feel the conversation dry up between them. "Are you doing anything exciting this weekend?" Dear God, I sound like a hairdresser, she thought.

"Not sure. I guess Pippa or Lumina will let me know. Look, Che says I'm done for today, so I'm going to make tracks. I'll see you next week," he said to Kate and then turned to Marcus, "I'll let you know about Sunday, okay?"

"Of course, hopefully see you then," replied Marcus. Kate was getting more confused by the minute. One moment Tim doesn't know what he's doing, the next he might see Marcus on Sunday, and it's something Marcus clearly knows about.

On the train, Kate listened to her messages. There was one message from Andy saying he'd put his washing on before he left, so it would still be in the machine when she got home. One from a neighbour asking if they could look at her deeds so that they could compare boundary lines. And, finally, one from Sarah asking if she'd have Amy while she went shopping for her birthday present. Back to normality and normal-ish people, she thought as she relaxed into her seat for the journey home.

Sarah had been woken early by an over-excited Amy, who was very keen to show Sarah the surprise in the garden. A very tired Sarah dragged herself out of bed, shrugged on her dressing gown and plodded downstairs like a stroppy sleep-walker. She hit the switch on the kettle as she passed, as she was in desperate need of caffeine to get her kick-started. Amy was trying to open the back door whilst jumping up and down on the spot, which made it completely impossible to get the key into the lock.

"Give it here," said Sarah, taking the key. Sarah opened the door and Amy ran past her and blocked her way.

"Stay there, Mummy," she instructed, before running round to the back of the house and exclaiming, "Yes, he did it, woweee!" Sarah woke up a bit at this. Amy came scurrying back.

"Close your eyes, Mummy, and follow me," said Amy, taking Sarah's hand. Sarah instead put her other hand over her eyes, but peeked down so that she could see where her feet were going. Whilst Amy was a sensible five-year-old, it still wasn't safe to put your entire wellbeing in her very excited hands. Sarah followed Amy along the old grey-stone path to the back of the house, where she saw the ground change. The grey stopped and, where there used to be grass, there were beautiful coloured slabs.

"Ta dah!" shouted Amy. "You can look now." Sarah took away her hand and took in the sight before her. Her old, grey concrete-slab path and part of the lawn had gone and in its place was a beautiful smaller version of Andy's patio, including the circle of stones. Sarah almost cried. "I helped Mummy. I filled in all of this bit and did the sand. Andy put the slabs on top."

"Amy, its amazing! Well done, you. I love it."

"So do I!" said Amy, hugging her mother.

Amy had her music on loud, so Sarah didn't hear the person slip through the side gate until they rapped a bony knuckle on the kitchen window. Sarah leapt away from the sink in alarm and looked to see who the rapper was. There was nobody there, but the back door flew open and in walked Irene. She was looking worse than usual, as if someone had wrung her face out and wasn't exactly sure which way it went back on.

"Where is 'e?"

"Hello, Irene. Let me stop you there. If you've come for an argument, you can leave now."

With absolutely perfect timing, Andy appeared behind Irene.

"Hi there. I saw your visitor heading down the side of the house, so I thought I'd come that way round too," and he walked past Irene to stand protectively next to Sarah.

"You still 'er are ya, must be some sort a record. So what's happened to my Shauny?"

"We don't know, we haven't seen him. I told you that," said Andy. Sarah turned to look questioningly at him. "Sorry, I forgot to say that she rang last night."

"When did you last see him?" asked Irene, her voice less confident than usual. Andy opened his mouth to speak, but Sarah got there first.

"Ten days ago, and I've not seen or heard from him since." It was Andy's turn to look surprised. "He came round here shouting the odds and I sent him off with a flea in his ear."

"Or an axe in his head! That means you're the last one to see him. What did ya do to him?"

"Nothing Irene. He was drunk, again, and shouting about me turning Melanie against him. He tried to get in, I threatened to call the police and he left. End of story."

"You're a lying c…"

"Hello, Nanny Irene!" shouted Amy, running into the kitchen, searching Irene with her eyes for any concealed presents. "It's my birthday next week."

"I know, Luvvy. Your daddy'll get you something special, I bet."

Sarah was thankful that Irene had the sense at least not to tell Amy that her father had gone AWOL.

"Nanny Irene is just going, so say good-bye," said Sarah.

"Bye-bye," said Amy dutifully, before returning to her music.

"If you've done something to my Shauny, I'll 'ave you," Irene said, as she stepped closer to Sarah.

"You're imagining things. Shaun will turn up like the proverbial bad penny that he is. You mark my words."

"I'll mark your face for ya if he don't."

"Okay, that's enough," said Andy, as he stepped in front of Sarah and gently ushered Irene to the door.

"Alrigh'! I'm goin'," she said, as she eyed Sarah. Irene then left, only pausing for a moment to admire the new patio.

"They're a lovely family, aren't they," said Andy, with a shake of his head.

"If you like tails, horns and cloven feet," replied Sarah.

"So you saw Shaun after the whole drink-drive thing, and after Melanie got beaten up?"

"Yeah, he came round shouting the odds."

"You didn't say that you'd seen him."

"I didn't realise I was tagged and had to report my every movement to you," Sarah said, defensively.

"Hey, I was only saying. Irene is clearly worried and it does look like you might have been the last person to see him."

"This is Shaun we're talking about. Shaun, who cares about nothing and nobody apart from himself. He will have gone off in a strop. He won't care that Irene is worrying about him or that he was meant to have Amy and didn't turn up again."

"Don't you think that's odd, to not turn up for Amy?" shot in Andy,

"For a normal human being, or even a laboratory chimp, yes, but for Shaun, no. He's an arsehole. Andy, if you've got something you want to ask, fire away."

Andy looked uncomfortable, but went for it anyway, "What happened, exactly, when he came round here the last time?"

"He was drunk. He was begging me to let him in and to help him. He said he needed my help because someone was going to kill him. I told him that I'd happily sponsor them, a pound a bullet. He got über cross and kicked the door. I shouted, so he kicked it some more. I opened the door… on the chain," Andy looked alarmed at this. "He tried to grab me, so I shut his hand in the door. Then he sat on the door step crying for a bit and he eventually buggered off. I had a large glass of wine, watched an old episode of *Friends* on TV, and hoped Shaun would spontaneously combust. Looks like dreams really do come true," said Sarah, with a forced smile.

Chapter 15

Kate looked at her computer screen for a while before completing a couple of chapters of her latest book, which made her feel rather pleased with herself. Unfortunately, her writing also got her thinking about the change of location for the setting for *Love.com*. Kate had only been to Bath once, a long time ago, and now all she could remember about it was lots of tourists and some nice shops. She googled Bath and a variety of hotels and details of the spa came up, but nothing that felt like somewhere that would have enticed Patrick to base himself there rather than London. Patrick was meant to be a ruthless character who softened on falling in love with Marcie. Someone who would take the high risk, do the deal and to hell with the impact on other people. A nice spa and lovely architecture didn't really seem to fit with his persona.

The more Kate thought about it, the more she thought she was unhappy with the decision. So she decided to give Marcus a call.

"Hi Marcus. Sorry to bother you. The thing is, I've been thinking about the location change to Bath and it's bothering me. It just doesn't feel like something Patrick would do."

"Oh dear. We're filming there in a few weeks' time. And to be brutally honest, I don't think we can influence a change."

"No, I know that, but I thought I might check out the filming locations in Bath with you and see if I felt any better about it." And she really did want to feel better about it as she knew it was all booked now.

"I'm afraid Niamh and I are fully booked this weekend; dinner and drinks at Fergus and Bunty's today, seeing friends tomorrow morning and then theatre in the evening."

"Not a problem, it was just a thought."

"You should ask Tim. He is very into the role of Patrick, so for once he could actually be quite helpful with this dilemma."

"I don't really like to ask him. He's always so busy with Lumina… and Jackie." Kate thought she would throw out the bait and see if he'd take it. There was a slight delay before Marcus replied.

"I think our Tim has rather got himself into a bit of a situation with the lovely Lumina. But aside from that, if he is free, I do think he would be worth taking with you. He'll definitely have an opinion," said Marcus.

"Okay, I'll try Tim and see if he wants to come."

"Good idea, have fun. I'll see you bright and bushy on Monday."

"Bye, Marcus."

"Au revoir," and he was gone.

She'd found out nothing about Jackie, and now she had to call Tim, otherwise Marcus would ask Tim if he'd gone to Bath with Kate, and he'd say he didn't know anything about it, and she'd look as if she was slightly bonkers. Kate sat at the kitchen table and thought through what she was going to say; she wanted to get things straight in her head before she spoke to him. Also, she was spending the day with Amy so that Sarah could do some secret shopping, so she could only do Bath on Sunday. She found his number and pressed the "call" button.

"He…lo, …lo, 'an… ear me?" said Tim or a really bad ventriloquist. This was such a great idea she thought sarcastically.

"Hello Tim, it's Kate. Can you hear me?"

"…lo?"

"Hello?"

"Kate, hello, is that better?"

"Yes! Hallelujah, I can hear you," she said, with a bit more gusto than it required. "Sorry to bother you. Have you got a couple of minutes?"

"Yes, fire away."

"I was thinking that I might check out the filming locations in Bath tomorrow and you said you thought you had nothing planned, so if you wanted to come along you'd be very welcome. I asked Marcus, but he's busy. Not that you weren't my first choice for a companion to Bath. I'd like your opinion as Patrick, I mean, to see if the location fits with the character."

"What time tomorrow?"

"Morning, I guess. I might make a day of it." Bath had very good shops and, if she was going all that way, she felt she might as well make it into a day out.

"Okay, I could meet you there at about lunchtime. Shall I call when I get there?" Tim's voice had a business tone to it.

"Okay, yes, that would be great. I'll see you lunchtime tomorrow."

"It's a date. Bye, Kate."

"A date"? Really? Did she have a date with Timothy Calder? Kate wished she knew what she was doing. This was not like her. She usually had a plan. Actually, she *always* had a plan. Plans were Kate's forte; it's what she did – she made a plan and stuck to it. Not this off- the-cuff, wander-off-in-any-direction and meet-up-with-famous-actors stuff. Kate wanted to talk it over with Sarah, but feared Sarah would get all excited and start planning what hat she'd wear for the *Hello* wedding photo shoot. So she decided to keep it to herself and enjoy a day in Bath with Timothy Calder. "Yay," she squealed excitedly.

Amy was deposited in a swirl of gravel, blue smoke and a flash of ageing VW Beetle.

"Mummy says she can't stop because she's doing flower deliveries. She gets to drive a van!"

"Wow, lucky Mummy," agreed Kate, as she was hugged enthusiastically by Amy,

"I've brought some books and some mini figures. What would you like to play, Kate?"   "I thought we would do some baking first, then have lunch while the biscuits are cooling down, and afterwards play whatever you like. What do you think?"

"Mummy said you'd have a good plan for today. Can I do the measuring?" Amy said, as she dropped her rucksack in the hall and headed for the kitchen.

The morning whizzed by, and Kate and Amy made a plethora of biscuits shaped like butterflies, hearts and flowers, and some fairy cakes of varying unregulated sizes. They played hide and seek inside and outside the house, did some skipping and generally had a good time.

Tim turned the corner with his phone held out in front of him and the little figure on the screen turned the corner, too, to indicate he was still going in the right direction. As he reached the end of a large wall, a small flag popped up to indicate he'd reached his destination. Tim looked around. He was wearing dark, fitted jeans, white t-shirt and his trademark sunglasses. He was looking for number 18, but on this side there was just a large wall. Tim looked over to the row of terraced houses on the other side of the road and crossed over to find some numbers. Most had names. He went along the row and saw "Lilac cottage", "Fairview", "The Berries", and number 25. Can't be far away, he thought. An elderly lady was bearing down on him, dragging a decrepit tartan trolley behind her. She looked up just before Tim leapt out of her path.

"Sorry," she said, but didn't look at all sorry.

"No problem. Actually, I wonder if you can help me. I'm looking for Kate Marshall?"

"Are you a friend of hers?" said the woman, suddenly stopping and looking interested.

"I'm a colleague, really. Can you tell me where she lives, please?" The woman's face changed and looked less friendly.

"But she's a writer, she doesn't work with anyone. She's written quite a few stories you know. They've got them at the library, but they're not my kind of thing. I like a good murder." Tim held his tongue. There was a temptation to offer to bring her closer to a real murder. "Unless you're her publisher," she added appraising him.

"Nothing so grand, I just need to talk to her about... a book-cover design." Tim amazed himself at his ability to confidently and convincingly lie to people. The woman seemed happy with the explanation.

"Poor Miss Marshall. Her fiancé was killed, you know. Very young he was. Tragic. He was a lovely young man. He always carried my shopping in for me, if he saw me," she said, looking from the trolley to Tim and then back again. There was a short delay before Tim sprang forward and picked up the trolley.

"Oh, you are kind. Now, where are my keys?" She fumbled in the bottom of a large handbag, took out a pair of woolly gloves, and handed them to Tim with a smile. A bit more rummaging produced a packet of tissues, a glasses case and a bag of toffees. Tim was about to lose his patience when she pulled out an Isle of Wight keyring, burdened with a lifetime's keys, and waved it under Tim's nose. "Here they are," she said and in a jangle she opened the door and pointed inside. "You can put the trolley anywhere in the kitchen." Tim walked through small rooms and into a narrow kitchen. He deposited the trolley and handbag items and went back to the front door.

"Thank you. Goodbye," said the woman, as she started to close the front door.

"Hey, just a minute. You were going to tell me which one is Kate's house," he said, nodding his head up and down the row of houses.

171

"Oh," she chuckled, "silly me. She lives over the road," and with that she shut the front door. Tim turned around and pulled down his sunglasses with his index finger so he could inspect the other side of the road. Just as he suspected, there was no sign of any houses on that side, just a large wall that seemed to go on forever. He could see that there was as a break in the wall further down, where there was a gated drive, so Tim decided he would go and see if there was any sign of intelligent life there.

As he turned in the gateway, Tim was impressed by the handsome house that stood at the end of the wide drive. It was a Georgian gentleman's residence, with three windows across the first floor and one either side of a large wooden door. It was beautifully symmetrical, with an understated grandeur. Tim crunched his way up the gravel driveway and climbed the two old stone steps. He knocked on the door and turned his back on it whilst he checked his phone for messages. There was a text from Lumina, "Surprise! We're going to Monaco in June!" Tim was frowning at the screen when the door opened behind him. Tim shoved his phone back in his pocket and turned around with a smile, ready to charm whoever opened the door.

"Tim?" said Kate, looking very puzzled by his presence on her doorstep.

"Hello," said Tim, as he glanced at the small cast-iron plaque next to the door, which read Number 18. "Hello, Kate!"

"What are you doing here? Sorry, that was rude. It's lovely to see you, come in."

"This is a great place you have here."

"Thank you. It's my family home, passed down the generations." Kate often felt she had to explain why she had such a grand home, even though she could have afforded it from the book sales. Even so, it was a large house for one person and her cat.

"You don't answer your phone, do you?" Tim scanned the rooms that were visible from the hall.

"Sorry, did you call? I was playing in the garden." Tim

172

looked quizzically at her and then he turned his attention to the skipping child, who was now joining them in the hall.

"Hello, do you like woodlice?" said Amy to Tim, opening a grubby hand to reveal a small tightly curled-up grey ball, rather like a ball bearing.

"Who doesn't?" said Tim, crouching down to get a better look.

"Do you want to come and find some more?" asked Amy hopefully.

"Amy, I don't think Tim came over to…" but Tim was already following Amy outside into the garden. Kate glanced out of the kitchen window to see if she could see Tim's car but there was no sign of it.

From the comfort of her steamer chair, Kate watched Tim and Amy playing jungle explorers. This didn't last long as she was soon roped into an impromptu game of football when Tim found a ball in the shed. They all took turns in goal. Tim made the most elaborate dives whenever Amy neared the goal and let the ball in every time, helping it on its way on a couple of occasions. When it was Amy's turn in goal, Kate found herself up against Tim in more ways than one. He teased her with the ball and then kicked it away when she got close. There was some contact that was deserving of a yellow card and lots of laughing. Apart from when the ball landed on Marmalade, who was asleep in the bushes. She gave them all a stern stare, flicked her tail in the air and stalked off to find somewhere quieter for her nap.

When they all got tired and out of breath, Kate made ice-cream floats and put them on the garden table. Amy came running over to investigate.

"Wow! My favourite!" exclaimed Amy, grabbing a spoon and digging into the nearest glass.

"Sit down please, Amy," instructed Kate, and Amy inched her bottom onto a cushioned seat without taking her eyes off her float. Tim sauntered over. His sunglasses were now resting on top of his head and, with the sun behind him, he looked as though he'd just stepped out of an aftershave advert.

"Has she worn you out?" Kate asked.

"No, I'm fine," he said, sitting down next to Amy. "Any good?" he asked, pointing at Amy's ice-cream float.

"The best!" Amy gasped in between slurps. For a while they all sat in silence exchanging glances and smiles as they tucked in. Amy finished first and was soon off to do more exploring.

"So is she from Rent-a-child or Ebay?" said Tim, flinching at his feeble joke.

"No, she's my goddaughter, my friend Sarah's little girl."

"She's a lovely kid."

"She is. She seems quite taken with you." It was a surprise to Kate that Tim was so comfortable with children, not having any of his own. They both watched Amy as she played happily at the far end of the garden, picking flowers and twirling around whilst chattering to herself.

Kate swept her hair off her neck and pulled it into an untied ponytail on one shoulder. Tim stopped watching Amy and studied Kate. Her mane of golden hair shone in the sun but had now moved to reveal her slender white neck. Tim followed the line of her neck up to her delicate chin and beautiful cheekbones. He was lost in her features, as if examining a painting. Tim felt so at ease in her company, even when they didn't speak. He had never been keen on long silences, but silence with Kate was peaceful. She turned to meet his gaze and smiled a warm smile.

"I'm sorry, Kate, I can't come to Bath tomorrow. Something's come up."

"Did you come all this way to tell me that?" she laughed.

"Well, if you won't answer your phone."

"Sorry about that, but a message would have been okay." Tim knew he could have left a message, but it didn't feel right. Kate deserved better and it had been a chance to see her, although not on her own, as he had hoped.

"Maybe we can go another time? One evening after filming, perhaps?" he said.

"Perhaps. It's okay. I'll see Bath soon enough."

Tim glanced at his watch. "Bugger. Sorry I need to dash," he said, getting to his feet.

"It's been lovely to see you. I mean, I know I see you on set, but…"

"Yeah, it's not the easiest place to chat." They stood looking at each for a moment before Tim cracked first. "Okay, best say goodbye to Amy," who, as if on cue, came skipping across the lawn towards them. Tim whispered something to her before he left and she giggled.

"Kate?" said Amy

"Yes," Kate said, feeling something ominous was about to happen.

"Knock, knock!"

Didi handed out the three cups of tea off the tray and walked steadily back to the kitchen, where one of the staff was washing up.

"Look at me – I can carry a tray of tea and not spill a drop. I must be ready to go home or are you keeping me here as slave labour?" Didi asked.

"Didi, we can't bear to lose you. You brighten everybody up."

"But I am completely better now, and you must need the bed."

"The doctor is seeing you this week about being discharged, so I think you'll be heading home very soon."

"Excuse me, I'm looking for the garden centre?" asked a very small grey-haired woman, with a hint of fear in her eyes.

"Hello, Alice, you've come to the right place. Let me show you to the tea rooms, then after a nice cuppa you can have a look at the plants," said Didi, with a wink as she helped Alice turn her zimmer frame around and head back out of the kitchen.

Chapter 16

Sarah was more than surprised to open her front door to a policeman early on a Monday morning. And even more surprised when they presented her with a search warrant. A friendly policeman had called the previous week, when he'd knocked at a few other houses in the road asking everyone when they had last seen Shaun, and she'd thought that was the end of it. Clearly she was wrong.

"Can I get dressed?" Sarah asked, as she pulled her dressing gown around herself.

"No, I'm sorry. You need to sit down, out of the way, while we have a look around." A policewoman came and sat with Sarah at the kitchen table whilst the other officer went from room to room methodically searching. Sarah was very grateful that she'd asked Kate to have Amy last night so she could work a late shift at the pub, otherwise she would be worried about the effect a police raid, however low-key, would have on her daughter.

"Can I ask what you're looking for?" asked Sarah.

"Anything that can help us in the search for Mr Greasely."

"He's still missing, then?" asked Sarah, and the policewoman nodded. "It's a lot of effort to go to for a missing adult, isn't it?" Sarah was sure there was more to it than that.

"We take all missing persons enquiries seriously."

"I'm sure you do. But you seem to be taking this one very seriously indeed," said Sarah. The policewoman didn't reply, but her poker face wasn't as good as she thought it was.

"Have you got a ladder, Mrs Greasely?" called the other police officer from upstairs.

"In the garden," she called back. He couldn't have been long in the loft as he soon returned downstairs with the ladder and took it back outside. He came back into the kitchen.

"New patio is it, love?"

"Yeah, it's Indian sandstone. Do you like it?" said Sarah.

"It's very nice. Done recently, was it?"

"Last week."

"Did you do it yourself, by any chance?"

"No, a friend of mine did it. Would you like his business card?" Sarah was always keen to drum up business for Andy. Even if this wasn't exactly his day job, it was still a referral.

"I'd like to have a chat to him, if we can," Sarah saw him exchange glances with the policewoman.

"Oh, come on! You don't seriously think Shaun's buried under the patio, do you? That's not very original, now, is it? Give me a little more credit! At least check out the batch of lasagne in the freezer," Sarah laughed, but both police officers scanned the kitchen until their eyes rested on the freezer.

"Madam, we're just making enquiries."

"Look, if you let me call Andy, I'm sure he'll come straight round and tell you about how he did the patio as a surprise. Okay?"

"Okay," said the police officer.

Sarah called Andy and gave him the basics of the story and he set off immediately. Sarah was pleased to be able to get dressed; it made her feel a little less wrong-footed. When Andy arrived, the male police officer was on his hands and knees examining Sarah's hall carpet. Andy introduced himself and went through to the kitchen, where Sarah virtually threw herself at him.

"The police officers are just doing their job. It'll all be okay.

Trust me," he said, soothingly, and she did. Sarah went to sit in the living room whilst the two officers talked to Andy about the patio. She could hear the conversation and it was best that she wasn't in the room as the temptation to butt in was very strong. Especially when they were asking the same question over and over again, "So Mrs Greasely approached you about the patio... It was Mrs Greasely's idea for you to build the patio... Mrs Greasely wanted the patio building quite urgently..." When eventually they finished, they called her into the kitchen and Andy gave her a friendly hug.

"I'd like to ask you about the damage to the front-door frame and the stains on the hall carpet, Mrs Greasely," asked the male police officer. Andy squeezed Sarah's hand.

"It was Shaun that damaged the door and frame. He was trying to get in the last night I saw him."

"What did he use?"

"He used a spanner," said Sarah, "I opened the door and shut his hand in it to make him stop."

"I see and is that where the blood on the carpet came from?" His stare was unblinking as he studied Sarah's response.

"Er, I think you'll find that's a coffee stain."

"I think we'll find that it's blood, Mrs Greasely, so it's best to tell us now," said the officer. Andy looked to Sarah for an explanation. Sarah ignored him.

"It's coffee."

"Did he come inside that night?"

"No, I told you already that he didn't come inside."

"So how did the blood get on the carpet?"

"It's coffee, but there may be blood from when I jammed his hand in the door."

"I think that's unlikely, given that the patch on the carpet is three feet away and you say he didn't come inside that night."

"It could be my blood," said Sarah, feeling her scalp start to prickle. "I locked myself out and had to smash the glass to get in. It was a while ago now, though. I cut myself, so there could

178

be some of mine. Andy repaired the glass for me," Sarah gave a half-glance in Andy's direction. Andy looked aghast and quickly tried to hide his reaction by staring at the floor.

"Okay, Mrs Greasely, Mr Shaw, I'll just take some samples of fibres from the carpet, if I may, and then that'll be all… for now. Thank you for your co-operation." When they left, Sarah broke down in tears and Andy held her. He didn't know what else to do.

After a few good scenes with a few retakes, Lumina made a strange squeaking noise, which Kate later discovered was actually a sneeze. Lumina called for her PA and was whisked off-stage in a flurry of drama and white fluffy robes. She then demanded that she be seen by a herbalist before she would continue. Everyone took a break whilst Che discussed options with his senior team. Tim jogged over and interrupted the group briefly and, after a short discussion, he bounded over to Kate with a broad grin on his face.

"Che loves your idea of us checking out the Bath locations whilst we have some down time, so I'm shooting two more scenes that we don't need Lumina for and then we're free to go." He stood there expectantly.

"Is this not going to put us hideously behind?"

"No. They're rescheduling the scene order and they'll carry on filming some scenes today that don't feature me or Lumina. I'm not in every scene, you know!"

"As long as I'm not needed." Kate was feeling increasingly superfluous.

"Marcus has it covered. You are free to go. Could you just track Pip down for me and ask her to get a chopper for about one o'clock?"

"Er, yes, okay," said Kate, feeling suddenly excited by the prospect of a ride in a helicopter.

"Great, you're a star," and he kissed her cheek. They both froze as if struck by something and then both looked to the floor. Tim mumbled something about the next scene and disappeared.

Kate just sat there wondering if anybody had noticed.

Kate tracked down Pippa, who was fielding phone calls with Lumina's new PA, who was looking very flustered and a little tearful.

"Hi, Pippa. I have a request from Tim."

"He'll have to get in the bloody queue!" she snapped.

"Problem? What can I do to help?" ventured Kate, pulling up a chair to show she meant business.

"Horse has swallowed the herbal aspirin that was put out for Lumina and now she's having a blue hairy fit," said Pippa, and at this Lumina's PA broke down and started to cry big heaving sobs.

"Pull yourself together or go home!" shouted Pippa, which only made the young woman sob harder. "Well?" she snapped. Lumina's PA ran out crying. "Do you see what I have to contend with?" barked Pippa.

"Yes, I see," said Kate, going into ultra-calm mode. "How about you tell me what needs doing? I make a quick list, we agree what order we do them in, and then we divide and conquer?"

"Right, okay. Emergency vet needed."

"I presume to put Lumina down," joked Kate, which only produced a weak smile from Pippa. Kate grabbed a pad and pen off the desk "Vet. Got that. Next?"

"Herbalist for Lumina, car to take her back to her apartment, release a press statement about her illness because they've already been on the phone." Kate raised an eyebrow at this quick response, but carried on scribbling. "Get someone, anyone, to go and calm her down before I shoot her, and cancel dinner reservations in Tim's name for tonight and… that's it, I think," said Pippa, who was screwing up her face as she mentally checked that she'd covered everything.

"And Tim wants a helicopter for about one o'clock," added Kate.

"Okay, that's one for Terry. He can sort that out and work

out his pick-up timings for it. Christ, who's he schmoozing now?"

Kate paused before answering. "It's a location check in Bath and, with the filming schedule up in the air, it was a good time-filler."

"Okay," said Pippa, but Kate could feel colour filling her cheeks.

"How about you sort out the vet, herbalist and the press and I'll sort out the rest?" suggested Kate, admiring the list she'd made.

"Brilliant."

"But first I'll get you a cappuccino. Do you want sprinkles?" asked Kate. Pippa gave an exaggerated shudder.

"No! Never again will that mean a nice little dusting of cocoa, thanks to that bloody dog!" And both women laughed.

Kate found that she really enjoyed the pressure of trying to sort out the things on the list and she also loved the feeling of ticking them off as they were completed. She quickly worked through the items, and was then left with only one thing remaining, which was to calm down Lumina.

Kate headed over to Lumina's trailer, which was her home while she was on set and, as she approached, she could hear the commotion inside. She steeled herself before banging with authority on the door. It was quickly opened by one of the young actors, who looked very stressed.

"I hoped you were the vet," he said, his jacket in his hand.

"No, sorry, but there's one on the way." The shrieking from Lumina went up an octave and the actor just stared at Kate. "Okay. You can go. I'll take over," and he gave a grateful smile before he disappeared. The trailer was very plush and draped in white from top to bottom. Lumina was lying on a bed wearing a white, towelling bath robe with Horse clutched to her chest as she wailed.

"Lumina, it's Kate," she said gently, as if talking to a child.

"He's dying and nobody will help."

"The vet will be here very soon and they've said that willow bark is usually safe for dogs. He's not going to die, Lumina." Kate sat on the edge of the bed and gave a very distressed-looking Horse a stroke.

"But he's sick. Look at him!" Lumina spat the words forcefully, as she turned the poor creature eyeball to eyeball with Kate. Kate took a deep, calming breath.

"He's fine, Lumina, they give dogs willow bark sometimes; their stomachs can handle it better than humans. He's okay, apart from looking very scared because you're making such a fuss."

Lumina stopped the tears instantly and gave Kate a cold look, "I am sick and I thought my dog was dying, I think I had a right to make a … to make people aware."

"Of course," said Kate calmly, "but it's upsetting Horse and that's the last thing you want to do." Lumina nodded and a few small tears escaped. "He is going to be okay, I promise."

"I love him," Lumina sniffed.

"I know," said Kate stroking Lumina's arm. "We get very close to our pets, don't we?"

"I do love Horse. But I meant Tim. I love Tim."

"Oh right, well that's nice, too. Did I say that the herbalist will be about an hour and then Terry will take you home?" said Kate, reverting to efficient mode and handing Lumina a clean tissue from her cardigan pocket.

"I think there's someone else," sniffed Lumina into the tissue.

Kate really wished the vet would arrive so that she could escape from this conversation, since clearly Lumina had worked out that Jackie was also a fixture in Tim's life. And Kate just wasn't comfortable discussing Lumina and Tim's relationship. Even though a curious part of her really wanted to know, there was a bigger part that just wanted to stick her fingers in her ears and chant la, la, la.

"You need to talk to Tim about that," Kate said, as calmly as she could manage.

"I can't," the wailing starting to return. "He won't talk to me. He's only with me to keep the peace on set. As soon as we finish filming he'll be off and I'll be d...dumped!" The wailing increased and Horse struggled to free himself; his ears had had enough noise-induced trauma for one day.

"Shh," soothed Kate, "you're upsetting Horse again," and thankfully Lumina did appear to quieten a little. She let Horse go and he jumped off the bed and went to eat some food from his handmade ceramic bowl, which featured his name and a series of paw marks. So he was clearly feeling fine and showing no signs of any after-effects of the herbal tablet he'd devoured.

Kate struggled to think of what best to say. All she could think of was that Lumina would get another ream of pages written about her when Tim dumped her for the second time, which she didn't think would help to stem the flow of tears. Kate could see that for Lumina this really wasn't just about the publicity, she looked genuinely upset.

"Have you told him how you feel?" Kate said, passing her another tissue as Lumina handed her the sodden one. Kate whisked it to the floor with barely a touch. This woman really was used to being waited on hand and foot and snotty nose.

"Huh, he's never here and when he is, he's watching his phone, waiting to pounce on it, like a cat watching a mouse." Kate knew this to be true.

"Maybe you need to talk to him about some time away together, just the two of you, so that you can work things out, understand where you stand with... well if there is someone else."

Lumina seemed to brighten up at this. "We are going away soon. To Monaco!"

"There you go. That will be ideal. I need to go now," said Kate, getting up from the bed. Lumina grabbed her hand and pulled her back.

"Thank you, Kate, you're a good friend." Kate gave a wan smile, but felt she barely knew her.

"Take care of yourself and Horse," she said, as she extricated her hand from Lumina's grasp and left.

Kate could hardly stop herself from jumping up and down on the spot when she saw the helicopter. Tim was striding ahead talking to Terry. Paul, the location manager, was following him, with Kate trailing behind. As nobody was watching her, she started to skip and felt silly for doing it, but it felt so good. At that second, Tim stopped abruptly and turned around. Kate managed to stop before she careered into the location manager, but she had been rumbled. Tim was grinning from ear to ear and Kate wanted the ground to open up and swallow her. Thankfully only Tim had seen her.

"Right, it's difficult to talk on board, so are there any questions before we go?" The response was shakes of heads all round. "Okay, see you later, Terry. We have to skip off now," said Tim, beaming at Kate, who thought the heat from her ears might actually set fire to her hair.

The flight was as exciting as she had hoped it would be. The helicopter was small inside, the three of them were sitting close together and she could feel the warmth of Tim's thigh against her own. Tim kept pointing out landmarks and checking she was okay and Kate was so enjoying the trip that it was disappointing when the helicopter came in to land. A large stretch limo pulled up alongside and they all filed in.

"Do you always go for the inconspicuous option?" she asked Tim.

"It's all they had. Terry arranged it, anyway," he said, giving her a playful nudge. "If we're talking about inconspicuous, I need to talk about your sk…" but Kate was quick and talked over Tim.

"So did you choose these locations?" she asked Paul.

"Yes. One of my team did the research, then we came here and whittled down the options. Then we presented them to Che."

They whizzed along, and soon they were in the centre of Bath, surrounded by Palladian and Georgian architecture. Paul's map had a series of yellow and red sticky spots on it and he was trying to follow where they were. Tim turned to Kate.

"Will you be walking around Bath, or will you be sk…"

"Here we are," announced the driver, and they all looked out of the window.

"I have a disability," said Kate, in hushed tones, as she returned Tim's nudge of earlier, "I can't walk when I'm happy. It's baffled medical science."

"I can imagine it has," said Tim, trying to keep a straight face, but his smile spread.

"Shall we get out, then?" said Paul, looking bemused by the exchange between Kate and Tim.

"Yes, please lead on," said Kate, and they all followed him. First stop was a magnificent regency building in Sydney Place that was going to double as the outside of Patrick's penthouse apartment.

"It is impressive and that's definitely something that Patrick would choose," said Tim.

"Does the super-modern interior set we have fit, though?" said Kate thinking out loud.

"I think it's actually a good descriptor for Patrick," said Tim.

"How do you mean?"

"Impressive on the outside and stark, stripped bare inside. Functional, cold almost, until Marcie comes into his life."

"Mmm, I think you could be right," said Kate thoughtfully, wishing she'd made that connection.

"I think these days you can have any interior you like and people accept it," chipped in Paul, making both Tim and Kate turn to look at him, as they had almost forgotten he was there. They walked up and down a bit and Paul took a few photos. Kate borrowed the camera and took one of Tim outside the front door. The look he gave her through the lens made something shiver inside her. She clicked the button quickly and handed the camera

185

back to Paul.

"So, all agreed on this one, then?" asked Paul.

"Yes, works for me," said Kate, and Tim agreed.

They all piled back into the limo and went off to inspect the office building that had been chosen as Patrick's office. The driver dropped them off nearby and they walked a short distance to the building in the city centre. Tim had his usual very dark designer shades on, and today he was wearing a fitted black shirt, long-sleeved but with the cuffs rolled back, and blue jeans. He always looked good, but then when you had people to buy your clothes for you and tell you what suited you best, it would be hard not to look good, mused Kate. The office was another regency building, but less impressive than Sydney Place. Kate, Tim and Paul stood on the pavement staring at it whilst a multitude of shoppers and tourists walked around them. Kate wondered if she'd be trampled in the rush if someone suddenly spotted that it was Timothy Calder.

"I don't like it," said Kate eventually.

"Why? It is an actual office building and we're planning to be filming inside this one too. It's all arranged," Paul said defensively.

"It's too ordinary, it's neither one thing nor the other. It's not an impressive regency building and it's not an impressive office building," she said flatly.

"Patrick would never choose this," stated Tim, as Paul puffed out a long, slow breath.

"It's Bath; all the buildings are like this, it's one of the best available," said Paul.

"I always had a very modern London-style office building in mind when I wrote it."

"With lots of glass," added in Tim.

"Yes, exactly," agreed Kate.

The conversation went round in a loop, with Paul trying to justify the choice and Kate and Tim maintaining their stance. Eventually, Paul agreed to look for other options, but firmly stated that he couldn't promise anything at such short notice.

The coffee shop was next on the list and this was perfect. Kate and Tim spent far too long there jabbering away to each other, agreeing fiercely on which was the cosiest table and where Patrick and Marcie would sit when they met. Tim slipped out the back to meet the owner, who was a woman in her forties. Kate watched as the woman stumbled over her words, turned red and stared in awe at Tim. It took her back to the first time she had met Tim at the cottage all those months ago. Next, they went to a bar that was surprisingly busy, so they just had a quick look and, to Paul's relief, were both happy with it.

Last location was the park. In the book, Kate had written about Patrick and Marcie meeting at the bandstand in Hyde Park, so the move to Royal Victoria Park in Bath was a big jump for her. The limo dropped them off, and the party of three headed off across the park, with the early-evening sun starting to fade behind them. As they were walking across the undulating grass, Kate almost lost her footing and in that moment she instinctively reached out for Tim's hand and it was there. She steadied herself quickly and then let his hand go. All the time she kept her eyes downward, inspecting the ground in her path, not wanting to feel the swim of emotions churning through her.

"There it is," said Paul, pointing ahead. In the distance was a small semicircular structure, open on one side and painted white on the other. In front of it was a low hedge and a variety of brightly coloured flowers.

"Is that meant to be the bandstand?" asked Tim,

"Of course it's a bandstand!" said Paul, who was still smarting after losing the office argument. As they reached the bandstand, Kate knew that despite it being quite different to the famous one in Hyde Park, which she had always pictured, this was the perfect place for the tender scenes between Patrick and Marcie. However, Tim was pulling faces.

"What's wrong?" asked Kate.

"It's not what I pictured and it's not as obvious. I think Patrick is an obvious character. And it's got filled-in sides – bandstands don't have sides."

"No, they don't usually, you're right. But the fact that it's not open will mean you'll have to focus on the two characters a lot more. It makes it more intimate, somehow. I like it."

"So, is that a yes, then?" asked Paul, looking at his watch.

"Hold on, give me a few minutes, will you," said Tim, as he went through the hedge and in one leap jumped over the decorative railings. Kate looked around; there must be another entrance to get onto the bandstand, but Tim was now offering a hand to help her up.

"I don't think you're meant to…" started Paul, but nobody was listening. Kate held onto her dress with one hand and with trepidation she took hold of Tim's offered hand. As she feared, the now-familiar shooting sensation seared through her body and she had to concentrate on getting over the railings without making an idiot of herself. Tim was strong and almost lifted her over and made sure she landed safely on the other side.

The view from the bandstand was a glorious one and made the perfect spot to sit and read or talk, apart from the distinct lack of seating. Kate couldn't control her excitement and she wasn't entirely sure that it was all down to the bandstand. She scanned the back of it, found the almost invisible door in the panelling where the band would normally enter, and pointed this out to Tim. "Look. Patrick will be waiting for Marcie and think she's not coming. But instead of seeing her as he's about to leave, as it was in the book, she'll appear through the secret door. Their eyes will meet, there's a fast-paced conversation and then Patrick sweeps her into his arms and kisses her and swings her around." Kate looked into Tim's eyes, those very green, expressive eyes and tried to make out what she saw there.

"Visually, I think it might just work. One question; why would Patrick pick here as opposed to over there by the lake?"

Tim said. Kate looked over to the lake, which was a very pretty spot and pondered this for a while as she leant on the railings.

"The bandstand makes a statement. He wants to control the situation. It's easier to walk away when you are in an open space, but here you are on show. Patrick lives his life on show; it's actually somewhere he's comfortable." She turned to Tim, who came and leant on the railings next to her.

"But he's changing. Being with Marcie is changing him."

"It is, but he'll still revert to his comfort zone when he's unsure of something. And being somewhere showy like this, where he can control what happens, is right up Patrick's alley."

There was a pause and they both let the amiable silence hang between them. "Okay, I'm sold. The bandstand works," Tim said, and they both smiled at each other. Tim leaned forward slightly and Kate's gaze was drawn to his lips.

"So, all sorted, then?" called Paul, and the moment was lost.

"No, sorry, we need to find an office building. Let's ask the driver," said Tim as he very smoothly jumped over the railings and lifted Kate over both the railings and the hedge, placing her gently on the ground next to him. He took her hand and this time he held it firmly when she tried to pull it away.

"I don't want you tripping over again," he smiled, "or skipping," he breathed quietly into her ear. Kate was surprised to find that her erogenous zones, which she thought had long since been packed up and archived, were able to spring into life in a split second, and she was thankful for the steadying hand to maintain her balance.

Back in the limo, the driver was very helpful and, much to Paul's annoyance, he knew of quite a few modern, glass office buildings around Bath, so they set off to view some. The first one was smoked glass with red frames, which reminded Kate of a fire station. The second one didn't have enough glass and was quite tired-looking. Number three was actually an NHS drop-in centre, which the driver apologised for, but number four fitted the bill completely. It was walkable to the city centre and had a mix of stark, white office building and dark glass, with a tall glass atrium. Kate and Tim took one look at the building and both said, "Yes". Paul went inside to find out some contact details, while Tim and Kate waited in the limo. Tim checked his phone and picked up some messages, so Kate decided to check hers, too, although she wasn't expecting to hear from anyone in particular. Her voicemail informed her that she had one new message. The message was from Didi saying that she'd been given the all-clear; she would be let out of the asylum at the weekend and was the offer of a lift still available? Tim looked over at Kate.

"My friend Didi. She's coming home at the weekend."

"Your mad friend?"

"Yes, well remembered! It's been driving her potty being cooped up. I've not been able to see her as much as I'd like, what with filming and everything, but I'll see her at the weekend."

"Take the chopper home tonight," offered Tim.

"How do you mean?"

"It's booked till midnight. It can fly at night and it'll have you home in no time."

"But you can't land a helicopter in my road," chuckled Kate.

"No, you land it on the field near the church," stated Tim, and Kate raised her eyebrows as she realised that this must have been what Tim had done at the weekend. "Or get it to land near the hospital and then take you home afterwards. Pip will sort it for you."

"Thanks, that's really kind. If it's okay with you, then, I will take it and I'll get the train back down in the morning."

"Of course, it's fine. Pip is a big fan of yours."

"I think she's read some of the books," said Kate, trying to appear modest.

"No, I mean after sorting out Mina and the chopper and stuff this morning," he said with a chuckle. Instant blush hit Kate's cheeks. I'll never need to wear blusher again, she thought.

"Oh, I was only helping out." The mention of Lumina brought

that morning's conversation back to her and a harsh reminder of the depth of Lumina's feelings for Tim. "You and Lumina, you've got something special there," she said rather awkwardly, as if she had to force the words out

"What makes you say that?" said Tim, a small wrinkle furrowing his brow.

"She's really in love with you, Tim." Perhaps she shouldn't have said it, but it was said now. Tim smirked and Kate knew that he wasn't aware. "Seriously, Tim, Lumina is in love with you. It runs deep for her. I'm sure she enjoys the media attention that you bring too, but the fact is that she's fallen hook, line and sinker for you."

"Now there's a phrase you don't hear very often. Only in films before 1970," he said, trying to lighten the moment, but he sensed Kate's solemnity. "She knows it's not serious. I've been clear with her all along."

"But you can't be logical about love." The atmosphere in the limo was a little strained when Paul returned. Little more was said and they headed back to the helicopter.

Chapter 17

Kate was quite shocked by how much she loved the excitement and opulence of travelling by helicopter, although it wasn't quite the same not sharing the experience with someone else. Travelling at night was different, too, because there was little to see as the helicopter slid through the darkness, so Kate gazed at the patterns of lights far below.

Tim was right that it was a surprisingly quick journey, and within about half an hour they were hovering and landing in the vast grounds of the convalescent home. The pilot jumped out and helped Kate down. She kept her head ducked low, as instructed, as the rotors were still turning. She promised the pilot she wouldn't be long and strode across the grass towards the home.

As she got closer she could see that the helicopter's arrival had caused a bit of a stir and there was a geriatric welcome party shuffling outside. Kate walked up the stone steps, where Didi was surrounded by about ten other residents in various states of undress, all jabbering excitedly and pointing from Kate to the helicopter. Didi was standing with her hands on her hips, "You're never taking me home in that?"

"No, sorry Didi, it's on loan just for this evening. I can't stay long. Shall we go inside? It's getting a bit chilly?" Didi ushered the others inside as the excited babble started to die down.

"Are they Nazis?" asked a small, frail old lady, who was leaning on a zimmer frame and staring wide-eyed at the helicopter.

"No, Alice, you're quite safe. It's just my show-off friend Kate. The war's over, Alice."

"Is it? How marvellous!"

"Come on, Alice, you had best get some cocoa and head off to bed," said Didi, with a good-natured roll of her eyes as she helped Alice turn her frame around.

It was lovely to see Didi fully mobile and able to help someone else. It gave Kate confidence that she was truly ready to go home.

"Ah," sighed Didi as she sat down hard in the large wing-backed chair, "so the celebrity lifestyle's not suiting you at all, I see."

"No, I hate it," said Kate, with a scowl.

"Must be terrible having to fly everywhere by helicopter. You must miss sitting in traffic on the motorway."

"I do, terribly." Kate picked up her tea cup and saucer, "Thanks for this."

"I figured I owed you a few," said Didi.

Kate gave her a summarised update of the last week or so and a few details about Lumina's meltdown and the trip to Bath.

"So why the visit by helicopter?"

"Tim's loaned it to me so we could see each other and sort out arrangements for the weekend."

"I see. And what does Tim want in return, I wonder," Didi said, giving Kate an old- fashioned look.

"He can want what he likes, but he's not getting it."

"Oh, so he is interested, then," said Didi, excitedly leaning forward.

"I don't think so," said Kate, wishing the conversation hadn't gone down this particular path. "We are becoming friends, which is a bit weird because he's this big, famous film star and I'm just me."

"Just friends?" Didi replaced her cup on its saucer without breaking eye contact with Kate.

"Yes, Didi, just friends. Nothing else."

"Nothing? With that hotty Timothy Calder? I don't believe it. You must feel something."

"Hotty? Really, you're using the word 'hotty'?"

"We've had some student nurses working over here for their geriatric training. It's amazing what you pick up," grinned Didi. "Don't change the subject. You must have felt something, having been that close to the man?"

Kate thought for a moment. "There is something. He can do that thing where he knows how to give you a tingly arm." Kate struggled to think of a better way to describe it without sounding too effusive.

"Uh huh, like electricity?"

"Yes! Exactly like thirty thousand volts sometimes. He must know pressure points or something, but whatever he does you can't not notice it. Must be a trick they teach you at the RSC," said Kate, feeling better for sharing it.

"You think it's a trick?" said Didi, looking very pleased with herself as she relaxed back into the chair.

"Well, it must be."

"You've not felt that before, then?"

"No."

"And it happens every time Tim touches you?" asked Didi, looking smugger by the second.

"Pretty much, yes. Do you know what it is?" asked Kate, feeling a little shiver, which was either the thought of Tim's touch or someone had left a window open.

"Oh, yes, I know what it is," said Didi with a wry smile. "It's static electricity. It's a bugger."

When the laughter had subsided the two women agreed that Kate would pick Didi up after lunch on Saturday. That would give Kate time to help out with tidying up after Amy's birthday party, which was in the morning, and would still give her plenty of time to make sure Didi was settled in before she drove back home. They kissed their goodbyes and Didi insisted on coming outside to wave off Kate's helicopter.

The helicopter had barely gained any height before it was landing again next to Kate's village church. She thanked the pilot far too many times, took her bag and almost skipped all the way home. If it wasn't for the fact that skipping was actually quite tiring if you did it for any length of time, she would have done. She was smiling to herself like the village idiot when she crunched up the gravel drive and was pleased to see lights on, which meant that Andy was still up. She turned her key in the lock and had a shock as the door stuck on the chain.

"Hello, Andy. Can you let me in, please," she called through the gap in the door. Andy appeared instantly, having been jolted to his feet by the sudden noise of the door. Sarah quickly appeared behind him.

"Hello," said Kate, when Andy opened the door, and she tried to mouth behind his back to Sarah to ask if she'd interrupted something. Kate quickly realised that couldn't have been the reason as Sarah was looking wretched. "What's happened?" Kate looked from Andy to Sarah and back again. Andy kept quiet. "Sarah, what's wrong?" Sarah gave Kate a hug and a few silent tears escaped, despite her best efforts to contain them.

"Amy's asleep upstairs. Come and sit down and I'll tell you everything," said Sarah. I bet you don't tell her everything, thought Andy, who had been waiting for Sarah to provide the missing details all week. He hadn't asked the direct question because he didn't want to push her, but the elephant in the room was growing fatter by the day.

Sarah explained about the police searching the house and questioning both her and Andy informally, about them taking carpet samples and being very interested in the patio.

"What's the plan now, then?" Kate said, releasing Sarah from another hug.

"Just wait for Shaun to show up, I guess," shrugged Sarah.

"But what if he doesn't show up? What if something has

happened to him, or if he's just gone off to start a new life? He may never show up. What then?"

"Kate, I can't magic him out of thin air! I'm not a magician!" Sarah's fragility was showing through.

"Someone must know something. He can't just vanish. And why are the police so keen to find him? That's not normal. Sadly, thousands of people go missing every year and the police aren't doing house-to-house and testing carpet stains for all of them."

Andy joined the conversation for the first time since Kate had come home. "I've asked around everyone I can think of and nobody has seen or heard from him."

"Do you think he'll turn up on Saturday for Amy's birthday?" asked Kate.

"I doubt it," said Sarah bluntly, which made Andy study her a little closer.

"I think that will be a really good indication of whether he's alive or not," said Andy, and Sarah turned to glare at him but said nothing. "I honestly don't think he would completely miss Amy's birthday if he could help it. I know you disagree, Sarah, but it's what I think." Sensing the increase in hostility, Andy stood up and air-kissed Sarah and then Kate. "I'll leave you two to have a catch-up." He paused at the door. "Your next-door neighbour was round in the week; he wants to talk to you about something."

"Oh dear. He wants to look at the boundaries on my deeds, but I can't find them. He'll just have to wait," said Kate as Andy avoided the look he knew Sarah was giving him.

"I'm off to bed. Night." And he left.

"You know you can stay as long as you like, but if you don't think he's going to show up, what made you move you and Amy in here?" Kate tried to phrase the question as gently as possible.

"It is a bit of a faff, but I can't sleep there any more. I keep having nightmares. I know it sounds childish, but here I'm able to sleep for a few hours and it makes a huge difference."

"What happens in the nightmares?"

"It's a mixture, really. Sometimes it's Shaun breaking in, sometimes it's the police raiding the house and taking Amy, sometimes… it's just rubbish, but I can't sleep afterwards." Sarah rummaged with difficulty in her skinny jeans pocket, retrieved a crumpled tissue and dabbed her blotchy face. Kate moved along the sofa and held Sarah tightly. Sarah let the tears come. They sat there together for some time and Kate gently rocked Sarah as all the emotion that had been building up was suddenly too much to contain any longer. Andy silently crept away from the doorway, wiped a stray tear from his cheek and went to bed.

In what felt like a blink, Kate found herself back on set surrounded by raised voices, and caught between a very stroppy Che and a tearful Lumina. Kate felt that her head was full of marshmallow today, as she had struggled to sleep properly after the overload of information from Sarah. It made her feel that these people really didn't live in the real world and had no clue what people like Sarah had to cope with day to day. Che was unhappy with what he called Lumina's lack of commitment to the scene, and Lumina was basically throwing a strop for being told off. Whilst Kate tried feebly to referee the situation that was unfolding, Tim seized the opportunity to take Marcus off for a chat. They stepped out into a warm sunny day and proceeded to wander off across the lot.

"So, yesterday went well, I hear." Marcus undid his buttoned waistcoat as they walked along at a gentle pace.

"Yeah, it was a great day. You know, just spending some time together, I'm calmer, I feel at ease. What did she say?" Tim was eager to hear Kate's take on the day.

"She? I spoke to Paul. He told me you approved all but one location and that one was easily resolved," Marcus continued to walk alongside Tim, but was now eyeing him speculatively.

"Right. Yes, of course. Yes, locations are fine. Kate felt exactly the same about each of them,"

"So, have you sorted out your, um, medical condition?" said

Marcus, slowing his pace and eventually stopping. Tim walked on briefly and then realised, so spun around on his heel to face Marcus. Tim took off his sunglasses and played with them distractedly. Marcus waited patiently.

"Marcus, I know you don't believe it but… I touch people all the time," started Tim.

"Yes, I know, I read the papers." Marcus had the look of a portly school teacher about him as he said this.

"No, you know all the lovey actor stuff, all the fake hugs and air kisses and such. But I have never felt this… this sensation I feel with Kate."

"Go on," he had Marcus's full attention.

"Yesterday, Kate nearly fell over in the park and we reached for each other at the same time and it's like zing, there's this amazing…"

"Sensation?"

"Yes!"

"Like electricity?"

"Exactly that," said Tim, pointing his sunglasses at Marcus, who rolled his eyes and took a small step to the side and started them off on their stroll again. "You know, I've read it a thousand times in scripts – 'the electricity' between them – and thought 'what a load of crap'. No offence."

"Some taken," said Marcus, his jaw tightening slightly.

"But that was what it was. It was electric. For that split second, we could have lit up Vegas."

"However, it matters not a jot unless Kate felt it too," Marcus said, in a sombre tone.

"She must have done. Every inch of me felt it," said Tim, as Marcus raised his eyebrows sharply and gave Tim a knowing look. "No, not like that," Marcus held his expression. "Well, yes, okay, but not *just* like that," conceded Tim.

"Did she react at all?"

"No, I don't think so, but I could tell yesterday she was holding back. Her guard is always up."

Marcus nodded. "Tim, we've known each other a very long time now and I know I can be honest with you. You love the thrill of the chase, and even more than that, you love obtaining the unobtainable, and I fear Kate is ticking those boxes."

"I won't deny that's how I've been in the past, but that's not what's happening this time." Tim was shaking his head for emphasis. Once again, Marcus stopped and looked as if he was in deep thought. He turned assertively on his heel and waved for Tim to join him on the return stroll back towards the set.

"What exactly makes this time different?" asked Marcus.

"Kate. Kate makes this time different."

"Hmm. Do you want my advice?" asked Marcus, glancing at Tim.

"Probably not, if you're going to tell me to leave well alone."

"Okay, good, here's my advice. Take it slowly. If there is something there for you and for Kate then it's worth waiting until you are sure. I don't want either of you getting hurt."

"Okay. Good advice, thank you."

"You're welcome. There is, of course, the matter of Lumina. You need to rectify that before it gets completely out of hand."

"Again, good advice, but it won't be pleasant. Kate seems to think that Lumina is in love with me."

"Kate is a very perceptive lady."

"Shit," said Tim with feeling,

"Precisely, dear boy," said Marcus patting him on the back, "precisely".

As they walked back inside, Tim caught sight of Kate. She was sitting with an arm around Lumina, who was sniffing and patting at her eyes with a handful of tissues. Tim didn't like the look Kate gave him as he approached.

"Is it all sorted with Che?" he said to both of them.

"Lumina is taking a short break, Che's gone to get a migraine tablet and we're back on set in 15 minutes," said Kate, nodding her head towards Lumina to indicate that he should speak to her. Tim took the cue like the pro he was and sat down on the other side of Lumina. He nodded to Kate to let go and he put his arms around Lumina, so that Kate could escape. Kate gave him a weak smile and left them alone. Lumina was in full Marcie make-up and wardrobe with a very long, patterned maxi dress and her hair loosely clipped up off her face. The make-up was subtle and made her look vulnerable. Lumina quietly snuggled into Tim's chest.

"Do you fancy dinner somewhere nice tonight?" Tim said softly and Lumina nodded.

The rest of the day's filming went well and almost without incident. Horse had escaped from his latest puppy minder and run amuck on set for a brief period in the afternoon, but apart from that everyone seemed happy, except Che, who was like a crocodile with toothache. As they set up for the final take of the day, Kate found herself in Che's firing line as Tim and Lumina were both missing. She placated him as best she could and went off in search of the pair praying, as she did so, that she wouldn't find them in a lovers' clinch somewhere. Not that it should matter to her.

Kate spotted them sitting together where they had been earlier. Lumina had her head in Tim's lap, which made Kate look twice before she realised that Lumina was asleep, so it was quite safe to approach them. Kate headed over to deliver the rather curt message Che had given her and, as she reached them, Tim's mobile rang. He pulled it from his pocket with his left hand and kept his other arm around Lumina. Kate stood and waited.

"Hang on, Mum, calm down and speak slower," Tim said, as he indicated for Kate to take Lumina. Kate shook her head and Tim removed himself as best he could without sending Lumina's head crashing onto the seat. She reluctantly sat up and walked off, pouting like a small child. Kate went after her.

"Che is setting up. Can you go straight over, please? I'll tell Tim when he's off the phone." That was the clean version of what Che had said, anyway.

"Did you see?" Lumina pointed her finger at Tim and then at herself. "Did you see us?"

"I did," smiled Kate. "Now get a move on or Che will fry your backside." Lumina giggled and trotted off towards the set and Kate returned to stand patiently next to Tim.

Tim was pacing and looked shocked by what the caller was saying.

"My God. I can't believe he's dead. How are the boys? And Mum, are you okay? No, of course you're not okay. How did it happen?" The words and the sorrow in Tim's voice grabbed Kate's attention and she watched him closely. She was frozen to the spot as Tim's face changed from concern to pain. Kate knew that feeling all too well. She gestured for him to sit down again and he did.

"Mum, I'll come up tonight. No, I want to. I can be back here for filming tomorrow. Is Dad there?" There was a brief pause as the phone was passed over at the other end. "Hi, Dad, I'm so sorry. Take care of Mum for me. I can't leave immediately, but I'll be there as soon as I can." Tim ended the call and sat thumbing the phone, looking shell-shocked. Kate sat down next to him and took his hand. Tim welcomed the contact and gripped it tightly and, after a long pause, he said, "It's Barney, he's dead."

"Oh, Tim, I'm so sorry," and, now the boot was on the other foot, Kate found herself just like all those people who had tried to comfort her. She was lost for words and she knew there was nothing she could do to help. Tim took his time to get the sentences out, as if he was going over them in his head first to check the information he had just received.

"He was playing with my nephews and he was hit by a car, died instantly."

"Oh, Tim, the poor children," said Kate, as she instinctively put her arm around his shoulder. Tim leaned in slightly to her and tried, but failed, to smile.

"Mum says the boys are pretty upset, poor little sods." Kate's grip on Tim's hand grew tighter as she fought to keep her emotions in check. Tim stared at their entwined hands.

"I can't think of anything worse than seeing your father killed." Kate had to get a grip of herself. The last thing Tim needed now was her getting emotional.

"Oh, um," said Tim, but the feel of Kate so close to him made him not finish the sentence. He let Kate hold him, enjoying the feel of Kate's closeness, her usual guard completely down.

Che came striding into view and Kate stood up to try to intercept him, but Tim stopped her.

"It's okay. Please don't say anything. I'll do the last scene and then leave." He looked into Kate's eyes. Her face was tense, but he could sense her craving to be close to him right now and to help. Kate threw her arms around Tim and hugged him, "I'm here, anything, anytime, just call." Tim nodded and then strode over to meet Che. Kate sat back down and stared at her shoes for a moment as she tried to compose herself. Her heart was racing, the tears were ready to fall at a moment's notice, and she needed to get things back under control before she went back on set.

Once she felt composed, she sneaked on set just before someone called out, "Quiet on set, rolling, action." Kate was mesmerised by Tim. She barely noticed the others in the scene; he was completely brilliant and gave a perfect performance. It never ceased to amaze her how he seemed to just step into Patrick's character and then step out again after the scene.

As soon as Che indicated it was a good scene and the filming day was over, Kate tried to make her way over to Tim. Unfortunately, Dennis had other ideas and was keen to speak to Kate before she left. She tried to listen to Dennis, but she was watching Tim over his shoulder. Tim was speaking to Lumina, holding both her hands in his. She was looking decidedly grumpy, and Tim had his apologetic face on. That wasn't the look of a supportive girlfriend; what was wrong with the woman? He kissed her briefly and she went over to Horse's play pen to retrieve him before leaving on her own. Tim stood scanning the set. He was looking for someone else now; was he looking for her? She caught his eye; he looked to the ground and then turned and left.

Kate returned her attention to Dennis, who was very keen to show her some emotional close-ups they had captured. She spent a few minutes trying to watch them, but it was pointless, her brain had been hijacked. Nothing was going in and nothing of any use was coming out. Kate made her apologies and headed back to the hotel in a complete daze. All she could think about was Tim.

Tim was in the back of his car with Terry, hurtling up the M1, when his mobile trilled into life and Marcus's name flashed on screen. "Hello," said Tim casually.

"Tim, thank God. Where are you?"

"On the way to my mother's."

"Tim, I'm so desperately sorry. Kate's just told me about Bernie's death. You must be utterly bereft. And those poor darling children, devastating…"

Tim stopped him mid-sentence, "Ah, hang on, Marcus. It's not Bernie who's died."

"What?" Marcus's voice conveyed his complete confusion.

"Bernie's not dead, it's Barney. Barney is dead. He was run over by a car."

"The bloody Labrador?" roared Marcus into the phone.

"Hey, I love that dog. I'm really upset about it. We all are. He was one of the family."

"Good God, dear boy! I doubt very much that you are as upset as Kate is right now. I went to see why she hadn't been down for dinner and found her crying in her room. Bloody hell, Tim! Kate was in tears because she thought you had lost your brother."

"Shit. There must be a slight mix-up over names, I think; Bernie, Barney…"

"Then why the hell didn't you put her straight?"

"There was a nanosecond where I realised and where I had that one chance to say something,"

"And you didn't take it?"

"By the time I'd realised, the moment was gone and it was always going to be awkward after that."

"Awkward! Awkward!" bellowed Marcus.

"Marcus, hold on. It's the first time we've really connected. She understood my pain. She cared enough to let her guard down, Marcus, and it felt great."

"Tim, you prize imbecile! She cared because she has been to hell and back because of the grim reaper and she thought you were feeling that same pain. You have to tell her. And tell her now!"

"I know, I will."

"Well, if you don't, I will. You have until tomorrow to sort this out."

"Okay. But when I tell her, she's going to hate me."

"If you're lucky, she'll only hate you. I'd kill you. You daft bastard."

"Thanks."

"Give my love and condolences to the family," said Marcus, his voice returning to its usual balanced tone and volume.

"Thanks. I will. Bye." Tim slumped back in his seat and saw Terry glance in the rear- view mirror. He recognised the look in Terry's eyes, too. He really had buggered it up this time. The only time it had really mattered and he'd royally buggered it up.

Chapter 18

Marcus knocked for Kate on his way to breakfast, but there was no answer. A phone call revealed she had left early. So he was relieved when he found her huddled in the script corner of the set frantically scribbling away.

"Darling girl," he said quietly, so as not to make her jump, but she jumped all the same, "What are you doing?"

"Writing. It's what I do," she smiled sadly at him. "It's quite perverse what triggers the ideas, isn't it? Book five is coming on a treat," and she flicked the completed pages of her notebook in front of Marcus. Marcus sat down next to her. She was wearing a pretty summer dress with a yellow cardigan and looked her usual elegant self, but the sadness in her eyes told a different story.

"Have you heard from Tim?" Kate said, putting the notebook down.

"I spoke to him last night. Has he not called you?"

"No. How was he?"

"He's fine. Still a complete idiot, but fine." Kate looked a little askance at Marcus's slight on Tim at this grave time. "He's going to talk to you today. It's for him to tell you, not me. But when he does, just remember he's an idiot and he's not malicious. Okay?"

"Okay, but none of what you just said made any sense at

all, Marcus. Are you okay?"

"Not really," and he hugged her.

Kate was back to scribbling in her notebook when she had one of those moments where you involuntarily have to look up, and far across the other side of set, she saw Tim. He was standing with his hands on his hips, wearing a plain black t-shirt and jeans. His hair was a mess and, even at that distance, she could make out that he hadn't shaved. He looked awful and anxious. Kate wanted to rush over, but knew that the last thing he needed right now was to be crowded or coddled. He needed space. She'd told him she was there if he needed her and she'd meant it. They looked at each other, their view only broken by the crew members walking across the set. A large panel was being manoeuvred, which blocked Kate's sight for a moment and when it was gone, so was Tim. Kate took a deep breath and carried on watching the comings and goings as everyone else got things ready for the day's filming.

Kate decided to get herself a cup of tea, where she found Marcus going over the running order with Dennis. When there was a pause in conversation and Kate was idly dipping her tea bag, she said, "Tim's here". Marcus handed the clipboard he'd been holding to Dennis and charged out of the room. As Kate wandered back to her little corner, she saw Pippa and Lumina talking. Neither looked happy and Horse was interjecting with the odd agitated yap. Lumina handed Pippa the pink dog-carry pouch, but Pippa wouldn't take it and marched off, leaving Horse to bark after her.

Kate heard Marcus's voice first and then realised that he and Tim were not too far away and were also having a heated discussion; she couldn't remember hearing Marcus ever raise his voice before. She wandered through the sets to Patrick's apartment, which wasn't being used today and there she found the pair. The exchange wasn't exactly enlightening – Tim just kept repeating the word "bugger", which he repeated as he saw Kate. A gentleman and two small boys joined them in the room and Kate smiled. Tim and Marcus both stopped arguing and stared at the man.

"I said wait in the sodding car!" said Tim, crossly, to the man.

"But the boys were driving Terry crazy. They were desperate to see the set." The man had dark hair, slightly unkempt, a little like the way Tim's went when it hadn't been coiffured and treated with the latest designer products. The man was quite broad, with a jolly face, and wore what appeared to be a very old beige jacket and threadbare navy trousers. He turned to Kate, smiled and offered his hand to shake, "Hello, I'm Bernie, Tim's brother."

Sarah woke up and was grateful that Amy had a teacher-training day and that she didn't have the mad rush to get her up, dressed and driven to school. Staying at Kate's was lovely but just a little too far away from Sarah's neighbourhood to make it work on a daily basis. Of course, Sarah could always set the alarm for earlier, but she was operating on minimum sleep right now, anyway, and Amy was always very grumpy if she was woken up.

Sarah lay there, enjoying the cool, white cotton and the weight of the duck-down quilt hugging her body. She decided that she would like to swap lives with Kate, but she would cut out the sad bits, obviously. She listened and she could hear that both Andy and Amy were awake and laughing downstairs. Sarah closed her eyes and tried to file this moment in her memory; she might need it for when everything went pear-shaped, as it inevitably would, because this was Sarah's life and that's what always happened.

She must have dropped off to sleep again, as she was brought back to consciousness by a knock on the door, before it was gently pushed open. Sarah sat up and watched as Andy hovered behind Amy, who came shuffling in wearing her Tinkerbell nightie and carrying a large wooden tray. On the tray was a plate of buttered toast, which was sliding one way and then the other, as if on the high seas in a very bad storm. Amy was biting her lip with concentration and inching her way to the bed, where she almost dropped the tray with relief.

"I made you breakfast, Mummy!" said Amy, excitedly clapping her now-free hands together. "Andy helped; he made you a coffee," which Andy presented to Sarah.

"Thank you, this is lovely. What's the occasion?" asked Sarah, quickly adjusting her Snoopy pyjama top to make sure that nothing inappropriate was on show before taking the hot mug from Andy.

"We thought you could do with a bit of fuss," said Andy, flopping down on the bed. Sarah clutched the mug as the hot liquid bounced around inside. Amy joined them and scurried up the bed and under the covers between the two adults. Andy gently ruffled Amy's hair and she giggled.

"This is lovely, but shouldn't you be getting to work?" Sarah asked, sipping her coffee and then flinching as she realised it was too hot to drink.

Andy shrugged. "I'm okay for a bit. They're not expecting me until later. So I thought I'd let you have a lie-in."

"Thanks." Sarah smiled at him.

"You're welcome. Stinkerbell here wanted to get you breakfast in bed. She said you missed out on Mother's Day because she couldn't manage it on her own." Sarah felt a lump in her throat and was pleased that Andy started to tickle Amy, which caused a distraction. Unfortunately Amy's writhing did jiggle the bed about, so Sarah held on tight to her mug. Amy squealed with laughter and managed to gasp out a couple of words.

"I'm Tinkerbell. That tickles!"

"It's meant to, Stinkerbell."

"Daddy!" squealed Amy not realising her mistake. The pair carried on the tickle fight and Andy gave Sarah a brief look. Sarah saw the pride in his eyes; he had got really close to Amy. Sarah swallowed hard and for the first time caught sight of her reflection in the full- length mirror at the end of the room. Sarah took a small gasp, but a voice inside her head screamed at the fright that looked back at her. She must have forgotten to take off her make- up last night, as her eyes looked as if they had been coloured in black, very similar to how Amy had looked when she'd had her face painted as a panda at the summer fête. There was a definite dark stain across her lips, having drunk too much red wine last night. The pièce de résistance was the hair – she looked like an electrocuted pineapple. Great tufts of blonde hair, which apparently were hers, were stuck out in a multitude of random directions.

"Are you okay?" asked Andy, seeing Sarah's look of alarm.

"I think I need to go straight in the shower, see if it has magical powers and can make me look human again." Sarah scurried out of bed and into the en-suite bathroom, only to be faced with another large mirror.

"Kate is a sadist," she muttered to herself as she sorted through the small basket of hotel-sized toiletries that Kate kept for guests to use.

"Sarah, if you're sure you're okay, I'm going to head off to work now. Amy is going to watch cartoons downstairs and I'll lock you both in, okay?" said Andy to the wood panelling of the en-suite door.

Sarah opened the door a fraction. "Thanks, for everything. I'm making the food for Amy's party today, but I'll cook something nice for dinner, too."

"That would be good. If anything happens, you call me, got it?"

"Yes, sir!" Sarah said, letting go of the door and saluting Andy. Andy leaned in to tickle her with one hand, but missed.

"Later, I'll get you later," he laughed as he shut the door and headed off with a spring in his step.

Tim's eyes flitted from person to person, as the nightmare played out in front of him. Kate stood transfixed, literally open-mouthed, and looked as if she'd seen a ghost, which she clearly thought she had. Kate heard the smash, but it took her a few moments to realise that it was made by her mug of tea. She was jolted back to the situation and surveyed the mess.

"I'm so sorry." Kate looked around for something to clear it up with.

"It's okay, you missed me," said Bernie cheerfully, brushing down his trousers and guiding the children away from the spillage. Tim opened out his arms wide and strode forward to embrace Bernie.

"You're alive!" Tim announced to a bewildered-looking Bernie, who patted Tim on the back whilst Marcus covered his eyes and shook his head. Kate stopped trying to mop the floor with her single tissue and stood up, which brought her very close and side-on to Tim. Her expression changed and her eyes burned into him. Tim let go of Bernie, who seemed rather overcome by the affection his brother was openly displaying, and turned to Kate with what he hoped was a conciliatory look on his face.

"I'm sorry, Kate. It was a simple mistake. Bernie is my brother, Barney is… was our Labrador; it was him that was run over yesterday." As he heard the whimpers from his nephews, he briefly turned to them, "Sorry, boys". Kate said nothing, but looked accusingly at Marcus, who held up his hands and pointed at Tim. She shook her head and turned and walked out of Patrick's apartment, slamming the door behind her, which made the frame shake and the handle pop out and land on the floor.

She strode off the set, out onto the lot and away from people before bursting into tears. The relief was immense. She hadn't even known Bernie, but the whole episode had again brought to the surface feelings she had been keeping at bay for such a long time. Thankfully, Kate found a small patch of grass behind some storage units and she just sat there and cried. She wished she hadn't wasted her only tissue on the spilt tea.

As the thoughts and feelings bounced around her head, she realised the sadness was only partly related to losing James. It was also that whatever she had had with Tim was now broken. After a while she was able to regulate her breathing and the noisy sobs stopped. She was glad there was nobody around to hear her. She wiped her face with her hands and resolved that the toilets would be the first port of call when she went back inside.

She was pleased with herself that she was going to go back inside. There had been a brief moment of temptation to just walk out completely and go home, but Kate was no quitter and she sure as hell wasn't going to let Timothy Calder spoil what, so far, had been an amazing experience.

Kate took in some more deep breaths and felt the anger surge through her; she'd never lashed out at anyone in her life, but right now she could understand how it happened. Kate didn't want to think about what had been Tim's motivation for leading her to believe his brother had been tragically killed. The best solution now seemed to be to ignore Tim and focus on the job at hand. She stood up, gave her face one last wipe, brushed some stray grass off her dress and left her little patch of grass.

When Kate walked back in, they were filming, so she scooted off to the ladies to sort herself out before anyone saw her. She studied herself in the mirror. She was a little pink and puffy around the eyes, but it could have been a lot worse. She wondered why you had to look so hideous when you cried, as if being upset wasn't enough. You also looked a total mess. Kate dabbed her eyes with some damp tissue and washed her hands, then popped a couple of clean tissues up her sleeve, just in case. Taking one last look at herself, she smoothed down her hair, which she'd let hang loose today, straightened her dress, pushed back her shoulders and walked out with confidence.

Kate managed to ignore Tim for the rest of the morning, which was fairly easy as he was filming most of the time. She gleaned from Marcus that nobody else knew what had happened, so at least she was spared the humiliation of being the butt of everyone's jokes, but unfortunately, it also meant that Tim had avoided being seen as the heartless tosser he clearly was. Marcus was equally, if not more, cross with Tim than Kate was, which made her feel better, although there was a small part of her that wished that Marcus had come and told her as soon as he'd realised her mistake. But it was very hard to stay cross with Marcus. He had felt that it was down to Tim to put the record straight, which was hard to disagree with.

At lunchtime, Pippa joined her in the queue and they sat down together to eat.

"So, you've escaped from the dog-sitting, then?" said Kate, pouring the salad dressing onto her lunch.

"Not completely. Lumina is a bit rubbish at remembering to take him out for... you know, the toilet."

"Pippa, do I detect a bit of puppy love creeping in there?"

"No! It's just not fair on him. He can't exactly cross his legs, can he?"

"So you're taking him for sprinkles, voluntarily."

"Just now and then, if Lumina forgets. He still yaps at me, the ungrateful little fur ball, but not as much as he yaps at Tim."

"That I understand," said Kate, with feeling. If she was a dog she could have happily bitten Timothy Calder and if the result was that she had to wear a muzzle forever, then so be it. It would be worth it. Kate pulled her bizarre train of thought back to Pippa. "So the rest of your time is still spent wet-nursing Tim?"

"Of course. He's had me ordering masses of flowers this morning to go to some mystery address. I hate to think what he's up to now. He's in a weird mood today, but it could be because he's got his brother and nephews on set. He didn't bother to tell me they were coming, so I had last-minute passes and clearance to sort out for them this morning." There was a pause in conversation while the women enjoyed their respective lunches. Kate had gone for a simple Greek salad, which was as good as it looked, and Pippa had chosen a jacket potato after checking in a small book how many points it was on her current diet regime.

"Lumina and Tim seem to have settled down, but knowing them, I think it's the calm before the storm," said Pippa.

"I don't think 'settled' is a word often used in the same sentence as Timothy Calder." Kate speared two olives firmly and ate them.

"Lumina is full of the joys; I think she thinks she's taming him. And, to be fair, he has been different of late, but it doesn't stop him buying gifts for other women."

"Oh, do tell," Kate said full of interest.

"I can't. Client confidentiality."

"You're not a doctor, Pippa."

"No, but it's the same." Pippa took a large forkful of jacket potato and waved it on her fork, "He has no idea the effect he has on women".

"Oh, I think he does," said Kate, her tone cool.

As she walked back from lunch chatting to Pippa about the joys of a good handbag, her mobile vibrated into life and as it was "home" calling she took the call.

"Hello," said Kate, thinking how odd it was to get a call from her own house when there was usually only her there, although of late it had become a little like Times Square on New Year's Eve. "Are you a burglar wanting to know where the good stuff is hidden? Because the bad news is, I don't have any!"

"Ha ha!" trilled Sarah.

"You okay?"

"Yes, we're fine. Andy is on red alert and there's still no sign of Shaun. I think the bastard has won the lottery and buggered off to the Caribbean. I wouldn't put it past him."

"Glad you're okay. I'm aiming to be home for seven tonight. Che has promised an early finish as it's been a long week and we are nearly back on schedule."

"Great. Reason for calling is that you've had a delivery." Sarah's voice was all excited now, like a child with a secret.

"I've not ordered anything for ages. How big is the box?"

"It's not in a box, it's everywhere," laughed Sarah.

"Sarah, spit it out, what's been delivered? It's not bricks for next door's wall?"

"No, it's flowers!"

"Flowers?"

"Yes. You know pretty coloured things on the end of green stalks, smell nice and keep me in a job. Well one of my jobs."

"Who would send me a bunch of flowers? Was there a card?"

"Kate, you might want to sit down."

"No, I'm fine."

"Right, but I did warn you. There are approximately 20 massive bouquets of flowers and every card just says 'Kate, I am truly sorry'."

"Twenty? But who… Oh crikey. Okay, thanks for letting me know."

"That's not all. There are another 20 or so baskets of flowers, five big outdoor troughs and a huge cake stand of cupcakes. They might not last the day, I'm afraid, as Amy already has her eye on them. Who are they from?" she could barely contain her excitement,

"Timothy Calder."

"No way! Careful, I might actually wet myself! Tell me why." Sarah was burning with intrigue.

"He's been an idiot and, well, I've been an idiot, too. I got upset over something and now he's trying to get round me."

"Did you shag him?" said Sarah excitedly.

"No! I bloody didn't. It's a dull story; I'll tell you tonight. But there was no sex involved."

"Sounds like my life."

"Look, keep the cupcakes for Amy's party tomorrow, pick out anything you want to keep, and please can you see if Esme will let you borrow the van to transport everything else up the convalescent home. Make sure Didi gets the best bouquet, would you?"

"Yes, ma'am."

"Sorry, that was really bossy of me. Have you got time to do that?"

"You need a PA! But it's fine, I'm sure I can fit it in somewhere. Are you sure you don't want to see them first, at least? They are truly amazing.

"No thanks,"

214

"Okay, it's your call."

"Thanks, Sarah. I have to go and kick Timothy Calder's backside."

"Can I kiss it better…?" offered Sarah enthusiastically, as Kate cut her off.

Marcus was playing with a pencil when Tim found him and he saw the look in Marcus's eyes as he stepped into the room and it saddened him. He knew he was a complete idiot, but if he'd stopped to think of the potential disaster this had become, of course he would have pointed out the error immediately. It didn't seem to do any good repeating the fact that it wasn't as if he had gone out of his way to upset anyone and he hadn't manufactured the story, it was simply that Kate had muddled the names. But blaming Kate for this wasn't the way to resolve it. Marcus stopped twirling the pencil.

"Look, I'll say it again in the hope that eventually you'll believe me. I am truly sorry."

"Yes, I know, dear boy, but what has been done cannot be undone."

"True. I need your help, Marcus."

"What now?" Marcus sounded tired.

"I need to talk to Kate, but she's ignoring me."

"Can you blame her?"

"No, of course not, but I wish she'd shout at me or something."

"Kate doesn't shout, she's a lady. There are very few of them around."

"I've sent her some flowers." Marcus looked down his nose at Tim, awaiting more information. "Lots of flowers. She'll come home to a house full of flowers, which should cheer her up."

Marcus just shook his head, "Will you never learn?"

"Clearly not, which is why I need your help. What else can I do?"

"Stop the overblown gestures, for a start. You won't

impress her by buying her things. You are just reinforcing what she already believes to be true about you."

"Which is?" said Tim cautiously.

"That you are a spoilt man who has been pampered and cossetted and thinks that he can buy or charm his way out of any situation. No offence."

"Some taken."

Chapter 19

Tim stood and stared out of his hotel-room window at a view he rarely noticed now. London was dressed in darkness and adorned with the sparkle of a million lights. Looking out over the River Thames he watched as the London Eye, a circle of bright-blue lights, turned imperceptibly. The bridges, all swathed in illuminations, drew his attention further downriver to Big Ben and the Houses of Parliament, awash with amber beams that highlighted its magnificence, even at this distance.

Tim sighed to himself. Eight years ago, this had all been so new and magical. He remembered his very first film premiere and the excitement he had felt. Also the fear and the thought that had flashed through his mind – so this is how a hedgehog feels when it's about to cross a motorway.

His jet-black limo had glided into position and the cameras had flashed their blinding-white blasts, lighting up the street like cheap fireworks. The crowd erupted into screams and the press jostled elbows in a last-ditch attempt to get the best position and capture "the" photograph of the night. A hotel footman glided forward to open the rear limo door and Tim had stepped out and beamed back a smile to out-blind the paparazzi. The Agent X film premiere had been a huge success. Anyone who was noteworthy had braved the crisp winter's evening to be a part of it and all were gushing the film's praises.

After years of small TV roles, he was finally a big-screen actor, a star before he was 25 and everyone was talking awards, fame, fortune and sequels. Days don't get much better than this, he had thought. He scribbled autographs, smiled confidently and gave a last wave. "Don't trip over, don't trip over," he recited softly as he bounded up the hotel steps and into the party.

So much had happened on the run-up to that night. He had been wrenched from wallowing in his trackie bottoms and slobbing around on his sofa onto a conveyer belt of promotional interviews and publicity shoots. This was exactly the sort of excitement he had wanted in his life. And exciting though it was, he was more than a little nervous, as very few people had actually seen the film. He had remembered how the doubt had crept in, actually not so much creeping – it had been more like a pissed teenager arriving home at 4 o'clock in the morning banging into everything and alerting everyone to their presence. Tim still harboured the fear that someone would find him out and uncover him as the average actor he was and the dream would be over.

Agent X had been how he had met Marcus, an already accomplished script writer that had taken him under his wing. He remembered Marcus at the party and how the briefest of nods had managed to convey the pride of a man watching his son lift the FA Cup. Tim had drunk far too much champagne that night. He recalled the taste of it and the sensation as the chilled liquid washed through his system.

Meeting one particular person had sent everything off on a different trajectory. He could picture the tumbling curls of blonde hair, the deep-blue eyes and amazing figure. The amount of alcohol consumed that night hadn't blurred the memory.

And that was it. That was the moment that had changed him forever, changed him into the person he was now and one he wasn't very fond of. Tim longed to bring back that naïve and unjaded person, the man unaffected by that night and the years of celebrity life that had followed. He stared again at the lights as London showed off in the dark and, for the first time in a very long time, he appreciated the sight in front of him and felt grateful.

Kate was ridiculously pleased to wake up in her own house and it was also lovely to have people staying, with the exception of Curry, the hamster, who had taken up residence in the study. He was putting Kate off from even venturing in, let alone working in there.

Sarah had been completely brilliant and had got rid of all the flowers, with the exception of the troughs, which had been too big and heavy, so Andy had lugged them to the furthest corner of the garden, where they were out of sight. Sarah had also given a basket of the most exotic flowers to Concetta, who had apparently been thrilled. They had shared a great meal and when they had finally got the very excited Amy up to bed, on her Birthday Eve, they had opened a bottle of wine and held a full trial and judgement of Timothy Calder. Sarah and Andy had been perfect friends as they had listened to the whole story of the name mix-up and had totally sided with Kate and slagged off Tim, which had made her feel a whole lot better.

Kate looked at the clock. It was only a quarter-past-six but she could hear muffled voices coming from downstairs. She slung on her dressing gown and slippers and went in search of the birthday girl. As Kate walked into her living room she was struck by the loveliness of the family scene she was presented with. Andy and Amy were sitting on the floor surrounded by ripped-up wrapping paper, both studying some Lego instructions, and Sarah was sitting in a chair reading Amy's birthday cards one by one. It looked the perfect picture of a normal, happy family.

"Happy Birthday, Amy!" Kate said, holding out a large parcel.

"Kate, you're up! Now can we put the music on?" pleaded Amy, as she skipped over to Kate. "Thanks Kate," she added, taking the big package and returning to her place next to Andy to unwrap it. "It's a Wii, it's a Wii! Kate got me a Wii! Wow, this is the best thing ever! Thank you!" and she came scrambling over the box, presents and paper to give Kate a hug.

"You're very welcome. What else did you get?" Kate sat on the arm of Sarah's chair so she had a view of the proceedings. Amy rattled through the presents, which also included a few new clothes, a new school bag and books from Sarah. Andy had clearly pushed the boat out and bought her lots of traditional games that he had enjoyed as a child and wanted to share with Amy. Kate found herself watching Sarah, who was, in turn, watching Andy and Amy intensely. When the living-room floor was cleared for the inaugural game of Wii Sports, Kate and Sarah retreated to the kitchen to sort out breakfast.

"Anything from Shaun?" asked Kate, trying to sound casual.

"No present, no card, no text, no phone call. Unless, of course, he's been to the house since midday yesterday, when I called in to put the jellies in the fridge."

"Irene?"

"No. Sadly, she *can* make it to the party, so we'll have the joy of her company later," Sarah made a snarling noise.

"So, you and Andy, what's going on there?" Kate gave Sarah a gentle nudge in the ribs as she started getting breakfast things out of the cupboard.

"Nothing," said Sarah.

"Don't you think that there should be something, though? Look at him with Amy. Look at the three of you. You make a perfect family."

"But we're not, are we? There's Shaun, and more baggage than Heathrow clears in a year!" Sarah was irritably pulling at her hair and trying to make it go in the right directions.

Kate turned around and leaned back against the cupboard, "So you would like there to be something with Andy?"

Sarah looked momentarily coy. "Might not be too awful," she

220

smiled, but it was brief. "But why start making up silly stuff like that when it's never likely to happen?"

"Stop being such a pessimist. You like him, he likes you and he adores Amy. It has got to be worth a go. What's the worst that could happen?" Kate handed Sarah bowls and plates, which she took from her, but just stood there holding them.

"Shaun. He's the worst that could happen."

"But he can't stop you seeing other people. Anyway, Andy can handle Shaun. Shaun has ruined enough of your life. Don't let him spoil something that could be... well, something special."

"Yuk. You writers are so schmaltzy," Sarah said, pulling a face before side-stepping Kate's pretend-swipe at her.

Kate and Sarah had a giggle making the food for the party. Kate was especially pleased with her cucumber crocodiles in a lettuce swamp, and Sarah's shark-infested fruit salad was quite scary. Kate had to admit that the cupcakes that had been delivered did look impressive and she was looking forward to trying one at the party, but just looking at them made her feel sad and cross at the same time. The cupcakes had had a small makeover so that they would fit in with the animal theme of the party and now had jelly snakes coiled on top of every one. There were also stacks of sandwiches, which, thanks to a set of animal cutters, were now shaped like teddies, ducks and dinosaurs – although probably pushing the theme a little, they were sure the children would enjoy them. The cake was a work of art and had taken Sarah most of the day before to perfect; it was a chocolate rabbit cake and trying to keep it a secret from Amy had been the hardest thing. They merrily loaded the things into Kate's and Sarah's cars and Kate could sense the change in Sarah and knew what was troubling her.

"Don't let him spoil it. If he turns up we'll just call the police and Irene won't cause any real trouble with Amy there." She put an arm round Sarah's shoulder and gave her a squeeze. Sarah gave a weak smile in return.

"I know, but even if he doesn't turn up, he's still this dark shadow looming over everything, peeing on any signs of fun."

"There will be no peeing on anything today, trust me," and she gave her another hug for good measure.

They all gave an inward sigh of relief when there was no sign of Shaun at the house, although Amy was a little disappointed that there were no more cards or presents waiting for her. Thankfully she was easily distracted by the prospect of another 12 presents arriving with her friends shortly. A flurry of activity saw balloons blown up, bunting hung in the garden, and the food, all carefully covered in clingfilm, laid out on the kitchen table with a space for the rabbit cake that was hiding in Sarah's bedroom until its grand entrance. Amy danced about the garden in her new dress, ignoring the regular calls from her mother to not get dirty before the party. Just as the adults all slumped onto the new plastic garden chairs, the door bell buzzed. A very hairy young man appeared carrying two large black boxes with carry handles.

"Hi, I'm Steve, Esme's nephew. I'm guessing this is the right house for the party?" He nodded at the balloons and large number six dangling around the doorframe.

"You're a good detective. Let's hope you're as good at entertaining a tribe of rowdy kids," said Sarah, ushering him through the house to the garden. Steve decided to set up on the grass so that the children could sit on cushions on the patio. He put up some hinged boards and placed a series of black boxes behind them. Kate and Andy were quite intrigued and made sure they were in a good position for when it started. Kate was feeling quite relaxed as she sat enjoying the intermittent sunshine that peeped out sporadically from behind the passing clouds. She would be on orange-squash duty once the children arrived, so it was best to enjoy the short spell of peace while it lasted. Her moment of peace was soon shattered by a thundering of knuckles on the side gate. Andy was up on his feet and opening the gate before Kate could even grab her mobile, just in case it was time for the emergency call she feared might be needed.

"Hello," said Andy with a deep sigh of relief as he opened the gate fully and stood back to let Irene and two large pound-shop bags come past.

"You took ya time! Didn't ya hear me banging?" Andy chose to ignore the ludicrous suggestion and offered to take the bags. "They ain't for you," she said as she marched around the patio, bumping Kate with one of the bags as she did so.

"Ow," protested Kate. "Hello, Irene," she added, sounding a lot friendlier than she felt, but Irene ignored her and headed into the house, closely followed by Andy.

"Nanny Irene!" shouted Amy when she saw her.

"'appy birfday darlin'. Nanny's got loads of brillyant stuff for ya." Irene put down the bags and gave Amy kiss and a hug.

"Hello, Irene, glad you could join us," said Sarah, with a very fake smile and her fingers crossed behind her back. "Can I get you a drink of anything?"

"Anyfin strong and large," she said, without looking at Sarah.

"One Incredible Hulk coming right up," Sarah said, as she went to source some grown-up drinks. She was just pondering over whether Southern Comfort ever went out of date, when she was aware of someone else in the room. She turned round quickly, looking startled.

"You livin' on ya nerves, are ya?" laughed Irene. "Wonder why that is?" She plonked herself down on the sofa. Irene appeared to have attempted to style her own hair today, which had made it look as if she had an Abyssinian guinea pig living on her head and it was having a particularly bad fur day. Sarah poured some Southern Comfort into a tumbler and handed it to Irene. Irene took the glass, but kept it held out and sniffed loudly. Sarah obligingly added more Southern Comfort until Irene nodded.

"So, any update on Shaun?" Sarah said, trying to sound

nonchalant as she busied herself with pouring wine for her and Andy.

"They haven't found him yet, but they will. They got people helping them wiv their enquiries." She took a large swig from the glass and grimaced.

"That's good, then. Hopefully he'll turn up soon." Sarah picked up the wine glasses and turned to leave.

"You won' get away wiv it, ya know that don't ya?" Sarah paused for a moment but chose to ignore Irene's goading and took the drinks out to the garden. Amy was busily unwrapping another of Nanny Irene's presents.

"So what have you got from Nanny Irene?" asked Sarah.

"Err, there's a man with no clothes on, a book of scary monsters..."

"How to draw mythical beasts," added Andy, trying to help.

"And this." Amy held up what looked like a doll attached to a kitchen-roll holder. Andy handed Sarah the box and she read out what it said.

"Polly the Pole Dancer, watch her twirl to the rhythm. Requires four AA batteries. I bet she does," smirked Sarah. "Let's see this man, then. Do they come as a pair? Has he got miniature ten-pound notes to put in her..."

"Sarah!" cut in Andy, "I think the man is meant to be Tarzan. There's pictures of chimps on the packaging."

"Course its bleedin Tarzan," croaked Irene as she appeared behind them, puffing on a recently lit cigarette.

"Sorry, Irene, we've got young children arriving any minute. Please could you go down the side of the house or, better still, not smoke at all." Irene huffed grumpily, but left the garden by the side gate as requested.

As if arriving by bus, all of Amy's friends descended in the following five minutes, all carrying neatly wrapped gifts, cards and broad smiles. Sarah was a little surprised that all the parents waved their children off without even offering to stay, or providing a phone number in case there was a problem. Look-e-likey Tarzan was soon forgotten once Amy started opening the latest toys, games and stationery. Kate did her first successful squash round and the children settled down for Steve to start the animal entertainment.

As it turned out, Steve was actually very good with the children. He told them interesting facts about the animals before he brought them out for them to have a closer look at. There was a gecko, a chameleon and a small bearded dragon, which held their attention well. Next up was a Dumbo Rat, which was quite simply one of the cutest things Sarah had ever seen. He was very unimaginatively called Dumbo and was very pale brown in colour with ears the size of chocolate buttons. Kate, on the other hand, was now wishing that she hadn't put her plastic chair in such a good viewing spot, as she was now only a small rodent's hop away from the action. Dumbo was handed around and was happy to be stroked by everyone and caused a simultaneous round of "ahhhh" when he decided to wash his face. An African hedgehog was up next and she was called Honey and was quite small and very blonde. Steve held her up to Sarah's face.

"There's a definite resemblance," he joked, looking at the two spikey blonde-topped females. Honey got a little scared of the children, who were now a little overexcited, and kept turning herself into a ball, so it was time for her to go back to the safety of her box. Last up, and the grand finale of the show, was a milk snake. One of the girls started to cry as soon as she saw him, but Steve was very gentle with them and within three minutes the same little girl had the snake proudly wrapped around her sleeve. Andy took a picture of each of the children holding the snake and one of the braver boys even had it wrapped around his neck like a tie.

Irene slinked back into the garden while the photos were being taken and stood on the grass near Kate's chair, breathing heavily. Kate looked over and smiled at Irene, who glared back at her. The children were all ferried into the house to wash their hands after handling the animals, and then back into the garden to have the food picnic-style. Andy insisted on humming the *Jaws* theme tune as he brought out the shark-infested fruit salad, but only the adults got the joke.

Sarah was busy sorting out party bags when there was a loud bang on the front door. She was in two minds whether to answer it or not but, deciding it was probably an over-eager parent, she opened it and was very surprised to see the police sergeant who had searched the house previously, standing there looking rather serious as only police officers can. The difference this time was that he had two other stern-looking policemen in tow and a small army of them coming up the path.

"Good morning, Mrs Greasley. This is my colleague, Inspector Chauvin, who would like to talk to you down at the station, whilst my colleagues here do some more detailed investigations of your property."

"But it's my daughter's birthday party. It's happening now." She stumbled over the words as the officers pushed past her. "Am I under arrest?"

"No madam, not at all, just helping us with our enquiries," said Inspector Chauvin, as he came into the hall and shut the door behind the last officer.

"Then please can you wait just 20 minutes whilst my daughter hands out the party bags? These children have been left in my care by their parents. I can't just leave."

"I quite understand. Twenty minutes is fine. Sergeant, tell the men to wait in the garden."

"No, not the garden!" Sarah followed them hastily outside to see the policemen moving the plastic chairs and tables off the patio and the children all standing open-mouthed.

"Can I have your attention, team? Mrs Greasley and her family will need just 20 minutes. So if you'd all like to just wait over there," said the Sergeant, indicating to where Steve was hastily packing up his boxes. Andy was putting his camera away when one of the boys came over to him, "Please can I have a photo with the policemen?" he asked, looking longingly at the row of uniformed men.

"I don't know if they're allowed to," said Andy, looking at the sergeant for some guidance.

"That's fine. Come on, stand in the middle," said the sergeant, and they all grouped together around the child for a photo. This set in motion a string of requests from the other children, which the officers kindly obliged. Amy had her photo taken, too, the birthday girl surrounded by smiling policemen. She was very keen to see their handcuffs, which caused almost as much excitement as the snake. The inspector stuck to Sarah like a bad smell and followed her back into the house.

Sarah waited by the front door in her desperation to stop any parents seeing the police, although the fact that there was a large police van outside and her neighbours were hanging out of their front doors was a bit of a giveaway. As the parents arrived, Sarah called out the child's name and Kate whisked them away from the police and through the house. She then thrust a party bag at them and away they went. When the last child finally went, Sarah realised that she was shaking like a leaf. Andy appeared and pulled her into hug. "It's okay, just tell the truth and it'll be fine."

"But I don't think it will ever be fine again," she spluttered. Andy gave a nervous smile at the inspector and they all went outside, where the sergeant was in a huddle with his team and Irene was puffing happily on a new cigarette. She grinned a yellow-toothed grin at Sarah and Andy as they came outside.

"Mummy, that was the best party ever!" said Amy, hugging Sarah, "It was just like the TV programmes Andy lets me watch sometimes when you're at work."

"Sorry," said Andy, as he gave Amy a pretend glare.

"Whoops, sorry Andy," she giggled.

"We need to go to the station now while my men work out here. Everyone else will need to leave," the inspector said to Sarah.

Kate stepped forward. "I'll take Amy and her presents back

to mine in my car. Andy, you can take Sarah's car and one of us will pick you up from the police station later." Kate was stroking Sarah's arm as she said it.

"Won't you need someone to stay and lock up?" Andy asked the inspector, as two of the others appeared through the gate carrying shovels and a strange instrument with a long handle and set them down next to the patio.

"No, you can leave the keys."

"If you're taking the patio up, please let me give you a hand. This cost a lot of money and when you find nothing, you don't want to have to pay compensation." Irene snorted in the background. "I can help you take them up quickly, without damaging them, and I promise to keep out of the way." The inspector was clearly torn by Andy's reasonable request; he looked to his sergeant, who shrugged.

"Okay, but if my sergeant says leave, you leave or you will be looking at a charge of obstructing the course of justice. Got it?"

"No problem, Inspector, you're the boss. Thank you." And he went over to the officers who had brought in the equipment to see what they were planning to use.

"Right, let's get these ladies out of here then, please," said the sergeant, indicating Sarah, Kate, Irene and Amy. Amy set about putting her presents into bags, Kate put a supportive arm around a stunned-looking Sarah and Irene stalked over to the sergeant.

"Carn't I stay, I am his muvver."

"Sorry, Mrs Greasley, I don't think that's wise," and he ushered her to the side gate. Irene looked furtively over her shoulder before speaking in a hushed voice to the sergeant.

"If ya find him, do I get a reward or somethin', for like givin' you the information?"

"No, sorry, Mrs Greasley, but I'm sure it has helped with our enquiries, so thank you."

"But you are arresting her, ain't ya?"

"No, Mrs Greasley, but we will be questioning her. If you'd like to leave now," he indicated the gate.

"But I told ya, she confessed it all to me, so what d'ya want to listen to more of her lies for?" said Irene in a whisper, but Irene's whispering skills were not as good as she'd thought. Sarah lurched forward and Kate failed to grab her. Thankfully Andy was quicker off the mark and took the full force of Sarah as she launched herself at Irene, fists clenched,

"You utter cow I'll…"

"No, Sarah!" shouted Andy over the top of her, to drown out the threats, "Sarah, think! For God's sake, think. This is what she wants!" Sarah wrestled against Andy, but held her tongue and soon lost her impetus and slumped against Andy, her whole body shaking. All the policemen were now standing a lot closer and the inspector, in particular, was looking as though he was on red alert.

"See? I told you she was a psycho, din't I?" sniffed Irene, as she sauntered out of the gate, being careful not to step on the patio as she did so.

"What's the matter, Mummy? Has Nanny Irene upset you?" asked Amy. Andy pulled Amy into a cuddle with him and her mother, as Sarah was struggling to speak.

"Yes, she has a bit, but it's going to be oksy. Mummy is going to have a chat to the policeman and sort it all out." He tilted Sarah's head up so he could make eye contact with her, and she nodded. "I'm going to help the policemen here and Kate and you are going to play at her house. Okay?"

"Okay," said Amy, looking suddenly not very okay at all. "I didn't get a birthday cake," she said, her lip starting to wobble,

"The rabbit is in my bedroom," said Sarah, and all the policemen suddenly looked interested again.

Chapter 20

Kate and Amy were both silent all the way back to Kate's house. A couple of times Kate opened her mouth to speak to Amy, but each time she judged that what she was about to say was totally banal and it was better just to smile at Amy in the rear-view mirror and keep quiet. Halfway home she switched on the radio, which helped a little. As Kate turned into her driveway and trundled up the gravel, she saw a hunched figure of a man sitting on her front- door step. Kate stopped the car a little abruptly until she registered who it was. She was still expecting Shaun to appear from nowhere, at any time. Kate recognised the figure and felt an instant spike of anger.

Tim looked up as he heard the car and jumped to his feet. Kate left the car in front of the garage and walked around to let Amy out of the car. Tim was now walking round in very tight circles and the look on his face was changing between a big, welcoming grin and a worried scowl; it was rather disconcerting. Thankfully, Amy came to the rescue and ran over to Tim, and they exchanged hellos while Kate gathered the things from the car. Whatever he was here for, Kate didn't need this right now.

"Would you like a hand with those?" Tim said, as he strode purposefully towards her.

"No, I'll manage, thank you," Kate said curtly, as she

struggled to retain her grip on Tarzan. Tim registered the still-open boot and headed over to Kate's car anyway.

"I'll bring the rest," he said cheerfully. Kate shook her head in annoyance and walked up the steps to the front door. She could hear the phone ringing inside. She fumbled with the key, but eventually managed to unlock the door, and she and Amy tumbled inside. Kate set down the armful of detritus in the living room and Amy settled down next to the pile and started going through her new things. Kate reached for the phone just as it stopped ringing. If it is important they will call back, Kate thought. Tim came in and shut the door behind him. Kate stood in the hallway and stared at him, cross at his presumption that he was actually welcome inside.

"Interesting," smiled Tim, looking at the pole-dancing doll.

"Birthday presents. Amy is six today."

"Happy birthday, Amy!" said Tim. "Here, have this in lieu of a present," he said pulling a 20-pound note from his pocket. Amy appeared at his side in a second.

"Thank you, Tim. This is cool! I'd rather have this than a loo present." She turned to Kate, "I can have the money, can't I, Kate?"

"Of course," said Kate, slightly puzzled by the question.

"It's just that Tim is a bit like a stranger." Amy whispered the last bit and Kate smiled.

"I see. Good girl for checking, but even if you don't know Tim very well, I do." She paused as she thought about this statement because she didn't actually know him well at all, but she wasn't going to explain all that to Amy. "So, yes, it's fine for you have the money."

"You look like you've got loads of presents there, Amy."

"I have and I had the best party ever."

"Great! Was there jelly and ice cream?" asked Tim.

"Yes, but there were lots of policemen and a snake!"

"Wow! That's exciting."

"We all had our photograph taken with them and they want

231

to talk to Mummy." She lost her excitement and went quiet again.

"So a police raid at your sixth birthday party! She's starting early," laughed Tim. Kate did a slow, meaningful blink for Tim's benefit, handed the things she'd taken from him to Amy, who went to the living room. Kate held her position in the hall and regarded Tim expectantly. Tim was still watching Amy, until he became aware of Kate's intense glare.

"I, err… I'm not sure why I'm here." Tim shoved his hands into his pockets, which made his shoulders hunch up and give him the look of a naughty schoolboy in front of the head teacher.

"Sorry, I can't help you there, I have absolutely no idea why you are here, either. Frankly, Tim, now is not a good time for me."

"Sorry. Why did the police raid her party?"

"I don't really think that's any concern of yours."

"No, you're right." There was a painfully long pause, during which Tim studied the neat black and white diamond-shaped tiles that covered the hall and Kate studied Tim. "I guess I just wanted to say sorry. Again. Make sure you understood that I meant it. Oh, and check you got the flowers," he said, scanning the rooms from the hall and not finding a single flower in sight, which made him blink involuntarily a few times. Kate had to admit that Tim did look as though he meant it. He looked dejected, not his usual commanding self, and definitely less self-assured.

"Okay."

"Okay?" said Tim, searching Kate's face for any signs of a reaction.

"Yes. Okay. I believe that you are sorry," Kate said with a shrug, unsure of what else he was expecting from her. "You know, that was a really low thing to do. You knew I'd got the names mixed up and still you…" Kate felt a pang of anger and stopped herself. She was not about to start shouting at Tim. Amy had witnessed enough drama for one day. She went to pull her cardigan around herself and realised she wasn't wearing one, so ended up crossing her arms instead.

"You are completely right. I'm not here to defend what I did, only to say that I deeply regret it and I know I've messed things up, but if there's any way we could still be friends…" Tim ran out of words and just looked hopefully at Kate. She found it was very hard to stay cross with Tim even if you really, really wanted to.

"Tim," she started, but she was interrupted by the phone. It was a welcome intrusion as she had no idea what she was going to say. "I'd better get that," she said as she went to answer the phone and noticed that Tim followed her into the living room and sat down on the floor next to Amy and started having a closer look at Polly the pole dancer.

"Hello," said Kate as she sat down in the neighbouring armchair so she could watch Tim and Amy.

"Kate, you are alive. You have not been abducted by aliens or sold into white slavery. Fantastic!" declared Didi.

"Didi!" exclaimed Kate with horror. "Oh, my goodness, I am so sorry!" How could she have forgotten about taking Didi home? Kate's brain raced ahead at high speed, trying to find a solution to the dilemma she now found herself in, but nothing came to mind.

"I take it there's a problem?"

"It's a long story involving a police raid at a birthday party, which I'll explain later, but I'm sure we can sort something out."

"Ooh, sounds like my kind of party. It's just that they're getting a bit twitchy here. There's already someone in my room, you see, so there's no room at the inn, as it were," explained Didi, so Kate's first solution of taking her home tomorrow was knocked out of the ball park. "I could see about a train?" offered Didi half-heartedly.

"Didi, can you give me five minutes? Just five minutes and I promise I'll come up with a solution and I'll call you straight back. Okay?"

"Okay," said Didi, brightening up. Kate put the phone down and surveyed the two pretty faces that were awaiting her update.

"I promised to take my friend Didi home to London this afternoon and settle her in. She's the one who has been recuperating." Tim nodded his understanding. Kate looked from Tim to Amy, fleetingly considered leaving Amy in Tim's care, and then dismissed it speedily as a very bad option. One call from Lumina or Jackie and Tim would be off in a helicopter, and Amy would most likely be abandoned here or dumped on Pippa.

"Can I help?" Tim said, as he got up and came and sat on the sofa, which was next to Kate's chair. He perched on the edge and waited for her response.

"Thank you, but I don't think you can help. I'll think of something," Kate tried to sound confident and in control but, with Sarah at a police station, Andy helping the police dig up goodness knows what in Sarah's garden and everyone else she was close to either in London or Australia, there was nobody else left that she trusted to do either job.

"Kate, please let me help." Tim's voice was soft and slightly pleading. "I could look after Amy. We get on, don't we Amy?"

"Can you cook?" asked Amy, with a small frown.

"Ah no, but we could get around that. My driver is just up the road in the pub. It's okay, he's watching the football not drinking," said Tim, quickly turning to Kate to reassure her.

"Sorry, Tim, Sarah has left me in loco parentis. I couldn't possibly let anyone else look after her."

"I understand. So that settles it, then. Terry and I will pick Didi up and take her home and settle her in. I need to be in London tonight anyway, so it's practically on the way home. Where does she live exactly?" He said pulling out his mobile.

"Somewhere near Hampstead Heath. She's given me the postcode for the sat nav. But, Tim, I couldn't really ask you to…"

Tim reached out and took Kate's hand. The familiar zing ran up her arm and they both flinched at the contact.

"No, stop, Kate, please let me do this. It's the least I can do. Please?" Kate gently pulled her hand away and took a deep breath. She knew that she had little choice and, to be honest, she fancied Didi's chances of survival with Tim a lot higher than Amy's. Anyway, Didi could most definitely give as good as she got, and it really was the only option Kate had right now.

"Okay," she sighed reluctantly, but then added, "Thank you, it's kind of you." Tim jumped to his feet and for a moment she thought he was going to punch the air. He looked quite elated. He patted Amy affectionately on the head as he left the room.

"Bye, Amy, enjoy the rest of your birthday," and he followed Kate into the kitchen, where she scribbled down Didi's details. Tim got on the mobile to drag a reluctant Terry away from the big match.

"Had you been waiting here long?" Kate asked as he was leaving.

"A couple of hours in the car."

"Right," nodded Kate.

"And another hour sitting here." He pointed at the step. "If I get piles as a result, you know I'll sue you, don't you?" grinned Tim, replacing his sunglasses before deftly jumping out of the way as Kate took a swipe at him.

"And then I'll sell the story of Timothy Calder's piles to the press and make a fortune!"

One of the police constables, who looked rather old to still be a constable, was setting up a strange-looking piece of kit on the grass. Andy went over to have a closer look. The equipment looked like a metal pole with a long, thin cylinder on one end. There was also a box with a small screen on the handle and some wicked-looking wraparound black glasses.

"That's an interesting bit of kit," said Andy eyeing the

strange contraption.

"It's a specialised type of laser ground scanner. It's really a bit of a hobby of mine. I do a bit of archaeology, but the kit works just as well for something like this," he said proudly.

"What's it do, then?" Andy picked up the special glasses and had a little look through them.

"It scans the ground and records any variances or disturbances in the layers underneath."

"Like a metal detector?"

"No," said the constable, looking put out and taking back the glasses, "not exactly like a metal detector. This is a sophisticated piece of kit. It can show you where alterations have been made to the natural lay of the land hundreds of years previously, like building foundations and burial chambers."

"What's it going to tell you here, then," he indicated the patio.

"Whether there is anything buried underneath it, however deep down it may be." Andy didn't say anything else; he just nodded and went to stand out of the way until the other police officers let him know when he could start moving the slabs. Andy hated waiting around and every minute he wasn't doing something he was worrying about Sarah. Wondering what they were asking her, what she was telling them and generally trying to work out what the hell was going on. He knew Sarah wasn't telling him everything and he was afraid of what she was leaving out. Andy wanted to protect Sarah, but he knew all he could do was wait to hear from her and then maybe he would be able to work out what he could do to help. For now, he'd just have to concentrate on saving her patio.

Eventually, they set about taking up the patio one slab at a time, with the officers taking photographs and meticulously recording what they were doing. Andy couldn't get over how much quicker it was to take up the patio than it had been to lay it. The sun spent the afternoon beating down on them and was only now starting to wane. The constable with the scanner had been walking up and down every time they moved a slab, but gave no indication whether he'd found anything interesting. Andy knew that all that was under there was rubble. When the slabs were all cleared and neatly set in piles around the lawn, the officers ushered Andy out of the way, so he went inside to get a long, cold drink, but there was only water. He leaned against the kitchen sink and enjoyed the cool draught coming in through the open kitchen window. He wondered if he'd be able to get the slabs back down again today, but he doubted it. He was knackered and emotionally drained as there was no word from Sarah or the inspector. Andy realised that the constable and the sergeant were having a conversation just by the kitchen window and were clearly unaware of Andy's close proximity.

"So, there's definitely something under there other than hardcore?" the sergeant asked.

"Yep. Do you see here there's a silhouette? It's probably only a couple of feet down. It sort of resembles a head and a torso, but it's vague, so that's only a guess. So he's either in pieces or he was very short, Sarge," suggested the constable. Despite the sweat he had built up moments earlier, Andy felt himself go cold, and all he could do was stand frozen to the spot and listen.

"Okay, I'll get the on-call SOCO down here. They'll love me on a Saturday. You and the boys had better get digging. Be careful – we don't want to damage any evidence."

"Right, Sarge," and Andy heard the clang as spades were picked up and the digging started.

Tim was very pleased with how things had panned out. At least Kate was talking to him and, better still, he was now doing something useful to help her and hopefully show her that he wasn't a total arse. He knew there was a lot of damage to mend, but this was a good start. Terry had clearly got over his annoyance at missing the end of the football match and had brought Tim a couple of ham rolls from the pub, for which Tim was very grateful. He had only just finished the second roll when Terry called out, "Here we are, boss". He turned the car into a side road and they followed a very neat line of beech trees to the front of an imposing three-storey Victorian red-brick building that was perfectly symmetrical, with an ornate clock tower in the middle, under which was a very over-the-top entrance with a large arched door, at the top of a flight of small stone steps. The many window frames were bright white and stood out against the red of the brick. There was a large, fancy sign outside, stating "St Gaudentia House – rest, recuperation and respite". Tim got out of the car and went to speak to Terry through the driver's window, which Terry duly lowered.

"Have you got your chauffeur's hat?" asked Tim, putting on his sunglasses and brushing crumbs off his crisp white t-shirt.

"Yeah," Terry said, as he reluctantly leaned over and retrieved it from the glove compartment. He clearly didn't like wearing it, even on the very few occasions that required him to do so, which were film premieres and when Tim wanted to particularly impress someone. Terry put the black hat with a patent black stripe on his head and was about to adjust it in the mirror when Tim swiped it.

"Thank you!" he said, and he put it on before bounding up the steps two at a time. Inside, the reception area had a hotel feel about it, with a large, highly polished wooden reception desk to the left, a series of large brown-leather sofas on the right, and an expanse of tiled flooring between the two. Tim approached the shiny desk and the young, smartly dressed receptionist looked up and beamed a welcoming smile; she looked a little startled by the vision in front of her, but soon recovered herself.

"Good afternoon. How can I help you?"

"Taxi for Didi," Tim said, with a tip of his chauffeur's cap.

"Well, well, well. Now this must be the surprise Kate was talking about," came a strong voice from the sofas. Tim pulled down his sunglasses so he could see better. Sunglasses were standard issue for all celebrities and must be worn at all times, in all situations and in all climates. However, sometimes it just wasn't practical. His eyes alighted on a slender, well-dressed woman of advancing years, wearing a smart, navy trouser suit with a bright-turquoise top underneath. Her hair was short and very neatly styled, and she had the face of a fifties' movie star. Tim was surprised; this wasn't the little old lady he had been expecting. He walked over and doffed his cap, before taking hold of Didi's wheelie case.

"Ma'am, Timothy Calder at your service."

"Oh my, this really is my lucky day," she winked.

"Do you have everything?"

"Knickers and passport," said Didi, tapping her shoulder bag.

"You're a minx, aren't you, which is exactly my kind of gal," said Tim as he linked arms with Didi and they strode out of St Gaudentia House with the receptionist staring after them open-mouthed. As they stepped into the fading sun, Terry was out of the car in a flash and opened the rear door, which he held whilst Didi got inside. He took his hat from Tim, as well as the case, and Tim got in the other side.

"Right then, Didi, we have the sat nav co-ordinates, so you now have my undivided attention for the next..." he looked at Terry as he was putting on his seat belt.

"Hour and half, depending on traffic," replied Terry. "Er, the address we've got, boss?" said Terry tentatively, but Tim was waving him away. Terry shook his head and started the car.

"So, tell me all about yourself, Didi," said Tim.

"In an hour and a half, you'll only get the edited highlights!" Didi laughed. That was to be the start of an hour and half of non-stop story-telling between the pair, which was frequently interspersed with laughter as they triggered memories for each other, and both had equally fascinating tales to tell.

By the time the scenery had changed from green fields to motorway and then to grey city buildings, they were chatting as though they'd been friends all their lives. Terry kept looking in the rear-view mirror in a feeble attempt to catch Tim's attention.

"We're nearly there, boss."

"Ooh, so we are," said Didi, recognising the streets out of the window. "My word, that was quick."

Tim looked out, too, but was not impressed by what he saw. They appeared to be entering a council estate, which was grimmer than the set he had worked on for the recent gangster film he'd been in. The buildings were grey concrete tombstones that had attracted the only grey clouds they had seen all day.

"Is this it?" Tim failed to hide the horror in his voice.

"Yes. If you drop me over there, I can go straight up in the lifts." Didi pointed to a pair of obscene, graffiti-strewn doors. It was impossible to tell what colour they had originally been painted as none of the paint was visible under the graffiti. On either side of the door were two groups of youths, who were now staring at the approaching luxury car. Tim was mentally running through the list Kate had given him about checking that the heating and water were working and settling her in before going to get her some shopping. She had failed to mention that Didi lived in a war zone.

"Right, Didi, I'm under strict instructions from Kate, so I need to check that the lift is working, then go and put the kettle on, so that when you come up you can have a nice cuppa. Keys?" Didi handed him the keys.

"Oh, you don't need to do that," she protested, but Tim was already out of the car and waiting for Terry to put the driver's window down.

"I'll check it out and you get ready to get her out of here if these guys kick off, okay?"

"I did try to warn you, boss, when I realised where it was," stressed Terry.

"Okay. Call me if you have any problems," said Tim, and Terry nodded and kept the engine running. Tim put on his shades and his best confident smile and he sauntered over to the double doors.

"Gents," he said, as he approached the two groups of young men, who appeared to be taking it in turns to spit on the ground.

There was no reply and, to Tim's utter relief, they didn't attempt to stop him entering the building.

Once inside, the smell assaulted his nasal passages and made him wretch. The urine of the ages was fermenting in the hallway. He quickly checked the scrap of paper from Kate: "Flat 524, fifth floor". Tim noted that one of the lifts had a large out-of-order sticker across it, but the other one was waiting with its doors open. He stepped inside and pressed the number five button. Nothing happened. He pressed it again and then spotted that there were no lights on and this one, too, was obviously out of order.

Tim stepped out of the lift, went through another set of double doors with matching graffiti and headed up the stairs. The concrete stairs were a strange affair as they were actually outside and zig-zagged upwards in blocks of ten steps. The stagnant city air was a blessed relief after the eau de urinal he had just encountered. Tim bounded up the stairs; his regular trips to the gym were paying off, but even so, he was very pleased finally to reach the fifth floor.

Each faded door had a number screwed to it and Tim mentally ticked them off as he went along the outside walkway, which was littered with rubbish and general filth. As he reached the door of number 524 and was about to put the key in the lock he realised something was missing. The lock itself had been punched out – there was now an egg-sized hole where it should have been and the door was slightly open.

Tim peered through the hole. It was dark inside and he could hear voices. They were young, male voices with local accents and lots of street talk. Tim stepped back and looked around him for inspiration. He quickly whipped off his sunglasses, expensive watch and t-shirt, tied the pristine white t-shirt in a knot and dropped it on the ground. He rolled it about briefly and then put it back on. He brushed off any obvious lumps of dirt and tried not to think about what it was exactly. He wiped his hands on his shoes to take off the shine and then messed up his hair as best he could. Taking a deep breath, he hunched his shoulders and stumbled inside flat number 524.

Chapter 21

Andy was still standing by the sink with his glass of water in his hand. His mouth was dry and although he could still feel the odd trickle of sweat running down his brow he no longer felt hot; if anything he felt shivery. He looked up as the back door was wrenched open and the sergeant came inside, jerking Andy back to life. The two men regarded each other. The sergeant faltered slightly as he saw the look on Andy's face. Andy had never felt so confused and afraid in his life. He stared at the sergeant, waiting to hear the next instalment.

"I'm afraid you need to leave now." The sergeant reached out an arm to usher Andy out of the kitchen and through to the hall. Andy didn't move. Aware of the dryness in his mouth he took a large slug of water and tipped the rest away. He could hear the sound of shovels digging into the ground outside. "You'd best leave me the keys," said the sergeant and he held his hand out expectantly.

Andy stared at his hand for a moment. He was finding it hard to think straight. He was still processing the conversation he had just overheard, still trying to find an alternative explanation. He couldn't believe that Shaun was dead and, even more, he didn't want to think about the implications for Sarah.

Sarah couldn't have killed Shaun, he was certain of it. She

couldn't have killed him in cold blood. Had Shaun wound her up? Had he threatened her? How could Shaun be buried under the patio? Andy had laid the patio himself; he knew that there was only rubble underneath it. Sarah couldn't have moved the slabs on her own, could she? Andy took a deep breath and tried to order his ridiculous thoughts, which were spiralling out of control. All he knew was what he'd heard, that the police believed that Shaun was dead, cut up into chunks and buried under the patio.

Andy gripped the sink and took another deep breath. He didn't want this to be happening; he wanted to press "pause" on his life so he could just take a few minutes to work out what had happened and, most importantly, why Sarah hadn't told him what she knew.

"Are you okay, sir?"

"Yeah, I'll be okay." Andy clearly didn't look okay. He turned the tap on and splashed his face with some cold water and dried it off with his t-shirt. "Actually, can I just wait in the car?" Andy pulled the window shut and locked it, partly for security and partly to block out the digging noise, which was now starting to disturb him greatly.

"I think it's best that you get off home now, sir. We may need to speak to you again, so don't go leaving the area now, will you?" The sergeant stepped forward, with his hand still outstretched, awaiting the house keys from Andy. Andy ignored the gesture.

"Have you heard from the inspector? Are they charging Sarah?" Andy knew that once he left they wouldn't tell him anything. He also felt he couldn't leave. In some macabre way he needed to see evidence that it was Shaun who was buried in the garden. He wanted to know for sure. He couldn't take half a story back to Kate and he couldn't think about Amy right now. Tears sprang to his eyes as he realised that with Shaun gone and Sarah on a murder charge, Irene was her next of kin. No child deserved that; least of all Amy.

"Sorry, I haven't heard from Inspector Chauvin, I expect

they are still interviewing Mrs Greasley. Keys please." The sergeant looked as though he was starting to lose his patience. He was obviously keen to get back to the excitement that was unfolding in the garden. Cases like this didn't come along very often in tranquil Northamptonshire and Andy knew from all the crime shows on TV that CID and SOCO would be taking over shortly. The local boys in blue would be off back to the station to write up their notes and move onto the next case, which would be considerably less interesting than this one.

"Look, how about I sit in the car for an hour or so and if there's no news by then, I'll give you the keys and I'll go home. Okay?"

"With respect, sir, we will not be providing you with updates," and the sergeant walked up the hall, opened the front door and beckoned Andy out. "If you want to wait, that's fine. Just keep away from the house," he instructed strictly.

"I'll be in that blue car, just there." Andy pointed to Sarah's Beetle, which was parked behind the police van.

"Okay, sir, but please don't bother my officers," and with that he shut the door behind Andy.

Inside Sarah's car, it was warm and the plastic seating was giving off a nauseating scent; no wonder kids got travel sick. He wound the stiff little handle and the window jolted down. He adjusted the seat so that he could stretch out his legs and looked around in search of something to eat. Andy realised that apart from a jam sandwich and a slice of melon that had doubled as a shark's fin in the fruit salad, he'd had nothing else to eat. All he found hidden at the back of the glove box was a small bag of jelly sweets, but they would just have to do.

His phone buzzed in his pocket and he took it out. It was a text from Kate to say that Amy was fine and asking if there was any news. He texted back "no", then looked around outside. The street was quiet and the smell of a nearby barbecue wafted through the open window; most likely some happy family was having a normal summer's evening and how he wished that the happy family barbecue had been him and Sarah and Amy.

Kate was pleased with the quick response from Andy, but not the content. Why didn't men make the most of the letter count on text messages? Kate thought. They always seemed to waste a text with short answers, which cost them the same to send as a full paragraph. Tim had taken one worry off her, but she was left with a whole other bundle of worries about what was happening with Sarah and why they were digging up her lovely new patio. From what Kate had witnessed, it seemed most likely that Irene was sending them on a wild-goose chase in an attempt to get Sarah into serious trouble. Kate had faith that the police would quickly realise that Sarah was the innocent party in all this, but it had already been a few hours and they couldn't have realised it yet or they would have let her come home. Perhaps Irene and Shaun were in it together; she wouldn't put it past them. For some reason they had spent a lot of time and effort trying to make Sarah out to be an unfit mother. Maybe this was another attempt at them gaining custody of Amy.

Thankfully, Amy seemed surprisingly fine. She hadn't mentioned the police again and hadn't asked Kate any questions. Her new toys and books had kept her occupied for quite some time and then a game of catch in the garden had occupied another chunk of time. When Amy started to look tired, Kate suggested that she watch just a bit of television and then they would make home-made pizza for tea. It looked more and more likely that it would be just the two of them eating together tonight.

Kate found a suitable children's channel and settled herself down on the sofa. Amy came and sat on her lap and snuggled her head into Kate's shoulder. Kate put her arms around her and cuddled her.

"Is my Mummy in trouble for shouting at Nanny Irene?" asked Amy, her eyes still glued to the television.

"No, sweetie, they just want to talk to your mummy, that's all."

"Is it about Daddy?"

Kate was growing increasingly uncomfortable with the conversation; she felt that how she answered these questions might stay with Amy for a long time, so she had to be as honest as she could without alarming her.

"Yes it is, because everyone wants to check that Daddy is all right."

"Daddy has run away, hasn't he?" Amy still didn't move her head. She looked as if she was talking to the television rather than to Kate.

"We don't know what has happened, that's what the police are trying to find out."

"I heard him shouting at Mummy. It was dark outside. He said he was in trouble and had to get away before someone killed him." Kate was a little taken aback by this. Amy seemed to be the one with the most information, all of a sudden, and it seemed that she might know more than Kate and Andy put together. But, in her desire to unearth the details Kate was still careful not to upset Amy.

"Were you meant to be asleep?" Amy nodded, rubbing her head up and down Kate's shoulder as she did so. "Did you hear Mummy and Daddy talking?" Amy nodded again.

"Daddy wasn't being very kind to Mummy. He was shouting a lot." Kate didn't know if it was wise to make Amy go over this, but she felt it was probably best if she heard it before the police did. "He said he had to get something from inside the house."

"Did he say what it was?"

"No. Mummy kept asking him, but he wouldn't tell her. Then he said he was taking me with him, but Mummy said I was asleep."

"Which you were meant to be," pointed out Kate.

"The shouting woke me up. Mummy got very cross with Daddy. Daddy called Mummy nasty names. He's not very nice to Mummy."

"No, that's not nice, you're right. Sometimes grown-ups aren't very kind to each other. It's a shame because I know they both love you very much."

"I love Mummy a bit more than Daddy."

"I think that's okay," said Kate, kissing the top of Amy's head and hugging her tighter.

"I think Mummy smacked Daddy because I heard him crying. Please can we make it a pepperoni pizza?"

Tim staggered into the dark, narrow hallway, the sickly smell of marijuana smoke giving his senses a jolt. Tim imagined he was on set and prepared himself for a performance; he put on his best street voice, as he had been coached to do, and called down the hallway,

"Dave, is that you, bro'?" There was a flurry of activity and the door at the end of the hallway flew open. A scruffy dreadlocked man, a similar height to Tim, appeared aggressively brandishing a decorative fruit bowl. Tim was delighted it wasn't a knife, or worse still, a gun.

"Who the fuck are you?" he barked. "Back up, fool!"

Tim was struggling to remember all the lines from the gangster film. Most of his had been fairly ordinary as he was playing the part of the gangland boss. What he needed to remember now was what those in his gang had said and pray that it was authentic. "Ah shit, I don' want trouble. I ain't bustin no one. I'm blud man, chill bro'."

"What crew yar in?"

"I ain't in no crew or massive man, I'm just a bum after a score. Dave said this was the place, but if I got it wrong, I'm sorry man," Tim said, putting his hands up in the air to show he wasn't dangerous.

"Dave who?" The fruit bowl was still raised, but his expression showed some recognition.

"I dunno, I met him in a pub. He wrote it down, see," and he showed the man the scrap of paper Kate had given him with the details of the flat on it. A voice from inside the room joined in.

"Was he tall?" the disembodied voice asked.

"Yeah, he was a lanky streak of piss," said Tim. Lots of laughter broke out inside and the man in the doorway lowered the fruit bowl. Tim relaxed a fraction.

"Yeah, that's Stretch. Come in, man," and he stood aside so that Tim could go into the small living room. Tim tried to hide his sigh of relief and his satisfaction that his theory, that everyone knew someone called Dave, had paid off. These guys might be occupying Didi's flat illegally, but they appeared to be "also rans" as opposed to hardened criminals, which was also good news for Tim.

The windows were closed and the curtains drawn, and Tim's eyes took a few moments to adjust to the dimly lit smoky room. There was a small, grubby sofa occupied by two other men, both white and younger than the fruit-bowl-wielding man. There was also an armchair strewn with takeaway boxes and packaging. Tim noted the position of the armchair, as it was facing a low television table that was missing its television. A couple of photo frames with colour photos that he couldn't quite see were lying in its place. On the wall above the sofa there was another photo, this time in black and white and of a man in uniform.

The two men looked Tim up and down and he suddenly wished he'd worked out a better plan than this. He shuffled across the room and stepped over a patterned rug that was now caked in grime and rucked up in a heap. Tim sat down gingerly on the arm of the chair. It was harder than he'd thought to stay in character when you knew nobody was going to shout "cut".

"Kotch man. S'up?" asked the fatter of the two on the sofa

who was wearing a thick hoody and an even thicker coat over the top, despite the oppressive warmth inside the flat. Tim wondered if he had bad circulation or perhaps nothing on underneath. He looked like a giant pupa. He was certainly sweating as the smell of body odour twisted with the marijuana in the stale air. His hair was shaved short, but there was a lightness of colour to what was visible. The other wore a dirty, red t-shirt and similarly shorn dark hair was just visible underneath a navy Yankees beanie hat, but Tim doubted it was genuine and even less likely that it had been purchased in New York.

"Me? I'm off the 'ook." Tim cringed internally as he said it, but quickly kept talking, "Nice drum, you got it goin' on here," Tim said, nodding as he scanned the room again. The fruit-bowl man was near the door, so he didn't like his chances of an easy exit.

"We jacked it. Ain't nobody livin' 'ere, and it's our yard," said the pupa. Tim stopped himself from pointing out that clearly somebody had been living here, hence the ornaments and photographs. Despite the mess it was now in, he could see it had once been a cosy home. He needed to get out of here and back to Terry and Didi and he needed a bloody good distraction to make it out in one piece.

"So, can I score some blow, puff, bash, Mary-Jane?" Tim stopped talking as, hopefully, he had made his point and was fast running out of slang names for marijuana. The three of them were staring at him now and he was feeling uneasy. "Don't vex me," Tim said, as menacingly as he could. "Don't do it. Don't vex me man or I'll flip out!"

"Chill, we ain't got stuff to sell till tomorra. I'll do ya a bomber?" offered Fruit Bowl. Tim thought this was a cigarette, but he wasn't sure, so he decided it was time to leave by the shortest route possible. He grabbed the two photos off the television table and jumped onto the back of the sofa. A lot of shouting and arm-waving ensued and the pupa made a grab for Tim's ankles. Tim kicked out hard and caught him square in the ear, which set him off swearing, whilst covering his head for protection. Tim grabbed the black-and-white photo off the wall and jumped off the end of the sofa. Fruit Bowl was waiting for him like a goalie in a penalty shootout. Tim put on his crazy-eye look and screamed in his face like a bee-stung banshee and then whacked him in the nether regions with the fruit bowl.

"Sorry, old chap," said Tim, in his best posh voice, as Fruit Bowl fell to the floor and Tim made a run for it.

As he ran along the outside corridor he pulled his phone from his pocket and dialled Terry. Above his racing heart and heavy breathing, he heard thundering footsteps coming up fast behind him. A glance over his shoulder told him that Beanie was quicker off the mark than he looked. Terry finally answered and Tim shouted fast into the phone,

"Pull the car under the stairs by the double doors. Right under the stairs because I'm coming down, right now!"

"There in ten seconds, boss," reassured Terry, as he revved the car into life and swung it around. "Trouble?"

"Shitloads!" Tim panted as he reached the stairwell and started down the stairs. He shoved the phone back in his pocket and clutched the photos to his chest with one hand. The small steps meant that he had to step on every stair very quickly and he looked as if he was doing some sort of strange dance or having some sort of fit. His feet were going so fast they were a blur, like a hamster in a wheel. As he made the second flight and reached the fourth floor, he heard the shuddering bang as Beanie jumped down the set of stairs in one go. Tim continued his hamster impression down to the third floor, but Beanie was gaining on him. As he touched down on the second floor so did Beanie, with a loud bang,

"You slaaaaag!" Beanie snarled as he lurched at Tim. With one hand clutching the photos to his chest, Tim used the other as he leap-frogged over the wall of the stairwell and disappeared. Beanie's eyes nearly popped out of his head and he looked over

251

the edge, expecting to see Tim splatter on the ground. Instead he saw Tim deftly land on the bonnet of a large black car and then dive headfirst into its open sunroof as the driver spun the vehicle backwards.

"What the fu…" Beanie kicked the wall in temper and then wished he hadn't as that had most likely broken his toe. "Oy! Get the fucker!" he shouted to the youths, who were gawping at the stunt show unfolding in front of them. Two of them responded with graphic hand signals, but the others pitched forward at the same time and started running towards the car, some of them throwing whatever rubbish was to hand. Terry reversed the car at speed, then adroitly did a handbrake turn and the car raced away from the scene as Tim's legs slid gracefully inside the car.

"Ah, hello there, Didi, terribly sorry about that. Are you okay?" he said, as he scrambled into his seat and relished the sound of the seat belt as he clicked it safely into place.

"Goodness me, it's like being in the movies," she said with glee.

"We aim to please, madam," Tim said, as he handed Didi the trio of photo frames he had gathered on his quest. Didi grasped them and examined each one in turn.

"Thank you," she said, and Tim gave her a smile.

Terry checked the mirrors a few times before he was happy that no one was following them. "We're clear, boss," he said, when he was sure.

"Terry, I'm getting too old for stunts. Nice driving, by the way. Remind me at Christmas when I'm sorting out your bonus."

"I will, don't worry," grinned Terry into the rear-view mirror.

"So what exactly happened back there?" asked Didi. This was a question that, surprisingly, Tim was not ready for. He had only just switched out of life-preservation mode and hadn't managed to conjure up a suitable story for the drama Didi had just witnessed.

"Oh, uh, there's a problem with your flat."

"I'd worked that bit out for myself. What sort of problem?"

"There's a gas leak," lied Tim very badly. "You won't be able to go back there for a while. But that's okay, I know a nice little hotel in London, so you'll be fine there whilst they sort it out."

"A gas leak?" questioned Didi.

"Yes. A bad one, apparently. It's all been cordoned off. It's not safe to go in. There's officials with clip boards and everything…" elaborated Tim, gesturing with his hands.

"That's astounding, seeing as the whole place has been electric since it was built in 1959." Didi shook her head in mock amazement. "Astounding," she said again. Tim threw his head back onto the head rest and gave up.

Chapter 22

Andy was jolted awake by the sound of people shouting. He pulled himself together and tried to get his eyes to open properly. He was in full yawn as he unfolded himself out of the car. The noise and kerfuffle was coming from the back garden and Andy felt compelled to find out what he could. He had expected to see mortuary vans, body bags, forensic experts in blue overalls, the whole performance, but it appeared that Andy had slept through it all.

He ran down the side of the house and could see that the back gate was ajar. His heart was thumping in his chest and he had an instant headache caused, most likely, by the sudden shot of adrenalin and the increased amount of stress he was experiencing. Andy hadn't acknowledged how stress-free his life had been of late and was now wishing he had.

He peered around the edge of the gate, knowing that when the officers saw him they would march him off the premises quicker than he could blink, so he had to take in as much as he could in the few seconds he had. As he looked through the gap he could see a pile of rubble on the lawn and the officers all standing around a huge hole where the patio used to be. A couple of wooden markers were pushed into the ground at key points. The sergeant stood nearby, rubbing his forehead with his hand and shaking his head.

As Andy watched, two of the officers started to lift a large black bag out of the hole. They did it quickly, so it didn't appear to be very heavy. Andy's stomach lurched, as he realised that it wouldn't be heavy if Shaun was in pieces. Andy had never thought of himself as a squeamish person, but right now he was having to take in deep breaths for fear of fainting if he saw anything too horrific.

He clutched the gate post as the officers placed the large muddy, black bin bag on the grass, giving Andy a perfect view. Suddenly, Andy realised that the volume from the police officers had increased but it wasn't shouting that he could hear, it was laughter. His eyes were drawn to them for a moment. This was wholly inappropriate, but perhaps that's how they dealt with the more traumatic scenes they encountered. He checked his watch; it was just gone half-five. He wasn't sure how long he'd been asleep, but he felt as if he'd woken up in a parallel universe.

Andy subconsciously took in another deep breath and dragged his eyes to look at the body. He stared at the large shape in the bin bag. There was something colourful spilling out of one end, which Andy assumed was clothing. He pushed open the gate and walked in, careful to tread on the grass and not to disturb anything. The officers continued to laugh, a couple of them holding their sides. The sergeant wasn't laughing; he was still shaking his head. They all looked at Andy, but nobody stopped him. Andy peered into the hole as he passed it. He wasn't sure what he was expecting to see in there, but he was very grateful there was just earth and a bit of rubble.

"Ah, Mr... sorry I've forgotten your name." The sergeant walked across the dishevelled earth and stepped over the body as he made his way over to where Andy was standing on the grass.

"Shaw, Andy Shaw." Andy was getting more alarmed by the minute by the lack of decorum they were all showing.

"We'll soon be all finished here, then you can lock up."

"What about all this?" asked Andy looking at the giant hole, the rubble and the body in the bag.

"I'm afraid it was a lawful search, so that's for Mrs Greasley to sort out, not us."

"I meant, was it Shaun?"

"In the hole?" grinned the sergeant, to which Andy nodded, and more peals of disrespectful laughter echoed from the other officers. The sergeant waved a hand for them to stop. "No, there's no body under the patio, but then you already knew that, didn't you?"

"Er, yes. Actually, no," said Andy tentatively.

"I could do you for wasting police time, you know, but, hey, it did give the boys a laugh."

"Look, I'm sorry, but I don't know what you're talking about. The last I heard there was a head and torso buried down there and we all thought it was Shaun. I helped you with the patio. I've done nothing to waste police time." Andy could feel himself getting het up the more he went on, so he stopped and waited for the police officer to fill the silence. The sergeant was looking at him oddly, now. It appeared that both men were confused about the situation. The sergeant cracked first.

"The clown," he said forcefully. Andy looked at him blankly. Was he referring to Shaun? He didn't know, but even Shaun deserved a bit more respect than this if he'd been butchered and buried. The sergeant bent down and pulled the muddy black bag so that the contents spilled onto the lawn. Andy stumbled back in shock, expecting to see something that would be etched in his nightmares forever, but instead he found he was staring at something colourful that had landed at his feet. "This big clown was buried in the hole. I take it that was your idea of a joke?" Andy stared at the grinning monstrosity of a toy.

"What? God no. Who would do that?" Andy paused. "Amy." The sergeant was looking more confused than ever. "Mrs Greasley's daughter, Amy. She got the clown from Shaun for Christmas. She hates it. I think she may have buried it in the hole when she was helping me with the patio, but I didn't see her do it. Honestly, I didn't know it was in there." Andy had a vague recollection of someone in the hall when he'd been distracted by Irene's telephone call, which must have been when Amy sneaked the clown downstairs.

"Oh, well, there we are then. We'll have to bag it up anyway, so it'll give forensics a laugh. You won't get it back for a while."

"That's not a problem, you can keep it." Andy was instantly overjoyed. "So does that mean Sarah is free to go? No charges?"

"I don't know, but I can radio in and find out for you," offered the officer, who was being quite reasonable considering the huge disappointment he must have had at finding a toy clown and not a mutilated body on his patch.

Andy hovered around the front garden after he'd locked up, waiting for the sergeant to update him. He stuck his head out of the side of the police van.

"She's free to go. You can pick her up now if you like, but don't either of you leave the area." He waved as the van pulled away from the curb. Andy rang Kate as he got into the car to relay the good news but didn't mention the clown; that was something he would need to tackle Amy over separately.

Andy started off his journey feeling overjoyed that Sarah was free to go, but as he got closer to the station other thoughts started to creep back into his mind. Shaun was still missing and Sarah was still their number-one suspect. He parked the old Beetle across the road and saw Sarah waiting just outside. As soon as she saw the car, she started to walk towards it and as Andy got out she quickened her pace towards him, fell into his arms and burst into tears. Andy held her and rocked her gently until the tears subsided. He gently tilted her head up to his.

"You know, I'll murder the bastard if he ever turns up alive," she laughed through her tears.

"Don't let the police hear you say that and don't let Shaun and Irene mess with your head."

"They should know better than to mess with me. They'd be

257

safer trying to sandpaper a tiger's arse."

"Come on, let's get you home. Apparently Amy is making your favourite meal for tea."

"Pepperoni pizza?"

"Yep," and he opened the rusty car door for her. She felt like a star as she got inside.

Back at Kate's, it was hugs and tears of relief all round and whilst Sarah was updating Kate on her questioning ordeal, Andy took Amy off for a chat. They went into the garden and Andy sat down on one of the garden chairs with Amy standing in front of him, so that they were virtually eye to eye.

"Amy, I need to ask you something and you need to tell me the truth. It's really important, okay?"

"Okay," said Amy, mirroring Andy's serious look.

"The policemen dug up Mummy's patio today."

"Oh no! Is it broken?"

"It's okay, we'll fix it. You and me; we did it once, so we can do it again. Do you know what they found when they dug it up?"

"Treasure? Fossils?" asked Amy excitedly.

"No, something else that someone had buried there. Something they might not want to see again," he suggested. Amy's expression changed in an instant as what he was asking registered. "Do you know what they found?"

"Daddy's clown." Amy hung her head. "I'm sorry, but it looks at me at night and it scares me. Daddy said it couldn't live at his house." Amy looked forlorn.

"Why didn't you tell Mummy or me that you didn't like it?"

"Daddy said not to. He said it was very special and I had to keep it safe."

"It's very safe now because the police have got it."

"That is very safe," said Amy, looking a little happier with the situation.

"Is it okay if I explain this all to Mummy later or do you want to tell her?"

258

"No, you can tell her," nodded Amy and she took Andy's hand. "Come and see the sunflower picture I made for you."

Didi stood in the large reception area of the hotel and tried to take in every detail of the fabulousness of it all. To think that she lived just a few bus stops away from all this was almost unbelievable. The floor gleamed beneath her feet, as if it were made of ice and the imposing chandelier sparkled and winked like floating jewels above her head. She knew she was grinning like an idiot, but couldn't help it.

She hadn't asked Tim what had really happened to her flat. She feared she had been burgled, but he had rescued her photographs, even the one of her old dad in his army uniform; they were the most precious things there. So, for now, she wasn't going to think about her little flat. She was going to pretend she was on holiday and enjoy it for as long as it lasted and try as hard as she could to remember every detail so that when she was back at home, these memories would make her smile.

As Tim approached the reception desk the young woman on duty recognised him.

"Mr Calder, lovely to see you again. Are you booked in with us or shall I check your usual suite?"

"Hi, I am booked in but I need another suite if you have one, ideally the one next to mine."

"Certainly," said the receptionist, tapping away on her computer. "The next-door suite is available. It's a connecting suite, if you'd like?"

"Brilliant, yes please. Can you also get onto Harvey Nicks,"

"The usual, Mr Calder? Evening dress and shoes, two sets of underwear and a change of clothes, size six is it?" smiled the receptionist, trying hard to keep the judgemental tone out of her voice.

"Just the evening dress and shoes," replied Tim slowly, "but I'm guessing in a bigger size," he said, lowering his voice and stepping aside so that the receptionist could see Didi, who was standing

259

patiently behind him. Didi smiled when she realised they were both looking at her. The receptionist would have fallen off her chair had she been sitting on one, as she stared at the mature lady, who was smiling so sweetly back at her. Tim beckoned Didi over and whispered the question in her ear. Didi looked at him shocked.

"You can't ask a lady that!"

"You'll need something to wear to dinner tonight."

"But I'm not telling you my size," Didi was insistent and the receptionist was fascinated by her. Tim reached for the pad and pen that was on the reception desk.

"Here, write it down, then. Top, bottom and shoes." Didi glared at him, harrumphed, snatched the pen from him and jotted it down begrudgingly. When she was done she folded the paper over and slid it across to the receptionist. Tim made a pretend grab for it and Didi smacked him on the arm.

"I think I may have been kidnapped," smiled Didi at the receptionist.

"Behave yourself or I'll have you sectioned again," Tim said, as he signed the form the receptionist placed in front of him.

"Harvey Nicholls have messaged back to say they'll be here with a selection of gowns in the next 30 minutes."

"Hurry them up, would you, I want to be leaving for dinner by then."

"Certainly, sir," the receptionist nodded and handed over the key cards. Didi took what looked like a white credit card, wondering what she needed it for, but accepted it graciously. As they walked away, Tim pointed Didi towards the lifts.

"I just need to book a wake-up call. Won't be a minute. Our lift is over there," and he strode back to reception.

"Actually, can you get her a couple of sets of fancy underwear, too, and some flowers? Women of all ages love that, don't they?"

"Certainly, sir."

Tim met Didi at the lift.

"What about my case?"

"That'll beat us up there, most likely. The porter will be bringing it up now in the service lift. Do you like Italian food?" he asked casually.

"Prefer French," said Didi.

Didi ran her hands over the soft fabric of her midnight-blue evening dress. It was the most beautiful feeling against her skin and she'd loved it the second the young lady had pulled it out of a suit carrier and laid it on the giant bed in her room. The room that most probably could have fitted her tiny flat inside it twice over. Didi felt the warm night air fan her hair and she took another sip of the exquisite champagne. She had never felt so utterly spoiled in all her life. She opened her eyes to see Tim watching her intently. He was leaning back on his chair, his dinner jacket open and his bow tie slung around his collar.

"That colour really does suit you. Are those sandals okay?"

"Bit higher than I'm used to, but they're surprisingly comfy, actually," Didi wiggled her toes to the side of the table so that Tim could see and he smiled.

"Don't go falling off them; that's how you break a hip at your age."

"Are you gay?" said Didi.

"No, but any longer with you and I can feel myself turning. Why?"

"Just wondered; the stories in the papers might have been an elaborate smoke screen."

"No, I'm straight. So you'd better be wearing your chastity belt."

"I'm not, but I've found incontinence pants are equally as effective at keeping men away." Tim shook his head and laughed. He had really enjoyed their evening together. It made a change for Tim to relax and just enjoy someone's company. He hadn't felt this calm since the cottage.

"Are you ready for dessert yet?" he asked.

"Ooh, now I think I could be tempted," grinned Didi cheekily. Tim nodded and the waiter appeared at their table, just as Tim's mobile rang. Tim saw the name flash up and then remembered that he was meant to update Kate after he'd settled Didi into her flat, but obviously the plans had changed a little since then.

"Hi, Kate, how are you? How's Amy?"

"We're all fine, thanks. It's been sorted. I think it has, anyway. Did you get Didi home all right? I can't get any answer from her flat, it just rings out," which was probably because the phone had been nicked, thought Tim.

"Oh, er, there was a slight change of plan. I thought I would take Didi out for a meal rather than leave her on her own…" he fumbled.

"Give me the phone." Didi held out her hand and Tim obediently handed it over. "Hello Kate, I'm fine. I've had a glorious meal with vintage champagne, on a fabulous private boat that's drifting up the river Seine, and the Eiffel Tower is just coming into view." Tim started to repeatedly bang his head on the table.

"Didi, you are a one," chortled Kate. "Well, as long as he's looking after you and you're okay."

"I'm fine. Tim is being the perfect gentlemen. He's even bought me new underwear!"

"Give me back the phone!" Tim said, making a failed attempt to take it from Didi.

"Didi, you're really teasing me now, so I know you're all right. Make sure he takes you right to your door and I'll speak to you tomorrow."

"Okay, au revoir!" and she handed the phone back to Tim, who was looking totally panicked. "Stop fretting. She didn't believe me for a second. She probably thinks you've taken me to the Beefeater."

"And I will next time, if you're going to behave like this. Look Stéphane is waiting for you to choose your pudding, then we need to get back to the airport."

"Spoilsport," and she kicked him gently under the table and he made a big fuss. The boat continued its slow path in front of the Eiffel Tower and Tim and Didi barely noticed that it erupted into a mass of flashing lights, as they were far too busy laughing.

When Amy was all tucked up in bed after a final round of "Happy Birthday", and the sixth time of blowing out her candles, the adults eventually retired to the garden and the warm summer evening with a bottle of Prosecco. Kate poured out the fizz and they "Ahhed" as they relaxed back in their seats. It was quiet for a while as they all sipped their drinks and listened to the garden birds calling to each other as they settled down to roost.

"I'm guessing you both want to know why I didn't tell you that I'd seen Shaun just before he went missing," Sarah said into her glass. She fidgeted in her chair before making eye contact with Kate and Andy.

"Yep, that would be good," said Andy, in a matter-of-fact manner.

"We've been worried about you, that's all. We know you didn't kill Shaun," Kate said.

"That's more than I know." Sarah took a quick sip from her glass. Kate and Andy were both looking at her closely now. "Don't worry, I probably haven't killed him. I've told the police everything now, anyway, and I have to say that I feel a lot better for it."

"So, tell us then," urged Andy.

"The night Shaun came round, that was the last time anyone saw him. He was demanding to come in and I wouldn't let him. I gave him some lip, but he didn't come back with his smart remarks like usual; he wasn't himself. I think he was frightened of someone and he kept saying that he was a dead man if I didn't let him in. Anyway, this went on for a bit and he got louder and more abusive and started trying to kick the door in. I lost my temper because Amy was asleep upstairs."

"No she wasn't," cut in Kate and Sarah stopped her story. "She listened from her room. She told me earlier today."

"Oh crap! That kid is going to need so much therapy when she's older," sighed Sarah.

"She won't, she's fine. Amy said Shaun was being nasty to you and wanted something from inside the house."

"Yes, he did, but the idiot wouldn't tell me what it was. He'd been drinking and was in such a rage, so there was no way I was letting him in. Shaun got a spanner from his van and was trying to jemmy the door open, and at the same time he was screaming that he was going to kill me and take Amy." Kate looked horrified and reached out to touch Sarah. "It freaked me out, so I went to the kitchen and grabbed a knife. I shouted to him that I had one and that I'd use it if he broke in, but he didn't stop. He managed to jemmy the door open and he came at me with the spanner," Sarah laughed at herself, "It sounds like a cheap version of Cluedo; Mr Arsehole in the Hallway with the Spanner."

"It's not funny, though is it?" Andy said gravely.

"No, sorry." Sarah composed herself. She'd always been able to find the funny side of even the darkest moments. "He was like a man possessed as he came at me, so I went for him with the knife. I stabbed him in the arm that was holding the spanner and he dropped it."

"Thank God," put in Kate, who could picture it happening.

"Exactly. Then he just stood there staring at his arm pumping out blood all over my carpet."

"Not a coffee stain, then," said Andy.

"I poured coffee on it later when I couldn't get the blood stain out," confessed Sarah, looking shamefaced. "I didn't know what to do, so I just pushed him outside and shut the door. I told him I was calling the police and pretended to give my details loudly so he could hear through the door. He sat on the step crying and bleeding for a bit, then it went quiet and when I looked outside he'd gone."

"Who fixed your door?" asked Andy.

"Some guy in the local directory came out the next day. He did the door but not the frame. And he charged me a fortune. I didn't sleep that night because I thought Shaun was coming back. When he didn't come back and nobody heard from him…"

"You thought he'd bled to death somewhere," Kate finished the sentence for her and Sarah nodded.

"I felt awful afterwards and I thought that if someone else was trying to kill him, like he said, then they might finish him off and I'd be off the hook, so I daren't tell anyone."

"Why?" asked Andy gently. "It was self-defence, he could have killed you with the spanner." Sarah shrugged. Andy continued, "Nobody would blame you for that."

"You clearly weren't trying to kill him or you'd have gone for his body," pointed out Kate.

"I just couldn't tell anyone." Sarah looked down and her forehead creased.

"But, why not," pressed Kate.

"Because I wanted to kill him. In that moment, I really did want to kill him and I could have done it. I've never been so angry. I could have killed him with Amy in the house."

"Don't worry, she's seen worse on the TV," said Andy with a smile, and he hugged her close.

"What did the police say about it?" asked Kate.

"They said it's not murder, even if he's died from his injuries, so they're not pressing charges at the moment. They are very keen to find Shaun. He's in some sort of trouble, but they wouldn't say what."

"I'd love to be there when they call Irene," smiled Kate.

"How could she have lied like that to the police? She told them I'd confessed to murdering him and buried him under the patio! She really is a witch. I hope they charge her for wasting police time, but I guess while her son is still missing they won't."

"She's just jealous of your patio, that's all," grinned Andy. Kate saw the look that passed between them and thought it was probably a good moment to make her excuses and leave them to it.

Chapter 23

Sunday had been a very quiet day after the emotional overload of Saturday. Only Amy had appeared to have her usual energy levels, so Andy had taken her off to Sarah's to start sorting out the patio. This left Kate and Sarah with a few hours to themselves before Sarah had a shift at the pub. Sarah had a long soak in the bath and then padded into Kate's bedroom to borrow her array of beauty products. Kate was just out of the shower and was towel-drying her hair. Sarah tightened the belt of the borrowed dressing gown she was wearing, then climbed onto Kate's bed and lay back against the many cushions that were neatly rowed up across the top of the bed. Sarah grabbed one of the large ones and threw it at Kate and missed.

"You weren't in the netball team, then?" Kate said, as she concentrated her drying efforts on the ends of her long hair. Sarah picked a smaller cushion and made a direct hit.

"Oy!" Kate folded her towel and reclaimed the cushions from the floor and returned them to their usual positions.

"Your bedroom needs to see more action than cushion-arranging," said Sarah, as she watched Kate.

"Not very likely. So what happened with you and Andy after I went to bed?"

Sarah moved quickly to sit up, crossed her legs, and spun

around to face Kate "We finished the bottle and went to bed. Separate beds!"

"You're kidding, I only went to bed so that you two could have… some private time."

"Do you mean a snog?"

"You have such a way with words. So did you have a snog?" said Kate.

"No!"

"Why not? It's obvious you two really like each other."

"I'd love to bump fuzzies with Andy, but there's Shaun…"

"I didn't know you were into threesomes." Kate raised an eyebrow in mock surprise. "What's it got to do with Shaun?"

"Andy and Shaun used to be good mates and, with Shaun missing, it doesn't seem right."

"So you're going to save yourself until Shaun reappears?"

"I don't know." Sarah flopped back onto the cushions, "I don't even know if Andy's interested."

"Get your eyes tested! He adores you and Amy."

"He could just feel sorry for us. It's all too complicated."

"Life is complicated. Get over it," Kate said, as she bopped Sarah playfully on the head with a cushion. "Don't let Shaun get in the way, he's spoiled too much already."

"Would you? You know, dance the horizontal tango with Andy?"

"Why can't you just say sex?"

"You are such a grown-up," groaned Sarah. "So would you have sex with Andy?"

"No! That's virtually incest. He would have been my brother in law if… well, you know. If I were you I wouldn't leap into bed with him; I'd check he wanted a relationship first."

"Still, not had a one-night stand, then?" grinned Sarah.

"No!" squeaked Kate, as she started to batter Sarah with any cushion she could grab.

It felt good to get back to the relative normality of filming on

Monday morning, although it was all very different as they were out on location in Bath for the next few weeks. Kate was keen to speak to Tim as she'd only managed a brief call with him the day before and he was being cagey about something. There was still no answer from Didi's flat, so Kate just wanted to check that she was okay. The weather had taken a sudden turn for the worse, with a chilly wind and drizzly rain making the soggy Monday feel more like November than June. It was hard to believe that they had been sitting in the sunshine only two days earlier. Her taxi pulled up outside the park and she could see a huge marquee had been set up for them. Some casual-looking security guards were patrolling the area and a few groups of fans and onlookers were clustered about despite the miserable weather.

Kate showed her pass and, thankful that she'd gone for the skinny jeans and mac rather than a dress, was heading for the marquee when she saw Didi at the entrance, laughing with Marcus. Didi was wearing a smart black-and-white dress and black heels, and looked every bit like one of the cast.

"Hey, look who it is," Kate said, as she stepped out of the rain and Didi gave her a warm hug. "Don't you look well?"

"I feel fabulous," grinned Didi, looking a good ten years younger than the last time Kate had seen her. Her make-up was flawless and her hair had been cut and styled. "Tim said I could be an extra!"

"Did he, now?" laughed Kate, wondering what Tim was up to and she felt a little bit guilty for automatically assuming he had an ulterior motive.

"She's going to be in the café scene," said Marcus, giving Kate a brief kiss on the cheek. Kate couldn't get over how amazing Didi looked.

"I've been in hair and make-up already. Didn't they do a good job?"

"Amazing. Remind me to see if I can get a walk-on part and have the same treatment," said Kate, looking around for Tim.

"Tim's in make-up now," said Marcus, answering her thoughts. "I take it you two have made up, then," he said, ushering her and Didi further inside.

"I wouldn't go that far, but he was a big help this weekend. Not that I could get an update out of him."

"I won't hear a word said against him. He's been marvellous," extolled Didi. "He is an utter sweetheart." Kate gave Didi a disbelieving look. "He is! I've had the best time ever."

"Is he paying you to say that?" Kate said. She had thought Didi was a better judge of character, but then, if she'd only experienced Tim in full-on charm offensive, that would explain her current point of view.

"No. I've just spent some time with him and, talk of the devil." Tim walked purposefully over to them, wearing one of Patrick's expensive handmade suits and his own sunglasses; it was a deadly combination. Pippa was marching up behind him, looking bedraggled, thanks to the weather, and running through a long list of things, but Tim didn't appear to be listening.

"My favourite girl, you look stunning," said Tim as he air-kissed Didi. Kate had felt a momentary flicker, as she couldn't see through the sunglasses who he was looking at, and for a moment she thought it was her, but thankfully the feeling left her just as quickly. Pippa gave up and stomped off. "Marcus, Che is looking for you. Kate we need to talk," and he took her by the elbow and marched her back through the marquee, out into the rain, over the grass and to his car. Terry waved through the glass and Kate waved back. "Get in," Tim instructed.

"Why?" Kate stood next to the car and felt defiant. The rain was falling harder now and it was running off her mac in resolute lines.

"Because I don't want anyone to hear what I'm about to say."

"Right, okay," and, feeling a little silly for her pointless churlishness, she got inside the car.

"I'll have to cut this short," started Tim, "but, basically, Didi's flat has been ransacked and drug dealers are living in it."

"Oh, my God!" Both Kate's hands flew to her mouth.

"I guess the place was left empty too long. Did you know it was in a seriously bad area?" Kate shook her head, her hands still at her mouth. "I had a run-in with the drugs gang, but I escaped, thanks to my stunt training and Terry's impressive driving." He wasn't going to miss an opportunity to be the hero in this story. "I've set Didi up in a suite at my hotel in London, but we need to sort out something permanent for her. Shall I get Pippa onto it?"

Kate looked puzzled. It was a lot of unexpected information to have fired at you, especially when you'd assumed that Didi had been tucked up in her own bed for the last couple of nights.

"Can't we get the council or police to sort out the drug dealers, so she can go home?"

"Kate, nobody of Didi's age should be living there; it's gangland hell. I'm amazed she's stayed there this long."

"I had no idea. I thought she had money. St Gaudentia's isn't cheap."

"Her niece paid for that. Apparently she never visits and obviously wasn't about to put her life on hold to look after Didi, so paying for the convalescent home was the easy answer."

"I think I probably need to talk to her niece, then. I'll get her details and call her in the next couple of days." Kate looked at Tim to see if he agreed.

"Why put off until tomorrow that which you can delegate today?" Tim recited in a thespian manner, but catching the look that Kate gave him, he added, "I'll ask Pip."

"So, if you were planning to sort this all out, why are you asking me?" said Kate, not sure why she was feeling so niggled with Tim, as he had clearly gone over and above with regards to looking after Didi.

"She's your friend. I didn't want to just take over."

"Not until you'd asked if you could take over first. I see." Kate got out of the car, and walked away with as much dignity as the driving rain would allow. Tim watched her leave, his face showing the expression of a man who was damned whatever he did.

The rain caused all sorts of problems for filming, so most of the day was spent holed up in the café and only a couple of usable scenes had been shot. Che was in a foul mood and was barking at everyone; woe betide anyone who suggested that they abandon filming for the day. Dennis had implied it and Kate had thought that Che was going to spontaneously combust with fury. At least the script was working well, and Lumina and Tim were both doing an amazing job. Patrick was letting his guard down and Tim played it brilliantly.

Didi was enjoying every second of her 15 minutes of fame. She was ushered here and there under a large umbrella by a runner and brought countless cups of coffee. Didi was an instant hit with everyone and Kate thought that she could detect a little bit of jealousy from Lumina as Tim fussed around Didi instead of her. Eventually, Che admitted defeat at four o'clock and everyone set about packing up. As Sod's Law would have it, by four-thirty the rain had ceased, the sun was starting to peek out from behind the clouds and the wind had disappeared completely.

After a few autographs for those who had been patiently waiting, they all retreated to the hotel bar. Kate crashed out in what turned out to be a surprisingly low chair overlooking the gardens and considered jotting down some more of her novel; the fairly blank day had given her a few good ideas. She was just resting her head on the back of the seat with her eyes closed when a tap on the shoulder made her spring up.

"Good grief, Lumina, you frightened the life out of me," said Kate.

"Sorry, just wanted a private word." If it was about her and Tim again, Kate really didn't want to know.

"It's about me and Tim," said Lumina. Kate wanted to hide. She even looked outside to see if that might provide an escape route. Pippa was walking Horse around the grass just outside and gave a faint smile and a half-hearted wave in Kate's direction. Kate grimaced back.

"I don't really think I'm the right person to talk to." Kate went to get out of the chair, but Lumina gently put a hand on her shoulder to keep her where she was, and the look in her eye was the final persuasion she needed. Kate relaxed and accepted the inevitable.

"Okay, how can I help?"

"I haven't seen Tim all weekend. I knew there was someone else…"

"Has he not explained that he was helping Didi most of the weekend? He's been a Good Samaritan. Her flat has been taken over by drug-dealing squatters." She hoped it sounded dramatic enough to get Tim off the hook.

"I know. It's Didi I'm worried about. Look at him! He's obsessed with her." They both looked over to the bar, where Tim and Didi were perched on bar stools cackling their heads off.

"Oh," was all Kate could manage in return.

"He cancelled our weekend in Monaco for her. I mean he can't really prefer that to me, can he?" Lumina looked disdainfully in Didi's direction, as Kate realised that actually he had ditched Monaco in favour of her doorstep.

"No, I really think you've got the wrong idea here. They just get on really well. They're similar characters; they both put on a good front to hide what they really feel. Sort of playing a part most of the time, keeping the real them under wraps. Sometimes you see a glimpse of it and then, before you know it, the masquerade is back in full swing." Kate paused and saw that Lumina had a look about her of a chimp trying to do applied mathematics, but slightly more pained.

"You don't think he and Didi…"

"God, no!" Kate was horrified at the thought and dismayed by Lumina's paranoia.

"Good. But you think Tim is acting all the time?"

"That wasn't exactly what I said… but have you noticed how he's different when he's one to one?"

Lumina shook her head slowly and turned to look out of the window. "Watch him!" she shouted as she banged on the glass, making both Kate and Pippa flinch. Horse was merrily chewing on a trailing geranium and looked rather pleased with himself. Thankfully, Lumina stormed off to reclaim her pet and left Kate to work out how best to get out of the ridiculously low chair without looking as if she needed a hip replacement.

Kate found Pippa with a mobile glued to her ear. She was sitting on a damp-looking bench in the courtyard garden and waved to indicate she wouldn't be long, so Kate perched tentatively on the edge of the soggy wood and hoped it wouldn't leave a wet patch on her trousers. Pippa's hair was not looking its usual sleek self. The rain had obviously unleashed a natural kink that was usually kept in line with a daily dose of hair-straighteners. It suited Pippa to be a little less angular, thought Kate. Finally Pippa ended the call with a big sigh.

"Think I've got the answer to Didi's problem."

"Great, what is it?"

"The niece is a harridan, couldn't give two hoots about Didi. She said something about promising her mother that she'd look after her. She was all for putting Didi in a nursing home." Kate looked shocked. "Exactly. Anyway I spoke to Tim's accountant and he's got a couple of Docklands apartments, one of which is vacant." Pippa looked at Kate to indicate that was apparently the end of the sentence, but Kate was looking blankly at her.

"And…" Kate encouraged.

"And Didi could live in one."

"How much rent does the accountant want? I don't think Didi has much of an income, you see."

"Not the accountant, Tim. It's Tim's apartment and he bought it for capital appreciation rather than rental income. God knows, he doesn't need the money."

"But, you're going to check with Tim first?"

"As a fait accompli, yeah," Pippa grinned. Kate daren't think what Lumina would do when she found out.

Andy was getting twitchy about the speed at which his house was coming along, so decided to take a couple of days off to have a concerted effort at making it one hundred per cent habitable. He also needed a few nights back in his own bed. Sleeping under the same roof as Sarah was driving him slightly crazy. Shaun dominated virtually every conversation and, with Kate away, there was an awkwardness between the two of them. Being in his own house felt good and reminded him that he was meant to be a carefree bachelor.

A couple of days of hard work really brought the place together. Andy had been flat out on the decorating and snagging, and a mate in the carpet trade had done him a good deal on carpet for upstairs. The kitchen hadn't needed much, but the finished tiles had made a strong statement and the solid-oak table and benches made it look complete. He looked around the bare walls and had an idea. Andy retrieved the screwed-up piece of paper from his glove box and set about ironing it. Once it was in a picture frame, the picture that Amy had drawn him of three sunflowers was quite impressive and totally original. He hung it above the seating area, where it would have pride of place. It had taken a while, but Andy had finally fathomed out what was missing from his new home. It was the finishing touches, the things that actually made it feel like a home rather than a nicely decorated box.

He bounded upstairs and took a good, hard look at his bedroom. The bedroom, he had thought, was finished. The fitted ash wardrobes were still simple but elegant, the wrought-iron bed still a classic and the white walls, white blinds, white duvet and matching pillow cases could offend nobody. The single hanging light bulb, on the other hand, wasn't the prettiest sight and gave off a harsh light. Andy stared around the room,

"Yep, I've got the sterile hospital look perfected," he muttered

275

to himself. If he thought, and it was a big "if", if we ever do get it together and we make it up here she'll think she's been admitted to A&E. He pulled out his phone, "Google to the rescue". After a few hours thumbing through miles of over-the-top bedroom looks that popped up and assaulted his eyeballs, some of which he thought he should bookmark for Concetta, he finally alighted on a look he could live with.

Two hours and a mammoth shopping trip later, Andy surveyed the bedroom. Rich navy-blue curtains hung at the windows, a small chandelier twinkled above and, thanks to the newly fitted dimmer switch, the level of lighting was easily controlled. A large picture of an impossibly blue flower was hung perfectly in the exact middle of the wall and small vases of white roses and an array of candles of varying sizes lined the dresser and chest of drawers. Perfect, he thought.

Chapter 24

Sarah was rushed off her feet, thanks to extra shifts at the pub and a three-wedding weekend for the flower shop. Andy had been a great help ferrying Amy to and from school, but like Andy, she felt she should probably be returning home soon and trying to get back to normal. Who knew when, or if, Shaun would return? Friday lunchtime was always a busy affair in the Blacksmith's Arms, but when you'd been up since five o'clock conditioning, dicing and arranging wedding flowers, it was like trying to run a marathon with your laces tied together and your head bubble-wrapped. Melanie was particularly perky, which only highlighted the contrast with how Sarah felt. When the last of the food orders had gone out and there was a brief pause at the bar, Melanie sidled over to Sarah and Phil and straightened the half-pint glasses.

"Can I get off 15 minutes early?" she asked.

"I'm not a charity," grumbled Phil. "You're not running off, too, are you?" he asked, turning to Sarah.

"No, but I need to go on time, for school pick-up." Phil nodded to both of them,

"Go on, then, you can clear off and abandon us. I 'spose you want your wages?" and he disappeared out the back.

"I've got a new man," Melanie said. She was jittery with excitement.

"Ooh, exciting, do tell!"

"I've not exactly got him yet, but I know he's interested and it's just a matter of time. He's really sweet. He keeps calling round to check I'm okay and he's got his own company."

"So this one is human, then. That's a big step up. And a big boss of a company means he can keep you in shoes. I like the sound of him already."

"He's just texted to say he'll call round if I'm in, so if I leave a bit early I can change and touch up my make-up, so I look all natural." Sarah wasn't sure that that made sense. Phil reappeared and begrudgingly handed over the pay envelopes. When Melanie had checked the clock for the tenth time in two minutes, Phil handed Melanie her handbag and pointed at the door.

"Go. You're making everyone restless." Melanie took her bag and almost skipped out of the pub, waving at them as if she were emigrating.

"New bloke, is it?" Phil was refilling the crisp boxes.

"Yeah, he sounds okay and she seems happy."

"Just need to find you a decent one and we can all relax." He banged the empty box flat and carried on with the salt and vinegar.

After lunch, Kate was ready to fall asleep as she sat outside the marquee in the sunshine. She checked her watch and decided a quick walk into town would be what she needed to recharge her batteries for the afternoon. She'd already promised herself a nap on the train. Tim sat down on the grass next to her and balanced a plate of salad on his knees.

"I'm just off into town. Do you want anything?" Kate saw his face fall as she stood to leave. "It's nothing personal. It's just that I'll nod off and start snoring and dribbling if I sit here any longer."

"Ew, fair enough. You'd best go, then. Apparently I need pictures and ornaments, according to Didi."

"That was quick. Has she moved in?"

"No, but Pip is trying to get it sorted as soon as possible."

"How's Lumina?" Kate asked tentatively, as she could imagine how she was, especially having seen her stomping about the marquee earlier demanding French bottled water and not the local "muck", as she'd referred to it. Tim put down his fork and looked up at Kate.

"I'm going to talk to Lumina over dinner tonight. Let's say I don't expect to get past starters before she throws a hissy fit. But it needs to be done," he said, his expression serious.

"Good luck with that, then," and Kate put on her sunglasses, brushed the grass off her plain, yellow dress and headed off across the park.

Kate enjoyed her potter around the shops and was pleased with her purchase of a Bath fridge magnet for Amy and a sketch of the cathedral for Didi – hopefully it would be a nice reminder for her. She couldn't be bothered to get her purse out again, so she held the few pence change in her hand. There was bound to be a collector for some charity further up and she'd be happy to donate it to a good cause. She walked back up John Street with the crowds of shoppers and tourists going at all speeds and in all directions. The only people not moving around were the Big Issue sellers and the occasional street beggar.

Kate was wondering whether to get a cardigan she'd seen as she dropped her few coins into the cup proffered by a man sitting on a piece of dirty cardboard, wearing equally dirty shorts and a black baseball cap. Kate carried on walking, when her brain tuned in to a familiar voice.

"Fanks, love," the beggar said. Kate took another couple of steps before she spun around only to see the man disappear into the crowd and start to run. She went back to where he had been sitting and looked at the dirty patch of cardboard. There was nothing left behind, no evidence, but Kate knew that it was Shaun.

"Kate, calm down, you're freaking me out." Sarah took herself and her mobile away from the pricked-up ears of the pub regulars and Phil, who was blatantly listening.

"It was Shaun. I gave him money and he said 'Thanks, Love' and then he ran away."

"How much did you give him?"

"About 70 pence," puzzled Kate.

"Oh, good, I thought you meant he demanded money with menaces."

"No, he was begging, but he's gone. I could give the police a description of what he's wearing."

"Did you see his arm?"

Kate had to think. "No, he was wearing long sleeves, with shorts, which is an odd combination. But he's not dead, Sarah."

"What did he say when he realised it was you?"

"Nothing. We didn't look at each other. He must have recognised me as I walked away and I recognised his voice."

"You didn't see his face, though?"

"No, but Sarah, it's him. His build, his voice, the way he ran. It was him, I'm sure and, anyway, why else would he run off?"

"He was desperate for a latte? I don't know."

"Can you give me the details of the policeman you've been dealing with and I'll report it. It's up to them what they do next. But Sarah, you can relax. You didn't kill him and he's miles away."

Sarah texted Kate the details and then texted Andy the revelation, but was careful to add that Kate only thought it was Shaun, she was not quite as confident as Kate or ready to celebrate just yet.

Sarah was waiting outside the school gates, busily checking her phone for messages and was frustrated that there weren't any. It didn't matter how many times she checked her phone, nothing popped up. She wanted to know what Andy thought and she needed an update from Kate. Also she badly wanted to enjoy the tiny little ball of relief that was sparkling inside her at the thought that she wasn't a murderer and wasn't going to prison. She knew that Kate was good with details and only acted on facts, unlike herself. A hand on her shoulder startled her and her phone jumped about in her hands like a slippery bar of soap.

"Sorry," said Andy, looking as if he'd won the lottery and Sarah couldn't help but hug him.

"Did you get my text?"

"Yeah, I was only around the corner and I knew you'd be here, so I thought I'd meet you."

"Why didn't you text to tell me that?"

"Dunno, didn't seem worth it, when I'd be here in a few minutes," he shrugged, still smiling. "So tell me what you know."

Sarah recounted, word for word, what Kate had said and Andy agreed that it was highly unlikely that Kate was mistaken. He was all for breaking out a bottle of bubbly.

"Should I tell Irene?" Sarah bit her lip.

"Do you *want* to tell Irene?"

"Yes and no, mainly I want to say 'ner, ner, ner-ner, ner!'"

"I think leave it to the police. She's unlikely to believe you, anyway." The school doors opened and children tumbled out with anxious teachers trying to eyeball the right parents for the right child. Andy and Sarah both raised a hand at the same time when they saw Amy's teacher with a firm hold on the little girl's shoulder. The woman was clearly terrified of letting Amy leave with the wrong parent. She looked relieved, released her grip, and Amy charged across the playground towards them.

Kate was on a high by the time she got back to the marquee and was bustled into a car with Marcus and back up to the offices for another round of filming. Kate relayed the exciting events to Marcus, who shared her excitement, but was not completely abreast of the whole story so kept asking too many questions and interrupting. Kate had insisted on speaking to Inspector Chauvin, who had called her back within a few minutes. He seemed like a nice, sensible sort of person and he listened carefully and asked some good questions. He asked her not to go looking for Shaun and said that his officers would be liaising with the local force in Bath and he would update Mrs Greasley if there were any significant developments. It wasn't quite the big police swoop she had hoped for, but it made sense.

When filming ended for the day, Kate was ready to skip to the train station. Tim came over as she and Pippa were sorting out who else was going to the station, to minimise the number of cars ferrying people in that direction.

"Tim, are you seeing Didi this weekend?"

"Yes, I was going to ask you something."

"Me first. I bought her this picture for her flat, well, your flat, actually. Can you give it to her, please?" and she handed Tim the bag. He didn't take it.

"Pippa wants to sort the apartment out before Didi moves in, so I thought a bit of sunshine would do us all good. I wondered if you fancied spending the weekend at my villa in Italy? You, me and Didi." Tim was looking expectant and Kate lowered the bag with the picture in it. Her brain was a mass of questions and she didn't know which one to voice first, so instead, she said nothing. "We'll fly out early tomorrow and back Sunday evening. Think about it and let me know if you can make it."

"Thanks. I'll let you know," she managed before he went off to speak to Pippa.

Tim was quiet in the back of the car as they inched their way through the Friday- evening traffic to pick up Lumina. She appeared on cue and sashayed towards to the car in a little black dress with a wrap elegantly arranged over her shoulders, her tiny feet squeezed into pointy patent shoes that increased her height by a good four inches. She had a bag in each hand; a tiny luminous-yellow clutch bag in her left and a small white bowling bag in her right, with a little furry head poking out of one end. It was simultaneous; as soon as Tim saw Horse he started to groan and as soon as Horse saw Tim he started to yap, even before Terry had opened the door.

"No," said Tim, "it's dinner for two; you're not bringing him!" But it was in vain, as Lumina was already swinging her sleek legs into the car.

"Sorry, what was that? I can't hear you over Horse."

"I think he'd be better off if you leave him here," Tim raised his voice in order to be heard.

"No, he gets lonely. Don't woo, baby boy? He would miss his mummy." Thankfully the interaction and kisses from Lumina distracted Horse for a few moments, and Tim slumped back in his seat in defeat. The car journey to the latest celebrity chef's restaurant was a short one, but by the time they got there, Tim feared that his ears might actually be bleeding due to the high pitch of Horse's incessant yaps. As they walked inside, Tim headed for the cloakroom attendant, who was already staring in their direction, having been alerted by the noise. Tim handed her a rolled-up note.

"Please offer to take the dog," Tim pleaded. The young woman's face was already apologising, but a quick glance down at the 50-pound note had the required effect.

"Thanks, I shouldn't, but I will."

"Thank you," mouthed Tim and, as Lumina approached, the young woman stepped forward to make a fuss of Horse.

"Aren't you a gorgeous girl?"

"Boy!" chipped in Tim.

"Boy, then. You like a fuss, don't you? Would you like me to look after him while you have your meal?" Tim thought she did a convincing job and was nodding frantically at Lumina.

"He does seem to like you," said Lumina with a pout, as Horse licked the woman's fingers and scrabbled to get out of the bag to get to her. "Okay," and she handed over the bag and stalked off.

"Thank you, we won't be long," smiled Tim.

It was early for dinner but the restaurant was buzzing with chatter, and smart waiters and waitresses sped around looking slick and efficient. A tall waiter showed them to their table, which was nicely positioned, not too far from the exit and not in full, public view – perfect if Lumina decided to throw a strop. They studied the menus in silence. The waiter returned and took their orders. Tim checked his watch and then his phone.

"Tim, are you taking this relationship seriously?" Lumina's words were forceful and she was leaning forward in her seat.

"It's not a relationship… actually, Lumina, I did want to talk to you."

"Oh no, not the 'I'm not ready to settle down' speech again. I don't want to settle down either."

"But I think you do. Maybe not this week, but sometime soon and I'm just not that guy. It's not fair on you to make you think I will ever be that guy. Because I won't."

"Tim, I'm not listening and we're not ending this. I won't let you, we had a deal." She threw down her napkin like a toddler throwing down a toy and walked off. Tim watched her go for as long as his stretched neck would allow. He waited for a few minutes and was about to ask for the bill when Lumina reappeared. The disappointment in his face was visible, but he tried to hide it with a smile.

Before they could continue the discussion, the starters arrived. An uncomfortable silence fell around their corner of the restaurant, as if in quarantine from the rest. Tim mulled over how else he could say it. He finished his starter and took a sip of water and went to speak. Lumina held up her hand to stop him and shook her head. This was hopeless. Tim checked his watch and then his phone. It had been the longest 30 minutes of his life.

"Have you enjoyed Bath this week?" Tim asked. Lumina stared at him as if it was a trick question.

"Yes, I have."

"Didi was a giggle, wasn't she?"

"No, she's old and boring. I don't know why you are friends with her." Tim was pleased with the negative reaction and saw an opportunity.

"She's moving into my apartment this weekend."

"What? You're moving in together?"

"More of a flat-share."

"That's ludicrous! I won't…" Lumina stopped herself and waved her hands up and down in a floating motion, as if trying to calm herself down. "Fine, it's your apartment. That's fine." Tim was stumped again. He checked his watch. His phone rang and he jumped on it in relief; he was thrilled to see who the caller was and leaned back as far as he could in his stiff, high-backed chair.

"Hi, Jackie, how are you? I've missed you, too," he glanced at Lumina. Her eyes were boring holes into his head, so he continued, "Did you like the clothes I sent you? Did they fit?" Another glance across the table showed that Lumina's usually ceramic complexion was turning crimson and the rage in her eyes was borderline psycho; he knew he had nearly cracked it. "I can't wait to see you wearing them, Jackie," he said, and that did the trick. Lumina screamed at him. There weren't any words, it was just a noise. She grabbed her glass of mineral water with a slice of lime and threw it over Tim with such force that for a second Tim thought the glass was coming at him, too. The slice of lime bounced rhythmically down his front. She stood up quickly, knocking her chair over backwards.

"You utter bastard! It's over."

"Hang on, Jackie," said Tim, brushing off some of the liquid from his face and covering the phone, "Okay, Lumina, if that's what you want. I take it the deal is off, too, then. I'm sorry it didn't work out. Terry will take you home."

Another stifled scream of frustration signalled her departure and she stomped off. The chatter in the restaurant had dwindled to a muffled titter.

"No, Jackie, it's nothing for you to worry about. Tell me what you've been up to," Tim said, as the waiters quickly rearranged the table and chair and proffered napkins for Tim to dry himself. Tim finished his phone call, paid the bill and walked out with his head held high. He was just reaching the doors when the cloakroom attendant called to him.

"Sir, your dog?" Tim spun around to see the young woman cradling a snarling Horse and holding up the small bowling bag.

"But he's not mine."

"Look, if the manager sees him, I'm in trouble. Here," and she popped Horse into his bag, zipped it up to his neck and offered it to Tim. The snarling turned to yapping as Tim approached.

"Right. Thanks," said Tim curtly, and he made a couple of failed attempts to grab the handles as Horse swivelled his head in an attempt to bite Tim.

"Now, listen, mutt. Unless you want to spend the evening in left luggage or the Battersea Dogs' Home, I suggest you start being nice." Tim's face was a bit too close for Horse's liking and he lunged forward and successfully nipped his nose.

"Ow!" Tim grabbed the bag and strode out of the restaurant. He was surprised but thankful to see that Terry was waiting nearby. He passed the yapping bag to Terry, "Boot," he said.

"I'll put him on the front seat. If he can't see you, he might shut up. Did she hit you?" asked Terry, as he noticed that Tim was holding his nose.

"No, let's take him back to Lumina before I sell him to the nearest kebab house."

"Okay, boss."

Terry's plan was a good one. Horse was happy sitting in the front, especially after Terry had put a couple of cushions from the boot onto the seat so that Horse could see out of the windscreen. Tim checked his nose in the rear vanity mirror and, although it was very red, the bite hadn't broken the skin. Tim called Lumina's mobile, but as expected, it went to voicemail. They pulled up outside Lumina's apartment building and Terry leaned over the

286

driver's seat to talk to Tim.

"Shall I take him in, then?"

"Please," winced Tim, rubbing his nose. Terry was only gone for a couple of minutes and he returned with Horse and replaced him regally on his cushions,

"She's not back yet," said Terry.

"But didn't you drive her back here?"

"No, she got in a cab."

"Just leave it with the concierge, then."

"I tried that. They won't take him."

"This is bloody brilliant." Tim dialled her number again, but this time left a message. "Mina, I am truly sorry about this evening, but sometime soon you'll realise it's for the best. Anyway, you left the dog at the restaurant and I'll have to take it back to my hotel. Can you pick it up as soon as you get this message?"

Back at Tim's hotel, things didn't improve between him and Horse. It took Tim a good 15 minutes to undo the zip of the bag without being bitten. He had been tempted to leave him in the bag or, better still, do the zip up tighter. However, despite what people thought, Tim did have a heart and he didn't think animals should be treated as fashion accessories, unless of course, in Horse's case, you were thinking of making him into a stole. The least he could do was let the thing have a run around the suite and have a drink of water. Horse had other ideas. As soon as he was free he started a full on attack of Tim's toes, which were on display since he'd taken off his shoes and socks to relax.

"Argh, get off! It's not far to Battersea, you know!" shouted Tim, to no avail. He ran into the bathroom and shut the door. Horse found this particularly frustrating and sat and yapped and whined outside while Tim made a number of phone calls, including another one to Lumina, one to Terry and lastly Pippa.

"Pips, darling Pips, I need you," pleaded Tim into his mobile.

"Before you ask, I'm having an evening off as I'll be working most of the weekend sorting out your apartment," said Pippa quickly. She was snuggled up in bed with a large glass of white wine, a box of Maltesers and the box set of her favourite Sci Fi show.

"But Pips, I'm being held hostage in my own bathroom." Pippa dropped the Malteser and clutched the phone.

"What do you need me to do?" she breathed huskily.

"I need you to come over now and rescue me."

"But I'm in my PJs." She could feel the panic rising.

"Just put a coat over the top, no one will know."

"Shall I call the police? Are they armed?"

"No, it's the sodding dog that's holding me hostage. Listen," and Tim held the phone to the bathroom door, outside which Horse was still going apoplectic and was now also scratching frantically at the door and carpet. "The size-to-volume ratio on that thing is way out of proportion."

"Tim! I thought you meant… Grrrr," Pippa growled at him in frustration.

"Look, I can't take this in stereo. Terry will drive you here and back; it won't take more than half an hour and then we'll all be happy."

"Okay, I'll do it for Horse," sighed Pippa, pressing "pause" on her DVD. "Ask Terry to pick me up in 20 minutes."

"You're a legend. Terry is waiting out the front of your place now, so get a move on, he wants to finish for the night," and Tim ended the call before she could protest.

Horse continued to yap and scratch. Tim found that the more he shouted at Horse the louder he got, so he decided to keep quiet. He put the shower on in an attempt to drown out the sound, but the combined volume was more annoying and the water just made Tim want to pee. Tim tried tying a towel on his head to drown out the noise, but it didn't work and it was a lot harder to do than it looked. After a few minutes it went quiet outside and Tim found himself doing a little happy dance until he caught sight of himself in the mirror and quickly sat down on the edge of the Edwardian bath.

A few minutes later, there was a knock on the main suite door. Tim peered out of the bathroom to see if the coast was clear, then tiptoed over and let Pippa in. She was wearing a short black mac, bare legs and red heels.

"This is actually one of my fantasies," said Tim, "Did I say that out loud? Sorry."

"Calm down, underneath I have my PJs on."

"Spoilsport, you didn't need to tell me that."

"So where is he, then?" Pippa was looking around the suite for Horse.

"Good question. He stopped the torturous yapping about five minutes ago."

"I'll find him, shall I?" Pippa raised her eyebrows and started checking the room, "Horse, come on Horse, it's Auntie Pippa. I've come to take you away from the horrible man." Tim gave a not-so-amused smile and got himself a beer from the fridge. After a few minutes of searching, Pippa called out, "Here he is. Poor little soul is hiding under the bed. He looks terrified!"

"Don't blame me, he was the one doing the terrorising. I've got the marks to prove it," said Tim, pointing to his nose and feet in quick succession.

"Come and help me. I can't get him out of here on my own, he's too scared."

"What am I? The bait?" Tim reluctantly joined Pippa, who was on her knees with her backside stuck up in the air and her head under the bed. "Actually, I just need to take a photo of this," laughed Tim, angling his mobile. Pippa was just about to protest when a shrill voice rang out behind them.

"Oh, my God! You are a sexaholic!" screeched Lumina.

"It's not what you think," said Pippa, reversing from underneath the bed and banging her head in the process. As she shuffled inelegantly backwards, her mac ruched up, revealing her rolled-up pyjama bottoms.

"Pippa! Not you too?"

"No, not me, too. I'm just here to get Horse."

"But I'm here to get Horse."

Tim sat back on his heels and laughed. He couldn't help it and he knew it wouldn't help the situation, but it was one of the funniest sights he'd ever seen. Pippa ignored him and tried to have a normal conversation with Lumina.

"Horse is under the bed and he won't come out."

"Horsey," called Lumina, and a shaking Horse crept from under the bed, to be hastily scooped up by Lumina, who shook her head briefly but violently, like a swimmer with water trapped in her ears. She turned on her Jimmy Choo heels and left without another word. Tim could have sworn that the dog stuck its tongue out at him as it left.

"I'm off back to bed," said Pippa, standing up.

"Oh Pips, just one more thing before you go."

"Whatever it is, the answer is no!"

After Pippa had left, Tim decided he'd have a quick drink in the bar. He put on some clean socks and slid his feet into his shoes. The sound of the squelch and the sensation of something soft oozing through his sock hit him simultaneously, closely followed by the smell.

"Little shit!" shouted Tim in anger and disgust, which summed up the situation on so many levels.

Chapter 25

Kate had lain awake most of the night, mulling over the proposed weekend away. She knew if it had been Sarah, or probably any woman, for that matter, they would have said yes in a heartbeat, but that wasn't Kate. She thought things through; she often wished that she didn't, that she could be spontaneous, but that just wasn't her way. She had done plenty of thinking and the only downside, which was also a big plus, would be her proximity to Timothy Calder in swimwear. But, if Didi was there she knew she wouldn't do anything she'd regret and it would definitely be a giggle.

Kate slunk out of bed and tried to be very quiet. She found herself tiptoeing from room to room. Unfortunately, it appeared that someone had turned up the volume on her otherwise mute house, because now every floorboard had a squeaky song to sing and every door a creaky tale to tell. She hadn't realised she was living in a sound-effects department. She fired up her computer, which beeped loudly into life and made her shush it. She printed off her holiday checklist and procured her wheelie case from the back of her walk-in wardrobe. Kate happily ferried all her essentials from their winter homes and placed them neatly in groups on the bed, with a separate section for hand luggage, obviously. When she was happy she had everything she could possibly need for one night in the sun, she placed them in the case like an elaborate three-dimensional jigsaw, marking each one off on her list with a satisfying tick in marker pen.

Kate checked the clock. It was still before seven, but she could hear movement in Amy's room, so she would be appearing soon. Kate decided now was her chance to call Tim in private. He had said they were leaving early, so she guessed he would be up.

Kate settled herself in the conservatory with her mobile and rang his number. It barely rang before he answered it.

"Hi, Kate, hang on a second," said Tim, and Kate waited patiently, her excitement bubbling away inside. "Okay, fire away."

"Count me in for the trip to Italy." As there was no imme- diate response she added. "Please."

"Er, thing is, Didi changed her mind, she's sorting the flat out with Pippa." Kate's bubble of excitement was reaching boiling point. If she went to Italy now, she'd be alone with Tim. This was one of those decision points in life, where you either made the right decision or the one that you regretted forever.

"Just the two of us, then. That's okay with me," she said as breezily as she could muster, despite the fact that she was now scrunched up into a small ball in an attempt to hold her nerve and contain her excitement.

Tim carried on almost as if he hadn't heard her. "So, because Didi changed her mind and I hadn't heard from you, I flew out last night…" An odd silence followed, where Kate's mind was wondering if she would look desperate if she suggested getting on the next flight out. Her train of thought was broken by a woman's cheery voice in the background.

"Come on, Tim, Jackie's waiting to have breakfast in the jacuzzi!" she called. There was a strange echo-ey noise, which Kate assumed was a hand covering the phone.

"Kate, are you still there?" Tim said anxiously.

"Is that Lumina?" Kate's voice was barely a whisper.

"No! It's not Lumina. God, no," Tim said emphatically. "That's completely over. Finished."

Kate ended the call and switched off her mobile. She sat and stared out at the early-morning sun dancing over the garden; a single cloud moved slowly in front, to cast shadows and finally block it out completely. She didn't notice the tears until they dripped onto her tightly folded arms. Kate felt kicked and foolish. After losing James, she knew what it was like to have your heart crushed, but this was a masterpiece of origami. She didn't know how much more manipulation her poor heart could take and the thought make her hug her knees tighter in an effort to protect herself.

Kate said she was coming down with something, so Andy, Sarah and Amy left her to have a duvet day while they spruced up Sarah's house ready for her and Amy to move back in. Sarah decided to start with the kitchen. She thought her house was generally clean, but when you had a really close look, from a down-on-your-hands-and-knees perspective, it was actually a bit mucky.

Sarah thought the quickest answer for removing the dirt was probably to torch the place, but given her recent scrape with the law, maybe some scouring pads and a selection of multi-coloured cleaners was the answer. Kate had said, "Help yourself", so Sarah had loaded just about every cleaning product she could find into a box and brought them over.

She started with something called "multi-purpose cleaner", which sounded a lot like her, so must be good. Sarah longed for a time when paper plates and sawdust flooring became acceptable. She put the radio on and, a few songs later, she found that the tiles and worktops had been easy and the sink was looking shinier than Irene's nose at Christmas. Sarah took a deep breath and decided it was time to tackle the floor, which thanks to a stampede of police boots, looked dirtier than a Glastonbury porta-loo.

"Sarah, is it okay if I just nip out for 20 minutes?" Andy popped his mop of sun- streaked hair around the back door. Sarah liked that he asked her, especially as he had no reason to.

"No problem. What's Amy doing?"

"She's dusting sand into the gaps between the slabs. Should keep her occupied for ten minutes or so."

"Okay, I might know what colour this floor is by the time you get back." Unfortunately, the floor had other ideas and the super-power floor cleaner that had promised so much was now just a mass of dirty foam that Sarah was pushing around the floor. She looked up to see a very superior look on Amy's face.

"Mummy, you have made a big mess!"

Andy returned, as promised, 20 minutes later and thought twice about entering the foam party that was now the kitchen. "Shall I get some sandwiches?"

Sarah looked up. She was hot and bothered but she was smiling. "How absorbent are sandwiches? I think we need sandbags!"

"Three sandwiches and a truck full of sandbags coming up," and he disappeared again.

They sat in the garden and had a picnic of shop-bought sandwiches, Hula Hoops and carrot cake, with a large bottle of lemonade to wash it all down. Andy cancelled the incoming call on his mobile for the third time.

"Someone's keen to get hold of you," Sarah nodded at his mobile, in between eating Hula Hoops off her fingers, just as Amy was doing. Andy's mobile replied with a double beep to advise that a text had also been received.

"Yeah," Andy frowned and switched it off.

"It's not…" Sarah tried to think of a way to say "Shaun" without Amy catching on, so she pointed at the patio instead. Andy shook his head and concentrated on his sandwich.

Kate tried to ignore the front-door bell, but when the caller resorted to banging on the door she knew she would have to drag herself out of bed. She had already had to unplug the house phone, thanks to Tim's incessant calling. She didn't want to hear his excuses, and why he was so bothered about relating them to her she couldn't fathom, either. She hoped it wasn't her neighbour wanting to know about the boundaries again, because she had turned the house upside down looking for the deeds and they were now officially lost. She pulled on her dressing gown and plodded downstairs as the persistent visitor continued to ring and knock. Kate opened the door to find three very trendy-looking people grinning at her.

"Hi, you must be Kate. I'm Ace." Kate liked people who had faith in themselves, but felt this was going a bit far.

"I'm a bit rubbish today, actually, so if you're selling something…" to which they all started to laugh rather hysterically.

"You're funny!" said the very tall young woman next to him. "His name is Ace, I'm Zoe and this is Chad," she indicated to the two thin men.

"How can I help you?"

"We are here to help you!" said Ace overexcitedly. "I'm a stylist, Chad is a hairdresser and Zoe is a make-up artist."

"Was this that magazine competition?" said Kate, really wishing she had got dressed as they all started to laugh again.

"No, no, no," waved Ace. "We work with top celebrities and today we are going to give you a complete make-over thanks to…" he gave a dramatic pause, but Kate feared she knew what was coming next, "Timothy Calder!"

"Sorry, no thank you," and Kate shut the door and went to get dressed.

As Sarah was out for the afternoon, doing flower deliveries straight after she finished at the pub, Andy was put in charge of sorting out the loft. Sarah had told him that there were distinct piles for charity, to keep and to throw away. After a quick look through the hatch, Andy resolved to board up the loft as he went, balancing on joists was always dangerous and, for a man of his size and limited balancing ability, it could easily end in disaster. He was no Billy

Elliott, that was for sure. A quick trip to the DIY store with Amy provided them with the chipboard flooring they needed.

Whilst Andy was busy in the loft, Amy set about sorting out any clothes that were too small for her and also any toys that she no longer wanted so that they could go to the charity shop, too.

After three hours at the pub and two more in the Back to the Fuchsia van, Sarah opened her front door to see Andy and Amy sitting on the bottom step of the stairs looking just as tired as she did.

"Mummy!" Amy immediately brightened up and flung her arms around Sarah. Andy held up a small box and gestured for Sarah to look inside. She peered over the edge and flinched, before she recognised the poor mangy stuffed otter inside.

"He's for the charity shop. He might be of use to someone, I think!"

"He's for the police station. He's full of cocaine, I think!" Andy said in a phlegmatic tone.

"What?" Sarah stuck her head in the box to get a closer look. There was more white dust than before, spilling out of the otter and part of a plastic bag was now visible where Andy had had more of a rummage about, "Oh fu...dge," modified Sarah.

"My thoughts entirely."

"What's coking, Mummy?" asked Amy, peeping into the box.

They were all quiet in the car on the way back from the police station and still silent as they walked into Kate's. Kate was curled up on the sofa staring at a switched-off television, but at least she was up and dressed, which was an achievement. The three dejected figures all wandered into the living room and slumped down on the sofa. Amy crawled onto Andy's lap.

"You all look tired. Is the house cleaner than a dentist's smile?"

"It's better than it was and we'll be able to move back in tomorrow. I'll fill you in later, but we've had a bit more excitement."

"I take it not in a good way," said Kate, as all three of them

296

shook their heads in response. "Okay, so how about takeaway for dinner, then? My treat, unless you'd like caviar?"

"Caviar?" queried Sarah.

"Yes, I have a whole Fortnum and Mason's picnic basket of the stuff. Oh, except for the space where the magnum of vintage champagne was."

"Explain?"

"Timothy Bloody Calder," said Kate, pointing to the kitchen. Sarah and Amy ran out to investigate and there were whoops of delight from both of them,

"That's not the half of it," said Kate to Andy. "Thankfully I managed to get them to take away the Vespa scooter and the West Highland White Terrier puppy called Marlon," she said, rolling her eyes.

"A puppy!" shouted a flabbergasted Amy.

The hammering on the front door had the whole house awake in seconds, hearts beating fast and dressing gowns being grabbed. Andy was first downstairs.

"Who is it?" he shouted to the closed door.

"Police!" Andy turned round to see Kate and Sarah freeze on the stairs. He opened the door on the chain.

"Can I see some ID please?"

"Yes, sir, I'm Police Sergeant Harris and this is Police Constable Bentley," said the impossibly tall policeman as he passed their badges through to Andy, but a quick glance behind them revealed a police estate car in its full reflective glory. "We're looking for a Mrs Sarah Greasley."

"Come in," said Andy, stepping to one side. Amy huddled up to Kate on the stairs and Sarah padded across the cold tiles.

"I'm Sarah Greasley." She looked terrified.

"Sorry to trouble you at this late hour, but we couldn't get any answer on the phone numbers you left us," said the very tall policeman. Kate took a sharp intake of breath and they all looked round.

"I'm so sorry, I unplugged it… too many sales calls."

"Don't worry, Kate, the mobiles were all switched off, too," said Sarah. She turned her attention back to the police officers. "What do you want me for?"

"I'm afraid there's been a break-in at your property." He paused instinctively to let the assembled citizens react, which they all did on cue. "It's difficult for us to tell if anything has been stolen, but the obvious items are still in place; television, DVD. We've secured the property but we'll need you to meet us there tomorrow and sign some forms.

"Is there much damage?" asked Sarah.

"Just a back window and a bit of mess upstairs, but nothing you can't tidy up."

"We were at the station earlier today," ventured Andy. "Do you think the two things are connected?"

"It's possible." Sergeant Harris shrugged. "Apologies for the disturbance. Here's my number. Call us in the morning and we'll sort everything out."

"Thank you," said Andy, as he locked the door behind them. "Tea and chat or back to bed?"

"No tea for me, thanks. I'll put Amy back to bed," said Kate, guiding a barely awake Amy back upstairs.

"Go on, I'll have a coffee. I couldn't sleep now even if you banged me over the head with a mallet," said Sarah, following Andy into the kitchen. She sat down and pulled her legs up onto her chair. Her feet were freezing.

"So, do you think it's Shaun or someone else looking for the otter's stash?" said Andy as he put the kettle on.

"My guess is Shaun. Who else would know it was there?"

"Fair enough. So, you're not going home tomorrow, then." Andy spooned coffee into the mugs and collected milk from the fridge as he waited for the kettle to finish boiling.

"No, but you can."

"I'm not sure. I don't like to leave you three, you know…"

"We'll be okay. The police and you aren't far away. I know you want to get back to your place now it's all finished."

"Not completely finished, but it is looking good. I'd like you to see it; you can give me a woman's verdict." He finished making the coffees and passed one to Sarah.

"I'd like that. How about tomorrow?"

Andy looked a little wrong-footed, "Uh, yeah. Okay, if you like."

"Well, while I've got a built-in babysitter."

"Good call! I'll cook us a meal."

"That'll be lovely. Thanks for everything, Andy. You've been brilliant," and she leaned over the table very inelegantly and planted a kiss on his lips. They both let the kiss linger. Andy gave a shy smile and Sarah sat back down and sipped her coffee whilst they both stared at the table.

Sunday was a miserable, rainy day, so Kate decided she would take Amy swimming and then to a particularly good indoor adventure playground that had near-vertical drop slides and rope swings. It was just the thing to take Amy's mind off stuff and for her to burn off some energy. Then they would grab a hamburger and finish off with the cinema. All in all, it would be a good kid's day out.

Andy and Sarah met another group of police officers at her house, as planned, and, due to the weather, Sarah gave them the option of either standing in the hall or taking their boots off as she had no desire to be scrubbing the kitchen floor again anytime soon. Despite a lot of fingerprint dust on Sarah's recently cleaned windowsill and worktop, the police hadn't found any evidence to implicate Shaun with the break-in. But Sarah did. An old cocoa tin was lying on its side near the sink.

"That tin was in the cupboard; it's where we kept the food money. It was empty, but only Shaun would have known where to look." The young officer smiled weakly and scribbled a note on his pad. Apart from the damage to the kitchen window, downstairs was unscathed. Upstairs was a different matter. The loft hatch was open and half of the remaining contents were strewn across the landing, including the pink tinsel, which Sarah quickly bundled into a carrier bag as Andy sniggered. The biggest shock was Amy's bedroom. It had been totally trashed. Everything that had been in the wardrobe or drawers was now flung around the room. Even the bed had been stripped and dragged away from the wall. Thankfully nothing appeared to be broken.

"So here or the loft stuff? I'll toss you for it." Sarah tried to smile.

"Let's do both together. Come on," and Andy got hold of one end of the bed and beckoned for Sarah to take the other and they moved it back into position.

"It can only be Shaun, so why on earth has he done this to her room?" Sarah put the bed down.

"Beats me. I'm just glad she won't see it like this."

It didn't take them long to tidy and straighten everything up in Amy's room and return the loft to some resemblance of order.

"I'll drop you back at Kate's, then I'm off to do some shopping for tonight," said Andy with a boyish grin.

"Okay," said Sarah feeling a little apprehensive, for the first time, about their planned evening together. Neither of them had mentioned last night's kiss. It hadn't been wild and passionate, so maybe it wasn't worth mentioning, but Sarah wanted to know what it meant or if it meant anything at all. At least he'd invited her over for a meal for two – or had he? When Sarah thought it through she realised that she'd invited herself over. Too late now, she thought.

Back at Kate's, Sarah was still mulling it over. All she could do was go with the flow, let Andy lead the way and see where they ended up. Just in case that meant bedroom activity, she went wild with the hair remover and did lots of neat topiary with the razor. Sarah found it particularly hard to drag herself out of Kate's giant bath tub, but on hearing a commotion downstairs, she was out in a flash, wrapping a towel around herself and heading onto the landing, her heart racing.

There was someone crashing about downstairs and they weren't worried about who heard them. Sarah heard the tea and coffee jars being knocked over in the kitchen, closely followed by what she guessed was the knives, as whoever it was worked their way along the kitchen surface.

She didn't know whether to confront whoever it was or just go straight for the phone. In her heart she knew it could only be Shaun. The sensible thing to do was call the police. Sarah went for the middle ground and grabbed the phone from Kate's room, tapped in 999, but didn't press the call button. She cautiously headed partway down the stairs.

"Shaun, I'm calling the police!" she shouted. She couldn't hear anything for a moment until, all of a sudden, there was the sound of more of a kerfuffle, which was heading her way. As she came eye to eye with them, she screamed. Sarah was met on the stairs by a green bird in mid-flight. It was about the size of a pigeon, with an impressive wingspan and a flash of red on its head. It was closely followed by a very determined Marmalade, who was bouncing up and down underneath it as if she was on springs. Sarah dodged the bird and threw the towel over Marmalade, who let out a screech of annoyance. Sarah, now completely naked, grabbed the struggling bundle, shoved it in the conservatory and shut the door. She was just wondering how Marmalade had managed to get in when she heard a scream behind her and spun around to see Concetta. Sarah decided to brazen it out.

"Hi, Concetta, welcome to naked Sunday. Are you going to join me?" and she did a little catwalk pose. Concetta's mouth opened and her jaw moved as if she was talking, but no noise was audible.

"Can I help you? We don't usually see you on a Sunday," she said, a little slower this time.

"No, I look for Endy."

"He's gone home. Try calling him. Don't let the pyscho cat back in and I'll sort out the bird. Bye," and Sarah walked upstairs trying hard to stifle her laughter. The poor bird was sitting on the windowsill in the bathroom, looking terrified. Up close, Sarah could clearly see that it was a woodpecker and was amazed by how beautiful it was. She had a little look over it and could see no signs of any injuries; Marmalade was gentler than she looked. Sarah opened the bathroom window as wide as it would go and then left the room, taking another towel with her. As she reached the door, the bird saw its opportunity for escape and was gone.

Chapter 26

Tim banged on the front door again as the ginger cat swirled itself around his legs.

"Why don't you have a key?" he asked it. "That would be useful, wouldn't it?" Marmalade stalked off in disgust and disappeared around the side of the house and Tim put down the carrier bags, which were starting to cut into his fingers. He tried Kate's home phone and he heard it ring inside. He tried her mobile again and it went straight to voicemail. A quick look round told him there were no cars on the drive, so it was likely that nobody was home.

He stood for a moment and tried to think. He wished he did more thinking, wished he thought things through better. He was impulsive and most of the time it worked out well for him, but where Kate was concerned, it just seemed to end in mini-disaster after mini-disaster.

Tim thought he heard something, so he peered in through the letterbox. There was no sign of anyone, but as he let it snap shut, he thought he saw some movement inside. He opened it and peered in again. There was a ginger cat, identical to the one that had just been wrapping itself around his legs, and it was sitting in the hallway staring at him. "How did you get in? Or are you a body-double?" The cat turned around, twitched its tail and sauntered off.

Tim felt a rush of excitement; if the cat had got in, maybe he could, too. He picked up his carrier bags and almost ran around the house. On the side of the house was a large semi-circular Victorian conservatory and there was one small window that was open. Tim tried the door, but to no avail. He put down his bags and studied the window. It wasn't too high up, about level with his head, and there was a ledge at knee-height, which must have been where the cat had jumped from. Marmalade appeared and settled down on the wicker furniture to enjoy the show, her unblinking gaze instantly putting Tim off his thought process.

Tim picked up the first carrier bag and started to post the contents through the window. First of all, a couple of onions, a bag of carrots and some parsnips. Marmalade sat up in alarm and watched intently. Stock cubes, garlic, sage and artichokes rained down next. Tim let the two handfuls of large tomatoes go at the same time as his brain kicked into gear and he and the cat watched them explode as they hit the floor, sending juice in every possible direction. The conservatory now looked like a budget version of La Tomatino, Spain's tomato festival.

"Bugger!" Tim held the butternut squash in his hand and he and Marmalade stared at it. Tim had a bad feeling about this. If the impact of the tiled floor had done that to the tomatoes, then this one looked as if it could be a big problem. Tim put the butternut squash through as far as it would go and then swung his arm. The vegetable left his hand and he and Marmalade followed its trajectory until the cat realised it was heading her way and, with a brief squeal, she leapt out of its path. The butternut squash landed safely on the soft cushions of the wicker chair. Tim punched the air and Marmalade glared at him. He did the same successful lob with the lemon and the steak but, deciding he would have to get by without the glass bottles of olive oil and red wine, he left them on the step.

It was now his turn to follow the ingredients inside. Marmalade resumed her seat to watch him. The first part was okay. He could balance on the ledge quite well and had already managed to unhook the latch so he could open the window to the full. Now came the hard part. He let the window rest on the back of his head whilst he wriggled in as far as he could. He gave a push with his feet and found himself being cut in two by the window frame and the window arm digging painfully into his back. Marmalade got a little bored and decided to investigate the items on the chair. The lemon and butternut squash were quickly dismissed, but the steak was a lot more interesting. She started to claw at the cellophane.

"No, you little sod, leave it alone. That's dinner!" Marmalade had a look at the shouting man who was stuck in the window and decided he was noisy but clearly not a threat. "I'm warning you!" he said, as he did some more wriggling and tried to lift himself off the window edge, which was trying its best to slice through his ribs. "Bugger!" he shouted as he hauled himself through, being careful not to balance any sensitive parts on the window edge. Tim now realised that even when he did think things through he didn't do a very good job. He was now tilting precariously towards the tiled floor. Marmalade stopped clawing the meat packet for a moment to watch.

"Do you know how much this face is insured for?" Tim asked a bored-looking Marmalade, who quickly returned to the meat packet, this time deciding that she'd give it a chew and see what happened. Tim realised he had to make a move now, and it was probably worse to think about what might happen than to actually do it. He pushed the rest of himself through the window and, as expected, he landed with an unceremonious and very painful thud. His hands broke the fall, but landing head-first onto Victorian tiles was never going to be a soft landing.

"Bugger!" said Tim, as he hauled himself into a sitting position and leant against the chair to get his breath back and inspect his injuries. Marmalade had failed to get into the steak and was now rubbing affectionately around Tim's head to see if

305

he might like to help her. "And you can bugger off, too. You were no help!"

After lots of inspecting, Tim decided that it was only bumps and bruises, but his right forearm was swelling up a bit. He collected his ingredients and ferried them into the kitchen, wishing he'd thought to bring the bag. Once inside, he realised that he could now go out of the front door and walk round and retrieve the olive oil and red wine, and he so wished he'd thought to do that for all the ingredients, especially the tomatoes. He gave a sigh, propped the front door open with a chair, just in case the bloody cat decided to shut it after him, and collected the bottles.

Some time later, Tim found himself in a steamed-up kitchen, up to his ears in chopped veg and in charge of a very angry, spitting pan.

"Didi, help!"

"Tim, I can't talk right now. We're deciding where to put a picture."

"On the sodding wall. Now, listen, this is important. I've burnt two onions and I'm on my last one, the sage has gone all stringy and the beef is now covered in what looks like glue. What do I do?" Tim stood dressed in a spotty apron he'd found, with the phone tucked under his chin and a wooden spoon raised in the air, ready to leap into action.

"What are you talking about? I thought you were in Italy."

"Change of plan. The casserole recipe you told me about, I'm making it now."

"Oh, heaven preserve us! Who are you trying to poison?"

"Not helping! Onions still spitting at me here!"

"Turn the heat down and stir them."

"Right, yes, that's a little better. It didn't say stir it."

"Maybe not, but it probably says get an adult to help you. You should have started off with chocolate crispie cakes."

"Again, not helping. What about the beef?" he said topping up his wine glass. He was glad that the recipe only needed a small amount of red wine.

"Did you pat it dry in kitchen roll and then roll it in flour?"

"I just rolled it in flour."

"Which explains the glue. Rinse it off under a lukewarm tap, pat it dry and try again. You did peel the veg before you chopped it, didn't you?"

"I'm not completely stupid! Thanks, bye," said Tim, surveying the vegetables, and wondering how he was going to peel them now they were cubes.

It was the smell that hit Kate as she opened the door. It wasn't altogether terrible, but there was sharpness to it. She wondered if Sarah and Andy had changed their plans and decided to stay home, but realised there were no cars on the drive. It was all quiet, so she ushered Amy upstairs.

"Do your teeth and I'll come and run you a bath in a minute," said Kate to a weary Amy, who simply nodded and went upstairs.

Kate went into the kitchen and surveyed the devastation. It looked like closing time on market day, when everything that's left ends up scattered everywhere for someone else to clear up. The oven was on and it appeared to be the source of the smell, which was considerably stronger in the kitchen. She opened it tentatively and was hit by a wave of smoke. She switched off the oven and opened the window. What was going on?

As she walked towards the stairs, she saw that someone was in the living room. There, on the sofa, lay Tim, wearing her favourite Cath Kidston apron and sound asleep, an empty wine glass on the table next to him. There was a second where she was pleased and relieved that it was Tim, but that feeling passed at lightning speed and left her feeling livid. How dare he break in and cook? She felt the anger bubble up, but she had to contain it just until she'd got Amy into bed; then she could deal with Tim, reclaim her apron and kick him out.

Amy was almost asleep in the bath, so did not complain when Kate suggested that she make it just a quick one tonight as it was school tomorrow. She was soon dried off and into pyjamas. Kate kissed her goodnight and suspected that she would be asleep before she had closed the door. Kate metaphorically rolled her sleeves up and thought through what she was going to say as she went downstairs. She strode into the living room ready for a confrontation, but Tim was gone.

"Wine before dinner?" Tim said smoothly. Kate spun around. Tim was leaning against the kitchen doorway holding out a glass of red wine. "I've cooked," he said, failing to contain the pride in his voice.

"No, you've burned," said Kate, marching over to the cooker and releasing another cloud of smoke.

"Bugger! How? I followed all the instructions." When the smoke cleared, Kate grabbed the oven gloves and removed her cast-iron casserole dish and placed it on the granite top. They both looked at the strange bubble-burping mass with its thick, black skin.

"Was it a casserole?" she asked,

"Yes. Is it dead?"

"I'm afraid so. Had it been in there long?"

"About two hours."

"With no lid and on at two hundred and twenty!"

"I wanted to cook you a meal to say sorry and to explain." He looked contrite, but Kate was still furious about the spoiled weekend away, the ridiculous gifts and now this.

"That hasn't gone exactly to plan, has it?" Kate's attention was suddenly drawn to Marmalade, who sauntered into the kitchen, jumped onto the table and left a trail of wet, red paw marks. Kate gasped and rushed to her. Tim saw an opportunity.

"It's okay, let me sort her out." He grabbed a cloth from the sink and went to wipe Marmalade's front paw. She thought it was a game and tried to grab the cloth.

"Where is she bleeding from?" asked Kate, grabbing kitchen roll. Tim paused.

"It's not blood, Kate, she's fine. It's tomato juice from the conservatory."

"Oh, right." She was still very confused as to what he was talking about, but she saw that he had avoided an opportunity to lie and come across as the hero, which was a good thing.

"I should probably get going." Tim sensed this was not going to be the panacea he had hoped for.

"No, I think there's some tidying up to be done." They both looked around the kitchen, "and apparently there's tomato sauce in the conservatory." On cue, Marmalade licked her front leg and then proceeded to try to spit out a tomato pip and shake the remainder off her paw.

"Tomato juice," corrected Tim before registering the irate look from Kate. "Yes, of course. Um, where to start?" Kate reluctantly handed him back the apron and a cloth and left him to it. After 30 minutes she found Tim on his hands and knees in the conservatory, wriggling his bottom as he tried to wipe up the tomato.

"Did you throw them at the cat?"

"No!" Tim was shocked that she'd think that. "I dropped them through the window."

"Because?"

"It's a long story. Look, I know I've ballsed up… yet again. How can I say I'm sorry?" Kate thought for a bit.

"I don't think you need to." She knew Tim was never going to change. They'd had an odd friendship and Kate wanted to hold onto that, even if it was going to hurt her.

"But I have to." Tim stood up, the apron looking as though he'd murdered someone. He took Kate's hand and she snatched it back, but she sat down next to him all the same.

"Come on, Kate, anything you want, you just have to say and it's yours." There was a long pause as Kate stared out at the garden in thought and Tim stared at Kate.

"I'd like to stay friends," she said.

"I'd like that, too. I'll always be there for you, Kate. I know you don't believe me, I'd think you were mad if you did. But I do mean it. If you need anything, I'll be there." It was a good speech; she couldn't place it, but it sounded good. "You must come to the villa another time."

"Maybe." Kate smiled, even though she thought it was never going to happen. She'd been caught once; she wouldn't let that happen again. Tim wasn't at all his usual relaxed self, he was sitting up very straight and kept looking around the room. Marmalade appeared and made straight for him, leaping onto his lap in an effortless bounce. She walked around in circles, flicked up her tail and gave him a close-up view of her behind. Tim grimaced. Marmalade settled down and started to rhythmically purr and knead her claws into Tim's knees.

"Ow," said Tim flinching. "Thank God, it's stopped. Oh, no it hasn't! Ow and again. What's with the rhythmic needles of pain?"

"It's what they do," explained Kate.

"What were you? A medieval torturer in a past life or one of the Krays?" he said to the cat.

"You can stroke her. She's friendly. She likes you," offered Kate amused. Tim stroked her and she stood up again and paced around in a circle.

"You do that when you're being friendly. Christ, what do you do when they piss you off?" he addressed Marmalade, who promptly settled back down, facing Tim this time, and proceeded to bury her claws in his scrotum by way of silent reply.

Sarah finished her lemon mousse and relaxed on the bench, looking once again at Amy's framed picture. "I'm impressed, Mr Shaw, you sure can cook. Who knew?"

"I live on my own and I like food. Don't tell anyone, but I sometimes watch *Saturday Kitchen*." He looked a little shy all of a sudden and started to clear the table.

"I'm shocked!" Sarah said in mock horror as she screwed up her face as the Fleurie and the sweet aftertaste of the lemon mousse met in her mouth. "I hate that bit, I always forget."

They'd had a great evening. They had just talked and talked about everything and nothing, but they hadn't talked about them or last night's kiss. Sarah checked her watch – it was nearly eleven.

"I'll need to get a cab before midnight or they'll sting me."

"Yeah, sure," Andy looked hesitant. "So that's the kitchen diner," he indicated with a sweep of his hand, "and you've seen the hall. Would you like to see the living room?" Sarah followed him through to a large room painted in neutral shades. It had a simple fireplace with a huge wooden beam above and a log burner beneath. Two chunky burgundy sofas sat facing the fire and a lone, matching chair, pointed half at the fire and half at a large flat-screen TV. A cream rug lay on the polished wooden floor in front of the fire. As Sarah sat down, Andy switched on his music system as he went past and some swearing rapper blared out.

"Sorry!" he said, switching it to something more melodic. Sarah cackled with laughter. He sat down on the sofa next to her, took a deep breath and turned to face her.

"Sarah?"

"Yes," she said.

"When I kissed you…"

"Technically, I think I kissed you." Sarah grimaced at her correction, as now really was not the time.

"Right, um, so when we kissed. I liked it," Good grief! Is that the best you can do? thought Andy, dismayed.

"I liked it, too. I like you." Sarah paused, feeling as awkward and unsure as Andy, "A lot."

"You do?" Andy looked genuinely surprised and she loved that about him. She saw the tension in his shoulders disappear.

"Yep, really, I do." There was a moment when Sarah heard

church bells ring, but she shook her head and tried to stop the wine from taking over.

"So, do you want to try the kissing thing again? I'm sorry, I sound like an idiot."

"You don't and it's okay." She reached out a hand and touched his arm. They both followed it with their eyes. "We could uh…" she didn't spell it out, "you haven't shown me upstairs yet." She knew she was being a total floozy, but she wasn't hurting anyone and she was due a bit of fun. Andy's smile spread really slowly as he stared at her.

"Are you sure about this?"

"Yes, I'm very interested in DIY," she grinned, with a tilt of her head, which made it swim just a little.

"Okay, give me two minutes." He kissed her quickly, half on the lips, as he jumped up and dashed upstairs two at a time. Left alone, Sarah wondered if she was sure about having sex with Andy. She figured it would be okay. She liked the closeness, even with Shaun – it was never like the films, but she expected that was the same for everyone. Her mother had warned her, "It's all hype. You'll be disappointed and you'll need tissues." As it turned out, that was actually quite good advice. Andy reappeared, still beaming his beautiful smile and took her hand.

She followed him silently upstairs, but as they neared the top a thought struck her.

"Do you have tissues?" she asked, Andy looked taken aback, but he laughed.

"Ever the romantic. Yes, in the bedside drawer." He stood behind her, rested one hand on her shoulder, then leaned into her ear and whispered, "From this moment on, it's all about you," and he opened the door.

Sarah was glad that Andy had a steadying hand on her, as she wasn't expecting to see what greeted her. Loads of twinkling candles in small groups were dotted around a good-sized bedroom, their vanilla scent mingling with the perfume of the roses that were

312

placed in small vases. A huge bed with cushions took centre stage and the room was flanked by floor-to- ceiling wardrobes.

"You can go in," Andy said softly, "if you want to," he added quickly, still unsure. Sarah stepped inside and ran her fingers over the ash wood of the wardrobes.

"Nice finish! Do you do flat-pack?"

"No, but I do made-to-measure." God, thought Sarah, that sounded so sexy! Who knew DIY could be a turn-on? Sarah started to feel her confidence return and in two steps she was on the bed.

"Ooh, I love your lamp-shadey chandelier thingy." The words squeaked out. Was that nerves or too much wine? Probably both. Andy joined her on the bed and then, very gently, he was kissing her. She felt a melting sensation, as if she was just going to liquefy down to nothing, like the candles. Damn! He was good at this. Andy continued his gentle but commanding kisses and then she felt his fingers in her hair and she figured that was her cue to get involved. She reached for his trousers and started tugging at the belt. Andy stopped kissing her and slowly took her hand as he shook his head. His eyes bright and sexy.

"No, I said it's all about you." He let her hand drop.

"What does that mean exactly?" Sarah said, propping herself up on an elbow and killing the moment slightly for Andy. He looked a tad exasperated.

"It's not a question-and-answer session. Please, just trust me. You can stop me at any time, okay? It's fine to change your mind."

"Are you into something a bit kinky? 'Cause it's okay. Well it might be okay. I'd just like to be forewarned."

"Sarah, there is no kinky stuff. You just need to relax. I just want to focus on you having a good time."

"So what shall I be doing?" she asked, her brow furrowing. Andy's eyes widened, this was not going the way he'd rehearsed it in his mind.

"You'll be enjoying it. Now shut up, take your clothes off and get into bed," he said, as he tried to tickle her. Once they were down to their best underwear they slid under the cool white-cotton covers. They kissed some more: long, gentle, exploring kisses as their bodies felt the warmth of each other. Andy leaned away and gently stroked Sarah's cheek. She opened her eyes slowly.

"So, that was starters. Are you ready for the main course?"

"I'll have the sausage, please," she said with a giggle. Andy couldn't help but laugh, although this probably wasn't the oh-so romantic moment he'd hoped for. Here we go, thought Sarah, brace yourself and she quickly thought she shouldn't be so unkind; men couldn't help it, that's just the way they were programmed. Kissing, shagging, snoring.

"You really are gorgeous, Sarah. You have a frightful gob on you, but you're amazing. Now, close those beautiful eyes." Sarah stared at him. She wanted to ask why she had to close her eyes, but apparently it wasn't a question-and-answer session.

"Close them," he whispered, as he leaned over and kissed each eyelid, and she automatically closed them. She felt him throw off the duvet. She felt his warm breath against her cheek and then small, soft kisses were placed slowly along her bottom lip. Her mouth had now fallen open and she was aware that she was breathing heavily. The trail moved painstakingly slowly to her neck and then to her ear, "Please relax, Sarah, trust me."

"I do," she breathed and the church bells chimed in her head again. There were more soft kisses and then there was nibbling, sending an alert to her nether regions, which until then had been in deep hibernation. Andy took his time and very gradually took his trail of kisses to her breasts. She giggled involuntarily and opened one eye. Andy gave her a stern look and she closed it again. Andy tugged at her nipple through her best lace bra, whilst his fingers gently circled the other. This was a revelation – Sarah had always thought that they weren't that sensitive. Shaun had squeezed them in the past, but it had always been a little too hard and it certainly hadn't had the effect this was having. This was unbelievable; apparently her nipples were directly wired to her girly bits. She realised that her back was arched, so she quickly returned it to the bed. Wanton hussy, she thought, as she smiled to herself.

Andy saw her smile and it gave him the reassurance he needed to continue. She was happy and that was all that he wanted out of tonight. Andy's kisses moved slowly to her tummy button.

"If you laugh at the stretch marks, I'll burn your bum with a candle," she said, still keeping her eyes closed.

"You'll set off the smoke alarm if you do, and I'll have to stop."

"No, don't stop."

Andy relentlessly traced kisses all over her body until she thought she could stand it no more. He was now near her shoulder and he whispered, "Turn over," which she did in a flash. If he likes it doggy, that's fine, Sarah thought, although she'd never liked it that way with Shaun. It had felt even more impersonal than it usually was. Sarah's thoughts were pulled back to the moment when she smelt a strong waft of vanilla stronger than the candles.

"I'm going to use some oil," said Andy softly. Sarah was about to joke about lubrication and then decided against it. She was aware that she had killed a couple of moments already this evening with her sharp tongue. He undid her bra. Then she felt Andy's hands on her back, sliding over her shoulders. She felt the warm oil on her skin as he proceeded to give her the most amazing massage, which went on and on. Andy was sitting astride her, his warm legs pinning her to the bed, his firm hands sweeping over her body. He moved himself further down and snuck his hands under her pants and started to massage her bottom. Although a little surprised, she found she liked it.

"I bet they don't do that at Fancy what's its name Hall Day Spa," she muttered. He worked his way down both hips and then up her inner thighs. Her back was arched again. Total hussy! How did she not know she was doing it until her arse was stuck up in the air like a sleeping policeman.

Sarah wanted sex more than she'd ever wanted it in her life before. Andy was kissing her neck. "Sit up now," he breathed and she shot up quickly, keen to oblige, but very close to knocking him out with the back of her head. He slid off her bra and concentrated his attention on her breasts, which merrily sprang back to attention.

Sarah didn't know how much of this she could stand, but was keen to find out. Andy shifted a little and she felt the cloth of his boxers at her back and there was something very interesting being restrained down there. Andy tantalisingly slowly slid his hand down her stomach and into her pants. Oh, sweet torture, this should be illegal, or at least very heavily taxed, it's that good, she thought, as a small moan escaped.

Her body didn't know which way to move; her left nipple was about to go into orbit like an errant firework and her groin wasn't hers to control at all -- someone must be operating it by remote control because she certainly couldn't control its writhing. Something was happening the like of which she'd never known before.

"Ready?" gasped Andy.

"For what?"

"Dessert," he smiled against her ear and the expelled air sent another shiver through her, all heading in one direction. Andy looked at her for a moment, kneeling there, softly panting. He'd done that to her and he was amazed; this was a first for him.

"If it's anything like the lemon mousse, then yes please."

"I didn't get these tips from James Martin, but I think it'll be on a par. Turn around and open your eyes." Sarah opened her eyes and blinked as they quickly adjusted to the flickering candlelight. She couldn't stop herself throwing her arms around Andy's neck and pulling him to her.

"Pants," she said.

"What's wrong? What's pants?" Andy briefly pulled away to check Sarah was still happy with where this was heading.

"Mine are still on," they both glanced downwards.

"Okay, let's take them off together," suggested Andy and they both quickly removed them and had a quick look at each other. Both sets of eyebrows raised in unison. What happened next was a bit of a blur but they remained kneeling and Andy set the rhythm – slow at first and then building pace. Sarah could hear someone half-shouting and half-screaming, but it was a good sound. Oh crap, she thought when at last she realised it was her doing the screaming. When it happened, she thought her whole body had sneezed, and when she thought she could take no more she felt Andy tense and she knew he was there too. She held onto him tight, sobbing uncontrollably.

"What's wrong? Are you okay?" Andy was breathless, but the worry in his voice was clear.

"Never better," she spluttered through the sobs and the giggles that were now taking over. Andy's strong and slightly sweaty arms were still holding her tightly.

"Sarah, please tell me. What's wrong?" Sarah wiped her face and caught a glimpse of her mascara-strewn face in the mirror. Oh God! He'll think he's shagged Alice Cooper.

"Nothing is wrong," she said at last, "everything is right. You're a sex god with a magic penis!" she exclaimed, as she playfully thumped his shoulder.

"Who knew?" he grinned. They lay there, arms and legs entwined, Sarah still feeling mini sneezes as she wrapped her legs around Andy's thigh in a vice-like grip. "We used to have a poodle like you," he laughed as he gently ran his fingers down her back.

"Shut up or I'll make you do it all over again."

"My pleasure," Andy said pretending to sit up.

"No, I need to sleep and dream about it," she said, giving his leg another squeeze with her thighs.

"Night, Sarah." He kissed the top of her head.

Chapter 27

"Come on, Amy!" called Kate as she put on her sandals, "I've got a train to catch."

"Sorry, I just need to get..."

"Time's up," Kate said as she gently steered Amy out of the front door, answering her phone as she went.

"Good morning, Sleeping Beauty! I got your text. Thank goodness it wasn't an email, it would have been impounded for crudeness!"

"Are you taking Amy to school?" asked Sarah.

"Yes, Ma'am, I'm on the way now. I'm dropping her in early as I need to get the train to Bath."

"Kate, I forgot. I'm so sorry!"

"It's not a problem. Well, maybe it's a bit of a problem, but I love you and you owe me big-style."

"Talking of big-style, I must tell you about last night."

"Yes, but not now, I need to be driving," she said, doing up her seatbelt with great difficulty. "I'm coming home tonight. I'm sick of hotels, so you can tell me then," and she switched off the phone. Amy was a "Stepford child" and happily went into school to join the breakfast club without a word of protest, waving Kate off with a big smile. Kate was just pulling into the traffic as she saw Andy's van go in the opposite direction. She waved and hooted, but he was looking quite grim and didn't respond. That's the effect of not having enough sleep, she thought.

Bath was a bit grey, which Che was very unhappy about, but was stopping short of blaming anyone in particular. There was a mix of inside and outside scenes planned that week, but the weather said that today was indoors-only. Tim, wisely, was keeping out of Lumina's way and had brought Didi with him for protection.

Lumina did look every inch the tragic actress – she was not looking her sleek, slender self, but gaunt and scrawny, which was not a great look. She was wearing a belly top and leggings with heels, which only served to highlight the lack of meat on very prominent bones. Her face was sour, her lips narrow and her skin was so smooth it looked as if she'd been airbrushed. Kate thought her sunglasses were growing of their own accord, as these ones were bordering on the ridiculous; they covered half her forehead and most of her cheeks. Either that or her head was shrinking. Lumina avoided eye contact and stalked past.

Didi, on the other hand, was wearing a comfy-looking pair of jeans with sensible but stylish white ballet pumps, a white t-shirt under an open, orange shirt. There was a little extra padding visible around her middle, but it suited her and for seventy she was looking trim. Didi had plenty of wrinkles around her eyes, but they were barely noticeable when her face lit up with her usual smile as she waved enthusiastically at the sight of Kate.

"Kate, my dear, you really must come and see my lovely new flat, it's amazing!"

"I'd love to Didi. We'll have to work something out."

"I could cook my famous beef casserole for you and Tim; he only lives upstairs."

"Upstairs? I thought he lived in hotels."

"So did I, but apparently he owns the penthouse suite in the same block of flats."

"Block of flats?" Kate smiled to herself. She suspected that Didi's description might be a little less glamorous than the reality, and most likely not the same way that the other residents referred to them.

"Yes, it's a big block. Much bigger than where I used to live, but the lifts are so fast they make your tummy tumble over. I rather like that feeling."

"Here you are," Marcus said, looking out of puff. "There's some dialogue I need you to look at for the bar scenes. Are you free now?"

"Yes, no problem. Bye, Didi."

The day went by like so many others, in a whirl of scenes and conversations about scenes, changes, and changes back to how they were originally. Che shouted at Lumina, Lumina cried. Lumina shouted at Tim and Horse yapped. It was all a bit familiar. Thankfully, Kate was soon back in her own house, tired but happy and very keen to catch up on the gossip with Sarah.

"So how was your day?"

"Breakfast in bed, then minding the shop on my own, picking Amy up from school and taking her to Freya's for a sleepover," Sarah said in a rush. "Now can we talk about last night? The sex! Oh. My. God!"

"First things first, tea or wine?" Kate pointed to the kettle and the wine rack in turn,

"I had enough wine to drown a blue whale last night and this morning my mouth felt like I'd spent the evening licking the chalk off the white cliffs of Dover, so I'll have a coffee please. Now, can I tell you?" Kate was tempted to make Sarah wait until she'd told her about her day first, but that would just be cruel and she didn't have any excitement to impart anyway. Tim had gone all aloof again, so no change there.

"When we're sitting down in the living room."

"Okay," Sarah said like a recalcitrant teenager. "It was quite frankly the laziest sex I've ever had. Not the usual wham, bam, fart, snore, which was Shaun, in case you were wondering. Sex is my new favourite pastime and, best of all, it's completely free!"

Kate carried the mugs through and they settled themselves at either end of the biggest sofa. Kate got herself comfortable as she expected this was going to take a while. Sarah started at the beginning and took her through the three-course meal in detail and then through the three courses of sex, in equally meticulous detail.

"I still had my eyes closed, so then he said are you ready? And I said for what? And he said… Are you even listening to me?" Sarah's tone startled Kate out of her trance. Her palms were damp and clammy and she felt almost faint as she gripped her tea, her knuckles white with the pressure. She looked at Sarah, whose face was alight and alive, radiating pure happiness.

"Yes, I'm listening… dessert," she said, meeting Sarah's gaze.

"Yes, dessert, good guess," said Sarah.

"Not a good guess, I know what comes next."

"Have you slept with Andy?" Sarah blurted out, almost in a shout.

"No, I have not!" Kate's reply was equally vehement.

"Then how? Read the same book? Seen the same film?" Sarah's speech had speeded up. Kate paused to give them both a chance to catch their breath.

"James," Kate said, "I had sex with James. That was what we did. You've just described in meticulous detail," Kate repeated the words for emphasis, "meticulous detail, what we used to do and exactly how we used to do it."

"Okay, so what happens next, then, if this is now your sex story?" said Sarah huffily, folding her arms. Kate sighed. If she wanted proof, then here it was.

"Okay. Then you turned around, opened your eyes. You both took off your underwear. You kissed some more, then he took hold of your backside and lifted you onto his…"

"Stop. I believe you." Sarah waved her to stop.

"Sorry," Kate said quietly, before taking a sip of her now-cold tea. Sarah shrugged.

"Bloody hell, you must miss sex if it was always like that." She gave a brief smile, which disappeared quickly.

"We did other stuff," Kate blushed at the memories, "but what you just described, so vividly, was what we called our 'standard recipe'. We spent a lot of Sundays perfecting it."

"Sorry." It was Sarah's turn to feel bad, as if she'd stolen something and been found out.

"So the question is…" Kate paused.

"How the hell did Andy know about it in such detail? Did you ever film yourselves?"

"Sod off! Of course we didn't."

"Don't be so alarmed, I quite like the idea," winked Sarah. "So, are you going to tackle Andy or should I?"

"Together," said Kate, leaning forward to squeeze Sarah's hand.

"We could go over there now. He should be back from Cambridge by now."

"Cambridge?"

"Yep, he left early. He's been there all day."

"That's odd. I saw him when I dropped Amy at school."

"But you couldn't have. He wouldn't have gone anywhere near there…" Sarah sat up "I think we have a few questions to ask Andy. Come on." After a bit of a debate, which Kate eventually won, they decided to call Andy first rather than just storm over there. Andy answered on the first ring, but sounded agitated.

"Sarah, is it urgent? Is something wrong?"

"No, but Kate and I need to see you about something quite important," she heard a muffled voice in the background. "Is there someone there?"

"Yeah, they're just leaving."

"Is it a woman?" Sarah hated herself, but she couldn't help it. She had just found out that one of her best mates was shit-hot in bed, about to become her boyfriend, and now within 24 hours it was all starting to unravel.

"Er, yes, but she's just a friend."

"I thought it might be a customer about a quote," Sarah voiced the straw she'd just clutched at and had had wrenched away. There was a pause whilst Andy most likely thought through that that would have been a far better line to go with. There was an almighty slam of a door, "I take it your friend's gone now."

"Er, yeah, you can come over or shall I come to you? I need to go out in about an hour anyway."

"Okay, we'll see you soon, then," and she switched off the phone and ran upstairs to make herself look fabulous, because if she was going to have to dump him for being a two- timing dogging pervert, she wanted him to know what he was losing.

As the song went, Andy was "A Whiter Shade Of Pale". Fight-or-flight adrenalin had kicked in, but his brain couldn't make a decision between the two, so he just stared at the two women, who in return where glaring back at him from the other side of the kitchen table.

"Say something, Andy," Kate said softly.

"Yes, for Christ's sake, say something!" added Sarah crossly.

"We deserve an explanation. I like what you've done to your hair, by the way."

"It's gel. Someone recommended it," he said. Hair questions he could answer easily. Why having sex with him was exactly the same as sex with James was a bit trickier. "Where's Amy?"

"Sleepover," Sarah said bluntly.

"Just tell the truth, Andy," urged Kate.

He ran a shaky hand through his uncharacteristically styled hair and it instantly reverted to his usual tousled look.

"I'm rubbish with women, with sex actually. The whole thing: it bothers me. I worry about… you know, hurting people. I'm a big bloke," his cheeks coloured and Sarah felt hers do the same.

"But you're not rubbish," offered Sarah.

"But I was until I asked for help." There was a long pause, during which Andy sighed a lot, "I asked James for help."

"He would never have told you what we did," Kate snapped. "That was way too personal. He just wouldn't."

"Kate, I'm sorry. He was always saying how amazing it was for you two." Andy looked down at the table, the embarrassment and guilt coming over him in waves, "I had to badger him before he'd tell me anything. Then one Sunday he came over." Sarah and Kate exchanged knowing looks, but Andy was oblivious and carried on. "He turned up at my old place. He had no socks on, his hair was a mess and he had a grin that stretched to Scotland and he had this way about him. He looked like the happiest man alive." Kate took a sharp intake of breath. She could picture James. Sarah reached out and put her arm around her shoulder.

"Go on, carry on, I'm fine," said Kate.

"He just went on about how brilliant you were, and the sex, and I asked him why, what was so different? He said it was because you were in tune with each other and that he'd only tell me once and I must never breathe a word to another living soul." Andy paused and looked upwards. "Sorry, James."

"So he just spilled his guts and gave you all the intimate details of their sex life and you did what, just memorised them?" Sarah was shaking her head.

"I wrote it all down after he'd left and I kind of read it a lot, but I never used it before last night. I was waiting."

"For a publisher?" Sarah snapped.

"For someone I truly loved, heart and soul."

"So that would be me?" Sarah's tone softened. Andy nodded shyly, "It's me! He loves me!" Sarah thumped Kate on the arm in her excitement and then saw her expression and tempered her enthusiasm.

"I can't believe James told you. Andy, it's not your fault that he told you."

"I'm still sorry. I just never thought you would find out."

"Yeah 'cause we never tell each other anything!" laughed Sarah. "I had the best time ever and my first…" Sarah whistled.

"Seriously?" queried Kate.

"Yep, first time ever."

"You know, I think I should be making tracks," said Andy looking very uncomfortable, but at the same time a little proud. "You sure you're okay, Kate?"

"Yes, just make some amendments next time. You know, make up a new recipe, okay?"

"Sounds like my sort of challenge," Sarah said, going around to Andy's side of the table.

"And wherever it's written down, please burn it!"

"I will, I can remember every detail of last night, so I don't need it any more," he said, grinning down at Sarah and kissing her.

"Get a room!" Kate said throwing a tea towel at them.

"Sure you're okay?" said Andy again.

"Come on, Kate's fine." Sarah turned to Kate, "You knew James wasn't completely perfect, right?" Andy flinched and shot a warning look at Sarah. Kate looked at the guilty-looking pair, but Sarah quickly bustled Andy out of the house.

"I know he wasn't perfect, but when someone dies young like James did, suddenly everyone thinks they were. And there is absolutely no way you can ever say anything a fraction derogatory about them," said Kate, voicing how she'd felt for two years. "I just mean he was fallible, like the rest of us." Sarah fidgeted about and picked up her coat.

"I think I'll go after Andy."

"But you don't know where he's gone."

"No, but when he said the nice stuff, I forgot to ask about the bloody woman he had there. I need to know what that was all about. I'm sure it's nothing, but I want to check," and she left, too.

Kate looked around the empty kitchen. It had been an odd day, thought Kate, finding out that the most private moments of your sex life had been shared. But hearing Sarah describe it perfectly, step by step, had Kate remembering what it had been like. It had been sensual, and so much fun, and she missed it. She pondered over whether she'd ever feel like that again. Possibly not, but perhaps there could be something similar, one day, with someone else.

Kate opened a bottle of wine and sat and thought about those Sundays. She was pleased that she didn't feel sad; they were good memories and she was grateful to James for them. She sat there after quite a while and thought to herself, So here I am lonely, slightly drunk and really quite horny – bugger! She thought through her options:

Option 1 – a cold shower.

Option 2 – drink self into oblivion and a deep sleep.

Option 3 – As Sarah would say – a damn good shag.

This made her laugh out loud as it was so unlikely. Marmalade sprang awake as if she'd just been electrocuted and, realising there was no danger, covered her eyes with her tail and went back to sleep. Kate took a sip of wine and thought over Option 3 again. It was an interesting thought. In her current situation, where would she go for Option 3 if she was so inclined? Not that she was saying she was, of course, it was just a bit of fun. Kate lay back on the sofa and closed her eyes to help her think.

Who would be on her shortlist? It took a moment to conjure up Andy and then instantly dismiss him. Maybe before he and Sarah had got together he might have been an option. He had been such a good friend, he would probably have done it as a favour, but it would have been complicated and a little bit like incest.

Okay, so who was kind and liked to do favours? Marcus sprang to mind and her face contorted. Definitely a "no". That would be like sleeping with another relative and he was married, so definitely off the list. She thought of, and crossed off, another two married men. There was always the man at the corner shop, but she was fairly certain he was gay, so he was out too.

Another sip of wine, but the glass was empty and so was the bottle. Option 2 was looking the most likely now and it was only a quarter to eight. Kate decided tea might be the answer to sober her up and dampen her ardour, but while she was waiting for

the kettle to boil she had to accept that the first person who had
honestly popped into her head had been Tim.

Sarah's car was not the best vehicle for surveillance –
there weren't many original Beetles on the roads and hers you
could hear coming a mile off. She could see Andy's van ahead at
the traffic lights, so she relaxed a bit. She looked about her; she
was only ten minutes from Kate's, but it wasn't an area that was
familiar to her. She continued to follow Andy at a distance and
then lost him for a moment. As she turned a corner, she pulled
over quickly behind some parked cars as she could see that Andy
had stopped outside some terraced houses and a figure was just
shutting the passenger door.

"Shit." Just a couple of seconds earlier and she would have seen
who it was. Sarah was grateful when another car overtook her and
she could pull out behind it; keeping a car between them meant
that Andy was less likely to see his new barking-mad girlfriend
stalking him. Unfortunately, the car in front was being driven
by someone who obviously felt that 25 miles an hour was fast
enough for anyone and she lost Andy at the lights. She strained
to see where he went. She opened the car door and stretched out
to see him take a right turn further down the road.

"Come on!" Sarah beeped her horn the second the lights
changed. "You want the pedal on the right, for Christ's sake. Push
it down!" she shouted. She took the right turn and found herself
in another residential area that she didn't know. She crawled along,
searching either side of the road for Andy's van. Then she saw it
parked further up, outside a community centre. Sarah sat in the
car for a minute trying to work out the scenarios that could play
out, and then gave up and stormed inside.

Kate sipped her tea. It was a poor substitute for the wine and
wasn't having the desired effect. She started to think about how
Tim might react to Option 3. Kate wondered what sex with him

might be like. She conjured up the scene in her mind like she did when she was writing, but erotica was not her genre. There were enough ladies plastered all over the tabloids claiming that he was very good. No complaints that she was aware of. He wasn't with Lumina any more, so she wouldn't be hurting anyone, well, at least, nobody she knew, anyway. Also anyone who was seeing Tim must have realised that it was very unlikely to be exclusive.

She checked the clock. The constant movement of the second hand played on her mind; time ticking away. Her time was ticking away. Was she really going to spend it analysing everything and doing not very much? What's the worst that could happen if she asked him? He could say no. So what? That was no big deal. This was Timothy Calder and she was not bad looking, with a pulse, and she was asking him for sex with no strings attached, so the likelihood of him saying no was probably quite slim. It really was a no- brainer. Don't think about it, just do it, she urged herself.

She put her tea down with such force that a perfect globule jumped up and splashed back down again. She reached for her phone and texted him. It was a cop-out, but it was so much easier than calling. 'Hi Tim, Are you doing anything exciting tonight? Kate. And she pressed "send".

As she put the phone down on the arm of the sofa the screen lit up and a quick glance confirmed her fears; it was Tim. She hadn't thought this bit through. She'd assumed he'd text back, not call. What was she going to say? Answer it! A voice in her head screamed and she picked it up.

"Hi, Kate, I saw your text and thought I'd call you back." Great, he chooses now to become all efficient, thought Kate.

"Thanks. So, are you doing someone… sorry, something exciting tonight?" Kate cringed at her faux pas, scrunching up her knees underneath herself. The wine was seriously fogging her brain.

"No, not really. Why?" He sounded curious. Okay need to pique his interest and sound alluring, thought Kate. Who was she kidding? She was no actor; that was him.

"I was wondering if you fancied," small pause for effect, give him a second to think what he might fancy.

"Hello? Kate, are you still there?" Bugger. Left too big a pause.

"If you fancied coming over," she quickly added. She knew Tim was looking at the time, and she didn't even know where he was. Kate was going to need a reason why he should bother to turn out at that time of night. Option 3, she thought, which was the honest answer. Kate believed honesty was always the best policy. Tim cut across her thoughts.

"It would be getting late by the time I got there, Kate. Are you okay?"

Come clean. Tell him. Option 3.

"I need you." She clenched her eyes tight shut. She'd said it. It was job done.

"You need me for what? To make up a bridge pair, hold up a wonky table, look over tomorrow's script?"

Be sexier, thought Kate, make it clear this time. "No, Tim," she breathed slowly into the phone, in what she desperately hoped was a sexy way and not an asthmatic-stalker kind of way. "I need you. Just you here, with me, tonight." More cringing and this time the heavy breathing was real. There was a reason she didn't write erotica. Her pulse had quickened and her cheeks were flushed.

"Kate, are you serious?" his voice was warm and smooth and he was interested. Bingo! Reel him in.

"Deadly serious. Will you come?"

"I'll be there about ten."

"Perfect!" she said a bit too excitedly.

"Kate, thank you for… I know this is a big step for you." And the line went dead. Big step? It would be the first sex she'd had in two years. She wondered if it had all changed and if she'd remember what to do or if she'd mess it up and look like an idiot, or what if things just didn't work like they should do? Cars and dishwashers often broke down if they weren't used frequently. She'd soon find out if she needed a full service and MOT herself and Tim was the man to do it.

Kate had a quick tidy-up, put champagne in the fridge and glasses on the table and went upstairs. After a speedy shower, where she defuzzed in all the right places, a quick pin- up hair- do, a touch of make-up and a fitted, dark-purple dress, she was ready. It was ten to ten. She smoothed out the bedcovers and put the bedside light on its dimmest setting, hoping for a soft-focus effect. A loud knock on the door echoed through the house.

"Bugger!" Suddenly very nervous, she bolted downstairs and nearly missed her footing in her silly heels and had a quick mental chat with herself. Calm down. It's only Tim. You're doing each other a mutual favour, mutual benefit, meaningless sex, no strings. Only, could sex ever be completely meaningless? Now was not the time for her to start asking herself questions like that, when he was standing on the other side of the door. Kate pasted on her best idea of a sexy smile and opened the door.

Sarah swung open the double doors and found herself in a small, empty lobby. So it wasn't quite the dramatic entrance she'd thought it might be, which was probably for the best. She went through another door and couldn't see anybody. She could hear voices upstairs, so she made her way up. She opened a door and found herself in a bar with a dance floor beyond. She stood there for a moment, feeling more than a bit foolish, and scanned the room for Andy. Sarah didn't see him.

She went to the bar and ordered an orange juice, then went and sat down at the side of the dance floor. There were quite a few people and more were arriving. They all seemed to know each other and there was lots of kissing and hugging. The lights dimmed and a disco ball started to spin overhead.

Sarah started to panic. She really didn't know what she was doing there. This was completely stupid. Andy wasn't here. She must have got it wrong; that must have been another van that just looked like his.

She was about to down her drink and leave when the music started. It wasn't anything she recognised and she didn't think much of it. Some doors at the end of the room opened and out came couples all lavishly dressed; the women, who were of a certain age, in very elaborate layered dresses and their hair pinned up. As the third couple pranced past her she recognised the woman. It was Concetta. Her head was held high and she was pointing her toes and splaying out her arms as she went past. Sarah's mouth dropped open and she had to work very hard not to start guffawing.

"Are you following me?" Andy sat down next to her.

"No, absolutely not! How could you think that?" Andy raised one eyebrow. "Yeah, okay, completely rumbled. Sorry."

"No, I'm sorry I've not been straight with you."

"Shhhhhh!" someone leaned over to Sarah.

"Sorry," said Andy. "Come on, let's go downstairs." They waited until the dancers were over the other side of the dance floor and headed for the exit, Sarah giggling as she went, partly through seeing Concetta in full-on flamenco gear and also with embarrassment at stalking Andy.

"Look, I'm sorry I followed you. I know that makes me look like a crazy loon, but I heard that woman at yours and after last night I needed to check it out. I know you're not Shaun, I know that. Do you understand?"

"Yeah, I do. I should have told you before, but it was nothing."

"I know that now."

"You do?"

"Yeah, I figured it out," she lied. "So you and Concetta. I never would have guessed."

"She was missing Spain. I helped her find a local Spanish group and they introduced her to the dancing. She really enjoys it, but she wouldn't want people to know."

"That's really sweet of you." Sarah hugged his arm and wondered if it would be very teenager-ish to have a snog.

"Sarah, I am sorry. I should have told you, about… her getting close to me."

"Hey, it's only Concetta."

"No, not Concetta, I mean Melanie."

Chapter 28

Tim couldn't believe how life could change so quickly. One minute you're at some event, as dull as a seaside town in January, and the next the person who has totally captured your heart is on the phone saying that they feel the same. Well, not exactly. She didn't use those words, but her intentions were pretty clear; she said she needed him. Their discussion last night must have made her think and, thankfully realise, her true feelings.

Pip had got him out of the charity evening; Colin Firth was standing in as host for the second half. The chopper had been ready to go and here he was standing outside her door, waiting. Waiting for the missing piece of his life to finally click into place.

As the door opened and he saw Kate, he had to quell the urge to whisk her up into his arms and twirl her around. He didn't want to rush her or freak her out – he'd made too many mistakes with this relationship and he could not afford to make any more. Kate looked perfect. Her slim figure, with curves in all the right places, was shown off to its best in a sleek dress, but he would have been just as mesmerised had she been wearing a sack. Tim looked into Kate's pale-blue eyes, rimmed with grey, and there was something different about them tonight; they were warmer, more welcoming, than before.

"Thanks for coming," she said. She sounded as if she'd

been running.

"Kate, I said if you need me, I'll always be there." Tim gave her a gentle kiss on the cheek, took her hand and kept hold of it. Kate felt herself relax at his touch, his fingers linked with hers. She shut the door and turned to face him. He was just smiling at her. She needed her hand back for the champagne, so reluctantly she let go,

"Champagne?"

"Please." There was a definite lack of conversation tonight. Kate got the champagne from the fridge and Tim took it from her. "Let me."

"I'm guessing you were at a function," said Kate, nodding at Tim's dinner suit as he expertly twisted the bottle and the cork eased itself out with the most delicate of pops.

"Yes, some charity do. I'd done my 'funny' speech and Pip got me out of the auction."

"You didn't tell Pippa, did you?" Kate was alarmed. This was what happened when you hadn't thought things through. Why hadn't she waited until they'd finished filming? There were only a couple of weeks to go. She'd waited two years, for goodness sake!

"No, I told her I had a relative who had been taken ill. Nothing serious, but I wanted to see them."

"Oh, good," she said hastily and a little too loudly. Lying came easy to Tim, it would seem. "I didn't mean to bark at you. Sorry," she said and he handed her a glass of champagne.

"To us," he clinked glasses and there was something in his eyes that drew her in.

"To us," she repeated. To Option 3, she thought.

Sarah had wanted to scream and shout at Andy, to come up with some suitably cutting comments, but she couldn't think of any. She just stood there like the dumb blonde she felt she was, and said nothing. Andy just kept repeating her name, as if she'd gone into some sort of vertical coma and he was trying to wake her. She didn't know how long she'd stood there, but when she felt the tears drip off her chin, she knew it was time to leave. And in a very un-Sarah way she simply shrugged off Andy's grip on her shoulders and walked out, no slam of doors, no last word. She merely walked away.

Sarah could hardly see to drive, the tears were streaming down her face and there was no off-switch. She wasn't sure where she was, but she wasn't about to stop and ask for directions. When she realised that she was completely lost, she pulled the car haphazardly onto the pavement and switched off the engine. She slumped against the steering wheel, but her forehead sounded the horn, which made her jerk in alarm. She decided to curl up in a ball across the two front seats. And there she stayed, sobbing and sniffing, until she cried herself to sleep.

"Come on." Kate had had enough of them smiling at each other and led Tim to the sofa. She knew there was no need to rush things, but she wished Tim would take charge a bit more. He must have done this sort of thing a million times, maybe not a million, but probably not far off. She'd check the *Guinness Book of Records* tomorrow for the exact number. Marmalade opened one eye as they entered the room.

"Evening, Reggie," said Tim to Marmalade, who stretched and showed off her claws. Tim avoided the cat and sat slightly turned towards Kate.

"You're really quiet," Kate said. If anything, he looked nervous, which was interesting.

"I think I'm in shock," Tim blinked. "I can't stop thinking I'm the luckiest person on the planet." Kate thought this was a touch over the top, but it was a nice thing to say.

"Me too. I'm lucky to know someone like you who's prepared to do this." She broke eye contact and sipped her champagne, the embarrassment getting the better of her. Tim looked at her warily.

"Prepared to do this?" he repeated as he raised his left eyebrow slightly, in that Agent X way he was so famous for, usually just before he killed the bad guy.

"There's not many people that you could…" she searched for an appropriate word, "proposition." Tim looked downright puzzled now. He put down his glass and leaned forward.

"So, what's your proposition, Kate? Why did you ask me here tonight?" His eyes were searching her face for some acknowledgment that he hadn't got this all horribly wrong, that she felt about him the same way he had felt about her for so long. What had been a nagging doubt was now a giant one stomping around in his head, stamping on any trace of happy feelings that he may have had, like nasty little kids stamped on sand castles.

"There's a little bit of a story."

"I think there always is with you."

"Sarah was here today. She was on top of the world. She and Andy have finally got it together and she was so happy, all because she'd had fantastic sex with Andy." Kate couldn't believe she was having this conversation with Timothy Calder. It was quite bizarre.

"I'm guessing it's not just the sex, though."

"Probably not, but still, after she'd recounted every last detail to me, it made me think about it… sex." She looked at Tim shyly. Surely this was the moment where he picked her up, or at the very least, took her hand and led her upstairs. Or perhaps he could just kiss her here and now. She wanted to be kissed. She wanted to be kissed by Tim. Well, who wouldn't?

"So you texted me, because…"

"I thought, who can I ask who would want the same as I do?" said Kate. Tim's expression was blank.

"And what is it that you want, Kate?"

"Meaningless sex, with someone I trust not to blab and who can trust me not to run to the tabloids or demand my 15 minutes of fame in the Timothy Calder spotlight." She smiled. She

336

was proud of her bravery. It was all there, totally honest, and they both knew where they stood. So can we have the sex now, please? She thought. The champagne had increased her confidence levels and most probably accounted for the deep attraction she felt for Tim right now. Tim reached out and held her hands in his. The familiar electric current pulsed through her.

"Is that what you want?" his voice hushed.

"Yes." Kate was emphatic. His thumbs stroked her knuckles and sent shivers through her.

"That's how you think of me? Someone who just wants meaningless sex with you?" His eyes were so sad. She was about to answer, but when she opened her mouth her brain stopped her dead as Tim's face was now ashen. A little frown flickered across his forehead and then disappeared. "I get it, Kate. I'm sorry, but I can't do that. Not with you." Kate opened her mouth to reply, but brain connection had been totally lost.

Tim continued to rub his thumbs over her knuckles, as his famous green eyes studied her. He leaned forward and kissed her cheek. It was all too brief. He let her go and headed for the door. Kate was thrown into confusion, but got up and followed him. Once outside, he turned to look at her standing utterly bewildered in the hallway. He swallowed hard, turned and walked away. Kate stood holding the door and watched him until he disappeared out of sight. There was no movie moment, where he turned to have one last look. Kate stood staring at the empty night before she closed the door and slumped down on the floor.

Sarah couldn't feel anything from the waist down. She tried to move, but everything was locked into a very unfamiliar position. She wiped the boulders of sleep out of her eyes and tried to sit up. She blinked a few times and reality gave her a slap in the face, which brought her round quite quickly. The sun was just coming up and she needed to get back to Kate's. She set off and tried to study the road signs. Thankfully there were very few cars about at this stupid time in the morning and things did look more familiar in the daylight. Sarah was pleased when she swung the car onto Kate's drive and let herself in as quietly as she could.

The piercing beep of the alarm was physically hurting Kate's head as she rolled over and tried to focus on the impossibly small "off" switch of the alarm clock. Kate lay back on the pillows, closed her eyes and listened to the rhythmic thud of her head. In the end she had gone for Option 2, having finished off the rest of the champagne.

Thankfully, it had assisted her in a good night's sleep, but this morning the memories of last night's fiasco flooded over her. She thought she was about to prove that it was actually possible to die of embarrassment. The one time in her life that she was impulsive and unpredictable, spontaneous and unstructured, and it all went horribly wrong. She still couldn't believe that she had read Tim so wrongly. She'd had no explanation as to why he had come all that way and then said no.

She hated the fact that you always thought of the things you really wanted to say after they were actually of any use to you. The humiliation was painful, just like her head. Worse still, she had to face him today. She could call in sick, but that wasn't her way. She couldn't leave Marcus stranded with Che in one of his moods; it was best to face up to the situation. Kate rolled out of bed, avoided the mirror, and headed for the extra-strong paracetamol. Her own problems ebbed away when she saw the sorry sight that was Sarah hunched up at the kitchen table hugging a mug.

"Painkillers?" asked Kate.

"Got any cyanide?"

"No, I'm all out, I'm afraid."

"Andy's seeing Melanie," stated Sarah, her eyes still focused on the table.

"Crikey!" Kate paused. Oh well, if they were sharing disastrous evening stories, "Tim turned me down for sex," countered Kate.

"Shit," Sarah swung her legs around.

"What is wrong with us?" Kate sat down on the chair opposite, popped out two tablets and pushed them across the table.

"Bastard-magnets… apart from James," there was a long pause.

"He wanted me to mortgage this house." Kate concentrated on her tablets. She hated saying it out loud. She had tried not to think about it for two years, but it just wouldn't go away. It wasn't the crime of the century, but it had been a significant argument between them at the time.

"I know," Sarah cringed a little. Kate looked up, surprised.

"Andy knows too, then?"

"He's got the deeds."

"I've been looking every sodding where for those," and they both smiled, despite everything.

"I might become a lesbian. Women are so much nicer," said Sarah, taking her tablets.

"I'm not marrying you – you're a nightmare."

"You're not meant to say that."

"Are you working today?"

"No, I'm resigning from the pub. I can't face Melanie. She's taken two men from me." She noted Kate's expression. "Okay, one drug-dealing arsehole and one very decent man."

"Then come to Bath. I need the moral support. I might be able to get you in as an extra, but no promises."

"I don't know."

"You'll get to meet Tim and, who knows, he might shag you," Kate said.

"Then why the hell not? I'm in!"

The marquee was buzzing when they got there, despite the grey clouds overhead. Even so, the darkest things in Bath were Kate and Sarah, like little clouds of doom shuffling into the marquee. Kate wore her favourite dress, sunglasses and a smudge of lipstick. She had thought briefly about going "all out" to look fabulous, to show Tim what he was missing, but quite frankly, she couldn't be bothered. Sarah had gone for ultra-casual in her ripped jeans and a red t-shirt, which made her look really young. Kate spotted Marcus and they headed over to him.

"He's so very gay," whispered Sarah as Kate dug her in the ribs.

"Good morning, darling girl, I need kisses. And remind me who we have here?" He air-kissed both of them and Sarah raised a knowing eyebrow, as if she'd seen proof enough.

"This is my friend, Sarah."

"Delighted," he quickly turned his attention back to Kate. "Oh dear," he said tapping the sunglasses, "hung over, are we?"

"A tad, but I'll survive. Have you seen Tim yet?"

"Not yet. I dare say he'll be crawling from under some long-legged beauty he met last night." Marcus was the only one who laughed.

Tim sat in the back of the limo and stared blankly out of the window at the slate-grey sky. It looked how he felt: lifeless and sad. He was full of regret and felt as if he'd been kicked squarely in the chest. They talk about heartache, but he hadn't expected it to hurt physically. He had been awake most of the night, torturing himself. He had thought it had been the right thing to do, to walk away, but in the early hours of the morning he hadn't been so sure. Plenty of relationships started with a physical encounter and grew from there. Perhaps he'd just passed up the one-and-only chance for that to happen for him and Kate.

What hurt him the most was how he must have made Kate feel – he'd spurned her, turned her down flat. Why hadn't he just talked to her instead of walking out? Over the last few weeks, Tim had tried to show Kate the person behind the famous mask, but he had very obviously failed. It was clear how she saw him and he couldn't blame her for that. The damage was done, and all he could do now was try not to make today too torturous for either of them.

When he entered his trailer, he saw it. A single walnut whip with a post-it note stuck on the mirror behind it, which read "Sorry X". Tim peeled off the post-it and smiled. Me too, he thought.

Kate didn't have too much convincing to do to get Sarah in as an extra, as she was one of the youngest there and ideal for the bar scene. Sarah was a bit put out that wardrobe made her change her clothes because hers didn't meet the criteria for a young, affluent professional. She cottoned on quickly that if she drank her large glass of wine during the scene she would get it refilled when they had to retake. She kept giving Kate the thumbs-up, which Kate studiously ignored.

"I think she's drunk the prop department dry," Marcus said, under his breath.

The morning was tedious. The weather had been patchy and so had Tim's acting; they had had to retake a number of scenes, much to Che's annoyance. Despite digging deep he was failing to be the consummate professional he prided himself on being. The first scene after lunch was to be the bandstand scene and, as Tim and Lumina went over it Tim felt that this scene needed some subtle changes. He'd discovered a new level to Patrick, the depth of the character had grown as he'd played him. Tim caught up with Che and explained his idea for the scene change. In conclusion he stated,

"He's not the guns-blazing kind of guy at this point. He's nervous, gentle even. So I want to tone it down, okay?"

"I'm not sure. I want close-up face shots on this from all angles. Where's Dennis?"

At that point, Lumina came striding over.

"No, no, no! You can't change this scene, it's a key scene. It says here," she stabbed the script for effect, "he engulfs her in his arms and kisses her passionately. We have to do the kiss." Her eyes were wide with anticipation.

"Oh, Mina, let it go! This scene needs to change. It's not about you and me."

"How dare you! I never thought for a moment, I'm so…" Tim waved for her to stop, but she just carried on ranting. Then Che chimed in and the volume escalated. Marcus grabbed Kate's arm and marched her in the direction of the noise.

"Creative differences that we need to resolve," he muttered.

"Can't you sort it?" asked Kate, as the voices grew louder.

"No. Come on, nearly there. It will soon be all parties and premieres." Marcus was keen to highlight the imminent fun stuff, but all Kate could think of was having to avoid Tim at all those events. Kate braced herself as they reached the warring trio, but Tim broke away as soon as he saw her and called over his shoulder to the others.

"Che, come with me. Let me show you what I mean." In seconds Kate was whirled around and was being guided back out of the marquee and across to the bandstand. Most of the park was cordoned off and crew were liberally scattered around. Tim's hand was gripping her elbow and the scent of his aftershave swept over her in ripples. Neither of them spoke. There was a steely determination in Tim's eyes and the firm grip on her arm showed he was serious. Che followed them, muttering to himself. As they reached the bandstand Tim lifted her up into his arms, their eyes briefly met, before she was deposited onto the bandstand. Tim vaulted the hedge and the low rail and spun her around to look at him. Kate smiled a shy smile.

"I'm sorry," she said in a small voice, because she didn't know what else to say. Tim shook his head briefly.

"Forget it. This is about the script. The whole feeling is of Patrick controlling the situation, of him going in guns blazing and sweeping Marcie up and engulfing her in a kiss."

"Yes," was all Kate could think to say.

"I agree," chimed in Che, who was now sitting on the grass.

"But he's not like that, not now, not with Marcie. He's unsure. He wouldn't risk blowing his chance with her."

"But that's his character, that's how he copes – he puts on a front, takes control of the situation." Kate could feel herself getting defensive. She was drawn into the debate now.

"It's worked in the other scenes," said Che. Tim raked his hands through his dark hair.

"I know it's your film, Che, and it's your character, Kate, but I've played him, I know him too and I think on this occasion you're both wrong,"

"Okay, how so?" said Kate.

"He's stripped bare…"

"No, that was an apartment scene weeks ago," joked Kate, but Tim wasn't laughing.

"The real Patrick is getting exposed, it's difficult for him, but that's the only way he's going to connect with Marcie, the only way he stands a chance of convincing her that he's the right man for her."

"But Patrick wouldn't do that," called Che from the grass, making them both turn to look at him.

"He would because…" Tim exhaled deeply. "This is getting us nowhere." Exasperation made him fidget about the bandstand, turning in circles. "Let me show you."

"Nice try, but once it's filmed, it's all done and you win, so no." Kate glared at him.

"No, not film it with Lumina. I mean let me show you, here. Both of you. Kate, you be Marcie. She only says two lines and you know the script, right?" Kate nodded. "I'll be Patrick."

"So, how does that solve it?" asked Kate.

"Try to be Marcie, and see if it feels right or wrong when Patrick approaches her how I want to play it. After everything that's happened between them, would Marcie fall for this Patrick? That's all I'm asking. If you hate it, we stick with the original. Deal?" he smiled for the first time and simultaneously Kate's stomach flipped.

"Okay, deal," said Kate and they shook on it. Che nodded his agreement and lay back on the grass to watch.

Tim explained where he was going to walk in from, where he was going to stand, just like Che did before a scene.

"Ready? Action," he said, taking a deep breath and Kate saw a change in Tim, in how he held himself, how the character of Patrick appeared before her eyes. Concentrate, she thought. She had to remember her two lines in the right places; this acting lark was terrifying, even without the cameras.

"Hi, Marcie." Patrick stepped forward on the bandstand.

"Hi," said Kate feeling that was 50 percent of her job done.

"I need to talk to you and I need you to listen." He said it calmly, but with warmth. That wasn't how Kate had written it – it was meant to be commanding and fast-paced and exciting, so that Marcie didn't stand a chance, so that she was caught up in the emotion. She had to hear him out now, they'd made a deal. Kate nodded on cue and Patrick smiled at her, but oh, that smile, his head was tilted down, he was looking at her through his eyelashes, and it was a lopsided smile, no beaming teeth. This was honest and vulnerable and she was mesmerised.

"Ah, Marcie," he sighed heavily, still standing gazing at her from the other side of the bandstand," his words thoughtful and slow, "the time we've spent together recently, it's like a dial has been turned and now everything is in sharp focus. I see life distinctly differently from before. I see what matters." He paused and took a step closer. "I see you." That smile again, his eyes locked on hers as he lifted his head and Kate felt her own chin lift involuntarily, too.

He slowly started to move towards her. "Marcie, we could both walk away now and settle for an ordinary life with the next person that comes along or we could grab this chance at something extraordinary." He was close now, his eyes fixed to hers, looking into her soul. His breathing was faster, but his words were smooth and gentle as he slowly lifted his hand to glide his index finger under her chin as he uttered the last line, "I'm not going to wait for the next one to come along when I've already found the only one I could ever need." He breathed against her lips," and paused, "and that's you, Marcie. You're the one." Every one of Kate's nerve endings was on fire. "The question is, am I the one for you?" And with that, he leaned in and kissed her, the side of his index finger lifting her face to his. She was lost in the kiss, his mouth controlling hers. Kate couldn't feel her legs and prayed her knees would hold up. Very slowly he ended the kiss and she opened her eyes. He was so close to her she was sure their hearts were beating the same fast rhythm. He looked anxious, as if he was waiting for something.

"Your line," he said bluntly. Kate look momentarily puzzled.

"Oh, uh, sorry… Yes, Patrick, you are," Kate fumbled.

"Then they kiss again and just hold each other, rather than the swinging-around thing. What do you think?" said Tim, turning to their audience of one.

"I like it," said Che, "Kate, what do you think?" Kate was only just registering that Tim was back, not Patrick, and was struggling with the question. Her brain had been hotwired and someone else was in control. As there was no response from Kate, Tim continued. "What did you feel? Is Marcie more likely to say yes to this Patrick or the one that barrels in, machine guns the words at her, engulfs her in a kiss and swings her around?"

"No contest, you're right. Warm and anxious Patrick wins the lady every time."

"Really?" he was pleased. "Great. You can tell Mina. She's still pissed at me."

"Wimp," she called after Tim as he leapt off the bandstand and jogged back to the marquee as the victor. Che got up and followed Tim.

Kate was alone in the bandstand, going over what had happened.

She found herself lost in that kiss again and those words. Oddly they were her words. She'd meant them to be brash and controlling, not gentle and so very sexy. And that kiss. Tim had kissed her. No, Patrick had kissed Marcie. Was that kiss all acting?

Chapter 29

Kate gave Sarah a big shove and she finally snorted into life.

"This is our stop, come on," she said, trying to nudge Sarah out of her seat. Sarah picked up her bag and tried to stand up. "Quicker than that, I don't want to end up in Wolverhampton!"

"Keep your wig on," Sarah said as she stumbled off the train. "What's the plan?"

"Pub for your pay, your house to collect post, pick up Amy, back to mine to eat and sober up."

"Great plan. Shall I just wait in the car?"

"No, come on." Kate linked arms with Sarah and bustled her off to the car park.

Sarah drank all the warm bottled water Kate had in her car and tried to stay awake and not vomit. Kate parked outside Sarah's house and they walked, or in Sarah's case, swayed, down to the pub.

"Oh, shit." Sarah spun around to walk in the opposite direction as she saw Melanie come out of the pub.

"You can handle her." Kate spun Sarah back around.

"Hey, this isn't *Strictly*, you know," said Sarah, trying to stop the spinning.

"Hiya!" called Melanie, as she quickened her pace towards

them.

"Great, a gloating Melanie. Just what I need." Sarah rubbed her eyes in an attempt to sharpen her senses. "Melanie, how lovely to see you. Are you off to Kleptomaniacs Anonymous?"

"Er, sorry?" said Melanie smiling, although she didn't know why.

"You keep stealing my men."

"I've said sorry," said Melanie, a little annoyed.

"Have you? I must have missed it. Did you whisper it through the letter box or write me an invisible letter?" snapped Sarah, which made her head hurt. Melanie looked at Kate for some help, but Kate was keeping out of it.

"Look, I'm sorry about Shaun and everything," said Melanie.

"Shaun?" Sarah was nearly shouting.

"Ooh, did you know he was back, by the way?" Melanie was wide-eyed.

"Yes, I did, thanks. He rearranged my house for me."

"Have you had a bump on the head?" Melanie tilted her chin and studied Sarah more closely.

"No, but I should give you a bump on the head for stealing Andy!"

"Andy? Do you know Andy?"

"Hold me back, Kate, or I'm going to slap some sense into her and that could take some time." Kate stepped forward just in case Sarah meant it.

"Sarah is still understandably upset, because you've hoovered up the only crumb of happiness she had left," said Kate, but Melanie just stared at her with a total lack of comprehension. "You and Andy getting together," added Kate.

"Oh, right," Melanie nodded and then shook her head. "But we're not together." Melanie was looking more confused than ever.

"You troll bitch from hell, you've dumped him already!"

Sarah lurched at Melanie, but Kate quickly grabbed her arm, which in her still-unsteady state was enough to have Sarah pirouetting out of the way.

"He kept coming round to mine. I thought it was just a line when he said he was just checking that I was getting better, but when I made it clear that I liked him, he said he was in love with someone else and it was serious."

"Serious," repeated Sarah in a smug tone.

"I think he's gay," said Melanie.

"What? Do I look like a bloke?" Sarah glanced down at her chest and shrugged. Looking down did not help her spinning head.

"Are you sure she's all right?" Melanie asked Kate, as she stepped a bit further back from Sarah. "Anyway, Andy must be gay to turn this down," and she waved her hands up and down her body and did a little pout for good measure." Sarah opened her mouth but Kate was quicker off the mark.

"Melanie, thanks for explaining, but I'm sure you're very busy, just like we are," and Kate started to walk Sarah towards the pub. Melanie waved after them and trotted off.

Sarah had decided that, since Melanie wasn't seeing Andy, she could still work at the pub. So it was an interesting conversation between Sarah and Phil, where Sarah denied all knowledge of ever resigning and Phil shook his head a lot. Thankfully he hadn't replaced her, so he was happy to have her resume her job once she'd sobered up.

Back at Sarah's, Kate was sweeping up the post from the floor and Sarah was leaning against the wall waiting for the stairs to stop spinning, so that she could get on them. There was a knock on the door and Sarah reached out and opened it without thinking. The door was swung open hard and crashed into Sarah's face, sending her reeling back against the wall. Shaun stepped inside and slammed the door shut.

"How convenient. The two people I hate most."

349

"Don't be an idiot…" started Kate.

"Have today off," muttered Sarah, as she tried to work out which part of her face the blood was coming from.

"Shut up, both of you." Shaun's eyes were wide and staring and they darted between the two women. "Where's my gear?"

"If you mean the otter, he's helping police with their enquiries," said Sarah.

Kate was desperately trying to think of a way to get to the door, but Shaun was in front of it and she doubted she could beat him to the back door, which she knew was locked. She started to edge her way down the hall and backed herself up to the hall table, where her bag was.

"You stupid bitch! Where's the clown?" Shaun shouted.

"I'm looking at him!" both women said at once and Sarah went to high-five Kate, but Kate wasn't playing. Shaun grabbed Sarah around the throat.

"Don't get smart! That clown is my ticket out of here. It could have been our ticket out of here, if you hadn't…"

"Come to my senses?"

"You'll never get another man like me, Sarah." Shaun's tone softened momentarily.

"God, I hope not. Nobody could be that unlucky twice!" she croaked.

"There's about two hundred thousand pounds worth of gear stuffed inside that clown. So, tell me where the fucking thing is?"

"He's also helping the police with their enquiries. It must be like the Royal Variety Performance down there." Sarah managed to squeeze the words out, but it was difficult as Shaun's grip was tightening. She wasn't sure if it was the alcohol, but she didn't feel as scared as she thought she should be, or as scared as Kate looked, for that matter.

"Let her go, Shaun!" shouted Kate, but he ignored her.

"You need to get the clown back, and quick." Shaun was leaning close to Sarah's face.

"Leave her alone," Kate said, calmer this time. "Leave now, before I call the police." Shaun started to laugh. It was a mocking snort. He kept hold of Sarah and turned to glare at Kate.

"You have no idea. I couldn't give a crap about the police. I've screwed over some major dealers and, if I don't get out of here, they're gonna kill me." He said it slowly, as if talking to a child.

"I really don't care," said Kate, equally patronisingly. Shaun lashed out quickly with his free hand and the force of the back-hander across her cheek knocked Kate into the hall table, sending it toppling over, with its contents scattered on the floor and Kate on top of it. With Shaun distracted, Sarah kicked out and caught him in the stomach. He let go of her throat and doubled over. Sarah started bashing him around the head, but one well-aimed punch from Shaun had Sarah's head ricocheting off the wall and she slumped to the floor. Shaun turned to Kate. She tried to shuffle backwards away from him, her head pounding and her ribs and wrist painful from the fall.

"You've got money! I want cards and PIN numbers now!" he shouted as he leaned over Kate with his fists clenched.

"Drop dead," said Kate, her chest heaving. Shaun grabbed Kate by the throat and raised his fist to hit her again. Kate reached for the yellow object on the floor and, with all the power she could muster, she swung it at Shaun's head and scored a direct hit. Shaun fell half on top of Kate and he lay still and silent.

"Shit! I've killed him," Kate looked at the heavy object in her hand and tried to bring it into focus, "with a pineapple!" There was a groaning from near the door. "Sarah, are you okay?"

"I've been better. My head hurts. That wine really was the most awful shite."

"I think I've killed Shaun." Kate nudged Shaun's body off her own and he didn't respond. A trickle of blood slid from his hair down his face.

"On the bright side, I still have his insurance policy… but

351

Andy is going to be mightily pissed off ... if we dig up the patio again," said Sarah in between gasps as the pain kicked in.

Kate reached for her mobile and realised that her hands were shaking to a comedic level. Sarah dragged herself up the hall towards Kate, who got a good look at her for the first time.

"Christ! Sarah, your nose!"

"I know, it's Dad's side of the family... they all have big noses."

"Sarah, don't be so flippant. This is serious," said Kate, as she dialled 999 on her mobile and then winced as she tried to lift it to her ear with her right hand. Someone answered very efficiently on the second ring and offered her a choice. "Please can I have police and an ambulance? Can I do that?"

"And an undertaker," said Sarah kicking Shaun's body in the ribs. Shaun groaned. "Hold the undertaker, the arsehole's still alive. Oh, hang on, I can remedy that," and Sarah reached for the pineapple. Kate gave her a nudge and she dropped it. "Spoilsport!"

The paramedics and hospital staff were all lovely, but the long wait they had to endure was not. Sarah had to stay in overnight so that they could monitor her head injuries, but they kept repeating that it was just routine. The police took photos of both Sarah's and Kate's injuries and hovered about for most of the evening. Shaun was being kept in due to his head injury, too, and police were outside his room. They weren't sure if that was for their protection or for his. The police were confident Shaun was going to get a hefty prison sentence, thanks to the now-lengthy list of evidence they had. They had been monitoring him in connection with a drugs' ring for months.

After Kate's arm was plastered in an unattractive orange cast and they had confirmed that she had bruised, but not broken, her ribs, she was able to sit at Sarah's bedside, where she fell asleep. She was aware of someone talking to her and had to think for a moment before she remembered where she was.

352

"No wonder Tim wouldn't sleep with you, your snoring is shocking," grinned Sarah, as she ruffled Kate's already dishevelled hair. Kate stretched one arm and yawned, and tried to release the tension in her neck. She looked at Sarah, whose face was a patchwork of purple and pink with a smattering of bloodied stitches for good measure. Sarah saw the look on Kate's face, "I know my face probably looks like a dropped pie, but you don't look so great yourself."

"Thanks, that's helpful." Kate gingerly touched the swelling on her cheek with her good arm. "At least I have a bona fide excuse for my editor." She raised her plaster to Sarah.

"Make yourself useful and track me down a coffee, will you? I'm thirstier than a marathon runner in the desert," said Sarah.

As Kate stood at the coffee machine trying to work out how she was going to carry back two hot drinks, she heard a familiar voice close behind her.

"Shall I help you? They don't have a burns unit here." Kate turned round.

"Andy!" Kate gave him a hug and he kissed her lightly on her unbruised cheek.

"I'd love to see what you did to Shaun, if you say he came off worse."

"It's amazing how much damage you can do with a pineapple."

"How is she?" Andy's smile faded.

"It's not as bad as it looks; they've been checking her every two hours. Come on, it's just down here."

The shock on Andy's face was clear, but he did his best to hide it as he put the drinks down next to Sarah's bed.

"Where's Amy?" Sarah asked looking behind Andy.

"Breakfast club with Freya. Hello, how are you feeling?"

"Oh, sorry. Hi, yeah, I'm okay. Head's a bit sore, but I've had worse hangovers than this." Andy leant over and very tenderly kissed Sarah.

"I'm really sorry about Melanie. She got the wrong idea and I didn't like to upset her, but I didn't want to lose you and... it all got into a bit of a mess..." Andy ran a hand through his already untidy hair.

"You have my tea, Andy. I'm off to St Gaudentia's. The walk and fresh air will do me good," said Kate.

"Subtle, she ain't," grinned Sarah.

"Kate, before you go," said Andy, "Tim rang for you last night, so I told him what happened and I've kept him updated with things. He's a nice guy. He was dead worried about you. We've swapped mobile numbers." Andy waved his mobile as if it now had a new celebrity status.

Chapter 30

Kate was right; the stroll to St Gaudentia's was a pleasant one. There were a few fluffy white clouds moving slowly across the sky, but otherwise it was a warm morning, which held the promise of a bright, sunny day to come.

She made a brief call to Marcus, to let him know that she wouldn't make it on set today. Marcus was already in a high state of drama, thanks to a call late the night before from Tim and he took a lot of convincing that Kate didn't need to be admitted to St Gaudentia's herself. When he was finally happy that the ruffian – Marcus's term for Shaun, not Kate's – was locked up and that none of her injuries was permanent, he at last let her go.

As Kate walked up the steps into the familiar building the receptionist did a double- take at Kate.

"I'm just visiting, if that's okay?"

"Of course… it's just that it's a bit early."

"Sorry," Kate checked her watch; it was almost eight-thirty. "I'll sit in the garden for a bit."

"Would you like a drink?"

"Tea would be lovely, thanks," said Kate and she headed through the building, out of the French doors, and onto the shaded patio.

After some time, Kate was woken by someone shaking her gently. The sun had moved and was now in her eyes; she had been asleep for a while.

"Thank goodness for that. The vultures were circling," said Didi, "and your tea's cold. Would you like another?" Kate blinked a few times.

"Hi, Didi, are you visiting me?" said Kate, feeling confused.

"Sort of. I came with a friend." Didi stood up and kissed Kate on the forehead before she went inside. Kate tried to sit up on the bench, but it was not easy with one arm in plaster. She felt a strong arm ease her up straight as Tim sat down on the bench next to her, his face crinkled with concern.

"Hi. What are you two doing here?" Kate said, licking her lips and wishing she'd drunk the tea, although a toothbrush would be the best thing for her right now.

"Can you see two of me?" said Tim, alarmed.

"No, I meant you and Didi, you fool. I'm fine, really, I'm fine," Kate grinned, which made her cheek twinge.

"I have something to tell you."

"Okay," said Kate, still trying to wake up. She waited expectantly as Tim shuffled along the bench and took her hand.

"Kate…"

"Yes," she said slowly, trying to un-fog her sleepy mind.

"Right, I'm just going to say it. Christ it's so much easier with a script. The thing is… I think you and me would be good together." Kate instinctively inched back; this was not what she expected and all sorts of alarm bells were going off in her head. This was Timothy Calder! Why on earth would he say that? Especially as he'd already turned her down once. "Kate, did you hear me?" Tim was looking concerned by her reaction.

"This on-off thing with Lumina, is it definitely over?"

"That was over months ago. I agreed to keep up the pretence of a relationship and, in exchange, she promised not to wreck filming."

"Okay, but what about Jackie?"

"Jackie?" Tim looked wrong-footed.

"Yes, Jackie. Who is she?"

"Look, everyone has a secret and this is mine." Things flashed through Kate's mind: hooker, drug-buddy, secret wife? The suspense was like waiting for the winner of a talent show to be announced.

"Tim, I need to know if she... I just need to know ..." Kate said, feeling very tired of everything.

"Okay. Jackie is not a she."

"Not a she?" said Kate waking up. "What then? A he-she, a lady boy? You read about it in the papers, but you never expect..." Tim interrupted her by gently placing a finger on her lips to stop her, his eyes wide with panic.

"No. Please stop jumping to conclusions." He paused and started again. "Jackie is an eight-year-old boy." This time, Kate's eyebrows jumped so high they nearly left her forehead behind. "For Christ's sake, please don't even think anything until I've finished. Seriously, just listen." Kate nodded, his finger still touching her lips.

"Jackie is an eight-year-old boy. I have kept this a secret for Jackie's sake, and no one else's. Jackie's mother was called Donna. I met her at the first Agent X film premiere party. She got in as a waitress and then changed in the ladies' loos halfway through the night. She was out to sleep with someone famous that night and I was the naïve, self-absorbed idiot that didn't see it coming. We drank heavily and passed out in my hotel room. Nothing happened." Kate's eyes flickered at this. "Honestly, Kate, I was not capable of anything. But, seven months later, she threatened to go to the papers if I didn't pay her a large lump sum and main- tenance for the baby she was about to have. I wasn't going to pay up because I knew I hadn't slept with her, so my legal team demanded a paternity test. Before she had the baby Donna sold her story to a paper for a couple of grand, but it didn't go too wide because they were worried about being sued. When she gave birth the test was negative, as expected. But what we didn't know until he arrived was that he had Down's syndrome." Tim paused and took a deep breath. "God, this is hard. I've never had to tell

357

anyone before." Kate took Tim's hand away from her mouth and held it tightly.

"Go on, carry on," she said softly.

"Donna called the baby Jack. She left hospital, facing a life in a one-bedroom, high-rise flat with a baby that needed special support. She had debts and my legal team were threatening to sue her and the newspaper who'd run the story. She had no family to speak of and no one to turn to. She was desperate." Tim willed Kate to understand with his eyes, which were filling with tears. Kate felt hers doing the same.

"Donna fed Jack, put him on his face in his cot and covered him over. She wrote a note and then took an overdose. A social worker found them the next day. It was too late for Donna but, amazingly, Jack survived." Tim wiped away a tear, "The lawyers told me to stay away, but I couldn't get this little baby out of my mind. I went to the hospital to see him. He was so tiny and helpless. I told myself it would just be one visit. He went into foster care, just a temporary measure before he would be adopted and I kept track of him. I sent some money, a few toys, just to tide him over until he had a proper family. But it never happened; nobody wanted to adopt Jack." Kate stifled a sob and Tim continued. "I kept in touch with his foster carers and became his kind of buddy. I see him whenever I can. If you could see the love in that kid's eyes. I don't have to care for him, but I do."

"Why keep it so secret?"

"If the press got hold of it, it's only Jackie who would get hurt. He'd discover things about his mother that no child should know. He would be thrown into the spotlight and it would destroy him. They would assume he was my son and then, when they discovered he wasn't, no one would understand why I spend time with him. There would be all sorts of accusations. Trust me, this way is best. His foster parents think so, too."

Kate had so many questions flying around in her head and one of the less-obvious ones popped out. "Why do you call him Jackie?"

"He's obsessed with Jackie Stewart, the racing driver. He saw a TV documentary and he was hooked. From then on we've all had to call him Jackie."

"So what does being his buddy entail?"

"We talk a lot on the phone and I see him when I can. I paid for him to have a heart operation he needed in America. He comes to the villa in Italy; that's easiest as there are fewer paps. I took him and his foster mother there that time that you and Didi blew me out." Kate retraced her memory and pieced together that the woman's voice she'd heard call Tim must have been Jackie's foster mother.

"So I guess you want to think about it," said Tim, searching Kate's pale face for a clue as to how she was feeling.

A frail old lady shuffled out onto the patio with her zimmer frame, closely followed by Didi.

"Ooh, Didi look – isn't that that famous actor chappy?" she said.

"I see no one Alice, you're hallucinating again," said Didi, guiding her back inside.

"I should be getting back to Sarah," said Kate, standing up. Her head was spinning. Tim stood up too and shoved his hands into his pockets.

"Can I call you?"

"I'll be back on set tomorrow." Kate paused and tried to order her thoughts. "It was nice of you to come, and you've done a lovely thing with Jackie." She gave him a brief kiss on the cheek. They looked at each other in silence for a moment before Kate turned away and set off back to the hospital in a daze.

As Kate wandered up to the main entrance, her muddled thoughts were shattered by a hiss of a voice, like water hitting hot oil.

"Bleedin' 'ell, what appened to you?" Irene chortled and sucked long and hard on a crumpled cigarette. She threw the butt down and ground it into the concrete with her studded plastic sandal.

"Your son happened," said Kate, staring Irene straight in the face, feeling brave.

"He's turned up, he ain't dead but he's been roughed up a bit. Police won't tell me nuffin and he ain't talkin' 'cause they're hanging round like a bad smell all the time." Irene did look thrilled at Shaun's return.

"He attacked Sarah and he attacked me, because he was after the drugs he had hidden in Amy's toy clown." Kate knew it was blunt, but Irene didn't seem the sort for flowery sentences.

"He's been stitched up then, ain't he?"

"No Irene, he's done this all himself. He could have killed one of us last night, if I hadn't…"

"Did you hit my Shauny?" The screech had returned to Irene's voice.

"Yes, I did. He had already hit me once. I was lying on the floor and he was about to hit me again so, yes, I hit him!" Kate's voice was getting louder. She wasn't sure where her confidence was coming from. Irene looked crestfallen; she looked again at Kate's face and her arm.

"My Shauny?" she flinched as she said it.

"Yes, your Shauny. I'm sorry, Irene."

Sarah didn't look overjoyed to see Irene coming into the ward, but Kate was doing her best to gesture a thumbs-up sign behind her.

"The grim reaper's mother has come to visit, oh deep joy," muttered Sarah to Andy, who brought over a couple of chairs for Irene and Kate. "Hello, Irene, what a delight," said Sarah. Irene waved Andy and the chair away.

"I ain't stoppin'."

"Now, there's a shame," said Sarah, and Kate shot her a look.

"I saw your posh mate artside and she told me what 'appened. I'm sure he didn't mean it but, anyways… he should never have hit ya. Thas not right and well… I'm sorry I said you killed him."

"And told the police I'd buried him under the patio," added Sarah.

360

"Yeah, that n'all." Irene looked contrite. "Can I still see our Amy sometimes?"

"We'll see," said Sarah but, as she saw the shock and sadness on Irene's face, she added, "I'm sure we can sort something out, Irene."

Tim sat on the grass next to Jackie, with his face in his hands. Jackie had listened carefully to what Tim had told him.

"So, what did she say, when you told her that you loved her?" Jackie asked. Tim looked at him and laughed; he shook his head. Jackie kept his gaze on Tim, waiting for an answer. Tim's expression changed from flippant to deadly serious, as realisation dawned.

"I didn't actually say those words as such," Tim said slowly.

"Tim!" Jackie shook his head. "You have to tell the girl that you love them, everybody knows that." Tim jumped to his feet, kissed Jackie on the forehead and ran up the garden.

"You're a genius, Jackie! I'll call you later."

"I want to be the best man!" shouted Jackie after him, but Tim was already striding through the house, speaking into his mobile.

"Pips, I need you to pull a few strings…"

A number of very bewildered porters were waiting with a stretcher when the helicopter landed on the hospital helipad. The door opened and Tim bounded out, running clear before it quickly took off again.

"Sorry, boys, I've got my own emergency," he said and he ran off towards the main entrance. A quick stop at reception for directions resulted in four autographs, one photograph with the reception staff, and another with a boy who had a broken leg from falling off a skateboard. Tim extricated himself and made a bolt for the stairs. A wrong turn had Tim in the maternity unit, surrounded by emotional woman and crying babies. He had to stay for five photographs and one woman changed her baby's name on the spot from Orlando to Timothy. Thankfully, a large nurse shooed people away and escorted Tim out of maternity and through to

Sarah's ward. He gave the nurse a peck on the cheek and she blushed furiously.

"You put your arm in there, and I'll pull it over your head," said Kate, her voice coming from behind a curtain drawn around a bed.

"Ow, mind my nose with your bloody concrete arm!"

"Stop complaining, you've flashed your bum at me a dozen times in that gown. Why you couldn't put your pants on first, I'll never know."

"Thanks for announcing it. These curtains aren't soundproof, you know! And anyway, Andy has gone to rinse them in the sink."

"It must be true love," giggled Kate.

"Knock, knock," said Tim as he reached the curtain. Both Sarah and Kate froze. Kate mouthed to Sarah *It's Tim* and she dramatically mouthed back *I know and my arse is hanging out!*

"Who's there?" said Kate, as Sarah quickly wrapped the hospital gown around her bottom half.

"Olive," said Tim.

"Is he taking the piss?" Sarah said, in hushed tones.

"Olive Who?" obliged Kate, waving her unplastered arm at Sarah, as a fit of giggles came over her. Tim opened the curtain just enough to step inside.

"Olive you too or, more precisely, I love you, Kate Marshall," said Tim as he took her hands in his and gently ran his thumbs over her knuckles.

"Tim, what's this about?"

"It's about me mucking it up this morning and going for a second take. So, please shut up and listen. When I think about you, I smile. When I see you, I want to kiss you. When I touch you, my body sparks and when I'm not with you… it's utterly shitty. I love you. What I want to know is, do you feel the same?"

Kate could feel her heart beating faster, she wanted to ask more questions, check and check again but this time she didn't. Kate pulled him towards her and kissed him. It was shorter than she'd planned as Sarah started whooping with delight and dropped her hospital gown, which was a distraction for all of them.

"Is that a yes?" he asked, as he held her in front of him.

"On two conditions."

"You name them."

"No secrets and no overblown gestures; we try to be normal. Agreed?" Kate had a tone of seriousness although she was smiling.

"Agreed," said Tim firmly and he pulled her to him and kissed her again. The sound of the helicopter could just be heard over Sarah's squeals and a quick flick of the curtain blocked the sight of it hovering outside with a large heart-shaped sign inside saying 'Timothy Calder loves Kate Marshall'.

Epilogue

Another nurse sneaked a peek through the door. The staff at the private hospital were used to the rich and famous and even royalty but it seemed Kate was of particular intrigue today.

"I could sell tickets," grinned Sarah, who apart from a neat pink scar on her nose, looked fully recovered. "This coffee is better than the cost-a-lot stuff," she said, glugging down a cup full, "I'll have another one of those." Kate gave her a look.

"What? It's free!" she protested. "If I'd have known, I'd have brought a flask and a bigger bag," she said squeezing the packet of complimentary biscuits into her already full handbag.

Sarah set off on her coffee mission and Kate picked up a nearby magazine. There on the cover was Tim. He was escaping from the back of a London restaurant and Kate smiled as she remembered the evening well. It was one of a few they had attempted to share together in a public place as they had tried to see as much of each other as possible over the last six weeks. Eventually a very short man with thinning hair and a serious smile appeared and she put down the magazine.

"Hello again, Miss Marshall. X-Rays look fine, let's take that off and see what we're dealing with shall we?" he said pointing firmly at her cast which was adorned with Amy's masterpieces and a stickman that Tim had drawn so that she could think of him whenever she looked at it. Soppy git.

Kate lay down on the bed with her arm on a rest. The doctor produced a small but lethal looking tool that was very like a mini circular saw, and she gulped hard.

"Ooh, be careful!" said Sarah, returning from her coffee run and making Kate jump.

"Please," said the doctor firmly directing Sarah into a chair, "there is nothing to worry about, Miss Marshall won't feel a thing."

"Oh, it wasn't that. It's just that we've promised the old plaster to my daughter's hamster to use as a play tunnel," said Sarah, with a broad smile as she sat down and began fiddling with another empty coffee cup. The Doctor stared at her for a moment.

The plaster removal was quick and painless just as the doctor had promised. When he left the room to get some forms, Kate and Sarah studied the arm. It was pale and the skin was very dry and flaky and it looked a lot weedier than her other arm due to lack of use.

"That's disgusting," said Sarah, "this is cool, though." She held up the cast, "Amy will be chuffed and so will Curry." Sarah quickly held it at arm's length. "It reeks by the way!"

"I couldn't wash properly with it on," said Kate feeling a little defensive, but she couldn't deny there was an unpleasant smell coming from her arm, which meant the cast was probably worse.

Sarah bundled it into a supermarket carrier bag, "Oh, well Curry smells too so it'll be fine."

"I wonder how long it'll look like this?" Kate twisted her arm about to get a better look at the withered limb.

"Hope it's better by your birthday."

"Why? What's happening then?" Kate looked instantly concerned.

"I don't know. I assume Tim is whisking you off somewhere exotic. You don't want photos of that shrivelled thing on the front of the newspaper. Even with a beautiful backdrop it'll still look gross." Sarah wrinkled her nose. "I bet he's plotting something totally lavish and amazing for you. You really are the luckiest bugger in the world," said Sarah, oblivious to the small frown making its way fleetingly across Kate's forehead.

At six thirty on her birthday Kate found herself in the back of Tim's car, cutting through the countryside with a small rapidly packed case in the boot and her passport in her handbag. She wasn't entirely sure how she felt. Tim had arrived on time and announced that he'd planned a surprise. He looked thrilled with himself and she had had to fight hard to hide her disappointment. It had turned out to be a quiet day with no visitors at all which was most likely because everyone had known she would be going away with Tim. All she had wanted to do was curl up on the sofa with him and a takeaway, like they'd discussed on the phone earlier that week, and maybe a piece of chocolate hedgehog cake that Sarah and Amy usually made for her on her birthday.

Tim put his hand over hers and squeezed gently. She squeezed back and looked into his stunning green eyes that were so famous around the world and that so many women swooned over. It was like living in a film. Here she was, simple ordinary Kate, being whisked away somewhere exotic by the man of her dreams. So why did she feel like something wasn't quite right?

Kate rested her head on Tim's chest, it was her favourite place to be. Cuddled up with her head nuzzled under his chin, his arm wrapped around her. She drifted off to sleep.

When she opened her eyes she realised the car had stopped and Terry was rummaging about in the boot. Kate looked out of the window, expecting to be at an airport but she wasn't. She sat up quickly and stared out of the car, she turned to Tim who was grinning inanely.

"Is this the surprise?"

Tim nodded and guided her out of the car. They followed Terry across the car park, round the back of the pub, in the back door and up some stairs.

Terry knocked on a door and then stepped back. It opened into a dark room, Tim almost shoved Kate inside and as he did so lights flooded the room. The assembled cast of Kate's life erupted into "Surprise!" as Amy launched herself at Kate closely followed by Sarah. Marcus handed her a glass of champagne and kissed her cheek lightly "Happy Birthday, darling girl," before whispering to her, "it's all his own doing, you know."

Didi fussed over her as did Andy and a variety of assorted friends. Amy gave Kate a guided tour of the buffet table including the centrepiece chocolate hedgehog cake and the mini crème brûlée that Amy had her eye on.

Kate turned back to Tim who was stood in his full dinner suit looking gorgeous and rather proud of himself. "Did I have you worried?" he said pulling her into his arms, her champagne glass tilting precariously.

"You might have done," said Kate, kissing him lightly on the lips.

"This lot are staying at the pub but you and I have Sunset Cottage to ourselves for the night." And right there at that moment she realised just how much she loved him.

A Q&A with Bella Osborne . . .

Kate retreats to gorgeous Sunset Cottage in the Cotswolds to focus on her screenplay. Where is your favourite place to write?

I am lucky enough to have a writing room as we converted our smallest bedroom into a study. I have my own desk (named Duncan – it's a long story), a corkboard with my plot points pinned to it and lots of stationery! However, I don't always have the luxury of large chunks of time so I will grab five minutes wherever I can to write a few sentences or ideas down. I always carry a pen and notebook for this.

Why did you choose the Cotswolds as the setting for Sunset Cottage?

We are very lucky to have some beautiful parts of the United Kingdom and many quaint villages and I think the Cotswolds is a great example of that. As so many of the buildings in Cotswold villages are made of the golden-coloured Jurassic limestone quarried nearby, it makes them unique and particularly picturesque. Coupled with rolling meadows, tree strewn hills and terrific sunsets it really is the perfect location for Sunset Cottage.

What was your inspiration for the novel?

The character of Kate came to me first. Someone whose life had been blessed and yet so quickly had her world turned upside down. I was also very keen to have an ordinary heroine and by that I mean someone that isn't quirky, accident prone or gets herself into silly situations, I wanted someone straightforward whose life becomes extraordinary. Very simply I asked 'What if?' What if one of her books was made into a film? What if she met someone else? At which point Tim barreled in with his charming exterior, mesmerizing eyes and deeply held secrets and I had myself a story!

Did you use a lot of your own author experiences when writing Kate's part? Can you relate to her character at all?

From an author experience perspective, Sunset Cottage is a bit 'which came first, the chicken or the egg?' This is my first full-length novel and I had no experience before this. I learnt an awful lot about being an author through writing Sunset Cottage. I think Kate is, by choice, more isolated than I am. I have terrific writing support from my local writing group and other writers of the Romantic Novelists' Association. However, Kate doesn't take risks and she skips when she's happy which are things that I can definitely relate to!

What was your favourite thing about writing It Started at Sunset Cottage?

I loved, that despite my well plotted out story, the characters still went off and did their own thing and surprised me. For example Irene (Shaun's mother) was just a walk on part. But as soon as she appeared I knew I had to give her a bigger role as I just had to see more of her!

If It Started at Sunset Cottage was made into a film, which actors would you choose to play your main characters?

Great question! I think Keira Knightley (in her long golden hair phase), would make a very good Kate. Keira Knightly does 'reserved British' particularly well and is also talented at touchingly portrayed comedy. Anne Hathaway has the small frame, delicate features and quirkiness to make a perfect Sarah once she's had her hair cut short and dyed blonde. Picking someone to play Tim is hard. It's all about the eyes with Tim so I think Ian Somerhalder or someone equally gorgeous would work quite well but they would have to have a flawless English accent to pull it off. Let's hope some day I have this conversation for real! That really would be amazing!

Discover more from your favourite authors . . .

Rebecca has chosen the most luscious, five-tiered, wedding cake. The wedding singer is on speed dial. The deposit on the white sand honeymoon is paid for in full on Barry's card. The down payment may require her to sell a kidney, but isn't that why you have two?

But there's one small problem: Barry is yet propose. And now Rebecca's feverish wedding plans have sent him bolting out the door! Depressed and alone, she'll do *anything* to get back the man she loves. But what if Rebecca's driven Barry into the arms of someone else? Will she *ever* get to say 'I do . . .?'

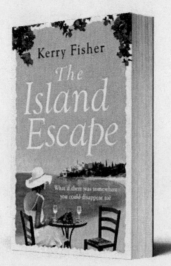

Octavia Shelton thought she'd have a different life. One where she travelled the world with an exotic husband and free-spirited children in tow.

Instead she's married to safe, reliable Jonathan, and her life now consists of packed lunches, school runs and mountains of dirty washing. She's not unhappy. It's just that she can barely recognise herself.

So as Octavia watches her best friend's marriage break up, it gets her thinking. What if life could be different? What if she could escape and rediscover the person she used to be? Escape back to the island she visited years ago? And what if the man she used to love was there waiting for her?

Charlotte Bristow is worried about her husband Will. With her 16-year-old daughter Rosie newly signed to a top modelling agency, and Will recently out of a job, things are changing in their household.

As Will dusts down his old leather trousers and starts partying with their new, fun neighbours, Charlotte begins to wonder what on earth is going on.

So when Fraser, Charlotte's ex – and father of Rosie – suddenly arrives back on the scene, she starts to imagine what might have been . . .

Honey Jones has a problem – she's never had a boyfriend who's really done it for her . . . Luckily her best friends Nell and Tash are determined to help, and so the hunt for Honey's perfect man begins.

But when a stranger moves into the flat opposite, their plan soon goes awry. Hal is secretive, bad-tempered, and ticks none of Honey's boxes.

Except maybe one . . .